MIDNIGHT ON THE
RIVER GREY

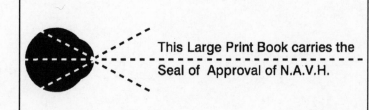

This Large Print Book carries the
Seal of Approval of N.A.V.H.

MIDNIGHT ON THE RIVER GREY

ABIGAIL WILSON

THORNDIKE PRESS
A part of Gale, a Cengage Company

Farmington Hills, Mich • San Francisco • New York • Waterville, Maine
Meriden, Conn • Mason, Ohio • Chicago

LIBRARY OF CONGRESS CIP DATA ON FILE.
CATALOGUING IN PUBLICATION FOR THIS BOOK
IS AVAILABLE FROM THE LIBRARY OF CONGRESS

ISBN-13: 978-1-4328-6865-9 (hardcover alk. paper)

Published in 2019 by arrangement with Thomas Nelson, Inc., a division of HarperCollins Christian Publishing, Inc.

Printed in Mexico
1 2 3 4 5 6 7 23 22 21 20 19

*For my mother
My best friend, my first librarian,
my biggest fan
Thank you for showing me what selfless
love and true courage looks like and for
being one of the few people with whom I
share my hopes, fears, and dreams*

PROLOGUE

1811
The Scottish Highlands

"Who's there?" My mother's haunted whisper drew me to her bedside. Sickness clung to the air around her bed as grief entombed the space.

She spoke again. "Rebecca?"

My heart lightened, and I grasped her frail hand. She'd recognized me only once a few months back, but she hadn't spoken my name since our move to the highlands six years ago. "Yes, Mama. It's me."

She squinted in the flickering candlelight as if she hadn't seen me for some time. "How lovely you look tonight."

I curved my lips into a small smile, for I knew I looked a fright. Heavens, I'd not left her bedchamber for nearly two days, which wasn't all that uncommon of late. This particular illness, however, this sudden worsening of her condition, felt different.

I dabbed a wet cloth against her forehead. "Are you in pain? We have a draught for relief if you require it."

She lay stone still, a ghost of the vibrant woman she once was. I tried again. "Perhaps some water? You must take something, surely."

I'd made a habit of talking to her as if nothing had changed, even though I knew she wouldn't respond as any normal person might.

Veiled by the night's scrambling shadows, I could just make out the slight shake of her head before she cleared her throat. "Have you heard from Jacob?"

I froze at my brother's name, and my gaze slipped to the letter I'd been reading. How did she know? My hand found my throat, my next words cautious. "I received a note from him only yesterday. He writes to say he's arrived at Greybourne Hall, and Mr. Browning is just as he imagined — cold and inhospitable. Yet, he does plan to stay for some time."

"Cold? Fanny Browning's boy? I don't doubt it."

My heart lurched. She'd remembered something — something from our past. I held still in anticipation. Could she be *lucid*? My hands trembled as I returned the cloth

8

to the water bowl.

After years of caring for little more than a childlike stranger, it was far too much to hope for — one night, one moment with my mother, the one I had been so close to as a girl. I didn't dare move an inch for fear the moment would pass.

"You alone accompanied me here." She glanced around as an owlish look took over her hazy eyes. "To this awful place away from all my friends . . . when *he* never would."

"I-I . . ." What could I say? She'd spoken the truth. In a way we had been left — forgotten — but there was so much more. I turned away, determined not to spend another moment dwelling on all we'd been through. "Such fustian. I don't think it awful here. I wish you could see the mountains, Mama, the plunging sweep of the land, the sharp cliffs, and dithered meadows. There is nothing in the world like the beauty of Scotland. I suppose the cottage is a bit small perhaps, but where better for you to rest? I do not regret for one moment coming here with you." My shoulders sank. "And please, do not speak so of Jacob. He loves us dearly. With Father gone he has had many responsibilities."

The half-truths flowed so easily. I'd said

them often enough in London. *"Is your mother well?"* Society would ask. And every time I'd reply without hesitation, *"Well enough, thank you."*

But she never had been.

I cringed at the memories — the pitiful looks from our supposed friends. Even now on her deathbed, I found them too painful to contemplate.

"Rebecca." She tried to sit up. "There is something I must tell you before . . ." Her voice slipped into a faint whisper.

I settled her back on the pillow and leaned forward. "Yes, Mama?"

Her head lolled side to side. "I'm so sorry, so sorry for . . ." Tears coursed down her cheeks, drowning out her words.

"Shh. You mustn't speak so." I touched her wispy gray hair and remembered a time when she had done the same for me.

Tears welled in my own eyes. I knew quite well what she meant to say. She was sorry for London, for her condition, for all the years I'd been forced to nurse her. But she needn't say such things aloud. We'd always had an unspoken bond, and as I sensed her passing, it was all forgotten. "I love you, Mama."

Her fingers tightened around my hand like a claw. "I'm so sorry . . ." She forced me to meet her icy glare. "So sorry . . . that someday . . . you'll be just like me."

CHAPTER 1

Two years later
London

"I have news, Aunt Jo." I sealed the drawing room door behind me and leaned back against the heavy wood. "But it's not what I'd hoped."

Magazine pages fluttered. Muslin rustled. Aunt Josephine floundered across the drawing room. " 'Pon my word, Rebecca, I've been beside myself with worry these last few hours. Come and sit at once. I've something important to tell you."

I untied my bonnet and tossed it onto the sofa. "I do apologize for leaving you this morning, but I went to the Court of Chancery . . . regarding Mr. Browning." I didn't think the man's name on my lips would cause the same pain it had nine months prior — when I'd sworn to despise him — but my heart lurched.

Aunt Jo fumbled the embroidered bell

13

rope, then took a seat, her lace cap askew. "The Court of Chancery? What are you getting at, child?"

This would be a bit harder to explain than I'd imagined in the wee hours of the morning. I took a quick breath. "I've been doing quite a bit of thinking about our, um, present situation, and I thought it might be prudent to appeal to the court for a new guardian."

Aunt Jo's eyes grew round.

"After all, when Papa named Mr. Browning years ago, no one dreamed he would later inherit the entailed estates. Considering everything that has happened, I thought the court might be willing to reexamine my case."

"Oh, Rebecca." Aunt Jo's response came out as more of a sigh. "But the scandal —"

"Is none of my concern. After all, I am determined to find a way for the two of us to set up our own establishment. I owe him nothing."

"My dear. Oh, my dearest darling." Her voice shook. "You do try to look out for your old aunt, and it does you credit, but . . ." The King Charles spaniel who'd been asleep under the table took Aunt Jo's hesitation as an opportunity and launched into her lap. She snuggled the dog against

14

her worn day gown without a glance. "But how are we to live on half a guinea a week?"

"Your jointure is a tad on the small side, but I do have some money from Papa if only my guardian will let me get at it. And please don't say the sum was meant to be my dowry, for I will have none of that. The two of us shall do well enough together. You and me . . . and Sophie of course." I stroked a floppy ear. "I'll hear no more talk of giving her away."

Aunt Jo's arms constricted around her furry bundle. "I don't think I could do it, even if I had to." She swallowed hard. "Give her away, I mean."

"Take heart, I am determined to find a way for us." I frowned. "But it won't be through the courts at present. The process is far more complicated than I had anticipated. If that horrid Mr. Browning will only allow us to —"

"Oh, my dear, there is something you must know at once."

"What is it?"

A line spread across her forehead, and her gaze shifted to the door. "It is what I have been trying to tell you since you arrived. *He* has been here."

My smile fell. "Mr. Browning? In London? I don't believe it."

"Yet, it is all too true. The monster himself. In our very house. He left his calling card this morning while I took my chocolate in my room. Oh Rebecca, I must confess, I didn't know what to do when Mrs. Fisher presented it to me but to respond with a card of my own." She pointed to the salver in the hall. "His card for you is still there. I hadn't the nerve to touch it."

My pulse tapped a steady beat as I walked to the sideboard. "Don't be ridiculous." And ferreted out the offending article.

Mr. Lewis Browning.

"Hmm . . . His name looks just as callous in print as I thought it would." I tossed the card aside. "It is no matter." I raised my chin. "This precipitous appearance gives me the opportunity to make a new proposition. I had already decided on my walk home to pen him a letter. Now, I shall just speak to him in person and, with any luck, never again."

"Oh, my dearest one. You are far braver than I. How your brother could have left you in such a difficult position, I will never understand."

A cold rush of memories surged to the surface, and my voice grew chill. "He could not have known he would be murdered."

"Rebecca! Hold your tongue at once. You

16

must not say such things. Besides, we don't know anything of the kind." Aunt Josephine pressed her handkerchief to her forehead before tapping her finger against the cloth. "Unfortunately, there is more to this wretched business than I thought only yesterday. I received a letter from your cousin Ellen this morning, and she does Mr. Browning no credit. No credit at all."

She lifted a white sheet of paper from the side table and unfolded it. "See here, she says the people of Plattsdale have taken to calling him the Midnight Devil — out all hours of the night yet a complete recluse during the day. Ellen says he has finally admitted some responsibility for causing Jacob's fall from the bridge but nothing more. What are we to make of that?"

"I . . ." I pressed my lips together and scoured the short missive, craving any news. If anyone had flushed out the details surrounding Jacob's death, it would be my silly, prattling cousin. But there was nothing beyond what my aunt had already told me. Slowly, I handed the missive back. "Perhaps we should visit Ellen as we once discussed. It would give me a chance to —"

"No, no, my dear. It won't do, for the entire family has left for Bath."

A loud knock sounded at the front door,

and our eyes met. Aunt Jo clutched her chest. "You don't suppose it is him already?"

Footsteps echoed down the hall, but neither of us moved. Beyond the wall, the front door clicked open then shut as the tick of the casement clock filled the charged silence between us. Another set of footsteps joined the first, and the drawing room door popped open. A man in a long brown cloak trailed on Mrs. Fisher's heels.

Somehow I stood and listened to her announce his name as if far away. How many times had I prepared myself for what I would feel, what I would say to the man who took everything? I'd practiced the moment in my room over and over again, but that was months ago. I glanced at Aunt Jo's equally stricken form.

Mr. Browning filled the room with a quiet stride, his bearing youthful yet refined. I was well aware my guardian was only nine and twenty, but my imagination had painted an old wrinkled crow. After all, due to my time in Scotland, I had not seen him for more than ten years. I could not have been more wrong.

He paused at the edge of the Aubusson rug as his shrewd eyes took in everything. His indifferent half smile dominated the uncomfortable silence. Removing his hat to reveal a mess of curly, dark hair, he bowed, then gestured into the air, a solitary ring on his right hand. "Cousin Rebecca." Then to my aunt. "And Miss Audley."

Due to Sophie's position in her lap, Aunt Jo remained seated, motioning to a slat-back chair, her fingers wiggling in the air. "Please, Mr. Browning, do have a seat. It is so good of you to call. Rebecca, some tea?"

I pulled the bell rope before edging onto the sofa, my back unnaturally stiff. I doubted Mrs. Fisher would respond. At least, I hoped she wouldn't. We were down to one servant after all, and this man didn't deserve the last of our cake.

Mr. Browning adjusted his coat and took the offered chair across from us before leaning forward and resting his elbows on his knees. A few seconds of silence passed, then his eyes flicked to mine. "I've come about some necessary arrangements." His voice was deep, his hands never far from his chin.

So, he had little use for pleasantries. Well, neither did I. "Yes, indeed. You have excellent timing, cousin. I had intended to write to you this very afternoon."

He froze. "Write to me?"

I forced a smile. Any man could be flattered, and all I needed was time to figure out my next step toward independence.

19

"My aunt and I have made a few plans we'd like to discuss with you."

"Plans?"

Did he intend to repeat every word I said with that insufferable mocking tone?

"Yes, plans." I took a deep breath. "You were in the right of it to leave us alone these last few months, as it has given me the opportunity to contemplate my future. Rest assured, I have everything in hand and require little from you. That is to say, my aunt and I will soon be completely self-sufficient. In the meantime, however, what I would ask of you" — I could feel my body quivering from within — "is permission for the two of us to stay on here in my London townhouse for another year or more until we have the means to set up our own establishment."

He lifted his eyebrows.

I responded by raising my voice. "I can fully understand how you must feel a bit unscrupulous having inherited my brother's entailed estates after his untimely death, but I will have you know, we mean to provide you some rent. That is, whatever we can afford until we are wholly independent. I am certain you comprehend the difficulty we've had adjusting to our sudden change in circumstances since you no doubt feel some level of responsibility."

A faint smile curved his lips. "And how exactly do you plan to go about paying me this rent?"

I didn't waver. "The details have not entirely been worked out; however, I assure you all will be taken care of."

"Indeed." He gave a slight shrug. "Though I applaud your determination, I'm afraid what you ask is, regrettably, impossible."

"Impossible?" I shot a look at Aunt Jo. "Why?"

"I leased the townhouse but two days ago, which was my express purpose in coming to London — to relay this information to you in person."

My lips parted, a surge of shock racing through my core. "You mean to tell me you leased my house?"

"No." He paused. "I leased *my* house." Then he glanced about the room as if he'd said nothing out of the common way. "I can certainly appreciate your enjoyment of this beautiful spot, but I haven't the inclination to keep a London residence."

I flew to my feet. "How dare you. Without even a word to my aunt or to me."

Startled by the sudden movement, Sophie sprang from my aunt's lap and scurried beneath the table before directing a slew of ear-piercing barks solely at Mr. Browning's tasseled boots.

Aunt Jo, constrained by propriety and her plump middle, swiped wildly beneath the table, but she was unable to reach the dog's collar. Frantically, she called her name, but Sophie had no intention of relinquishing her attack. She'd found her villain.

Mrs. Fisher bustled into the room at the same moment with a tea tray and the last of the cake. Terrified as she was of dogs, particularly angry ones, she stumbled upon entry, and I raced to intercept her.

Mr. Browning was there first, though. He grasped the tray and silenced the dog in one booming, "Enough!"

The room fell silent. Sophie groaned and laid her fluffy head on the rug as if in penance. The sudden stillness left me stunned and uncomfortably close to the man. So close that I caught a whiff of his tangy, orange cologne. I took a hasty step back as warmth rushed to my face.

"Thank you, Mrs. Fisher." I nodded to the housekeeper and grasped Sophie's collar, helping the dog into the hallway in one quick swoop.

"You've had quite enough enjoyment for one day, don't you think, Miss Sophie? Out you go."

I closed the door and turned back to the drawing room determined to affect the confidence I no longer felt. Heaven knows I'd not meant to, but I shared a quick look with Mr. Browning. Something in his witty expression brought my anger rushing back. "Where were we? Oh, yes. I had taken fault with your proposal to turn my aunt and me out on the street."

He cocked an eyebrow. "Not exactly."

I flashed a cold smile. "What else would you call it then?"

"Merely business." He held up his hand to stave off a reply. "Allow me to finish."

Ignoring the man's plea for civility and his outstretched arm, I found my way back to the sofa and my aunt's side without assistance. My next move would have to be planned carefully.

A hint of irony accompanied Mr. Browning's words as he once again took a seat across from me. "I do hope to make this transition as easy as possible. You will have a fortnight to collect your personal belongings, as I understand the rest is part of the estate."

The headache I'd been anticipating all day pounded its way across my forehead. He had thought of everything. What escape could there be for my aunt and me with

23

such short notice?

He went on, oblivious to the wild thoughts circling in my head. "My solicitor will present himself to you in a few days and provide the necessary funds to complete your move to Greybourne Hall at the end of the month."

Aunt Jo gasped.

"Greybourne Hall?" slipped out on my next breath. "You intend for us to live at your country estate?"

"Naturally, as I am your guardian."

My heartbeat turned sluggish as an ache swelled in the back of my throat. This man — the person responsible for my brother's death — expected me to live with him? In his house? Madness. "And if we refuse?"

"I'm afraid there is little choice in the matter at this point. The arrangements are already complete."

Mr. Browning narrowed his blue eyes, scrutinizing me, no doubt, as the numbing shock of his declaration faded to resignation across my face. He sighed. "I do realize Greybourne Hall might hold unfortunate associations for you —"

"*Unfortunate?*" My voice came out a bit louder than I'd expected. "Is that what you choose to call it?"

He gave a sideways glance at Aunt Jo, then

returned to me, a pained look hovering about his eyes. His voice, however, remained firm. "Forgive me if I startled you. I hadn't expected such a violent reaction to what I assumed was the logical next step. Perhaps I should make myself a bit clearer." He gave a curt sigh. "I only intend for you to stay at Greybourne Hall till some place more suitable can be arranged. Unfortunately, there are few options at present."

Ice enveloped my heart. I had no wish to travel to, let alone *live* at, that dreadful house, not even for a single night. In his letters, Jacob had described the rambling structure as a gray pile of stones fit for vampires, or worse. I could only image Mr. Browning, this dark-headed devil before me, at home in such a place. Oh, Jacob.

Aunt Jo's voice startled me from my reflections. "I daresay Mr. Browning's offer comes as something of a surprise; however, it is most generous, Rebecca, is it not?" Her fingers brushed my arm.

I opened my mouth to protest, but Aunt Jo's foot poked my leg. Cautiously, I turned to face her as she took a long sip of tea. Her astute gaze met mine over the rim of the cup. My heart pounded. She meant for us to go. To Greybourne Hall. But why? Though she had never agreed with me that

Jacob had been murdered, she knew very well what I thought of my cousin. What could she mean by supporting such a suggestion?

It was then I saw Ellen's half-opened letter on the table and the room shifted. How many times had I declared that somehow, some way, I would uncover the truth of Jacob's death? Did my resolution include traveling to Greybourne Hall? And would such an undertaking be worth dragging Aunt Jo across the country to the southeastern coast of England? Allowing my heart to see that bridge? I let out a slow breath and gauged my next move.

I would be in the house where Jacob had lived, free to look where I pleased, speak with whom I chose. And I was desperate for answers. Aunt Jo knew me better than I knew myself.

Mr. Browning dipped his chin, no doubt prepared for another outburst. I glared at the gentleman. "We shall do as you wish, Mr. Browning. You may have it all your way. My Aunt and I will vacate our home at your bidding and go to Greybourne Hall whenever it is convenient for you."

Something akin to disbelief flashed across his face. He tilted his head back. "As I said, my solicitor, Mr. Drake, will assist with

whatever is necessary to facilitate the move."
He stood. "With that settled, I will bid you
both good day."

I watched him vacate the townhouse with
the numb satisfaction that in a way I'd managed to get just what I'd hoped for — a
chance to investigate Jacob's death. Yet
somehow the look on Mr. Browning's face
as he took his leave left me cold — the wry
bend to his black brows, the piercing yet
lingering gaze. Had I just bartered what was
left of my future with the devil himself?

CHAPTER 2

One month later
Greybourne Hall

"Do you not think it odd that Mr. Browning was not present to meet us on arrival?" I took a seat in front of a darling little dressing table in my new room. "It was he who forced us to come here after all."

Aunt Jo's tired eyes rounded, and she spun to face the young maid unpacking my trunk. "That will be all for now. Tabby, was it? We'll ring for you in a few hours when we wish to dress for dinner."

"Yes, ma'am." The maid nodded, her cheeks filling with pink. She paused, then shuffled her feet as she rushed from the room.

Aunt Jo waited for the click of the door before collapsing on the bed's cream coverlet. "Oh, Rebecca! How could you say such a thing?"

"Quite easily, I assure you."

"But the servants —"

"Think no better of him than I do, I'm sure. You remember that ostler at the coaching house. One mention of Mr. Browning and we were treated as if headed to the guillotine. Clearly the townspeople think him guilty of Jacob's murder. And what's worse, they pity us for having to live here with him."

Aunt Jo gave me a sideways glance.

I picked up my brush from the table where Tabby had laid it and smoothed a few loose hairs back into place. "If Mr. Browning thinks bringing me here will change my opinion of him or my intentions for my own future, he is living in a dream."

Aunt Jo touched her chest. "Yes, I agree it was difficult to leave London and our home. But now that we are here, surely you see that you must try to make yourself more agreeable." A slow smile spread across her face, her idle finger stroking one of the bedposts. "I should think Mr. Browning might look quite handsome in his own home. You might consider . . ."

The hairbrush slipped from my fingers and crashed to the dresser. "What on earth do you imply, Aunt?" I spun to face her. "You cannot possibly think I came to Greybourne Hall with the least thought of *him.*"

"Don't be cross with me, Rebecca, and no, I'm not so daft. I know why you came. You and your plans. I only hoped you might bring your heart as well. I saw the way Mr. Browning looked at you in London, after all, and I did not think you wholly unaffected —"

"Looked at me? You mean when he glared at me like I was an unbroken filly he means to bend to his will? I only wish he might try. Heavens, Aunt Jo! Let me be clear. I came to Greybourne Hall for one reason and one reason alone. To discover Jacob's murderer." I whirled back to the looking glass. "Besides, I've told you before I shall never marry."

Aunt Jo rose and crossed the rug. "My dearest darling, forgive me for speaking so. I do hope a great many things, but I'll say no more on that particular subject. I am well aware what it would mean to you to know the truth about Jacob's death. However," — her eyes took in every inch of the rose-papered room — "you must be cautious as well as practical. I cannot countenance anything foolish or dangerous on your part. And as your chaperone, I forbid it." She cocked an eyebrow. "What do you plan to do?"

"Expose him, of course."

"By *him,* I assume you mean our host."
She reached around my arm for the powder
and applied a quick swipe to her nose. "You
still believe him responsible . . . even after
all of his fine condescension."

"With certainty."

She took a deep breath. "You must admit
he was quite civil to us in London. You don't
think . . . Well, *I* more than anyone stand in
his debt." She rested her hands on my
shoulders. "Your father proved to be the
best sort of brother-in-law while he was
alive, but I was not his family any more than
I am Mr. Browning's now. And, Rebecca,
Mr. Browning allowed me to accompany
you here without question."

"He knew very well I needed a chaperone,
so don't —"

"Anything we asked of his solicitor has
been supplied. Did Mr. Browning not also
instruct Mr. Drake to encourage us to
purchase these beautiful dresses before we
left? And Mr. Drake had nothing but wonderful things to say about his employer."

I pursed my lips. "Mr. Browning has been
generous, but I think it more to allay his
guilty conscience than anything else. My
cousin, or rather my distant cousin — goodness, I don't even know how the man is
related to me."

Aunt Jo cast a vague glance at the ceiling. "Hmm, let me think on that. He is your cousin on your father's side. Although I don't exactly remember how. I believe your great uncle Robert had three girls and a son, or was it one of Robert's second cousin's children who was his father . . . Oh well, never mind. Browning is the heir, and that is all there is to it." She crinkled her forehead. "I suppose you are right to be cautious, but I cannot get one thought out of my mind. What if Jacob's fall was simply a terrible accident, and you are doing the man a wretched disservice?"

I considered her words for a moment, my eyes on the looking glass. "That is precisely why I must uncover the truth, one way or another. Surely there must be clues. Someone who saw something."

"Oh, Rebecca. Clues?" She crossed her arms. "You sound like a Bow Street runner. And what do you plan to do if Mr. Browning learns of your investigation?"

I laughed. "You needn't be concerned. He won't. I'm far too clever for that."

She looked amused. "If only I could believe such a declaration."

I turned and took her hands. "Do you remember when Jacob and I were children and we used to play knight and princess in the folly? He was always the one to wield the sword and kill the dragon. I wanted to, of course, but he wouldn't let me. With that boyish grin of his, he'd remind me that he was seven years older and tasked by father to be my protector. I thought him terribly clever and resourceful." I paused. "Now that he's gone, I must protect myself and you. Finding out the truth of what happened is the first step in doing just that."

A tear slipped down Aunt Jo's cheek, and she swiped it away. "Jacob always did like to save the day, to rush into battle on a moment's notice."

The clock on the mantel chimed the hour. "Oh, dear. It's far too late, and I'd hoped to poke around the house before dinner."

"Poke around? Before dinner? What about rest? You must be as tired as I."

I threw a shawl around my shoulders and made my way to the door. "I think it a fine idea for you to take a nap. As for me, you know very well how I get. I couldn't close my eyes if I wanted to. I'll be sure to wake you in time to dress for dinner." I flashed a smile. "And take heart. I won't be long."

"Don't —" The heavy door muffled Aunt Jo's voice as I sealed it shut.

"My apologies," I said in a quiet voice. I hated to escape in such a way, but I knew she would be far too exhausted from our journey to put up much of a fuss, and these first few moments at Greybourne Hall were too important to waste. I had much to discover.

The shroud of twilight had fallen over the estate. I didn't need a candle, not yet at least, as the waning fingers of daylight forced their way through the window at the end of the hall. Alone with the faded carpets and the musty air, I retraced my steps along a series of paneled walls. I paused at each shadowed doorway but could hear no trace of life.

The corridor that housed my aunt and me seemed to stretch on forever, narrow and dark. Eventually I spilled out onto a landing that overlooked the vast entryway we passed through upon arrival. It took me a moment to catch my bearings, lost as I was in the scrambling turns of the house and the whispered gloominess of the corners.

I remembered the front gallery with its soaring paintings and parquet floors and descended the split staircase, my thoughts on Jacob's description of Greybourne Hall. If I remembered correctly, the main structure was built in the fifteenth century and passed through several owners over the years. Each had made their own additions, which created the crisscrossing network of halls and rooms around me, as well as the stone patchwork of turrets and angles at the exterior.

The air was misty when my aunt and I rounded the central drive earlier in the day, but Greybourne Hall's presentation had been no less impressive. Its blackened stones blighted the otherwise beautiful landscape, the storied structure rising from the manicured lawns with its sharp, pointed chimneys and windows that hid beneath crumbling trellises. It reminded me of a dark version of Strawberry Hill in London.

On the main level I kept to the interior wall's edge and crossed the open entryway amid the shadows where a biting draft from the back rooms snaked across the floor. Long, leaded windows surrounded the front door, but little light came through at present.

Continuing into the bowels of the old house, I glanced in each open door along the central hall. Room after room a heavy silence lurked, accompanied by dark furnishings, intricate moldings, and the airy symmetry of a medieval structure. The drawing room at the end of the hall was the only space lightened by delicate patterns and pale hues, though it, too, stood chill and lonely in the evening air, the scent of disuse betraying its otherwise soft loveliness.

I'd seen few servants beyond the groom, Mr. Browning's valet, and Tabby, and I wondered how much of the house was in use. Mr. Browning clearly ran the place as a bachelor's establishment and would likely not need a full staff.

As I crept into the back corridors, I was surprised to hear a set of voices, particularly one that I recognized. I lifted my eyebrows. Well, well. Was Mr. Browning in residence after all?

My determined footsteps turned sluggish as I approached the sounds. It was indeed Mr. Browning and another man deep in conversation. I'd always had an ear for private whispers, left out of important family discussions all too often, but never more so than when I heard my name. A coldness spilled into my chest. They were speaking of *me*. Driven by an overwhelming curiosity, I tiptoed around the stone column before narrowing in on a curved door, which had been left slightly ajar.

A hint of woodsmoke met my nose as warmth feathered against my skin. I melted into the shadows beside the door, all too conscious of my ill-advised intrusion. Of course, I had justice on my side. How dare they discuss me in my absence, and besides, anything I might learn could only help bring to light that which some might wish to remain hidden. I fell motionless and attended.

The second voice rose, and I was able to recognize the rich timbre of Mr. Drake, the solicitor who helped us in London. I placed my ear as close to the candlelit sliver as I dared.

Mr. Browning responded in kind, his voice sharp, his tone mocking. "Don't look at me like that, Drake. I've no thoughts of marriage, if that is what you are insinuating, particularly not with that girl."

"No? I thought her charming with her dark hair and green eyes — not beautiful, I suppose, but taking in a way, and in particular need of a husband at present." He paused. "With you summoning her here of all places, I did wonder."

My lips parted, and I covered them with my hand as I rested the side of my head against the cold doorframe.

Mr. Browning began again. "I have my own reasons for bringing her here, which have absolutely nothing to do with any interest on my part. I assure you. Gads, do you think me nothing but a young fool in danger of throwing my heart away on the first passable female to step through my door?"

"No, not you. The proud Lewis Browning is far too disciplined for such an emotional response, though I daresay the sentiment would do you a deal of good." The pitter-patter of fingers on a desk started, then stopped. "Though you do have me vastly curious. What is the chit doing here, and at such a time?"

"Enough with your questions. I am not at liberty to share at present, so you will simply have to remain in the dark."

A glass clinked against wood. "As you wish, sir. Keep your secrets. I have no use for them. I only hope this has nothing to do with that brother of hers."

I stifled a gasp.

"Dash it all, Drake! I hired you to watch my estate and keep your mouth shut, re-member? Not plague my deuced conscience all the time."

A laugh followed. "And I've had to do a great deal of that, I'm afraid. Nearly every day, if I'm not mistaken."

A deep breath. "You are not mistaken. You've stood a good friend, Drake. One far better than I deserve."

"As long as you acknowledge it, my boy,

as long as you acknowledge it . . . However —"

The conversation dropped to silence, and I adjusted my head against the wall, straining to hear footsteps . . . or whispers . . . or anything.

But what I got was Mr. Browning's voice booming through the slit in the door. "Would you care to join us, Cousin Rebecca?"

My nerves snapped. I'd been caught, and in the worst way. My heart pounded, and I took a wild step back.

"No need to run off. I can see the toe of your slipper through the reflection in the glass. Please, we would be obliged if you would join us."

The door popped open, and an equally surprised Mr. Drake extended his arm. "Why, Miss Hunter, it is indeed you, and what an honor." He cast a quick glance at Mr. Browning. "Only the devil could have guessed it."

Only the devil. Shaken by my own foolishness, I allowed Mr. Drake to usher me into what turned out to be a library. Or rather, some sort of office of Mr. Browning's. Whatever the purpose of the room, it was covered in books — some filed on shelves, others strewn about the massive central

39

desk, and the remaining stacked oddly in the corner. A floor-length window stood sentry over the darkened night.

Mr. Browning eased back against the edge of his desk, arms crossed, hair a muddle of black. He lifted a chin that hadn't seen a razor in several days. "So good of you to join us."

Still reeling from what I overheard, I found it difficult to meet his eyes. However, I had no intention of bowing to my guardian's censure, particularly when he felt at ease discussing me in company. "I apologize for the intrusion, but when my aunt and I were left to fend for ourselves upon arrival, I thought it natural enough to tour the house and perhaps discover our host's whereabouts."

He raised his eyebrows. "Indeed." He hesitated, drumming his fingers on the desk, before speaking again. "I must say I find such a hasty pursuit intriguing, considering I left explicit instructions for you to be taken care of in my absence. Do you mean to tell me my commands were not carried out by the servants?"

I stiffened. "Indeed they were, as you likely already know. Your housekeeper, Mrs. Ware, showed us to our rooms quite properly; however," — I smiled — "she left no directions regarding dinner."

Mr. Drake laughed. "There you have it, Lewis. I daresay you have sorely neglected your guests if they've nothing to do but wander Greybourne Hall alone searching for sustenance. I will admit, Miss Hunter, there is a slew of fine paintings and whatnot around this moldering old building, which I am told are of great interest. I would be pleased to show you some tomorrow if Mr. Browning has not already done so by then."

Mr. Browning shot Mr. Drake a searing look.

I nodded. "I shall be quite pleased to see the whole of my new home by the light of day." Then to Mr. Browning, "I do apologize if I offended you by roaming. I did not mean to imply you had been wholly remiss as host."

Mr. Browning dipped his chin, probably all too aware that was exactly what I meant to imply. "Nonsense. Greybourne Hall is your home now too." He flicked his fingers at the door. "You may feel free to *wander* at will." He paused. "Nevertheless, I would be cautious of the west wing since that section of the house has not been kept up as the rest. And, unfortunately, there is a . . ."

I waited.

"That is to say, I'm not certain the cellars

are all that safe either. Perhaps it is wiser for you to avoid anything other than the main living areas."

I took a small breath. "I thought you were about to warn me of a ghost, Mr. Browning."

"Not at all. I can see you are far too clever for such a Banbury story." He narrowed his eyes. "Although, I have not completely figured you out as of yet."

"Good." I smiled, but at the same time a wave of nervousness came over me. Certainly not due to Mr. Browning's striking demeanor or the questions in his eyes, but the feel of him, how his presence seemed to cross the room and disarm me. Looking away, I took a seat in the nearby chair. Greybourne Hall was his domain after all. I'd have to be careful if I meant to learn the truth.

Mr. Drake adjusted his bottle-green jacket and returned to his seat at my side. "And what do you think of this sprawling old structure?"

"I find it piques my imagination. Such dark and dreary halls. The history of this old place must be fascinating. An interesting study to keep one preoccupied." I took a quick glance at the door. "However, I do believe I would find it difficult to live here long, as I fear the house might swallow me up in time."

Mr. Drake smiled. "Interesting you should say so, as Lewis would declare it just the opposite. The man never wishes to depart this rickety old estate."

Mr. Browning cleared his throat. "Speaking of leaving . . . Drake, my friend, haven't you somewhere you need to be?"

Mr. Drake paused, then popped to his feet. "Quite right. Quite right. Till tomorrow then. Good night, Miss Hunter. Lewis."

I watched him leave with a bit of apprehension. Though I knew his departure would alter the mood in the office, I was unprepared for the cloying stillness that took over — and how Mr. Browning silently studied me.

What was he thinking? I couldn't guess. Attempting to distract myself, I laced my fingers together in my lap and focused on them.

He walked over to the fire. "You and your aunt are settled?" His gentle tone seemed at odds with the look on his face and our previous discussion.

"Yes, quite settled." I lifted my chin. "My aunt is resting at present. It was a tiring journey for her."

He released a deep breath. "You must

extend my apologies to her as well for my lack of hospitality. My business this afternoon took longer than I'd expected." He glanced back at the desk before grasping a dirty rag, which he buried rather quickly in a desk drawer. "And I'm afraid I shall miss dinner as well. I am needed elsewhere."

I hid my surprise at his statement. No sooner had I found my reticent cousin than he intended to dash off once again. "It is no matter." I stood. "My aunt and I are prepared to handle everything on our own."

He shrugged. "I've tasked Cook to await your orders, and you are free to run as much or as little of the house as you like. I have never taken much of an interest there, so you may find my household staff a bit remiss in some areas. I . . ." He watched me for a moment, then his lips parted. "We do have much to discuss — about your pin money and whatnot. However, I . . ." His voice trailed away again as he paced to the window, his eyes trained on the darkness beyond the glass.

Slowly, I made my way to his side and peered over his shoulder. He'd seen something, and it had put him on edge. I, too, felt the hairs rise on the back of my neck. Outside, deep within the sea of blackness, bobbed a small light, winking in and out of the trees.

Mr. Browning must have felt me close at his side, for he stepped away, brushing my arm. "I didn't mean to startle you. I thought I heard something. A dog's bark perhaps. But it is only Drake heading to Reedwick."

"Or Sophie. My aunt did bring her dog with us."

His rigid posture seemed to abate. "Yes. That's right. Sophie." Then something changed. Confusion? Sadness? Anger? He fought to conceal the emotions flashing across his face. "Just keep the mongrel out of my way and away from the horses."

"As you wish."

He raked his hand through his hair, turning to the casement clock. "I'm afraid I must beg your pardon and lapse into the poor host I've already proved to be. I am late for an engagement."

"Oh . . . certainly." I stumbled to the door, then turned. "And, thank you."

He paused. "Whatever for?"

"For providing my aunt and me a place to live." I don't know why I said such a thing. It couldn't be further from the truth, but it brought out a slight smile on Mr. Browning's face.

He advanced to meet me at the doorway, and my heart did an unexpected turn. The firelight had softened his otherwise sharp features; his eyes appeared devastatingly perceptive. Aunt Jo was right. The man was indeed handsome, but I wouldn't let him bewitch me.

He took my hand. I assumed to bid me good night, but his fingers tightened around mine. "I only hope you feel the same way at the end of all this."

CHAPTER 3

Years of history and neglect had left a steady hush throughout Greybourne Hall. Almost as if the soul of the house had left it long ago and what remained was a hollow shell. From the cobweb-decorated parlor to the abandoned chapel, a transient gloom roamed the halls, leaving my body yearning for warmth.

From the lawn, I couldn't help but glare back at the old, dark structure, battered by the hands of time. It loomed like a sleeping giant draped in fog. Trees clawed the corners of the blackened stones as creepers scaled the three-story walls. The wariness I'd felt on arrival still pricked my skin.

I sidled closer to Aunt Jo as we resumed our journey down the front walk. Past the unattended gardens and the empty fountain, I could see horse tracks from the previous night. Mr. Browning's, no doubt. I'd watched him through my bedchamber window at midnight, cutting through the mist like a ghost as he galloped across the east rise. It was curious that he was absent from the breakfast room this morning.

Aunt Jo had seemed unaffected by his neglect, but as we passed the stable complex, I caught her peering through the door, a strange look across her face. She was as confused as I.

I raised my eyebrows. "I don't believe he has returned."

Aunt Jo tended to wiggle when she walked, and today I found the sound of her swishing muslin a comfort. She smiled. "I'm certain he is a busy man, my dear, running such a large estate."

At midnight? "I suppose so." I took a deep breath of autumn loveliness. The scent of woodsmoke. The wayward breeze of wet leaves.

After a quick glance at my feet, I cast another look back toward the house. "Where is Sophie this fine morning?"

"That pup has run off again. Probably found something far more interesting to do than follow an old lady about."

"Nonsense. She's likely made her way to the kitchens again. I daresay a tasty treat always trumps a walk in the woods."

"My word, I hope not. If so, I'm sure I

shall hear of it at once from that butler, Knowles. He doesn't like Cook put out in any way."

I laughed. "Everyone likes Sophie." Then I remembered Mr. Browning's warning in the library. "Well, almost everyone."

The estate road turned east, and I urged Aunt Jo to follow the wider path. I had a purpose for our stroll and wasn't sure Aunt Jo would be all that pleased. "I must confess, Aunt. I asked you to accompany me on my walk for a particular reason."

"Oh?" She blinked. "I did wonder what you were about."

My stomach tensed. "I've a mind to go to the bridge . . . where Jacob died."

She stopped short, her hand finding its way to her chest. "My dear, what can possibly be gained by such a notion?"

"I'm not certain" — I reached for her arm — "but I *am* certain I must go. Seeing that place shall be difficult, knowing what happened there — for both of us. Only, I feel that it is necessary in our search for the truth. After all, we can hardly avoid it. What if it provides us with a clue?"

She glanced down the leaf-strewn road ahead before resting her hands on her hips. "I daresay if I don't go with you now, you'll only come back another time alone. Neither you nor Jacob has ever heeded my warnings, always dashing off without thinking. Goodness, I swore to your father on his deathbed that I would help you navigate the world, but I had no idea the merry ride you'd take me on. I suppose it was that wild Scottish upbringing. Running all over those hills. Going wherever you wished. Doing what you wanted without the hint of a chaperone. I'm afraid it's given you a sense of freedom you must not have in England."

"Yes, it's quite liberating." I smiled. "And I have no intention of giving it up."

She gave me a sly glance, then motioned ahead. "I suppose there is nothing for it but to relieve that horrid curiosity of yours."

I squeezed her fingers. "I knew you'd want to come."

The bridge stood less than a mile from the lawns of Greybourne Hall on the main road into the estate where it crossed the wide and sometimes torrential River Grey.

We had a pleasant walk with a crisp wind at our backs before the low bridge appeared. The stone structure stretched out like a curved blanket into the fog. Around us, nature fell silent but for the distant sound of the river and the occasional flap of a bird's wing. Autumn had already consumed the little gully. Trees stood bare, their naked branches immovable in the wind.

Aunt Jo's hand shook as she brought it to her mouth. "Such a terrible tragedy. I'm not certain I can face it."

I allowed her words some space as my eyes filled with tears. It had only been nine months. Could I face it myself?

Yet we plodded forward, arm in arm, driven by a mix of longing and dread, until we'd climbed to the very crest of the bridge. Consigned to my plan, I inched up to the traitorous edge and leaned against the stones, the small ledge barely reaching my waist.

The rush of water filled my ears. I allowed myself to think of Jacob, to soak in every painful memory. He loved lakes and rivers and brooks. He'd once had the notion to be a ship captain, impatient as he was to leave England in any way possible. He dreamed of taking on the world, and he was always in such a great rush to do it, as if he knew he didn't have much time. First it was the navy, then London society. Aunt Jo and I had only held him back, tethered him to England and later to Scotland.

I clutched my hands beneath my chin as a silent prayer drifted through my mind. Though I'd mourned his death these many months, I hadn't allowed myself to say good-bye, not completely. Here, where he lived his last moments, where his life faded away, it felt right.

Grief had taken many forms with me. Numbness with my father. The slow insipid acceptance with my mother. Shock with Jacob. It was an ever-changing process of finding a way to move on. But the one thing I would never let go of — my resolution to find the truth.

Minutes passed like a slow wind before I wiped my cheeks. "I suppose it all happened quite quickly."

Aunt Jo put her arm across my shoulders. "It does no good to dwell on such thoughts." She turned me to face her. "My darling, I'll help you uncover whatever we can, but you must consider that Jacob's death might have been nothing more than an accident."

My voice dropped to a whisper. "I know." Then I turned back to the fog-filled canyon, to the place where my brother lost everything. "But I have to be certain. I have to get these relentless questions out of my head." Rising to my toes, I stretched forward as far as I could to see below. "It must be a long way down. I cannot make out anything in this thick mist."

"No, I don't believe we shall learn anything here today."

I took a deep breath of dampened air. "Unless . . ." Wide-eyed, I crossed the remainder of the bridge before motioning for Aunt Jo to follow. "I don't believe it's as steep on this side. If we're careful, we can make our way down to the river."

Aunt Jo touched her forehead. "Don't be ridiculous, Rebecca."

"I'm never ridiculous," I said as I swung around the bridge pillar, clutching a loose tree branch.

"Oh, heavens." She, too, crossed the bridge. "You would put my declaration to the test first thing." She glanced down the wild slope. "I hope you don't break your neck."

"Nonsense." I had already sidestepped my way down below the tree when I heard Aunt Jo plodding behind me. I dared not look back for fear she might change her mind. "It's not that far really, and —" My boot slipped on a leaf and I hit the ground hard, the spindly brush scratching at my gown.

"Oh my darling, are you hurt? Wait for me there if you need my assistance."

"No, only embarrassed." I patted the dirt from the back of my gown and began again, this time throwing a look back at Aunt Jo. Though she was twenty years my senior and a bit soft about the middle, she could rival the best sportsman on a horse, and likely make short work of a hillside.

Wrapped by the insistent fog, we could see little to either side or out into the flowing river. The world felt suddenly small, as if we were being squeezed in on all sides. The narrow canyon blocked the wind and left a sickly stillness I didn't like. I forced my muscles to relax.

Aunt Jo's fingers curled tighter around my arm. "What do we do now?"

"Look about, I expect."

Together we crept along the bank, cautious of the mud and jutting rocks beneath our shoes, until Aunt Jo pressed my arm. "What is that?"

I stopped midstride. A large, dark shape took form in the distance under the bridge. Something *was* there. "Probably just a rock." But I wasn't sure, was I?

We skulked forward as if pulled by an invisible rope, our eyes trained on the unnatural lump before us. Perhaps it was the looming reminder of Jacob's death or the eerie calm of the river pulsating beneath the bridge, but all at once a sense of dread washed over me, and I knew it was not a rock. I pulled Aunt Jo back, but I was too late.

The shrill ache to her scream sliced

straight into my heart. "A person . . . a dead person!"

I swallowed hard, unable to tear my gaze from the body and the mud stains splattered across a fine bottle-green jacket — one I was quite certain I'd seen before. But where?

"I suppose . . ." I shivered. "We should make sure the man is indeed dead and doesn't need our help."

Aunt Jo nodded.

Bottle green? Where had I seen it?

Prying myself away from Aunt Jo's stiff arms, I made my way to the twisted figure lying half on the rocks, half in the river, his two black boots bobbing with the current. I looked up. Had the man fallen from the bridge? Or worse?

A painful thought struck. Last night in the library . . . a green jacket. My hand shook as I reached out and lifted the man's lifeless shoulder. His face was dull and swollen but unmistakable. Mr. Browning's friend and solicitor, Mr. Drake.

Shock swarmed my muscles, and my hand slipped away. Such a kind and gentle man — and to come to such an end.

"Who is it, Rebecca? Why do you stare so?"

I closed my eyes, hoping I was caught up

in a dreadful dream. "I'm afraid it is Mr. Drake, and you were right. He is deceased."

Aunt Jo's voice came out in a confusion of tone and texture. "Oh, my dear! How can this be? He was so kind and . . . so near my own age. An accident?"

"I don't know. We must find help — and quickly."

A distant pounding of horse's hooves echoed off the stone underbelly of the bridge.

Aunt Jo caught my arm as I flew by her. "Be careful. We don't know what happened. That could be anyone up there."

I nodded but continued up the bracken and rocky hillside without stopping. I had every intention of seeing who meant to cross the bridge. Louder, the pounding resonated until the horse and rider materialized in the fog.

A black stallion whickered as his cloaked rider reined him to a walk a few feet from the bridge. My pulse raced. I'd been seen.

Or, at least, I thought I had. The man's voice broke the silence as he directed his horse forward. "Easy, fella. Slow here, remember?"

Gingerly the horse pranced across the smooth stones, the rider glancing about him as if he, too, thought something lay in wait in the foggy soup below.

I inched around the stone pillar, meaning to watch as the horse and rider reached the other side of the bridge and all but disappeared into the mist. Yet, I couldn't help myself. I called out. "Mr. Browning?"

The rider tugged the reins hard, and the horse sidled around. I had been right.

"Who's there?"

I heard the cock of a pistol.

"It's me. Rebecca."

Slowly, the horse retraced its steps. "What on earth are you doing here?"

I paused before answering, allowing Mr. Browning to reach his own conclusions.

The smile faded from his face like a retreating wave. "Forget I asked." His shoulders slumped, and he added unemotionally, "Are you in need of assistance?"

I stiffened. "Indeed I am. There is something you must see under the bridge. My aunt is down there now."

He eyed me for a moment before slipping from his horse's back.

Aunt Jo called out from below. "Rebecca, you've been an age."

I raised my voice in answer. "Mr. Browning is here and will accompany me to see what has happened." I crossed my arms, as my guardian seemed to be taking a great deal of time tying off his horse.

At length he turned, and I couldn't miss the hostile look about his eyes. Such a glare was hardly lost on me. I knew quite well I was accompanying the very person responsible for my brother's death back to the scene of the crime. Yet a part of me couldn't help but realize that what Mr. Browning would find below could only bring him pain.

Or would it?

He offered his hand as we descended. But remembering the last time I'd taken it, I chose a tree branch instead. This time I had no intention of losing my footing.

"M-Mr. Browning." My aunt met him at the river's edge, gasping back a sob. "A terrible thing has happened." She pointed beneath the bridge as she led him closer to our shocking discovery.

I'll never forget the look on his face when he noticed the cloaked body. Dazed, then incredulous, his hand retreated to his mouth. It didn't take long for him to observe the bottle-green jacket. Shaking his head, he raced to Mr. Drake's still form. "Drake! Drake. Drake." He kept repeating his friend's name before turning on me. "When did you discover him? Did you see it happen?"

"No, my aunt and I found him just a few

minutes ago while we were . . ." My throat felt thick. What a blunder. I couldn't possibly tell him why we'd come, yet I could think of no other reason to give.

He waited for me to finish, but not for long. He turned back to his lifeless friend. "It must have been last night . . . the old, dear fool."

Carefully, he ran his fingers down Mr. Drake's arms then onto his legs before gently touching his friend's head.

Mr. Browning jerked his sharp gaze to the bridge above. "He has clearly broken nothing, yet . . ." He shot to his feet. "There will be an inquest. And you may be asked to give information."

"I'll help in any way I can." And I meant it. Mr. Drake had been nothing but kind to my aunt and me. And seeing Mr. Browning's swift and painful reaction had given me a bit of insight into his relationship with the man, as well as a great deal to ponder. Whatever role Mr. Browning had played in my brother's death, he clearly grieved the loss of his friend.

My aunt stepped closer to Mr. Browning. "Has Mr. Drake any family to notify?"

Mr. Browning's shoulders slumped. "No. He was an only child, married to his work. Leave it to me to see about the necessary arrangements." He glanced around, almost as if lost. "I shall see you ladies back to the house then handle the rest personally."

I made no argument, and Mr. Browning led us up the slope in silence. None of us had words, each lost in our own minds. I took Aunt Jo's arm and she squeezed my hand. The shock had taken its toll on both of us.

As we crested the bridge, the wind that had guided us to the river now beat against our languid movements. Mr. Browning untied his horse, and Aunt Jo and I stepped onto the bridge, where I took one last look into the murky gloom. Somewhere hidden below lay the remains of the amiable Mr. Drake.

Two deaths. One bridge. And the truth as elusive as the fog.

Chapter 4

Knowles, the butler, was waiting for Mr. Browning in the hall when we returned to the house, a curious look across his usually placid face. "Mrs. Browning is in the drawing room, sir. She asks to see you directly."

"Isabell?" Mr. Browning gave a sigh of irritation. "Beg my apologies, but I haven't a moment to spare at present."

"Shall I ask her to return at another time?"

"No." His fingers found his forehead, then he turned to me. "Cousin, would it be too much to ask after such a harrowing afternoon for you to sit with my sister-in-law? I don't believe she will be put off this time, and the visit shouldn't take long." He drew in a quick breath and released it. "You see, she is planning a small dinner party in your honor. I'm regretful I shall be unable to join you to discuss it at present, but I'm quite certain she'd much rather speak with the both of you."

Mrs. Browning? His sister-in-law? I took a peek at Aunt Jo. "I'm sorry, who did you say wishes to speak with us?"

He shook his head like he was flicking off snow. "I meant to introduce the two of you as soon as possible. She won't be pleased." He hesitated, then gave me a plausible nod. "Isabell Browning is my late brother's wife. She resides in the dower house on the north rise." He motioned into the air. "She does, however, spend a great deal of her time here. You will have the pleasure of her company on many occasions."

"Oh." So he had a sister-in-law . . . and one I wasn't certain he approved of. I liked her already.

He added quickly, "Please extend to her my gratitude for her efforts on your behalf and my apologies for deserting her now." His hands were back at his hair. "However, there is much to be done. I shall have to send a servant to Plattsdale for the coroner. Drake was the parish officer for the area. It shall take some time to summon him."

Aunt Jo stepped forward. "Don't think on it a moment longer, Mr. Browning. You do whatever is necessary for your friend. We shall be pleased to entertain your sister-in-law and help you however we can."

"Thank you." He gave us a quick nod, followed by a pale look of uncertainty, before he took his leave, hastening through the open front door.

Knowles cleared his throat at our backs. "If you would follow me."

The drawing room flanked the corner of the house, well situated to catch the morning rays followed by the afternoon's orange glow. Today, though, there was little sunlight to be had. The candles were lit, and the wide, scrolled fireplace emitted a wobbly haze. The room, wrapped in pale purple with white columns and matching brocade curtains, revealed a feminine touch, the only one in the house I'd found thus far. I couldn't help but wonder at the designer.

On entrance, a smiling woman of average height rose and seemed to float across the cream carpet to the door, her green velvet gown moving seamlessly as she advanced. Introduced by Knowles as Mrs. Browning, she bid us join her with a gentle roll of her hand.

Soft-spoken but firm, she exuded an essence one could hardly ignore. It was as if she knew she could command the room, yet she would never dream of doing so. She possessed a subtle beauty, charming eyes, and a fresh lavender scent. I thought we would suit quite well.

"And where is Lewis this fine afternoon?"

"Mr. Browning sends his regrets, but he has something quite important to attend to." My words came out rushed, and I wasn't sure how much I was at liberty to say. After all, he hadn't given us leave to discuss Mr. Drake's death.

She took my arm as if we were old friends. "Oh, men. They've always something." She twitched her lips. "I daresay I shall not forgive him this time. You know, he put me off yesterday as well. That man will never learn how to treat a lady. Come now, have a seat. You shall do very well in his place. I wasn't here to bother with him anyway. I only wish to know all about you."

Aunt Jo peeked back at the door as we made our way across the room, the wrinkle on her forehead betraying a hint of unease.

Mrs. Browning took no notice, for she barely spared my aunt a glance. She slid onto the sofa, the perfect location for her fair hair to catch the glittering firelight. Part of me wondered if she had planned it that way.

I followed her and took a seat, a touch of shyness sneaking up on me. "I can't say there is much to tell about me, not really. My aunt would be far better to —"

"Nonsense. I find you a delightful creature. That is certain. I can't imagine Lewis would have brought you here otherwise."

My smile faded. "What do you mean?"

Her laugh held an edgy, almost forced, quality to it. "What a dear you are, but don't look so shocked. I only meant to pay you a compliment. You shall learn soon enough that I simply say what I think, and I admire beauty in any form."

I tried again. "Mr. Browning only brought me to Greybourne Hall until we can find more suitable arrangements for my aunt and me."

"Hmm, is that what he told you?" Her eyebrows were rather thin and seemed to jump about when she spoke. "What a mull that man makes of everything." She took a long sip of tea.

It was then I noticed the tray and cake she must have summoned before our arrival. She evidently knew her way around the house. Of course, that is just what Mr. Browning had said, yet the thought rankled somehow.

"Lewis has given me leave to host a small dinner party in your honor. What do you say to that? He wants all the proper young men of the neighborhood in attendance, if you get my meaning." Her green eyes flashed. "It shall be such great fun."

Young men? Dread welled in my stomach, and I sent a silent plea to Aunt Jo in one sharp look.

Aunt Jo's teacup rattled on its saucer, agitated by her quivering fingers. She never liked to put herself forward, but she alone knew my resolve. "Why, Rebecca —"

Mrs. Browning seemed startled by Aunt Jo's voice, as if it grated on her nerves, her eyes widening and blinking.

Thankfully Aunt Jo paid her no heed. "How thoughtful of Mr. Browning . . . but I'm not at all certain . . . I mean, after the events of today, that we should be having any parties . . . for the time being that is."

Mrs. Browning stiffened. "What does your companion imply?" She directed the conversation back to me. "Whatever has happened?"

I took a deep breath. "There was an accident. Possibly last night. At the bridge."

Her face blanched, and for the first time I wondered if she knew Jacob and the particulars of his death.

"Last night?" Her hand found her chest. "Who?"

"It seems Mr. Drake fell to his death." I didn't mean to sound so cold and impersonal, but I knew no other way to disclose the news.

She pushed to her feet, her mouth slipping open. "Drake? Gone?" She turned away from us toward the window and fell silent for several seconds. "Who found him?"

Aunt Jo could see the hesitation in my eyes. "Miss Hunter and I did not long ago."

Ignoring my aunt, she spoke over her shoulder to me. "And Lewis. What is he to do? Is he implicated in some way?"

Surprised by her question and the continued insult to my aunt, I spoke a bit louder than I intended. "No. Not that I know of."

She shook off a chill. "Good."

Aunt Jo and I waited while Isabell paced the rug like a restless animal. I couldn't help but catch her wandering eyes, her thoughts so easily readable as they mirrored my own — same bridge, same accident.

All at once, she paused. "Such a tragedy." Then she draped the back of her hand across her forehead in a far more dramatic way than her initial reaction. "This must be a difficult time for you as well. Your brother, Jacob, and I were good friends."

"Were you?"

"I-I . . ." She ambled first for the door, then to the sideboard and poured herself a quick drink. "You must excuse me. I find that I am not myself. Give Lewis my regards, but I must return to the dower house at once. My brother, Adam, must be told what has happened."

Aunt Jo stood and offered her an arm. "Are you well enough to walk?"

She jerked away. "Don't be ridiculous. I never walk. My carriage will be brought round to the front." Recovering, she offered me a wan smile. "I'm so glad you are here, my dear Rebecca. I feel as if I already know you somehow. In future, you will call me Isabell. We're family after all, and I promise to return as soon as possible to plan your dinner party. I don't intend for this monstrous accident to affect your chances."

With that declaration, she strolled from the room.

I was waiting for Mr. Browning in the entryway the following day when the group that had gathered for the inquest emerged from the back of the house. One after the other, the men trudged by me on their way to the front door, each with a face of grave determination.

Mr. Browning lagged a few steps behind the others, leading the man I supposed to be acting as parish officer. A hush followed their heavy tread and settled into the gloomy corners of the room. The dusky afternoon light poured in through the open doorway, illuminating dust particles in the air. I shrank into the darkness of the wall.

Mr. Browning said little to the man as he bid him good day and inched the door shut. He rested first his hand against the dark wood, then his forehead. He remained that way for several seconds before trailing back my direction.

I cleared my throat. "What did they decide?"

My sudden words from the shadows must have startled him. His steps stilled, and his jaw clenched. He crossed his arms. "If you must know, they ruled it a blasted accident."

I moved forward. "But they didn't even speak with me."

"No. It was all over in a matter of minutes." He crumpled a piece of paper from his jacket pocket and threw it into the fire. "An accidental fall from the bridge, nothing more."

"But you don't believe them."

A vein twitched across his brow. "Do you?"

I could see Mr. Drake's body in my mind's eye, no broken bones, his face clear of the water. "No, I don't."

He snatched the poker from the wall and jammed it into the dwindling fire. Sparks popped and flew like small fireworks cascading over the logs, a few scattering against the fender. "Regardless of what we believe, it is done now. Unless . . ."

I moved in next to him, and the heat of the flames rolled over me. "Unless what?"

His eyelids narrowed, then relaxed. "Unless something definitive turns up to dispute their assessment."

I paused for a moment, weighing my next words. "You've learned something about Mr. Drake's death, haven't you?"

He met my gaze. "I have."

Emboldened by his openness, I leaned forward. "What?"

Footsteps sounded on the stairs, and he motioned to the back hall. "To the library? I have something I would prefer to ask you in private."

I followed him without thinking down the long corridor and into the paneled room I'd seen before, curious as to what he'd discovered. But as I entered the library with its towering shelves and dark walls, my confidence fled.

The remains of a fire smoldered in the grate. The scent of smoke mixed with the smell of books and old papers. Documents lay scattered about the huge desk. A decanter sat open on the sideboard, a cup tipped on its side. I remembered Mr. Drake's kind face and pleasing eyes. His absence was absolute.

Mr. Browning pressed by me without comment and motioned for me to sit. "Please excuse the disorder."

"Not at all." I settled into a large cushioned chair, but found my muscles unwilling to relax as a restless silence prowled about the room.

Mr. Browning leaned his shoulder against the bookshelf next to the fire, moving his hands first to the mantel then against his brown jacket. Eventually, he abandoned the idea and eased into the chair across from me. A strained resignation fell over his face. "I examined Drake's body."

"What?" I tried to hide the surprise in my voice.

He crossed a boot over his knee and watched me as he tended to do, assessing me. I fought back a sudden sense of panic. Neither of us trusted the other. I had been a fool to come alone.

He raised an eyebrow. "Perhaps I was wrong to involve you in all this." His fingernails dipped into the armrest's plush fabric. "However, my situation in town these past nine months has left me with few options, and you were a witness after all." A wrinkle formed on his brow. "If you'd prefer I speak with your aunt, I'd be happy to do so."

"Please, no." My words came out rushed. "Mr. Drake was very kind to my aunt and me in London. It is only natural I would hope for the truth to be found."

The dim candlelight made Mr. Browning's eyes a cool gray. He settled his elbows on his knees. "I believe he was murdered."

"How can you possibly know that?"

He rubbed his chin and relaxed the edge to his voice. "Several years ago, I spent some time in China where I met a man who worked with the bodies of the deceased. They have a fascinating knowledge of death over there. You would be amazed."

I tried to keep my reaction impassive, though *amazed* would hardly be the word I would use.

He went on. "The man utilized a book, which I had translated to English before I left. Since my return, I've had the time and the inclination to study it."

He rose to his feet and crossed the room to fetch a leather-bound stack of papers from his desk. "I believe I found something, but I wonder if I shouldn't spare you the details."

I suppose he meant to protect my innocent ears, but did he not know of my mother's descent into madness? I'd seen and heard it all. "Please, go on."

He ran his finger along the volume's edge. "My initial thought at the bridge was that Drake could not possibly have died of drowning. If you remember, his skin was yellow instead of white. His mouth and eyes were open. These facts didn't leave me, and on further investigation earlier today, I found no sand or mud in his fingernails. His feet weren't wrinkled as they should have been, and there were multiple bruises across his body."

I stared at the smoldering logs for several seconds, puzzling over his words. "He could have fallen."

"No," he said hurriedly. "Drake's face was swollen on only one side, which suggests not an accident but strangulation."

My gaze shot to his.

"That's not all. There was a mark low across his throat that was deep and black. It is my belief that whoever committed this brutal act did it from behind."

My stomach turned, and I closed my eyes. The images he had commanded were uncomfortable to digest. A bitter taste filled my mouth and burned my throat. The moment I had seen Mr. Drake's body replayed over and over again in my mind, meshing his battered form with images of my brother.

All at once I noticed that my fingers were shaking. I looked to the door, realizing belatedly I'd not been prepared for the truth.

Mr. Browning reached for my hand. "Perhaps I went too far. Cousin Rebecca, are you well?" His voice was kind, his grip secure. My ears buzzed and I held fast until my head cleared.

When able to breathe again, I found it difficult to meet his eyes, but I did so at last. "Yes, thank you." I slipped my hand away. "Did you tell them all of this at the inquest?"

"My findings were dismissed out of hand. I'm afraid the generalized distrust of me runs quite deep."

I thought for a moment. "I do believe what you say about Mr. Drake — that it was not an accident. But, do you know of anyone who would wish to see him dead?"

Mr. Browning turned and raked his fingers through his hair. "I have been pondering that very thought all day to no avail. There is no one who would wish him ill. He was such an amiable man. Tell me, did he meet anyone in London when he was assisting with the move?"

"Not that I am aware of. It all went quite

smoothly."

"As he reported upon his return." His next words came out carefully. "You do understand that I've taken you into my confidence as a member of my family. You will keep what I've told you to yourself?"

"Of course." I paused. "I do share your assumptions."

"I trust no one and neither should you."

I narrowed my eyes. "I cannot keep anything from my aunt, but I give you my promise beyond her."

A slow smile spread across his face. "That will do."

Surely it was the shock of all I'd learned, the danger his conclusions indicated, but as I returned his smile, a bit of warmth filled my cheeks. There was something awfully pleasant about his dark features and wild hair, which begged to be touched.

The small clock on the mantel chimed the hour, and I pushed to my feet. "It must be late. I should dress for dinner. Aunt Jo will be looking for me." I hurried to the door, then stopped cold as a thought ceased my movements in a way nothing else could.

I spun to face him, my earlier lightness replaced by a hard stare. "Tell me, Cousin. Did you examine my brother's body after *his* accident?"

The connection we had shared just moments ago drained from his face, and he averted his eyes. "No. It was several days before he came ashore and was located. He was miles downstream."

Numbly, I looked to the floor as the nagging pain of unanswered questions and blame filled my heart. I had much more to ask him about Jacob's death, but I had to be extremely careful. I'd no intention of revealing I was on a quest for the truth, or to alert him in any way. Slowly, I lifted my gaze. "I understand."

CHAPTER 5

My Dearest Rebecca,

I was relieved to receive your letter upon our arrival in Bath. Mother and I spent the whole of the journey discussing how very dreadful your move to Greybourne Hall must have been. What it must have felt like to face that man! I wish I had been there to comfort you, but Papa would not change his plans, and I know you've always preferred to handle things yourself.

As to your particular questions, I know little of what officially happened after Jacob's death was discovered. I plied Mother with questions, though, and I have been able to piece together a few things regarding Mr. Browning and the tragedy.

First of all, as I've said before, no one in town believes Mr. Browning innocent, as he has acted most peculiar since it all happened. Papa said Mr. Browning did not attend the funeral. And he was off to London to square away the entail before withdrawing into that awful house of his and refusing to see any visitors. Even Papa, who had business with Mr. Browning directly, was turned away.

There is more that I hesitate to write, for I have told no one thus far. You see, Jacob met me one afternoon only a week before he died. I had hoped to disclose this information to you in person, but I suppose a letter will have to do. At the time, Jacob begged me to keep our meeting a secret, and our being alone together would not have been looked upon well by my mother.

He was riding through our woods that day and came upon me painting a nearby hill. We sat for a bit as we used to as children. But, Rebecca, I found him distracted, edgy even, as if he knew something. Something about Mr. Browning? I cannot say, only that I hadn't seen Jacob in several months, and he appeared quite thin with dark circles under his eyes. It worried me a bit at the time, but now, now I cannot get the thought out of my mind.

During our coze he discussed his living situation at great length, but I could not understand what he meant. He spoke of a plan he had just in case — and money tucked away. I nodded and smiled, for I thought he was speaking of his debts of honor or the other ridiculous things he had involved himself in during his time in London. I daresay he cut a dash those two years he was there. I know he was forced to come to Greybourne Hall because his pockets were to let. He did tell me that much.

Later, he got quite agitated and said the whole thing had come to an impasse between himself and his guardian, that he feared what Mr. Browning would do. Did he owe him money? Or something worse? He asked me to write to you and make sure you'd settled in London, and then he kissed my hand in that dashing way he does whenever he wants something and was off.

I'm left with nothing but questions. What was Jacob doing on that bridge so late at night? And considering all he said, I cannot believe Mr. Browning uninvolved. Far too much of a coincidence, if you ask me.

I shall do my best to remember more and write when I can. I do hope you discover something. Please write and let me know of any information you come by. I miss him a great deal. And you as well.

Your loving cousin,
Ellen

"Good morning." A man's voice ripped me from my cousin's words.

I stopped short on the front path and folded the unsettling letter before thrusting it into my pocket. A gentleman I'd not met strolled down the lane. I gave him a cursory nod, but he didn't make way for me to pass.

He was a young man with fine eyes dressed smartly in a pale blue jacket. He dipped his chin. "I don't mean to sound impertinent, but would you be so kind as to tell me if Mr. Browning is available for visitors this morning?"

Distracted, I motioned back toward the house. "Why, I believe he is." I added a questioning glance.

A wide smile spread across his face, bringing out an attractive dimple. "Thank you, miss. You have done me quite the favor. Yes, a favor indeed." He bowed as if I were the queen but met my eyes as he straightened. "Considering Mr. Browning has been avoiding me these many weeks or more, I daresay I might have put you in a difficult situation." Then he laughed. "For I shall demand to see him now."

I could just imagine Knowles's disgruntled surprise when this man pushed by him. After what Ellen said in her letter, I doubted many visitors came to Greybourne Hall. Particularly ones so bold. However, considering this man had no more love for my guardian than I did, I decided to humor him and added mildly, "In return, sir, you must tell me why Mr. Browning sees fit to avoid you?"

He removed his hat to reveal a tangle of yellow curls. "I suppose I should, but first, allow me introduce myself. I am your neighbor, Mr. Galpin. And you must be Browning's ward."

I hesitated, then nodded. "Miss Hunter."

"Do not be concerned." He stooped forward. "I have no intention of telling anyone we met, since we've not been properly introduced. Isabell would have my head." He laughed again. "And on further thought, I say we keep this little meeting a secret. I have every plan of attending your dinner party, and now that I've laid eyes on you, I mean to have the first two dances."

My mouth felt suddenly dry. Goodness, I thought the party far from planned, even at risk of not happening at all. But it seemed Isabell had been busy since we spoke. Irritated by her presumption, my voice came out severe. "Thank you for your interest, but there may not be a dinner party at all." I cleared my throat. "Allow me to ask again, Mr. Galpin, why does Mr. Browning not wish to see you?"

He raised his eyebrows. "You make it sound as if we've a pesky argument brewing. I assure you, it's not as bleak as all that. I've a plan to renew my offer to buy Greybourne Hall is all, and Mr. Browning does not like to be reminded of his family's . . . shall we call them — shortcomings."

Buy Greybourne Hall? "Mr. Browning intends to sell?"

"Not at present. But I do bring a generous offer. And considering what Isabell has revealed to me about her living situation, I wonder if he might be waning on his earlier intention of never letting me have it."

I thought of the townhouse in London and the cottage in Scotland. Perhaps Mr. Browning had reasons for his hasty decisions. "Well, I do wish you luck, Mr. Galpin, but you must excuse me. It is time I am on my way."

A bark thundered at my back, and I turned to see Sophie plowing through the hedgerow. She careened to a halt, the hair on her back rising to attention before she launched headfirst at Mr. Galpin, teeth bared. I opened my mouth to call her back as Mr. Galpin shrank away in horror. "What a little beast. Control the dog at once."

I apologized as I seized Sophie's collar. "She really is quite sweet once you get to know her."

Off stride, Mr. Galpin straightened his jacket and spoke with an edge to his otherwise pleasant voice. "I suppose Mr. Browning has seen fit to set his dog on me. Pity the mongrel is not a bit larger." A smile played with his lips. "Reminds me of the pest he used to always have underfoot."

"Oh?"

Sophie barked and lunged at Mr. Galpin once again, but I held her back.

Mr. Galpin took a wild step back. "I do believe I shall bid you good day, Miss Hunter." He cast one last cutting look at Sophie and departed down the hedgerow toward the house, his hat gripped hard in his hand.

That night I awoke with a start, my heart thrashing in my chest, my head wet with sweat. For a breathless moment I had been back in Scotland. Lost in the long, dark winter nights that Mother never handled well.

My hands quivered. My muscles screamed in tension.

"It wasn't real," I said aloud, if only to give credence to the fact that I was awake now, and the shape I'd seen in the shadows had disappeared.

A small clock ticked from wherever it lay buried in the darkness, but the rest of the room remained still — an unnatural stillness that could only be found in the small hours when I'd had one of my "dreams" or whatever one called them. Mother had labeled them spells, but I refused to do so.

I rubbed my forehead and took a deep breath, staring at the end of the poster bed, the memory of what I'd seen like a sharp dagger, fresh in my mind. Her jasmine scent, the sound of her voice, it had all felt so real.

I eased into a sitting-up position, waiting for my mind to clear from the dreamlike state I tended to slip into all too often. Half-awake, half-asleep, my first unsettling experiences with seeing things began when I was a child. The first had been a snake in the folds of my covers. I'd panicked and screamed and tried to push it away, only to realize nothing was there at all. Later, people came, standing in my room, staring at me. They never spoke, but I feared them all the same.

Each time I would eventually fight my way awake, and the ghosts of my "dreams" would disappear into the night, leaving me with a sense of intrusion and dread. Over the years I'd told no one except Aunt Jo, for fear others would come to the same conclusion I had — that someday these visions would cease to be a nighttime occurrence and would creep into the daylight hours as my mother's had.

I lit the candle at my bedside, my fingers still jittery from my latest visitor. It was my mother this time, gaping at me from the foot of the bed. At least, I thought it was her, a much younger version, her hair done up as she used to wear it when I was a child. Although I could not see her face clearly through the darkness, I'd know those piercing green eyes anywhere.

It was the second time since I'd arrived at Greybourne Hall that I'd seen her, far more frequent "dreams" than usual. I tried to settle the flutters in my stomach. Perhaps the difficulty of the move and the murder brought them on.

A subtle draft swept the bed. The candlelight wavered, sending shadows dithering across the far wall. The hairs on the back of my neck lifted, and I glanced up. The door to my room was ajar.

I grabbed the coverlet as I leaned forward. "Who's there?"

My heart throbbed and I strained to listen, but there was no answer.

Suddenly I heard a scratch at the side of the bed, then a shuffle. A round ghost took shape in the gloom, pacing. All at once the figure hurled itself onto the bed, rushing straight for my lap. A scream bubbled up as I pawed desperately at the darkness.

The hairy, wet-nosed bundle licked my hand, and my pulse slackened.

"Sophie! You little wretch." Goodness. I took a long breath.

The dog panted a sort of smile before nosing under my hand.

"How ever did you escape Aunt Jo? Or get in here, for that matter?"

My gaze flicked back to the door, an eerie thought taking hold. I had shut it completely before bed. Hadn't I? There's no way Sophie could have nudged it open. I pulled the dog close to my chest, my eyes trained to the dark hallway beyond.

No sound. No movement. Nothing but my ingenious imagination.

My shoulders relaxed. "I suppose we

should seal the door, shouldn't we?"

Sophie licked my cheek, and I made a spot in the bed for her to curl up beside me when I returned.

A chill hovered on the floor, and my bare feet slapped against the icy boards as I raced to the door. I peered out. Moonlight cascaded down the hall from the windows, bathing the long carpet in white squares and crisscrossing shadows. Silence wrapped my thoughts as I watched and waited, yet nothing moved, nothing to warrant my nervous flight to the door.

Carefully I retreated inside, inching the door closed before turning back to Sophie and the bed. But my tense gaze shot to the window and the flicker of light beyond the glass. The hairs on my arms pricked to attention. I had seen something similar before.

I padded over to the glass and searched the dim horizon. A small light shone near the woods. Someone was prowling the grounds. Could it be Mr. Browning? He was known as the midnight devil after all, and I had seen him myself riding about the estate deep into the night. No, this person was not tall enough.

A chill tickled my arms as I remembered the glow Mr. Browning and I had seen through the library window the day I arrived at Greybourne Hall. Of course, it could have been anyone, but Mr. Browning had thought it Mr. Drake at the time. Yet now . . .

My breath caught as the dark figure turned into the moonlight to glare back at the house, and I shrank behind the wall and into the safety of my room. Whoever was out there wore a red rag across his face. He didn't want to be known.

"Sophie!" Aunt Jo called the dog, as we'd lost sight of her yet again on our morning walk.

"Do not be overly concerned. She knows where we are." I hoped what I said was true, for I intended to retrace the path the masked man had taken the previous night, and I hadn't the time to be forever searching out the silly pup. Sophie had made things decidedly more difficult — barking at nearly everything, rolling on the ground, and darting off in all directions, but I hadn't told Aunt Jo what I'd seen from my bedroom window. She would forbid me to leave the house, and I thought bringing Sophie along would provide a layer of protection, so to speak.

"That infuriating dog certainly has a way of trying one's patience; however, she is all

I have in the world, and I don't know what I would do if I lost her." Aunt Jo looked fretfully into the trees. "There is quite a bit more nature for her to explore here than in London, and you do force me to let her off lead."

I smiled, my hands still a bit sore from her artful tugging. "She was in need of a run, and you know it will do her a world of good. Knowles will be glad to have her enthusiasm spent by this afternoon, I assure you."

"I suppose you are right." A tumble resounded in the underbrush, then Sophie raced by once again. Aunt Jo raised her eyebrows. "Well," she said with a huff. "What are we about today? I daresay I wasn't woken early and forced to leave my warm bedchamber simply to give you a bit of company."

"Indeed, you are correct, Aunt Jo. But I daresay you are glad of the invitation — even at this time of morning." I nudged her arm. "Don't deny it."

She glanced up into the towering trees, the deep blue sky sweeping overhead like an endless painting. "I'll admit, I do love our chats, and it is rather pretty around here."

I kicked a rock with my half boot. "Now don't scold me, but I do have plans for our morning jaunt." I stifled a grin. "I've a mind to look for more clues."

I'd been doing some plotting. Since Mr. Drake's death occurred at night — the same time of day I had seen the masked man . . . and interestingly enough, Mr. Browning — perhaps someone had left something.

Aunt Jo pursed her lips. "I thought as much. Regarding Jacob's death, you mean?"

"No. Mr. Drake's."

"My word, Rebecca. Isn't one ill-advised investigation enough?"

After reading Ellen's letter, I had more questions than answers about Jacob's death, and I was determined to find an angle to pursue. "There may be a possibility the two deaths are connected in some way."

She touched my arm. "Considering they fell from the same bridge, I can't say the thought hasn't crossed my mind, yet —"

"That is just what I mean. Moreover, Mr. Browning and I believe Mr. Drake didn't fall at all."

She hesitated. "But Jacob certainly did. Why, Ellen said in her letters that Mr. Browning knocked your brother from his feet while riding by. Accident or not."

"Yes, but Jacob died over nine months ago, leaving us little chance of uncovering any evidence of foul play. Mr. Drake's sudden death may turn up something."

"You have a great deal of sense, Rebecca, but should you be trusting the very man who you feel responsible in the first place?"

"I do see your point; however, you must also concede that I cannot continue on without his involvement. Do not fret though, I shall be exceedingly careful, and it is equally possible he may eventually betray something — something that may lead me to the truth."

A twig popped at our backs, and we spun around.

"Good day, ladies." It was Mr. Galpin, dimple and all.

Aunt Jo's hand flew to her chest. "You startled us, sir."

He looked almost shocked. "Well, I hadn't the least intention of doing so. I was merely enjoying the fine autumn morning for a walk."

On Mr. Browning's land? I pressed my lips together, hoping he hadn't overhead our conversation, then gave him a smile. "As were we."

Aunt Jo took my arm. "Yes, Mr. Browning told us he has many fine walks in these woods."

Mr. Galpin moved to allow us to pass, but abruptly turned. "Browning suggested a walk? Egad, but that would astonish me. I cannot believe my neighbor has ever been out and about in daylight."

Aunt Jo shuffled a step. "And why not, pray tell?"

Mr. Galpin shrugged. "I daresay Mr. Browning cannot stomach the insults. As his unwilling guests, surely you are aware he has become the biggest recluse these parts have ever known. Not a soul sees him out during the day. Not for some time now."

I pressed my lips together. How did Mr. Galpin know we had come to Greybourne Hall against our wishes? Then I remembered my loose tongue in front of the servants. "What do you mean, insults?"

He frowned, but I did not think it genuine. "Regarding Mr. Browning's guilt, of course. Although, I'd rather not discuss the beastly details in front of two lovely ladies."

Aunt Jo dipped her chin. "Perhaps not. Good day to you, sir."

He gave us a nod, but I could not miss the amusement about his eyes. "Good day, ladies."

Aunt Jo and I plowed forward. Confident we were out of earshot, she leaned close. "What a bold sort of man to put himself forward in such a way. Do you think he knew you were Jacob's sister?"

"Yes, I do."

She wrinkled her nose. "Indeed. And he was quite definite in his opinions about our host."

I sighed. "I'm afraid the meeting he had with Mr. Browning must not have gone to his liking yesterday."

She grasped my hand. "What meeting yesterday? Do you know him, my dear?"

I related the events of the day before as we walked.

At length, Aunt Jo bit her lip. "I suppose that means we shall have a friend at the dinner party." She glanced behind her. "Perhaps the gentleman could be charming in another light."

"Oh . . . Aunt Jo . . ."

As we rounded the bend, the bridge over the River Grey loomed large before us. Our conversation was snuffed out like a candle in the wind, the dreary stone structure barring our way. Gingerly, we walked to the cliff's edge and explored the span of the bridge before descending to the water's edge.

I could still make out where Mr. Drake's body had been. The dirt was disturbed, a few reeds crushed along the bank. In the open light, the morning dew glistened in a line leading to the adjacent hill. My brow furrowed. Rocks were strewn about, the grass pressed and stretched. Almost as if something had been dragged away.

Perhaps when the people were moving the body. Or not? I followed the strange trail until it disappeared into the thick under-brush and dense forest. There, I took several moments to scour the space, certain the discovery would lead to something. But just as the gnarled oaks intertwined over my head, the fledgling bushes and trees sought to cover the ground. Nature, it seemed, had other plans.

Aunt Jo sidled over. "What is it, Rebecca? Did you find something?"

"Not much, I'm afraid." I shrugged. "It's just this odd rustling pattern on the ground. I thought perhaps Mr. Drake's body had been moved somehow, but the trail leads nowhere. It only disappears."

A sudden flutter of wings startled me, and I glanced up to catch sight of a blackbird darting in and out of the tree limbs. It was then I perceived a flash of white, hiding on the low branch of a nearby oak, so small I almost missed it — a handkerchief at eye level, hooked in the crook of the tree and forgotten.

I retrieved the ripped fabric and held it up to the light. It was well worn, with dark brown stains and a large tear, but I was able to make out a pair of initials embroidered in the corner. I moved the handkerchief to the side for Aunt Jo to see. "What do you make of this?"

She leaned forward. "Goodness, what a thing to find in a tree and of such fine quality. Hmm, do you think that could that be an *L*? The second letter is most certainly a *B,* but the third" — she squinted — "is far too ragged to determine."

I, too, could not decipher the first or last initials, but my guess on the second letter was as assured as Aunt Jo's. It was a *B,* as in Browning. Interesting. Of course, if the handkerchief were indeed his, the *B* would be the third initial, not the second.

Like a roll of thunder, a sudden cluster of shouts and growls reverberated through the trees. I spun around, realizing the sounds emanated from the bridge.

Sophie.

I tore back the way we'd come only to catch the fleeting sight of a dark jacket disappearing into the far trees.

Gasping for breath, Aunt Jo stopped beside me, her hand splayed across her chest. "Sophie, darling. Return to me at once."

Sophie trotted straight to us at the use of

her name, her pink tongue lolling to the side, but I spared her only a cursory glance as I ran the handkerchief's rough fabric between my fingers. Carefully, I slid it into my pocket, my mind on the retreating figure I'd seen moments ago. Suppositions twisted a path in my mind. Someone had been following us. I glanced behind me, then back to Aunt Jo. Far too many people utilized these woods. Aunt Jo's face was all too plain to read. She was on edge as well.

CHAPTER 6

Later the same day, quite by accident, I unearthed Greybourne's hidden garden. After the events of the morning, I had little interest in another long walk in the woods and was pleased to find the small iron gate concealed by brambles at the back of the house. A quick glance through the narrow opening, and I thought the solitary garden the perfect spot to lose myself for the afternoon.

Inside the gate, a slender walking path emerged that twisted its way in and out of hanging willows and berry-filled holly trees. A lush wilderness folded in around me. Curtains of creepers in muted tones reached out, urging me from my reflections. Elder shrubs lined the path, and the scent of fresh, dampened soil met my nose.

As I walked, the foliage deepened once again, and I had to lift a low-hanging branch to approach a curved bench. It backed up to an ivy-covered wall and circular pool. My presence was instantly noted by the resident frog, who leapt into the still water, sending ripples across the surface.

In awe, I took a seat. London had its vast parks and grand statues, but nothing to compare to the serenity of this beautiful place.

I took a long breath, and my eyes slipped shut.

"Why, Miss Hunter."

Startled, I nearly shot to my feet. I hadn't expected anyone to find me, lost in the heart of the garden as I was. Least of all *him.*

Standing near a birch tree, his arms loosely crossed, Mr. Browning had a wry smile across his face. "I see you found my thinking spot." A basket was looped over one arm, and he set it on the bench as he approached. "I had planned a solitary luncheon." He shrugged, a boyish quickness about his movements. "But perhaps you'd favor me with your company."

A fluttery feeling swarmed my thoughts as I pondered the implications of what he proposed. Slowly, I lifted my eyes to his. "Perhaps . . . I should not." I peered down the retreating path. "Servants tend to talk, regardless of whether you are my guardian or not."

He smiled, his easy grin quite natural in the sumptuous garden. "True, but I also get the feeling that you don't care a fig for what other people might think."

He was remembering my tour of the house, and I regarded him with a wary look. "I daresay you are correct in your assumption. I care little for the opinions of others."

He cocked an eyebrow. "So?"

It was a challenge, and I lowered my lashes. "However, I also do not intend to be badgered into doing anything I do not choose to do myself."

"Certainly not. I should particularly despise a man who *badgered.*" His cough hid a laugh, and he managed a pert look. "Considering that the callous term you accuse me of originates from the practice of badger-baiting, tell me, Miss Hunter, would that make me the poor badger trapped in the barrel, or the vicious dog that drags him out?"

I thought for a moment before meeting his searching gaze with a far more piercing one of my own. "The dog, of course."

"Of course." He slanted his chin. "However, I'm afraid that leaves you to be the badger, a miserable, aggressive animal at that."

My eyes widened. "Only when attacked."

He laughed. "Touché."

A volatile calm seemed to descend over the garden before Mr. Browning looked back up. "Well, I'm glad we have settled all that. Though I'm afraid you still have me at a disadvantage, for I haven't any idea whether you mean to stay or not. And trust me, Miss Hunter, I have no intention of badgering you any further." There was a humorous glint about his eyes as he lifted the basket lid. "Mrs. Dyer usually packs plenty."

The man was atrocious. He clearly meant to infuriate me, flirting like a boy gaining his first touch of town bronze, but my heart lightened all the same. Regardless of my conflicted feelings, such an opportunity might not present itself again for some time . . . and I had questions. I took a seat. "I suppose I could favor you with my company for a few minutes. We are family after all."

"Yes, family, though I don't know how the deuce that comes to be."

"Well, I certainly couldn't enlighten you, or my aunt, for that matter. We've been unable to piece together the connection at all."

He smiled. "So, you have discussed me."

Heat filled my cheeks, and unconsciously I inched backward on the bench. If the man

100

thought to wheedle his way into my affections, he was entirely deceived. "Only in the most formal way, I assure you."

Mr. Browning settled onto the far end of the bench, his dark blue jacket mirroring the brilliance of his eyes; the evergreen branches the perfect backdrop for his dark hair. He was more at ease than I had seen him before, tucked away from the world in this little wilderness of his. He was a natural host. I wondered how often he came here. Was it a place of refuge from his guilt? Considering the care the trees and bushes evidently received — I'd been a fool not to realize it before — this was his special place.

He took out some bread and cold meats and arranged them on a small blanket on the bench between us, followed by a cup he filled with punch. I accepted the drink, allowing our eyes to meet for a brief second as my fingers slid along his. My heart ticked a bit faster, but I was determined to keep it under careful control.

Why had Mr. Browning asked me to stay? I looked around. "This is a beautiful place. I can see why you come here often."

"I rarely seek out company, Miss Hunter. My soul is revived by nature."

"That is quite poetic."

"Please, don't accuse me of that. I assure

you, my brother would be vastly amused by such an assertion, if he were still with us." Mr. Browning flicked a fallen leaf off his breeches. "Charles was the artist of the family — not me."

Sensing an underlying ache to his words, I found myself curiously aligning with his sentiments. I, too, had been the forgotten sibling after all. "I daresay practicality has its place as well. I haven't the least use for Byron when I need a dress mended or a new hat arranged."

I liked his laugh — a soothing blend of amusement and pleasure. A wrinkle creased his brow. "What ever will you say next? Though, I suppose I am glad to meet with your approval in some way. That is, when I am not badgering you."

I lifted my chin. "Do not read too far into my words, sir. You did force me from the home I loved."

He cast a quick glance at the cloudy sky. "A task that was unavoidable, I'm afraid."

This was the first casual conversation we'd had since I arrived, and all at once, I didn't wish to spoil it. Yet, I had stayed for answers — difficult or not. Jacob would not be so addlebrained. "I, uh, met your friend, Mr. Galpin, on my morning walk yesterday."

He took a long sip of his drink. "Ah, my

persistent neighbor. And how did you find him?"

"Civil, I suppose."

"A favorite in the district. He's been eyeing my land for some time now. Rest assured, Greybourne Hall shall never be his."

Considering the two estates Mr. Browning had inherited from my brother, I believed his convictions would not be difficult to maintain.

The frog returned to the pond's edge, and I watched him waddle beneath a few rocks, while silence crept up like an unwanted guest.

Greybourne Hall. The townhouse in London. The cottage in Scotland.

For the first time I wondered who the heir to his holdings was at present. Of course, such a person would not inherit if Mr. Browning married and fathered a son. He was still young, and really, it was surprising he had not done so already.

Mr. Browning, it seemed, had not moved on from our discussion of Mr. Galpin, as if he had some need to explain himself further. "I'll have you know that I consider Galpin nothing more than a distant acquaintance. Isabell, however, is quite friendly with the gentleman. They are together often. I suppose I humor him for her sake — when I'm in the mood to do so."

"And Mrs. Browning was married to your younger brother?"

"Yes. Charles. He was killed by an accident at sea several years ago. He and Isabell had not been married long. I still miss him a great deal." He glanced up. "As I know you do your own brother and parents."

"Loss of one's family is indeed difficult." The words sounded empty, and I wished I could take them back the moment they spilled out.

I took a nervous bite of bread and a few wayward crumbs rolled down my gown. I brushed them away before catching Mr. Browning's sudden half smile from the corner of my eyes. The expression lifted the lines on his face and softened his usually sharp gaze.

He rested his arm on the back of the bench while the elusive wind played with a stray lock of hair. "What brought you out here today, Miss Hunter? No one has taken an interest in my little garden in years."

"The beauty and the solitude, I suppose."

He allowed a restful silence before responding. "I can understand that."

I selected a piece of cold meat, surprised by how comfortable it felt, sitting with Mr.

Browning alone. I could almost feel his thoughts, his quiet humor amid all the pressing concerns.

He dipped his chin. "Speaking of Isabell, you should know that I left her just moments ago. I fear she has it in her mind to have the dinner party at your earliest convenience."

"I thought she might. Do you think it proper after Mr. Drake's death?"

"Mr. Drake was not well-known in the district, and I do not believe she will be put off. I daresay a small dinner will not be deemed insensitive." He stared off into the distance. "When Isabell originally proposed the idea, long before your arrival, mind you, I saw no reason not to introduce you to Plattsdale society." He rubbed his chin. "But now, I'm not so certain."

I stiffened, stung by his words. "Why do you say that?"

He tapped the back of the bench. "I may be wrong, but I don't believe the idea interests you."

He had that haunted look about him as if he could read my mind, and the thought needled me. "Undoubtedly, I would be pleased to meet your friends. But allow me to be clear. I have no thoughts of marriage."

His eyes widened. "You shock me, Miss

Hunter. A young lady without money or connections . . . Have you any expectations at all? I am your guardian, and your future is heavy on my mind."

My hand went to my skirt, straightening it, dusting off any remaining crumbs. Such a topic was the last thing I meant to discuss, particularly with him. "I shan't be a burden to you, if that is what you imply. Aunt Jo and I shall think of something. We always do."

He raised his eyebrows, a light smile about his lips. "I'm assured you will, but Isabell is not so easily routed. The party will have to be endured for the both of us."

I pictured the great room filled with guests. Strangers looking at me, measuring my worth. Mr. Galpin and his ridiculous dimple and all it implied. The insults Mr. Browning might be forced to bear. Sympathy pressed my heart. I would not be the only one on display.

"As expected, I shall attend." I paused. "Although not to set my cap at some hapless guest. In fact, I would be far more at ease if you would be so kind as to lead me out for the first dance."

My heart pounded. I froze like a pond in winter, unable to look up or move away. What on earth had I just said? How presumptuous of me. I bit my lip — hard. Drat my Scottish independence. What would Aunt Jo think of such behavior? There I was thinking how awful it would be to dance with Mr. Galpin and his expectations, and the words just tumbled out.

Mr. Browning blinked, a peculiar expression rounding his eyes. "If that is what you wish, I'd be honored."

A heavy stillness descended and all I could do was chew. Not only had I chosen to dance with the man who had a hand in my brother's death, but I'd taken it upon myself to ask him to do it. What a miserable little idiot I was. Of course, it would only aid the investigation to get close to Mr. Browning, would it not? To gain his confidence?

I took a desperate sip of punch. Perhaps, in my ignorance, I had stumbled onto the very thing that could lead me to the truth. Mr. Browning and I could cry friends. I glanced up. Goodness, he was half there already. But what of me? Could I control my loose tongue? And my fickle heart?

"Mr. Browning?"

He cleared his throat. "Won't you call me Lewis? I have no patience for formality among cousins."

"All right. Lewis." The sudden familiarity felt an intrusion after my earlier thoughts.

"Thank you." What else could I say?

The luncheon dispensed with, Lewis returned the empty dishes to the basket. I stood, contemplating the dance and the dinner party. A curious mix of excitement and dread had filled my chest, when the crack of a gunshot racketed through the small garden. Lewis pushed to his feet and seized my arm, concern consuming his face.

"Your gamekeeper perhaps?" I asked, my feet tingling.

"Not this close to the estate." He thrust the basket into my hands. "Please return to the house at once and remain inside. I will speak with you there shortly." His eyes never left the far wall.

"But —"

"Do as I say."

"I . . ."

My sentence floated away on the breeze, for Lewis had already darted through the willow branches and disappeared.

Evening rolled into Plattsdale with a vengeance that night, lightning illuminated the walls, rain coursed down the stones of the house, the roof moaned above our heads.

Aunt Jo covered her face with her quivering fingers. "What if Sophie is missing all night? This dreadful storm has likely set in for hours."

I begged my aunt over to the large fireplace in the entryway and away from the recessed windows. The northern wind had turned cold, and she had been out in it far too long. I'd already dressed for dinner, but Aunt Jo was a mess. "Sophie knows her way around the estate well. She will find her way back or a safe place to bed down for the night."

I said rather than believed the words, for I had been worried about the dog since I learned she hadn't returned. And now it was full dark. "Perhaps Lewis can send one of the servants to ride around the estate."

Aunt Jo jumped at my use of Lewis's Christian name, but she made no remark. She was far too addled. "Mr. Browning has already done so. And I've been walking all over the grounds calling her name. She is nowhere near."

I was the one who had insisted that Sophie be let loose to run. If anything befell that maddening dog, I'd have no one to blame but myself. I rubbed Aunt Jo's chilled arms. "She'll be back."

The front door flung open, crashing into the adjacent wall. Lewis stormed inside, rain dripping from his wet hair.

Aunt Jo hurried to his side, and he led her

back to the fire. "I'm sorry to say, but there is no sign of Sophie anywhere." His fingers went to his hair, stopping at the back as he shook his head. His voice was strained. "My groom will continue the search; however, I regret to say I have somewhere I simply have to be."

I glanced out the window. "At this hour, and in this weather?"

"It cannot be helped." He glared about the room as if thinking on something. "If you will excuse me." He started for the stairs, then halted at the last moment, turning to face us. "You haven't heard any more shots hereabouts? It was only the one?"

I nodded, a twinge of unease crawling beneath my skin. "None whatsoever." I wished he hadn't said anything in front of Aunt Jo.

"Good." He hesitated, staring into the shadows for a long moment, then scrambled up the stairs. I doubted we'd see him again before morning.

Aunt Jo grasped my arm. "What did Mr. Browning mean? Shots? Here at Greybourne Hall?"

I shrugged off her concern, hoping to abate my own. "It was likely nothing, but Lewis and I did hear something while we were together in the garden."

110

She raised her eyebrows, dipping her chin. "Rebecca?"

My face tightened. "Yes, Lewis and I were in the garden today, but our being together was not what you imply. We met there quite by accident."

Aunt Jo crossed her arms and shook her head. "My dearest darling, I stand a poor companion for you — allowing you free rein of the house and grounds while I searched for my dog. What would your father say?"

A chill circled my heart. "Likely nothing. As long as I stayed out of his way."

CHAPTER 7

I set out alone the following morning on the hunt for Sophie. Aunt Jo had kept to her room, likely too exhausted from her vigil the previous night to face another day without answers. Isabell had arrived to see Lewis, but I had no time to humor her.

Dew glistened the tips of the yellowed grass and painted the bare bushes along the path. There was a look of disorder about the land, having endured the beating of the storm. A whisper followed each of my steps as yesterday's gunshot echoed in my mind. Could it have involved my aunt's dog? I pushed away the thought, unable to deal with another loss in the family.

"Sophie!" I called, my voice growing more and more urgent as Greybourne Hall's black pile of stones faded behind me. I entered the heart of the woods. There, the previous night's storm had brought with it winter's ghost, a glimpse of the chill to

112

come. My nose ached, and I buried my fingers farther into my muff.

"Sophie!" Wind whipped through the towering oaks like a bolting horse, stealing any chance I had of being heard.

A fine mist clung to the shrubbery and shadows as I walked, making any length of sight difficult. But I was determined to follow the same path my aunt and I had taken the previous day, if I could only figure out where I was. Surely, I was nearing the bridge.

"Sophie!" I tried again.

Ahead in the gloom, a figure appeared. I squinted, unable to determine just what it was in the distance. It was far too large to be a dog and traveling rather quickly. Broad shouldered, dark clothes. A man emerged, and the outline of a gun took shape against his jacket. The hairs on my arms wriggled to attention, and I glanced behind me. How far had I traveled from the house?

My shoulders tensed and in one swift movement, I retreated to the back of a large oak and sank against the cold, ridged wood.

The man's footsteps became audible, scraping against the gravel with a heavy tread. Louder, more persistent. The fleeting image of the jacket in the woods stole into my mind. Whoever the man was, he would pass by quite close to where I stood. My legs felt weak, and with a shiver, I pressed against the tree.

A small animal scampered into the brush along the path and I held my breath. The pounding footsteps ceased as well.

"Sophie?" The man's shout had an almost piteous quality to it.

My shoulders relaxed. The pent-up tension flowed from my muscles as quickly as it had come. I shut my eyes for a blessed second. What an imagination I had. It was daylight after all.

I moved into the foggy light. "Good morning, Mr. Galpin."

He smiled. "Ah, Miss Hunter. A good morning it is, but not for our little friend, I'm afraid." He stared off into the distance. "Isabell was a guest at my house for dinner last night. Browning told her of the unfortunate disappearance during his search. I promised right away that I'd help in the morning first thing."

I couldn't help but remember Mr. Galpin's utter revulsion of the dog previously. It was interesting he was out here searching. "We are all quite worried for the pup. It's not like her to run off like she did and not return."

"Isabell was beside herself with worry. I

mean, after Mollie's death and all, and the two dogs so alike. She knows how it might affect Mr. Browning."

My brows drew in. "Mollie?"

"Yes, Browning and his dog were inseparable until . . ."

I leaned forward, urging him to finish his sentence.

"Till I found her shot in the woods 'bout four weeks ago."

I shrank back. "Murdered? His dog? Who would do such a terrible thing?"

Mr. Galpin poked a rock with his boot. "We never did find out. I figure too many villagers still blame Mr. Browning for your brother's death." He looked away. "Sometimes people do awful things when they feel justified."

My heart ticked a bit faster. "Regardless of Mr. Browning's guilt, they should never have laid one hand on his dog. Monsters." I swallowed hard. "Speaking of guilt, what do you know about the night of my brother's death? Mr. Browning *was* responsible for what happened that day on the bridge, was he not? He said he knocked Jacob straight into the torrent of water."

Mr. Galpin hesitated. "No one has claimed to be present on the bridge that night besides Mr. Browning. He is the only one

115

able to say what happened." He hunched forward, his words tight. "It is unfortunately left for us either to believe him or not."

I didn't move.

"I'll warn you, though, if it is a quest for answers that brought you to Greybourne Hall, then I suggest you consider carefully how far you intend to search for them. There are some ghosts you might not want to summon back to life."

I suppose it was the unsettling meeting with Mr. Galpin or the continued absence of Sophie that caused me to have another vision of my mother that night. This time she stood before me for only a second, her eyes bloodshot, her gaze wretched. The room felt unusually hazy, and she stumbled toward the bed where I slept, her arms outstretched, her fingers gnarled.

Then I was awake — panting, sweating, crying.

The room fell empty as a hint of moonlight fought the shadows in my mind. I dared not move, dared not lose the feel of her presence, the aching intensity of being with her once again, even if she seemed angry with me.

I lay there for quite some time unable to return to sleep before rising and donning a dressing gown. I was drawn once again to the muted light of the window. In Scotland on such a night, I would have raced out into the adjacent field — no lamp, no reservations, only the brilliance of the stars for company.

In the warmer months, I'd have lain in the tall grass for hours, tracing the constellations with my finger, tracking the movement of the heavens and the waning moon. The infinite vastness calmed my fears in a way nothing else could. I'd not made the connection before Jacob's death, but the stars were the only thing that had remained a constant in my life. They reminded me of the time Jacob had risked his life for mine.

The feel of the wind that day, the sound of the leaves rustling in the trees, it was all still so real. One moment seared into my memory. I was only seven years old, adventurous and reckless. It had been an imaginative summer. And at the time, I saw no purpose for drawing rooms and embroidery. It was the wilds I wanted. To be like my brother — to be free.

As soon as it was dark, I fled our country house and followed Jacob beyond the front lawns. There was a full moon and plenty of light to aid my ever-increasing curiosity. I ran farther and farther into the trees until I was quite a way into the woods, which is where I saw it.

A large dog. Silver moonlight glistened off his raised fur. A low growl transformed the silence of the forest. I learned later the animal was rabid, but all I could think of at the time was how terribly in danger I was and how foolish I had been for darting out of the house the way I did.

The animal leapt for me, teeth bared, eyes fixed on my chest. I was struck immobile for a moment before I managed a strangled yell. Its claw struck first, beating me to the ground. I knew its strong jaws would inevitably follow, but a gunshot cracked through the night air. The heavy animal went suddenly limp at my side. I lay there on the cold ground, petrified for several seconds, staring at the stars, wondering what had happened to spare me. Then Jacob pulled me to my feet.

He roughly checked me over, livid I had followed him and put myself in such peril. Then he turned back to the dead body of the dog. Over and over again he kicked the lump of fur, shouting into the night like I'd never seen him before. Terrified, I clung to his arm and eventually the heat of anger ebbed from his face and his boot stilled. He was so strong at fourteen, and he lifted me into his arms. He carried me home pressed to his chest, my eyes turned to the heavens and the stars.

During that long walk, I had a great deal of time to ponder what I'd experienced. We didn't speak then about what had happened, or ever. But I knew from that day forward that regardless of our arguments, Jacob would do anything for me. We had a bond. If I ever needed him, he would be there. Of course, little did I know then how much we would both endure over the years. First Father's death and then Mother's two years later. And now I was alone.

I pressed my forehead to the cool glass of my bedchamber window and searched once again for the stars. But with the overhang of the roof, I couldn't make out a single twinkle. The stars, my stars, were out there just beyond my reach, and all at once I needed to be with them.

I secured my half boots, slung my pelisse around my shoulders, and snuck from the stifling air of Greybourne Hall.

I was careful to be sure the servants were all abed and the lights had vanished from the many windows facing the terrace. The last thing I needed was questions about what I experienced night after night, and I had no intention of being discovered, not in my secret indulgence. This alone was mine.

The night felt relatively still about me, the trees unnaturally motionless. Nature was stagnant, as if holding its breath. The heavy silence pressed my ears, the cold present, yet tolerable. I slunk my way through the shadow of Greybourne Hall to the wall of the terrace, using the chilled stones to steady myself, and looked up.

A smile emerged as I found Betelgeuse, the brightest star in the sky. I extended my free hand to trace the remaining stars that formed the Orion constellation. One by one, I pointed out the different formations I'd learned from a book in the cottage library. If only I could have brought it with me. I let out a slow breath. There was no need, for I knew all the constellations by heart.

As I looked up, I couldn't help but wonder who else in the world might be staring up at the stars, taking in the same beauty at this very moment. Somewhere, someone contemplated Orion as I did. It was a comforting thought. When I was sequestered with my mother in Scotland, I would think of Jacob gazing up at the same time. Of course, most nights he had been in London and far too busy to look at stars or think of me.

A glimmer of light caught my attention out of the corner of my eye. A glow appeared on the horizon, emanating from the direction of the dower house. Yes, it was the dower house itself. I could see it now, silhouetted against the gray night.

I'd not walked that direction since arrival, steered clear more like, purposefully avoiding Isabell and all her plans. It was interesting that I'd never noticed how close the small structure stood to the main house. No wonder Isabell visited so frequently.

I heard a door slam, then the hint of a faraway voice raised in anger, but I couldn't make out any movement in the darkness. Who else was up at such an hour? A second light appeared close to the first then diverged to the left. There were two people out and about. Was it Isabell and her brother, whom she'd called Adam? My mind raced through all the possibilities, ranging from an innocent argument to something far more sinister.

I strained for a better look, but it was useless. Whoever paced out there was simply too far away. A few more muffled sounds then the lights bobbed back and forth, vanishing as quickly as they had come, leaving the night air as undisturbed as it had once been.

I wrinkled my nose. What had I witnessed? Shouts at the dower house so late in the night?

Of course, there would be little hope of discovering the answer to my question, and I was hardly in a position to inquire. Isabell's business was none of my affair. Yet, I couldn't turn my gaze from where I'd seen the lights. With two deaths in the area over the last year, I could hardly disregard such an occurrence.

A bark broke my thoughts, and I jerked my attention back to the horizon. Another bark and the wonderful bundle that was Sophie barreled through the tree line, heading straight for me. I gasped, throwing my arms out to catch her, tears filling my eyes. Thank God she was back.

Lumbering across the terrace, her tongue lolling to the side, the dog didn't appear hurt. She leapt for me at the last second and smothered my face with her wet tongue and icy nose.

"Heavens, Sophie. Have you forgotten your manners?"

I set her down and held up my hand. "Now you must behave while I look you over." The front half of her body followed my directions. Her mournful eyes pleaded with me for affection, but her hindquarters wiggled where she stood, her tail flipping back and forth. "Yes, darling. I am quite glad to see you as well." I patted her head and down her back. "But I must make sure you haven't any injuries. Now hold still."

I ran my hands along her back and down her legs. Everything seemed to be in working order. When I reached to scratch her ears, I noticed a small cut in her fur. Concerned, I leaned closer. There was more. Much more. A line of blood had dried down her neck. Swelling circled the cut. I reached out to touch it, and Sophie yelped, jerking away.

My shoulders sank, and a cold feeling spread through my chest. Either Sophie had a terrible accident, or someone hurt her on purpose. "Come along, darling, let's get you something to eat and drink, then a bath first thing in the morning." I nestled my nose into her fur. "You're safe now."

I crossed back to the terrace door and set Sophie down. She wasted no time, racing inside, happy to be home, her world nothing but one jolly adventure. My own movements were not as steady. My skin tingled, and I hesitated as I moved to shut the door behind me. My gaze fell on the north horizon once again. Something had happened to Sophie out there. Where had she been the past two days?

My thoughts floated into the cold night air, thick now with more questions than answers. All at once a rider streaked across the lawn, heading for the stables. My heart slammed against my chest as I sank into the house, clicking the door shut behind me. It was Lewis again. I recognized his horse, but this time he wore a rag — like the man I'd seen from my bedchamber two nights ago.

Squeezing my hands at my side, I moved to a nearby window. So he was out and about again — with a mask. I dropped to my knees and peered through the glass. What had my guardian been up to? My hand found my necklace as I stared down the path to the stables.

Lewis Browning was involved in something far beyond simply running the estate. That was certain. Something that could have brought him face-to-face with Jacob that fateful night? Perhaps. I pulled my arms tight across my body. Either way, there was more to Lewis than he'd allowed us to know, and I meant to find out what it was.

CHAPTER 8

The house had awakened to Sophie's return, and to my surprise everyone seemed genuinely glad of it. Even Cook stooped to pat the little dog's fluffy head before thrusting her finger in the air and ordering us all out of the kitchen.

I took her *suggestion* and, on a lead mind you, accompanied Sophie for a walk out of doors. Aunt Jo was still abed as I had been unable to wait till morning to deliver her darling pet. It was a glorious reunion, and I daresay the two spent a great deal of time awake after I left, for I found Aunt Jo sleeping soundly late into the morning. I didn't dare disturb her.

So, it was left to Sophie and me to soak up the beauty of Greybourne Hall's vast estate. As I breathed in the subtle breeze, a part of me was glad I'd been blessed with a solitary ramble. With all the excitement of late, I needed a bit of time alone to process what I'd learned.

The sun was out, bright as a flaming ball, bathing the countryside in an unseasonably warm day. I decided to give Sophie the lead, which allowed her to drag me across the north lawn where she seemed determined to go. Considering the dower house lay ahead, I was curious just where she meant to direct our walk. And what I might find.

With Sophie's scrambling misdirection, I lost sight of Isabell's house rather quickly, discovering instead a delightful little brook and walking path. I gave her a pert smile. "Was this your intention from the start? You do love the water."

Sophie pranced along the slow stream, which trickled over smooth rocks and subtle banks as it wound its way down a hill, leaving a fresh scent about the air. Fallen leaves littered the path, dropped from the overhanging trees that had grown enormous beside the river. Sophie nosed her way through several wet clumps before darting back and forth across the trail, tugging me ever forward as if she had come this way in search of something.

Soon a rock outcropping jutted out of the hillside above my head and filled one side of the path in shade. At the top I could just make out the corner of a stone wall, likely belonging to the dower house.

The air felt cooler along the rock, and I pulled my pelisse tight around my neck. Moss climbed the weathered stone, filling in every dampened crevice. The brook seemed louder as the rush echoed off the looming sides of the rock. I ran my fingers down the coarse surface as we passed, my imagination pricked by a lonely crevice.

Nearing the end, Sophie jerked on her lead while her tail thrashed back and forth. "Easy girl."

I saw nothing ahead, but Sophie pulled again, then yelped for release.

"Rebecca." A dark figure pushed off the end of the rock and Lewis stepped into the light. "I didn't mean to startle you."

My heart leapt at his voice, and my eyes widened. He wore a strange look as if he'd been waiting for me all along. Had he? Of course, I knew that wasn't possible. No one knew where we meant to walk that day. His cheeks held a tint of color, his loose-fitting jacket disheveled as if he might have been running.

Without thinking, I let go of the lead and allowed Sophie the freedom to charge at him. Within seconds, she'd raced to his side, properly halting to sit on the ground at his feet as her tail swished the leaves behind her.

A smile emerged on Lewis's face as he stared down at Sophie. "I heard you'd returned to us, little one. I've missed you about the estate."

My gaze flicked to Lewis, my mind still fresh with the image he posed the previous night, but he continued to regard Sophie. "Most importantly, I need to know that you have learned your lesson."

Squatting, Lewis scratched under her chin, and Sophie's tongue popped out of her mouth as if to show some kind of remorse. He finally glanced up at me with a casual smile. "Perhaps the two of you would like to join me for the rest of your walk. It's quite beautiful along Middlebottom Brook."

His sudden boldness alarmed me. Mr. Galpin's comment popped into my mind — how Lewis hid in the house during the day. A recluse, he'd called him. Yet here he stood plain as day, an unrestrained air about him, steps from Isabell's home. Perhaps the neighbors were not completely aware of all of his habits — some things went unseen. I bit my lip. Had he been at the dower house the previous night?

I affected a smile as I reclaimed Sophie's lead. "Thank you for the invitation. We'd love to join you." I peeked farther down the path. "What brings you out here on this fine morning?"

His eyes narrowed slightly as if he'd noticed I agreed far too quickly. "Oh, I walk this way most mornings. In fact, Sophie here has joined me on several of my morning jaunts."

I lifted my eyebrows. So it was Sophie who'd arranged this tête-à-tête. The little imp. "I didn't realize the two of you were so close."

He chuckled. "She does grow on one, does she not?"

"Yes." I smiled. "A few years ago, when Aunt Jo moved into the townhouse to be with me in London, I thought I should scream with Sophie's ridiculous behavior, but I've found I don't like the thought of living without the silly dog. She's a great champion of ours." I paused, then grasped my bonnet ribbons. "I mustn't go on without thanking you for your help in her search. My aunt was quite overset, and —"

"Not at all. I was concerned as well." He shook his head. "I'm just glad to see nothing ill has befallen the little madcap." Then more to her than me, "Perhaps she will be more careful in the future so as not to get lost again."

Lost? Did he believe his own words? I wasn't sure. "You think she was only lost?"

He slowed. "What other conclusion should I come to?"

"None, I suppose. It was just all so strange." I glanced up, surprised to catch Lewis's searching gaze that showed no sign of abating. Heat filled my cheeks.

He must have noticed, for he turned quickly away, concentrating instead on the path ahead. "I do apologize, Rebecca. I didn't mean to stare. Only . . . I'm sure you've heard before that you look very much like your father. I can't help but feel at times as if I already know you. He spoke of you often when he visited Greybourne Hall about five years ago."

"Oh?" My chest grew tight.

"I suppose you were still in Scotland and —"

"Yes. Yes, I was. Conveniently put away for a time." I hadn't concealed the edge to my voice. What was it about my family that made me unable to discuss them with any sort of control?

Concern crept into those dark blue eyes. "That time was difficult for everyone, especially for your father. He stayed about six months after your mother's illness progressed." He touched his forehead.

130

"Your father and I . . . I don't know how to explain it exactly, only, we got along quite well."

In that, he likely spoke the truth. Two people who'd changed others' lives without a thought. They would have been well suited. "To tell the truth, I spent little time with my father during those last years. And when I did, he had no use for prattling on about his misfortunes, which does make me wonder what the two of you had to discuss. I mean, besides me."

A new expression took over Lewis's face — one of pity, or something else? "Your father was a complicated man, private in many ways. He said little to me about your mother, but I am certain he loved both of you dearly."

Not the answer I had expected, nor the way it squeezed my heart. "Then perhaps you can help me understand why he sent me back to Scotland when I came home."

A furrow crossed his brow. "I —"

"He didn't say too much about how I felt about my situation, did he?"

"A little."

"I came back to London over the holidays when I was sixteen to see Jacob and Father. I had ideas for my upcoming London season, but my father would have none of that.

He simply packed me up and sent me back to Scotland. Mother and I had to remain out of sight, you see." I gave Lewis a hard smile. "If you were so close, perchance you can answer a question I've had for some time. Why didn't my father ever visit us?"

A sigh escaped Lewis's lips before silence fell between us for several steps. "If I were to dare speculate, I would credit your father with deep feelings. I fear he was at a loss as to what was best to be done. He wanted to remember your mother the way she once was. And I'm not saying his decision would be mine or that it was right. However, if you try to see the world from his perspective, his profound pain, you might begin to understand why he was not able to bring himself to go to Scotland."

My throat felt scratchy, my arms heavy. I thought I'd trained myself not to feel anything for my father, not to care what he once thought, but I couldn't help myself. I had to ask. "Not even to see *me*?"

Lewis offered me his arm as we passed the side wall of the dower house, turning up a slight hill, away from my initial destination. He didn't spare Isabell's home a glance. Sophie ran happily along beside us. "I find what you say a bit remarkable. I had no knowledge of his relationship with you. I only assumed . . ."

Perhaps I felt relief at disclosing one of my family's many secrets, or I believed the empathetic scowl on Lewis's face, but I surprised myself by saying more. "I barely knew him, and then he died from pneumonia two years before my mother. One or two letters is all I have to remember him by."

Lewis let out a long sigh. "Though your words are at odds with the man I thought I knew, I will offer no defense for his actions." His jaw tensed. "Such neglect by a father, and a gentleman, is hardly excusable."

I'm not sure what I expected Lewis to say, but I found his words oddly comforting. I'd been around few men before, but Mr. Browning was altogether different. Goodness, he had turned out a far cry from what I'd expected to find. Jacob had described him as cold and inhospitable. Of course, Jacob had his own reasons for such thoughts. Lewis was Jacob's guardian until he reached the age of majority. And who could blame Jacob for feeling threatened by Lewis's tightfisted control of his purse strings? Father had even sung Lewis's praises to me, and Jacob was never one to share anyone's affections, particularly our own father's.

Of course, Ellen thought Lewis a devil like

the rest of Plattsdale, but what about me? I glanced over at my walking companion. I'd found a man — conflicted. Slow to speak, yet clearly riddled with secrets.

I'd come to Greybourne Hall intending to expose the wretch, but having dwelt in his home now for several days and shared his pain over Mr. Drake's death, my feelings had grown far more complicated. I paused. What was it about Mr. Browning that enticed me to know him better? His calm control in the face of heartache? The way everything around me shifted in his presence? I'd felt something in the library that night when he'd held my hand. Something I could not explore — not with him.

My shoulders slumped, my vision blurring the path in front of me. Likely, I was simply confusing pity with a curious connection. Either way, I would never rest until I knew what had happened between him and Jacob.

Lewis nudged my shoulder. "Allow me to add, however, that your father was kind to me during that same time. He taught me much of what I needed to know to turn around a failing estate, when my own father had imparted nothing but how to gain further debt. Things are much improved at Greybourne now. The last few years have been kind, and I have him to thank."

My muscles tensed. Kind indeed. I suppose inheriting and renting Jacob's holdings were only an added bonus.

Lewis's steps slowed, and he touched my hand in the crook of his arm. "I can also see now that the man I admired had his own share of flaws alongside his virtues. It was inexcusable that he hurt you."

I found it difficult to respond. "Yes, well, at least at the time I had Jacob. Now, I have no one but Aunt Jo."

His arm slackened, but he didn't respond, his eyes fixed on mine.

My heart pounded as I allowed myself to search the depths of that steady gaze. *What really happened that night on the bridge?* He'd told me his version in a letter soon after the accident, at least the one he meant for me to believe. Questions screamed in my mind, but I dared not give them voice. Not yet at least. I needed Lewis's favor if I were to uncover the truth. I turned away, continuing into the woods.

Soon the trees parted at a split in the path, opening the shady trail to long fields and crisscrossing hedgerows. Beneath the clear blue sky, a cluster of cottages poked up from the gentle swells, swirls of smoke rising from the chimney tops, the fiery scent riding on the breeze.

Halfway down the winding road, I caught sight of a man leisurely leading a donkey cart toward the cottages. I breathed in the beautiful countryside, my skin itching to bathe in the sun. Sophie tugged on the lead, but Lewis pulled me back.

"I do apologize, but it is time to return to the house." He took a quick look at the man coming toward them. "And I think it best you accompany me. I'd rather you not go on alone."

He was right of course. There had been gunshots and murders on this very estate, but I was determined to maintain my independence. It had taken me years to go back into the woods after the vicious dog attack, but I had then and I always would. If I gave in to fear now, I would be locked away in the house with little chance of ever learning the truth of Jacob's death. I straightened. "I have Sophie with me, and it was my intention to take a stroll alone from the onset."

"I've been meaning to speak with you about that. I prefer you take your aunt or someone else for an escort."

"An escort? For a short country stroll? Ridiculous."

"You mustn't fight me on this, Rebecca. You know there is more." His jaw clenched.

"I'd prefer not to list the reasons why you may or may not be received well in town. I daresay you can guess." His voice deepened. "Not only am I your guardian and under your father's orders to protect you, but I've lived here a long time. My judgment must remain paramount." He motioned back the way we'd come. "You shall return to the house with me at once. Trust me, if you are seen out and about with me, it could only put you in danger."

The sound of approaching hooves sent Lewis stealing behind a tree branch. My mouth fell open. Sophie barked, and I nudged her back with my foot.

The man reined the donkey to a halt. "Good morning, miss." He removed his hat and nodded, revealing a sweaty bunch of copper hair and a long face that resolved into a jutting chin.

I patted Sophie again to silence her barking. "Good morning." I could sense Lewis's distress beside me, but I forced a smile. He wasn't visible, and what else could I do?

Dressed in a worn work shirt and tainted trousers, the man steered his donkey cart to the edge of the path and squinted as he looked at Lewis's land. "Name's Miller. My wife and I wondered if we ought'n check on you." He shrugged. "Considerin' things."

"Thank you, but I assure you, I have been well taken care of."

"Have you now?" His face screwed up into a ball. "And maybe you haven't. Perchance you aren't even aware of everything going on in these parts." He motioned me closer.

Curiosity fought my better sense, and I took a step forward, leaving Lewis in the trees. I wanted to know what the man meant to say, but as I approached, the venom in his sharp green eyes sent shivers across my shoulders. His lips turned up at the corners, and suddenly I felt small beside his cart. Nevertheless, I had to know what he meant. For Jacob. I didn't dare look back at Lewis as I held Sophie tight. What would he think of my behavior?

The man in the cart swiped his shirt sleeve across his forehead. "We live just over yonder." He glanced right and then left, a hesitation about his movements. "You alone?"

"I have my dog, as you can see." It wasn't exactly a lie.

His voice dropped to nothing more than a whisper. "Listen, miss, you need to know that there was a death at that house you've been brought to, and more'n one. Un-natural they said it was. And the master might just ha' been responsible. He sneaks out all hours of the night, he does." He cocked his eyebrows as if I should run screaming at the news.

Of course, I'd seen Lewis myself, so I went on. "Do you have any proof as to what you claim?"

The man stiffened, his gaze flicking to Lewis's land once again. "Listen here. Don't go off in the boughs. Just stopped to warn you to be careful, is all. Some say Browning's got the devil in him, that one. But we know how to defend our own around here. He won't show his face in our town, not since the people started throwing things. So if you —"

My eye's widened. "People throw things . . . at Mr. Browning?"

A slow smile spread across his face as if he reveled in my discomfiture. "I got a rock by me front door just in case. They say he crawls around at night to do his bidding. Been seen, he has."

My tongue felt dry. An evening ride on a horse could hardly be called crawling around, but Lewis was up to something, something he needed a mask for. "Who saw him, um, crawling?"

"Couldn't rightly say." He slapped his donkey's reins and spoke over his shoulder as the cart pulled him away. "Just thought

I'd warn you, being dependent on him and all."

A puff of wind skirted through the trees as I watched the man leave. I rubbed the chill from my arms and turned back to the trail, my grip tight around Sophie's lead, unsure whether or not I should ask Lewis about the mask.

I needn't have bothered. Lewis had vanished.

CHAPTER 9

I didn't see Lewis again till the following day when I came upon him quite by accident on my way to the drawing room.

My steps slowed at the sight of him pacing down the hall. After what happened on the walk, I hoped to reassure him somehow, but he would have none of it, brushing by my shoulder with little more than a nod. The look in his eyes, however, lingered as he passed, causing my back to stiffen and my stomach to clench. Something had changed between us, something I feared I might not recover.

Had he heard everything the man said? Or was it something else? Something about Mr. Drake's murder?

I felt restless as I passed into the sun-filled hues of the rose-scented drawing room, my mind preoccupied, my emotions tight as a string. My fingers curled into a ball around my muslin slip as I took a hasty seat at the escritoire nestled in the crook of the bow window and gathered my thoughts for a letter to my cousin, Ellen. But how to explain all the strange occurrences?

There was the mysterious handkerchief with its possible implications and Sophie's strange disappearance. My fingers rested on the smooth surface of the desk, as still and silent as the empty room around me. My chest felt heavy.

And then there was Lewis Browning.

I touched my forehead, searching for the dull ache pounding within. I enjoyed our time in the garden and again in the woods yesterday. What did that say about me and my convictions? Was I actually attracted to the man?

My jaw clenched with the startling revelation as my father's crooked smile came to mind, wriggling its way under my skin. I'd never forget the last thing he said to me when he helped me into our family's carriage, happy to return me to Scotland.

"Take heart. You shan't need a season, for I have decided on the perfect match for you, my dear. Mr. Lewis Browning. He has inherited a nice parcel of land and an estate. I find him exceedingly agreeable, and I shall see about making the arrangements if it is in my power to do so. It would be best if you had a name

and a layer of protection . . . if . . . the worst were to happen."

I suppose that was my father's way of taking care of me, compensation for missing any chance I had of making a suitable match. However, I'd not met Lewis at the time, and though my father's offhanded words were meant to comfort me as I journeyed back into isolation, they did just the opposite. A far more jarring resolution seeped into my soul. If Lewis Browning were anything like my father, I had no interest in marrying him — or anyone, for that matter. I would find a way to provide for myself. After my "dreams" began, this decision was only enforced.

My conversation with Aunt Jo rushed into my mind on the heels of the memory of my father — the one we shared the day we arrived at Greybourne Hall. The things she said about Lewis haunted me like a white flame in my heart and spiraled me into the discussion I overheard between Mr. Drake and Lewis that same day. Had my father told everyone his intentions? Did they all have plans for me and *him*?

No. I shook my head. Lewis did not. He had been as repulsed as I was. At least there was that. No one could force an alliance between us.

I let out a calming breath and shifted my attention to the window, to the unbridled lawns beyond the front walk and the thick trees. I had need of an escape, an escape from myself. Mr. Galpin trudged around the front corner of the house. He had probably forced another meeting with Lewis. I paused. Perhaps Lewis's earlier coldness had a different direction after all. He might simply have come from humoring Mr. Galpin, his mind elsewhere. I rubbed the back of my neck. Why must I always read into everything?

Yet I could still see Lewis's strained jaw and tensed shoulders. He had been upset. If not about me, then about something.

I tracked Mr. Galpin's movements across the lawn to the folly at the edge of the trees where he stopped suddenly and glanced behind him. A woman emerged from the shadows as if she had been waiting for him.

Isabell. A smile, and she tugged him beneath the rounded roof of the old folly. Her hand lingered on his arm, but at last he drew away as if they rehearsed a familiar dance, their meeting a matter of course. She brushed a clump of dirt from his cloak before tucking her hand quickly back into her muff.

Mr. Galpin looked amused. Isabell leaned

144

close to speak, quite pleased with whatever passed between them. Then it happened — a quick embrace, her arm wrapped around his . . .

I felt the footsteps behind me before I heard them. I stiffened then spun in my chair to face whoever loomed behind me.

"Oh," Lewis ceased his approach. "I thought the room empty or I'd not have imposed."

I swallowed hard. My hands dropped to my lap. "You know you're quite welcome to come and go as you please in your own house. I'm simply writing a few letters." My rambling might have gone unnoticed if I had already taken out a sheet of paper and some ink.

Our eyes met. "As you say. I left some important documents in that drawer there." He motioned to my right then took a long breath. "Looks as if Galpin is interested in buying the London townhouse as well."

I rose from the chair, moving out of his way, and cast one last glance at the folly, now empty. "The townhouse?"

"It is a curious business. He means to have a permanent place to stay while in London." After retrieving the desired document, Lewis closed the drawer. "I must admit, I find his sudden interest surprising." His eyes sought mine. "Then again, perhaps I don't."

The depth of his look startled me, and I took a step back. Did he mean I had something to do with changing Mr. Galpin's mind? Ridiculous, yet the thought lingered. I spun away, blurting out the first thing that popped into my head. "Any news of Mr. Drake? Have you learned more regarding his death?"

Lewis hesitated, as if he knew that was not what I'd meant to say, then shook his head. "No. It has been a wasted case from the beginning. I brought my concerns to the new parish officer, but he is not willing to do more at present." He made his way to the window. "I believe the town only wishes to heal from all that has happened, and my dear friend is merely caught up in the aftermath."

We both knew he included my brother's death in what he said. "And you?"

He remained silent for a moment, his face turned to the misty afternoon, before speaking again. "I shall never rest . . . nor heal."

My chest tightened. I knew just what he meant by those hollow words. I opened my mouth, but a sound drew our attention to the door.

"How delightful I've found you two together . . . and alone." A wide smile brightened Isabell's otherwise pale face. She'd been out in the cold for too long and headed directly to the fire. "I should like some tea, if you please."

Lewis moved to pull the bell rope, and the strained look he wore around his sister-in-law settled onto his face. "You must have had a cold carriage ride, I see."

She laughed. "Would you believe that I walked?" She held out her fingers to the flame. "Charles would never have permitted it. He took prodigious care of me, but I shall say no more about him . . . at present."

A silent look passed between them. Their eyes held before Isabell stiffened and turned her focus on me. "The modiste should be arriving any moment to fit your gown for the dinner party in two weeks. We haven't any time to waste." She cast one last sideways glance at Lewis. "If the gown is as beautiful as my design for this room, no one will be able to keep their eyes off her."

Lewis shifted once again to look out the window, his expression as impassive as ever.

Isabell paid him no heed and led me to the sofa like a child. "Come, we must discuss who will be in attendance for our little party."

"I thought you already sent out the invitations."

She seemed taken aback, her willowy fingers coming to rest on her chest. "How did you know that?" She cast a quick glance at Lewis, her lips pressed tight. "What a clever young lady you are. Forgive me, my dear, but I did take it upon myself to select the guests and move forward with the invitations since there are so few people willing to attend anything at Greybourne Hall." She arched her eyebrows. "There is really no reason I should have waited."

I took a deep breath. "I see."

Isabell took my hand, then leaned forward, which created a forced intimacy between us. "I came today because I thought that you might like to know a little about the men before they arrive."

I couldn't get the sight of Isabell and Mr. Galpin out of my mind. Evidently, she knew a great deal about the men. "I suppose that would be —"

"Let me start by telling you of a dear friend I have in the neighborhood. He is a widower, terribly lonely, and far too handsome for his own good. He has given me leave to help him find a wife, and he will be a perfect match for you, my dear."

My heart sank.

Isabell laughed, reading my reaction as embarrassment rather than revulsion. "His name is Mr. Galpin, and he has a comfortable living but a few miles away."

Lewis pushed to his feet and crossed the room, silencing Isabell's delight. He halted before the sofa and narrowed his eyes. "If you ladies will excuse me, I have business to attend to."

Isabell tipped her chin. "Certainly. We would not wish to detain you." She patted my hand. "Rebecca and I have much to discuss, and we have little need of your opinion on the matter."

He stood as if frozen for a moment, digesting her words, then nodded and strode from the room. I was surprised he chose not to answer or at the very least defend himself. What power did she have over him?

The door clicked shut, and Isabell shrugged. "What a droll man Lewis has become. I find him almost unworthy of my notice these days. With you here, thankfully, I don't need his boorish company. And this party will give me such pleasure. I've had little enough since Charles died. And then there was your brother."

I glanced up at the mention of Jacob.

She seemed to sense my discomfort for she added quickly, "I believe Jacob loved entertainment as much as I do. I always thought him so different from Lewis. I can scarcely believe them related." Isabell's fingers were busy on the arm of the sofa. "It was such a shock that day when I saw him lying there so still and cold." Her words were clipped, but her gaze shot to mine.

What did she mean? My mind raced to understand. "You mean you saw Jacob's body after the accident?" My last word came out as more of a whisper.

She shivered as she folded her hands in her lap. "It was a ghastly business. I never should have mentioned it." But she went on. "He had washed downstream, you know, and I was visiting a friend in Reedwick." She pressed her hand to her brow. "I was asked to identify him. Everyone else was hours away. I crept into that room, scarcely able to breathe. Then I saw the scar by his ear. Oh, my dear Rebecca. It was too much to bear."

"That must have been difficult — to see him like that." I took a long breath. My gaze drifted to the floor. "He got that scar when he was only twelve."

"Oh?"

"A boy at Eton declared a large opening in a stone wall too far to jump. Of course, Jacob just rushed right in to prove the boy wrong. He did land his jump, at least that is what he told me, but his footing faltered and he fell, catching his neck on a nearby tree branch. He always did enjoy that scar. He thought it a distinguishing feature."

A slight smile graced Isabell's lips. "He never told me that story." Then her smile vanished, her fingers returning to the arm of the sofa. "I should never have agreed to go that day. The sight of your brother — lifeless — haunts me even now."

I took her cold hand into mine. "I'm sorry the task fell to you."

A knock at the door silenced my words as Knowles bustled through with the tea tray. On his heels, a man wearing a tailored jacket entered the room. A wry smile rounded out the gentleman's full face. His dusty blond hair had a touch of red that glistened in the sunlight. He had a lazy look about him as if he'd only wandered into Greybourne Hall on a whim.

Isabell sprang to her feet. "Adam. You are just the person we need to lighten up the room."

He shot her a coy glance, stopping by the side bar for a drink before collapsing into a cushioned chair and leaving one leg to dangle over the armrest. Belatedly he noticed me and drew himself to his feet in a somewhat clumsy fashion. I rose as well.

Isabell reclaimed my hand almost as if she'd forgotten she released it. "Miss Hunter, may I present my elder brother, Mr. Wynn."

He gave me an awkward bow, and we were back in our seats as if the thought of standing for any length of time bored the man. He held up his glass. "Charmed."

Isabell laughed. "Oh, Adam. Do behave yourself. What will my little friend think of you?" Then to me. "You mustn't take him seriously."

I didn't intend to.

He took a sip. "Isa, darling. I came this way about your, er, other friend."

She blinked. "What on earth do you mean, my other friend?" A nervous laugh followed her words.

"He's been looking for you and growing a bit impatient."

She still looked bewildered, so I couldn't help myself. "Do you by any chance mean Mr. Galpin?"

Isabell's sharp glare snapped to mine. "Mr. Galpin? What a notion. No. My brother is the biggest tease you shall ever meet. I'm certain he means my cat." She rose, turning to her brother. "I was under the impression you could handle the little dear."

He smiled. "Not my responsibility, pet."

She let out a long breath. "I am most displeased to have to leave so soon and in this havey-cavey way, particularly when Miss Hunter and I have yet to discuss the dinner party."

"Perhaps another time?" I offered.

She blinked rapidly. "I'm not certain when I shall be able to get away." She hugged her arms across her chest as she looked to the window and beyond. "And what of Mr. Galpin? I had so wished to speak to you about him. You will remember him at the dinner party, won't you?"

I nodded. How could I forget it?

She took her brother's outstretched arm. "If you promise me you will be agreeable to my friend, Mr. Galpin, I will say nothing more at present. I have great hopes for the two of you. Great hopes."

A cold rock settled into my stomach as I watched them leave. Any thoughts I'd had of enjoying the party vanished with her words. How on earth could I ever be agreeable to that man again after seeing what I had in the folly?

CHAPTER 10

I screamed. There was a man before me, his face blighted by shadows, his bulk looming over me. His hand sought my neck as he moved in closer, quickly, as if he meant to strike. I gasped for air. My pulse raced. I clawed at his arms, attempting escape, but I was pinned by a larger object at my back. What was it surrounding my head?

Then his fingers circled my wrist. Black spots appeared before my eyes. A crash resounded to my right. My muscles ached with tension. I screamed again, not like before, as if I had been startled, but like my life depended on it.

Clumsily, I batted his shoulder with my free hand, pressing my balled fist as sharp as I could into his side over and over again. Gathering my strength, I lunged forward, catching my attacker off guard. We both toppled to the floor, landing in a tangled heap on the rug.

I blinked for a moment, my thoughts clearing, the dark haze lifting from the room.

"What the deuce, Rebecca?" Lewis touched his forehead.

Slowly, I sat up, the truth dawning. I was in Lewis's office, the room that doubled as Greybourne's library. I'd come for a book when I couldn't sleep. Having found a copy of Mary Robinson's poems, I had nestled into the lush chair, and I must have drifted off.

Lewis eyed me from his spot on the rug, pressing his handkerchief against a cut on his head. "What was that, Rebecca?"

My stomach rolled. I'd had one of my spells. And he'd seen it.

Attempting nonchalance, I shrugged. "I suppose I was dreaming."

He shook his head, his eyes on mine. "That was a great deal more than a dream. You were awake somehow." He raised his voice. "You stared into my eyes, and you were terrified."

How could I explain it? For years I'd tried to clarify it to myself. The littlest thing could set me off while I was asleep. A noise, a person. One time in Scotland I had been unwell and my maid came by to check on me. I nearly toppled her from her feet in my race to the door. Luckily I had soon recovered and my silly actions were smoothed over.

I bit my lip. The last thing I wanted was Lewis Browning bearing my secret.

He took my hand in his, the other finding my shoulder. His eyes looked puzzled, and his face betrayed layers of concern. "Are you afraid here?"

A tingle pricked my skin. "No." I tried to laugh off his assertion. "I made a mistake is all."

He inched a bit closer to me on the rug. "I came into the library, unaware you were here. And when I shut the door, you started screaming — like a wild animal caught in a trap. I hurried over and . . ." He met my gaze. "You fought me as if —"

I held up my hand. "Please say no more. You don't understand."

"Indeed I do not." His voice dropped to a whisper. "Please enlighten me."

It was then I noticed Lewis's state of dress, his thin white shirt loose at the neck, his jacket and cravat discarded. He had not yet been to bed, yet he'd made himself at ease, the perfect mixture of boyish abandon and master of his domain. Instinctively, I touched the cloth covering the cut I'd caused on his forehead and took a peek at the gash, before inadvertently meeting his eyes. Lewis had brought only a guttering candle with him, but easily enough I followed the curious intensity behind those dark blue eyes and the moment his eyes changed. Suddenly, my world felt terribly small, like I'd experienced merely a handful of what it had to offer.

Inches from each other on the rug, we didn't move, captured by the unexpected intimacy. What would he do if I leaned forward? What would he say? I could almost feel him urging me closer, and for the first time I allowed myself to wonder what it would it be like to have someone share my struggles.

I pushed to my feet and retreated into the safety of distance, turning my back to him. He followed me, however, and his hand found my shoulder once again. "There is more to this business than just a bad dream. Tell me."

His voice was gentle, but he meant to force an answer. The casement clock ticked beside me as the wind tugged at the window. I spun to face him, unprepared for the concern in his eyes or the way the words fell from my lips. "You are aware of my mother's illness."

He nodded, a pained look washing over

his face.

"Well, I have my own troubles." I bit my lip. "Sometimes in the night, I find myself neither asleep nor awake. I see things that frighten me, and I respond." I fought back the tears that threatened my voice. "Each time I remember very little. When the spells happen, my body shakes. My heart means to burst in my chest. All my muscles scream out in fear. I believe somehow in that moment that I am dying."

"And you fight back." His hand moved to rub the cut on his forehead. A smile appeared for a moment then drifted away. "I don't mean to make light of your experiences. It must be quite difficult to live with these spells."

I could never stand a person's pity, particularly Lewis's. "I manage well enough."

Then he did smile, full out, a playful grin that brightened his eyes. "I daresay you do. I don't believe I shall be able to walk without wincing for a few days."

"I hurt you that badly?"

A laugh overcame him. "Do you by any chance box at Jackson's?"

"Don't be ridiculous."

He motioned with his fingers as he crossed the room to get the candle. "Come here."

I hesitated, disarmed by the edge in his

voice, but I went nonetheless. As I approached, he lifted the edge of his shirt to reveal marks on his side.

Red splotches littered his creamy skin in circular rows. I gasped. "I did all that?"

"And more." He touched his forehead. "I believe it was the table that caught my head on our way down to the floor."

The last few moments flashed through my mind. I'd landed on him before we sat up . . . on the carpet. Warmth filled my cheeks. "I must apologize."

"Don't. You have taught me a valuable lesson. Never underestimate your opponent." He reached out to touch my arm but stopped. Silence fell between us, pushing me once again into that place where my heart lightened and my head fought for control.

Lewis must have sensed my retreat, for he wandered over to his desk, a cautious air to his movements. "What were you doing in here so late, if I may ask?"

"I couldn't sleep. I decided to seek out a book." Turning to a nearby shelf, something familiar caught my eye. A red, tattered volume with gold print on the cover. *The Mysteries of Udolpho.* It was my copy from London. And there beside it, *Camilla.* "My books! They're all here." I ran my fingers down the spines, shelf after shelf.

"I could hardly let such a rich collection go to waste. I had them shipped here from London."

It was like a piece of me had been returned, my soul reviving as I never thought it would. I paused to meet Lewis's gaze. "Thank you for bringing them here."

He gave a disinterested nod, yet I noticed something else hidden in that vague gesture he used so often — pleasure. He was happy for me. The thought struck a strange chord, and I hardly knew what to say.

I averted my attention back to the shelves. "Jacob sent me all these books in Scotland. He enjoyed filling my head with novels. He had such a wonderful mind. He used to read to me when we were children. I miss his strong voice." I sighed. "He was so clever. He would change the words in the stories to make me laugh, and sometimes we would appear as characters. He the dashing hero, me the villain. I cannot read some of these books without hearing his voice."

I noticed a chill in the room. The utter silence brought about by my words.

Lewis stared at me like I was a ghost. "It's getting late. We should retire to our rooms."

His stilted demeanor invaded my own. "Yes. I suppose we should."

"Take whatever you want with you, and feel free to come back whenever you wish."

I grasped *Udolpho* and the book of poems I had begun earlier. "I'm not sure I shall be able to sleep." I touched the familiar edge of the book's cover. "I would rather read than have another spell."

Lewis's fingers sought his hair, his eyes never leaving my face.

At that moment, trapped in his heady gaze, I realized something. Throughout the entire conversation I had called my dreams *spells*. Like my mother.

I could pretend no longer. For that is what they were. The first step into madness.

On Saturday night, Aunt Jo and I gathered in the drawing room, the dark night lurking beyond the curtains, a chill hovering just beyond the reach of the large fireplace. The room felt different somehow now that I was aware Isabell had helped design it. Apparently she and Lewis were a bit closer than I originally thought.

Aunt Jo seemed anxious as we crossed the room. Lewis had startled us with his presence at dinner. Though a quiet addition, it was the first time he had joined us. I couldn't help but wonder why.

Aunt Jo settled Sophie on the sofa by the

fire, but I remained listless, my mind spinning. After circling the room, I stopped in the bow window and flicked open the edge of the heavy chintz curtain. Beyond the glass, a light flickered through the trees from the direction of the dower house. It had been a sennight since I'd seen Isabell and Adam in the drawing room. What had kept her and her brother so busy?

The drape slipped from my fingers like a slow-moving waterfall. The brocade pattern settled back into place, snuffing out the darkness beyond. The movement brought to mind the handkerchief I'd found weeks ago. I had given some thought to the torn initials and made a mental list of people's middle names. But after a quick look in the family Bible, I learned Lewis had been christened Lewis Michael. Isabell and her brother were crossed off soon after. I'd hit a wall. No one seemed to have a name that began with a *B* other than Browning — and that was a surname.

The other initials were far too tattered to make a solid guess. Yet I was determined not to give it up. The item still felt important somehow. Just one more unanswered clue. I'd encountered too many odd things to dismiss — the lone gunshot so close to the house, Sophie's strange disappearance, and the argument I observed at the dower house just before her return.

Isabell had acted unusually on more than one occasion. And Adam came to fetch her to take care of a cat? I didn't believe that for one moment. What was she hiding? Her familiarity with Mr. Galpin for one thing. *There* was a mystery. And Jacob. I stared hard at the corner of the room, allowing my mind to churn. Jacob hadn't mentioned Isabell even once in his letters, yet she led me to believe the two of them were quite close. So close that she'd been the one to identify his body. And Mr. Drake probably handled her pin money and other affairs.

I paused by the fireplace mantel. When Lewis examined Mr. Drake, he said the solicitor was strangled from behind. Could Isabell with her slight hand movements and willowy presence overpower the broad-shouldered Mr. Drake? Not likely. And what reason would she have for doing so?

I simply needed more information. Who knew Mr. Drake, and who might have wished to see him dead? Perhaps my little dinner party tomorrow night might provide a few answers.

Aunt Jo leaned forward. "It is a thought that will do you no good."

I shuffled back a step. "Whatever do you mean?"

"Oh, I'm not certain, not yet at least, but you're planning something. Something's turning in that beautiful mind of yours."

"Don't be ridiculous. I was only thinking about my upcoming party."

Her eyebrows arched. "I find that a little hard to believe."

"Well, it's true enough. For the first time, I have decided I should like to meet our neighbors — not to fall madly in love with one mind you, but . . ."

Aunt Jo dipped her chin. "To avoid Mr. Browning?"

A low voice emerged from the doorway. "I should hope not."

A lump hit my stomach, and I turned to the door. Lewis must have finished his port and decided to join us. What had he heard? I gave a little laugh. "Don't be absurd. My aunt was only teasing, as I believe she saw you standing there."

I thought Aunt Jo might drop her cup of tea, but she rallied a nod.

The formality of the dining room had faded from Lewis's demeanor, leaving a face eager to please and a lightness about his movements. It was clear he adored Aunt Jo . . . and Sophie for that matter. But what

164

he thought of me, I couldn't say. Nor exactly what I thought of him.

He crossed the rug and paused at the fireplace fender.

Aunt Jo smiled. "Why don't we have a song, Rebecca? I don't think Mr. Browning has heard you play."

The warmth in my cheeks vanished. Aunt Jo could not be serious. "Perhaps another time."

"I'm not certain there will be another time. Now go on, my dear. I shan't be persuaded otherwise."

Slowly, I angled a pleading glance at Lewis with hope that he might save me from utter embarrassment, but he held out his arm. "I would love to hear you play. Allow me to turn the pages."

I had never played the pianoforte for anyone but Aunt Jo, and she suffered from the same delusion many hopeful mothers did in drawing rooms all across London — that their children were brilliant. Well, I wasn't.

As I trudged to the beautiful instrument, the ivory keys twinkled in the candlelight, and my father came to mind. He of all people was an excellent musician, and I . . . well, I had never measured up.

Lewis took out a bundle of sheet music

for me to look through. He hesitated before handing me the stack. "If you'd prefer to sing, I'd be happy to play for you."

He had caught my discomfiture at last. But goodness, singing would be far worse. "No. I shall play." Resolve had taken root, and I grabbed the music with a firm hand, if for no reason but to show them all, particularly the ghost of my father.

Smoothing my gown beneath my legs, I took a seat on the bench. Luckily, the selections Lewis procured were not all that difficult, and I'd previously played one by Haydn. I let it rest on the music stand, and my fingers found the keys.

I can't say I remember much of the song, how I played, or how Aunt Jo beamed at me from across the room. No. All my faculties prickled on edge, my skin quick to detect any movement of Lewis behind me — the lingering scent of his soap, the feel of his arm brushing mine as he reached to turn the pages.

I held the last chord, and his voice was at my ear. "Lovely."

My hands retreated to my lap. "Thank you." Then I slid away and removed myself to the sofa.

Lewis glanced through the other songs, and I was just about to ask him to play when

Knowles hurried through the door. He held out a silver platter to Lewis. "This just came for you, sir."

A letter so late could only be something important. I found Aunt Jo's worried gaze. Lewis grasped the letter and strolled toward the window. He broke the seal before silently digesting the contents inside. "Excuse me," he said almost belatedly.

It was clearly none of our business, but Aunt Jo and I sat on edge. Knowles's footsteps drifted away and were replaced by the insistent tick of the casement clock and the occasional flap of Sophie's ears.

At last, Lewis furrowed his brow and refolded the note. "Peculiar business in London."

So he meant to include us. Anxious, I widened my eyes. "What is it?"

"There has been a robbery at the townhouse. No sign of a broken window or battered door, yet several rooms were left disheveled. Books on the floor. Drawers left open. Sofa cushions tossed about. Mr. and Mrs. Blakemoor were not at home when the terrible act occurred."

I gasped. "My poor house. What was stolen?"

"That's just it. Nothing has been found missing yet; however, they plan to take a thorough inventory."

Aunt Jo set her teacup on the side table. "Quite odd. I'm not at all certain I remember hearing of such a thing happening before."

"Nor I." My gaze sought the snapping fire. "It's almost as if they were looking for something."

Lewis rubbed his chin. "It is possible. But what?"

Aunt Jo pulled Sophie a bit closer to her rounded stomach. "It is upsetting. Upsetting indeed." Then to me, "Goodness, what if we had still been in residence? All alone . . ."

I took her hand. "Thankfully we were not, and it may all have something to do with the new tenants." I angled my chin. "Are you well acquainted with the people you allowed in my house?"

Lewis slid the letter into his pocket. "Very well." He smoothed down the jacket's superfine fabric. "More than likely, this whole business is a big mistake." To my aunt, "Please, do not think on it any further. It shall be investigated by my people in London, and I will let you know the outcome as soon as I hear back." He glanced at the door. "I, uh, have a few things to attend to this evening, so I shall bid you ladies goodnight."

We watched him leave before Aunt Jo leaned in close. " 'His people?' . . . in London?"

I was thinking the same thing.

CHAPTER 11

The night of the dinner party arrived on the wings of expectation and dread. Aunt Jo stayed in my bedchamber as I dressed, waiting to speak until my flighty maid left the room.

"You look positively lovely, my dear. Say what you will of Isabell, but she has a fine eye for gowns."

I smiled back at her, but hesitated before facing the mirror, unsettled by the unexpected surge of anticipation ticking in my chest. I'd held every intention of using the evening for my own purposes, but something else fought for the balance of my emotions. My eyes slipped closed, and I took a quick breath. What would the looking glass reveal? A lady on the threshold of her first real party? Or my mother's daughter — terrified and alone?

The fabric of my gown felt light and fresh against my legs. The quietest ruffle escaped as I approached the gilded frame and my reflection took shape. The lady in the glass who stared back at me looked poised yet tentative. But it was just me. Rebecca Hunter, draped in an expensive gown with beautifully arranged hair. Not my mother or the bright-eyed girl forced to return to Scotland so long ago.

The creation Isabell selected fit to perfection. I adjusted my shoulders and turned first one direction then the next. I ran my fingers along the soft pink crepe, which parted down the front to reveal a stunning white satin slip beneath. I leaned forward, and my green eyes glistened back at me, just as the modiste had predicted at the fitting. Or was it the sudden tears stinging my eyes?

Years ago I dreamed of such a moment — before my mother's illness, before London and my season were taken away. I would have worn just such a dress. I would have danced and fallen in love. I watched my reflection a moment longer before shrugging off the memory. I had buried such aspirations long ago, and over the years, I had become quite good at doing so, saddled with the need to be strong for mother and then for myself. Besides, what did it matter now? Such romantic notions were for girls barely out of the schoolroom. And I, for one, knew better. My hand slipped to my side. I had seen too much of life in my twenty years.

The white satin fluting at the base of the skirt swished as I backed away, my pearl-gray slippers hidden underneath. My feelings, however, remained at the surface, taunting me. Even so, I was determined to get through the evening, one way or another.

Aunt Jo must have sensed my distress. Her hand found my arm, and she turned me to face her. "It is only one night, my dear. Why don't you simply enjoy yourself?" She gave me a little shake. Her fingers pressed then released. "You bear everything on these shoulders like a heavy chain, weighing you down. This dinner party tonight, my dear, is only that — one night. Allow it to be what it is."

"One night." I breathed out the words like a flavored dream. A glorious moment I could never allow myself to have. My gaze fell to the floor. "I wish that were possible, Aunt Jo." My voice escaped into a whisper. "But I've been experiencing them again."

Her brow wrinkled. "What are you talking about?"

"The spells or dreams or whatever they are." I lifted my eyebrows. "I've had more than ever before — nearly every night."

Her fingers touched her parted lips. "Oh my darling, why didn't you tell me?"

"I don't know. I guess I hoped they'd go away. But they are not ever going to, are they? They shall only get worse."

"I — No one can be certain of that. Only God knows the future." She shook her head slowly as if trying to make sense of it. "Perhaps you should see a doctor —"

"No." I touched my stomach. "Not yet at least."

The lines on her face deepened, her voice taking on the tone I'd heard so many times as a child from my mother — resignation. "Then perhaps you must do what your father wanted and take a husband."

My hand shook as I reached for the pearl necklace around my neck. "I thought you understood my resolve. I don't wish to be a burden to anyone."

"I do understand — for that is just what *I* am . . . a burden." She pulled me down beside her on the bed. "But my dearest love, I can only imagine you want the best for everyone. Still, you must also be practical. Money . . . protection . . . You will someday need so many things that I cannot provide." Now she sounded like my father — all business, no emotion. A quick breath and she glanced about the room, her eyes seeing beyond me to the large estate hidden behind the walls.

I knew just what she was thinking, and inwardly I cringed. Lewis would never be my husband, regardless of his inheritance or his standing in society or even for his role in my brother's death. Marriage was not for me. I could not do it.

I turned to tell her so as a knock sounded on the door. "Come." I assumed it was my maid, but Isabell's smiling face appeared.

"Mr. Galpin is already here and quite striking in his formal attire. We shall make our entrance in a few minutes." Her eyes fluttered as she crossed the room. "Let me take a look at you." Nosing out Aunt Jo, she pulled me to my feet. "Stunning. I daresay you might be my greatest accomplishment. If only Jacob were here to see it."

Her comment caught me off guard. "Jacob? I'm not sure he would wish for me to be paraded about so —"

"Oh fiddlesticks. He spoke a great deal about you to me, and I assure you, he had high hopes for you finding a brilliant match."

My skin felt tight as I folded my fingers together. "You discussed me with Jacob?"

She laughed. "He was worried about you

at the time since he had been unable to pay for a season for you in London." She gave her shoulder a little shrug. "He thought I might help you someday. I suppose he saw that the two of us had a great deal in common."

"He didn't mention you in his letters."

"Well, it wouldn't have been proper to do so, now would it? And then everything changed." Her voice grew quiet, and I could read the sorrow behind her words. "But now is not the time to think on that, hmm?" She touched the braiding at the back of my head before examining the pile of curls on each side of my forehead. "I suppose this style will do, though I would have chosen something else entirely. Lud, I wish I could have sent you my maid. Well, it can't be helped. Are you ready? We shall enter together, of course." She gave Aunt Jo a sideways glance.

My aunt took the cue and wiggled to the door. "Yes. I probably need to hurry on down to ensure Sophie is tucked away." She took one last glance at me. "I will see you below in a few minutes. Try to remember what I said."

"Now." Isabell patted my hand, dismissing my aunt's heartfelt plea. "Mr. Galpin has delightful blond hair and a rather fine countenance. I daresay you shall know him at once. How could you not?"

So Mr. Galpin must not have told her of our prior meeting. He had promised as much, but I wondered on more than one occasion if they had not been discussing me that day in the folly.

Unable to stay still, she went on. "He shall be the one enraptured with our arrival — with you, I mean. I am certain of it." She glanced down at my evening gown, a hint of jealousy in her eyes. "I chose everything you are wearing especially for him. He takes prodigious care of his dress, you know, and I found out just what he likes. Come along, my dear," she said, taking my hand. "We have kept the room waiting long enough."

She spirited me from the bedchamber, and we descended the great, central staircase as if she were presenting me at court. I, however, couldn't help but imagine myself as an animal being led to the slaughter. I hesitated halfway down the steps, the banister cold beneath my fingers, nerves prickling up my spine. I could do this, couldn't I?

A transformation had taken place at Greybourne Hall in my absence. Light engulfed the entryway, glittering off the polished floor. Bundles of beeswax candles conjured dancing shadows along the heavy wooden panels. Hanging baskets overflowed with colorful flowers, marking our way as the sweet scent tickled my nose. The murmur of guests thrummed in my ears as we walked down the last of the steps.

Isabell tilted her chin. "Just a few things I arranged. Now, shoulders back, chin up. I hope you will do your best for me."

I swallowed hard. "Of course, I will."

Heavy footsteps drew my attention to the drawing room doorway where Mr. Galpin's dimple popped around the corner. Isabell squeezed my hand, my palm already a good deal sweaty.

Dressed snug in a black coat and breeches, Mr. Galpin's white, single-breasted waist-coat accented his light hair. His black pumps gleamed in the candlelight as he approached. Any other girl would have been enraptured.

I forced a smile as Isabell introduced us, and Mr. Galpin took the earliest moment to lean down to my ear. "You look lovely this evening, Miss Hunter." A look of conquest settled into his face as if he had just been declared the victor of some great battle and I the prize. A bitter taste filled my mouth. What had Isabell told him?

"I do believe pink is my favorite color." He glanced at Isabell. "I've said so often enough."

"I am pleased you like it." I blinked. I swallowed. What else could I say? Ultimately, I averted my gaze to the drawing room beyond. Mr. Galpin could not mean to marry me, not the real me. I had to do my best to put him off. "Shall we?" I motioned into the room and Isabell ushered me forward, her duty as hostess taking over any hopes she had of lingering in the hall with Mr. Galpin.

The *small* party still felt like a great many people to me, all lounging about Lewis's chairs and sofa engrossed in conversation. As expected, I was directed to each one and introduced like a puppet on display. There was the amiable Mr. Lovell, a landed gentleman, with a rounded middle and spectacles perched on his nose, and his wife, a thin, hard-nosed woman with little to recommend herself. Colonel Hatcher, newly cashiered, had brought his rosy-cheeked daughters and his elder son, who took my introduction with a blush.

Isabell whispered in my ear as we crossed to the other side of the room. "Unfortunately, this is the best I could do, considering Lewis's unfortunate reputation."

"Oh." At her pointed words, the sound of Lewis's strained voice came to mind, the way he'd retreated into the trees on our

178

walk. I glanced up and searched the room for him. How exactly did he feel about each one of these people, and they him? We were supposed to bear the ordeal together. Where was he?

Isabell pursed her lips. "He will be late, if he comes at all. The man is not to be relied on. Thank goodness my brother, Adam, is here to fill in as host if necessary."

With two more couples shown into the room, the party rounded out at seventeen without Lewis, and I was rushed by the remaining people in a whirlwind, seconds before Knowles announced dinner. Mr. Galpin appeared at my side, his arm outstretched. "It is my honor to escort you in."

I took one last look for Lewis before slipping my hand in the crook of Mr. Galpin's elbow. My jaw felt tight, my body twitchy. Surely Lewis wouldn't abandon me like this after what he said to me in the garden. The thought rankled as the various guests merged into a line and headed to the dining room, Adam at the front with Isabell, leading the way.

Muted light and a delightful warmth beckoned us through the door to the formal dining room, where the servants had laid eighteen symmetrical china place settings arranged at perfect intervals. A large candelabrum hung over the mahogany table, which was lit the whole of one side by a gray scrolled fireplace. A pale-red hue circled the room, broken only by wooden beams and plaster designs that reached up to touch a cherubim-painted ceiling.

Mr. Galpin had been purposefully placed to my right with Colonel Hatcher on my other side. Chairs shuffled, gowns swished, and everyone was seated, but not before I caught sight of Lewis sneaking to his place on Isabell's right at the head of the table. His gaze fell to mine and his eyebrow lifted as if in repentance before uttering something to Isabell that seemed to pacify her. I watched as her gloved hand came to rest on his arm for several seconds before she slowly drew it away.

I stared at the plate before me, my shoulders tight. To my right, Colonel Hatcher nudged my arm by accident, and it wasn't long before he launched into a vivid description of his stables. I decided to humor him. Anything to keep my attention on his side of the table.

"Bottom, my girl, bottom!" he blurted out between bites of soup.

"Pardon?"

"A good hindquarters." He slapped his outermost thigh. "Now hunters, that is my passion."

"I do love to ride, but I'm not certain I should like to hunt." I bit my lip. "Mr. Browning does keep a very fine stable though." A thought came to me as I swallowed. "It is my understanding he rides quite well. I've actually seen him from my window late at night flying across the estate in the moonlight."

Colonel Hatcher's corset creaked as he sat up straight. "Yes. Well. I know he's out and about at night. Can't say the wife and I haven't spent many an evening pondering what he is up to. But Browning and I don't speak at present. Came for Isabell tonight. Darling girl. Doesn't get out much."

I blinked. "Why is that?"

His brow furrowed. "Deuced awkward business, I 'spect. Married the younger brother after breaking the engagement with the elder. Now she's left under Browning's care. Deuced awkward, if you ask me."

My skin felt suddenly cold. "You mean to tell me, Mr. Browning was once engaged to Isabell?"

He pulled at the edge of his cravat. "Thought you knew. Don't like to spread gossip, you see."

"Not at all." I took a deep breath, hesitating, choosing my next words carefully. "Is it

181

possible you were acquainted with my brother, Jacob?"

He wiped his forehead with a handkerchief, smashing it back into his jacket pocket. "Delightful young lad. Full of spunk. Can't see him getting knocked off a bridge though."

I cast him a quick glance. "Neither can I. Mr. Browning claims it was an accident. I don't suppose, I mean, do you have an opinion on the matter?"

He wrinkled his nose. "The scandal cut up the whole neighborhood, but I can't say I have much to add. Keep to myself, I do." He motioned to my left. "Suppose you could ask good old Galpin. He was at the inquest, you know."

A prickle climbed my neck, and my soup spoon fell against the bowl with a clink. Galpin had been at the inquest. Why hadn't I been made aware of that? Frozen for a moment, I thought back on our prior conversations. Had he ever mentioned the inquest?

Lewis's steady voice cut through the lull of the table, stirring me from my reflections in a way nothing else could. He kept his head turned neatly to Isabell, but his eyes were on me. My heartbeat quickened, and my hands found their way to my lap. How long had he been watching me?

The first course was replaced by the second, and Galpin turned at once, smiling into my startled face. "A lovely dinner, is it not? Isabell has outdone herself once again."

"Yes." My voice had deserted me.

"Old Hatcher's been entertaining you, I see." A laugh hid behind his words.

"The Colonel has been most kind."

"Yes, but I must say you look a bit flushed. Are you certain you are well?"

"Quite well. Thank you." I took a quick sip from my drink. "My brother Jacob came up in conversation is all. I-I didn't know you were on the inquest that day."

"Ah. I see now your distress. What a topic to discuss at dinner. I didn't think Hatcher so indelicate." He rested his hand on the edge of the table, his fork loose in his fingers. "A terrible day to recall."

"Please don't speak so of Colonel Hatcher. It was I who brought up the topic. I'm still gathering information about my brother's time here."

His eyebrows rose. "Extraordinary. To what purpose?"

"To expose the truth." I blinked. "Whatever it might be. Have you any details about the inquest that might prove helpful, that might put my mind at ease?"

A slow smile spread across his face. "So,

you've heard the whole of the rumors."

My gaze flicked instinctively to Lewis. "I've heard enough."

"There is really very little to reveal. Browning declared the whole thing an accident. And as it took several days to locate the, uh, body. By then there was nothing to dispute that fact. It was afterward that people became suspicious."

I leaned in. "How so?"

"Well, I didn't speak up at first. You see, I didn't put the two situations together at the time. They seemed unrelated."

"What do you mean?"

"I had taken a drink that night with Jacob at the Boar's Head Inn where I found your brother in a strange mood, cursing about Browning and all that. At least three other men heard him as well." Mr. Galpin adjusted his fork on the table, then leaned in. "Jacob mentioned more than once your astute guardian meant to have it all." He angled his chin. "What, you ask? We don't know, really. Only your dear brother turned up dead that very night, and Browning . . ." He paused. "Inherited everything."

My chest felt tighter with every breath I took. "And no charges were brought?"

Mr. Galpin shrugged. "No real evidence. Mind you, things have a way of being brushed under the rug, especially when your good friend, Mr. Drake, is the parish officer." He tapped the edge of his plate. "But I can say no more . . . at present."

Mr. Galpin eyed me for a good many seconds before I slowly turned to Lewis, my heartbeat echoing in my ears. What else had he kept from me? Something happened that night on the bridge, and now more than ever, I was determined to figure out just what it was.

CHAPTER 12

Isabell had led the ladies back into the drawing room following dinner to await the gentlemen. Pacing from one end of the room to the next, she seemed a bit lost as to how to fill the time in their absence. As the party had been clearly designed for the sole purpose of introducing me to the local eligible men, Isabell had constructed a crowd full of shy young girls and aging women who preferred card games and fireside chats to the more refined notions of accomplishment.

One more turn about the room and Isabell herself was forced to an exhibition on the pianoforte. She played quite well, but I was glad to have a few minutes alone with Aunt Jo, who'd seated herself in the back corner and nosed into a book.

"What are you doing hiding in the drapes?"

Aunt Jo shrugged as a knowing smile

graced her lips. "I believe Isabell placed this chair here just for me." She slipped the book shut. "As well as ample reading material."

I couldn't help but laugh. "She very likely did. The wretch." I took Aunt Jo's hand. "But we shall not let her deter us." I helped Aunt Jo to her feet and accompanied her over to a row of salon chairs as close to the fire as the mingling guests would allow.

Aunt Jo smoothed out her skirt as she took a seat. "Really, Rebecca, Isabell is right. You should be making friends instead of humoring your old aunt."

I dipped my chin and mumbled beneath my breath. "With whom, pray tell? The stone-faced Mrs. Hatcher or perhaps one of her daughters, who I am quite certain are nearly five years my junior?"

Aunt Jo pressed her lips together. "You mustn't say such things aloud, Rebecca, even if they are true."

I lifted my head. "You are right, of course. I have always been a bit too free with my tongue. You are wise to keep me from regretting it." I leaned in. "I promise to say no more on that score, yet I am afraid I have something else to tell you that you may not like."

She looked up. "What now, my dear?"

"I have made a kind of discovery." I

paused to make certain our conversation was private. "Were you aware that Mr. Galpin was on Jacob's inquest?"

"On the inquest! That is indeed surprising. And a strange coincidence. You mean to tell me he told you all?"

"Not exactly. I have learned nothing more about what they found that day, not yet at least. I'm afraid I shall have to agree to some nonsense with Mr. Galpin at some point to get him to talk more. He seemed hesitant to do so fully at the table."

A slight shiver shook her back, and she cast a quick look at the door. "Or maybe not. It may surprise you, but I, too, have been busy this evening. Quite by accident, mind you. I haven't your incessant need for information, but I do believe you could find this bit of news useful and hopefully avoid a tête-à-tête with Mr. Galpin, if that pleases you."

I leaned forward. "What is it? Do not keep me in suspense."

"As you may have noticed, I have been enjoying Mr. Fernside's very fine company." A blush stole across her cheeks.

"Why, Aunt Jo." I couldn't hide the excitement in my voice.

She held up her hand. "He properly gave me his regrets about Jacob, but here is where it gets interesting. He happened to mention that he was the very person who came upon Jacob in the river."

My mouth slipped open. "Go on."

"Being quite amiable and thoughtful, of course, Mr. Fernside did not want to distress me at dinner; however, I am sure if we were to speak with him again, he could be persuaded to answer any questions you might have."

I took a deep breath, my mind awash with the possibilities. Aunt Jo must have read the eagerness in my eyes, for she grasped my hand. "Not here, love. Not tonight. There are far too many people that might take such a discussion amiss. Mr. Browning has been too kind for me to get the villagers restless in his own home. Goodness knows the man has endured enough."

Her words rankled, but I chose to ignore them. "Then how shall we meet with Mr. Fernside again and alone?"

"I have been giving that some thought as well. You see, Mr. Fernside owns the circulating library in Plattsdale. Perhaps if the two of us were to give the establishment a visit this week, we might be favored with his excellent company." She leaned in. "For a recommendation, perhaps."

"That is an excellent idea." I tapped my

muslin-covered knee. "It just might work. Yes, indeed. What if you were to mention to Mr. Fernside tonight about our possible trip into town, so we could be certain of his being in the shop and available?"

Aunt Jo's finger drew a pattern on the chair's armrest. "I suppose I could. He's been quite attentive, but I'm not sure he'll . . ."

I lifted my eyebrow. "I daresay he means to seek you out again and as soon as possible. How could he stay away?"

Her ears turned bright red. "Don't toy with me, Rebecca. I am too old for such nonsense."

My voice dropped to a whisper. "I wouldn't dream of it. Sit up straight and smile, for here he comes now, leading the rest of the gentlemen."

Her face turned white and then a cherry red as Isabell held the last note of the song on the pianoforte and Mr. Fernside arrived at our seats.

I stood and nodded, freeing up the seat beside Aunt Jo. "Why, Mr. Fernside, have you had a pleasant evening?"

A tallish man, his broad shoulders and bulk seemed to stoop as he nodded, his dark brown hair peppered with gray. "What an excellent dinner and fine company."

"I'm so pleased." I caught Isabell's pointed look from across the room. Mr. Fernside was not on her short list of men I was to entertain. "If you will excuse me, Mrs. Browning requires my attention just now." Aunt Jo could handle the rest. A small smile parted my lips. And I daresay, she would enjoy doing so.

I crossed the room, my feet a bit lighter, my steps more assured. Perhaps the dinner party would be a success after all, just not in the way Isabell had imagined.

She met my arrival with a huff. "Do not waste your time on a man in his dotage. Besides, Fernside has little to recommend himself, I assure you. Mr. Galpin, however, should be in here momentarily, and I have already asked Adam to play a song we can dance to. What do you think of that?"

I met her eyes. "I think it quite nice."

"Nice? Don't be absurd, Rebecca. Really. Dancing is the surest way to know one's heart." She hesitated. "What *do* you think of my Mr. Galpin?"

"I cannot say I've finished forming an opinion . . ."

She gave another huff. "Well, I suggest you hurry it along. I daresay he doesn't know what to make of you. And without a bit of encouragement, you will hardly secure him." She cocked an eyebrow, and a momentary flash of excitement lit her face. "You are far too stiff, Rebecca. Allow the music to guide your actions."

I lowered my chin and added a shrewd glance.

Isabell would have none of that. "Let me tell you, Miss Prim and Proper. You are hardly the expert on romance. While you have been hidden away in Scotland, the rest of us have been perfecting the art of dancing and flirting and finding love." She narrowed her eyes. "Music, my dear, has a way of invading your soul, stripping away any useless thoughts, baring the truth for all to see. Trust me, when your hand finds Mr. Galpin's and his touch suddenly feels different, look into his eyes." Her own eyes glistened. "Then you'll know." As an afterthought more to herself, she added on a huff, "It is how I realized I was engaged to the wrong man."

She peeked around my shoulder to the door. "Ah, here are the last of the gentlemen now."

Mr. Galpin wasted no time in locating us, charging across the Aubusson rug, a wry look about his eyes. If I cared at all to find a husband, I would have been flattered. He stopped just before us, almost posing.

"What a bore the last few minutes have proved to be without the two of you to entertain me." He took Isabell's hand and she laughed.

Lewis was the last to wander into the drawing room's muted glow. He hovered on the periphery like the stuffy men I'd seen in the paintings in the front hall, uninterested in all he saw. I watched as he sauntered to a nearby pillar and leaned against it. After what Mr. Galpin had revealed to me at the table, I couldn't help but appraise Lewis with a keen eye.

What were the days like at Greybourne Hall leading up to Jacob's death? What passed between him and Lewis? There was much I still did not know, and unfortunately Lewis held the key. I would have to be careful.

Bathed in shadows, his dark coat and hair all but disappeared into the dusky wood. Yet his blue eyes remained solid enough. They flashed in the candlelight as he assessed each person in the room until he looked at me.

I wasn't ready for such a direct glare and shied away. Did he know what I had discovered?

Isabell's voice was soft, but her words jolted me back to the conversation at hand.

"Thank you, Adam. I do agree a dance will liven up the room. Don't you think, Miss Hunter?"

They were all looking at me — Mr. Galpin, Isabell, Adam — but it was Mr. Galpin who took my hand. "Would you do me the honor, Miss Hunter?"

His grip was assured. He was, no doubt, confident of my answer. A commanding smile creased his lips. "I suppose a waltz would be a bit too bold to request in this sleepy little place." He squeezed my fingers. "However much I would enjoy the experience."

Gently, I drew my hand away.

Isabell's laugh rang out like a bell. "He is only teasing, Rebecca. We shall have none of that here."

My pulse quickened as my mind flicked back to the garden and Lewis. "I do apologize, Mr. Galpin, but I must beg your leave. I'm afraid I am not free at present." The little group fell silent, and I offered them a conciliatory grin. "Rest assured, it is not the selection that has me refusing. I should have enjoyed a waltz; however, I have already promised this dance to someone else."

Mr. Galpin held fast and controlled every muscle in his face. He did not believe me. Who else could compete with the dashing figure he presented?

Something grazed the small of my back, and I closed my eyes for a brief second. Lewis's voice was at my ear. "This is our dance, is it not?"

My fingers tingled. My gaze shot to Isabell's face. "Yes. I suppose it is."

The room settled into a blur of movement as Lewis led me to the set. I am quite certain there were other couples that joined us in line, the Hatcher girls, perhaps Mr. Galpin, but as the musical introduction began, I could see no one but the man across from me.

Lewis cut a fine figure, his black coat angled to perfection, his hair newly trimmed. Yet, it wasn't the clothes that made my nerves prickle up the nape of my neck, nor the way he moved forward in the dance. It was far more. The curious intensity to his presence, the questions that lay between us, the intangible pull that had been there since our first meeting.

I fought for control. "I was concerned you might not come to the dinner party at all. Perhaps there were people invited you did not wish to meet?"

"To my own dinner party?" He sounded incredulous.

"Isabell thought it likely."

"Have no doubt that when I give my word, I keep it." A line settled across his forehead as we began the figures, Lewis speaking in passing. "Isabell Browning is not my keeper."

I took his hand as the dance brought us close. His movements were smooth and composed. "And, I never would have missed our dance."

There was a moment of confused silence on my part, then the other couples were between us, allowing me a chance to breathe, to sort out Lewis's duplicity. His declaration felt sincere, but how could I trust the man after learning what Jacob had said just hours before his death?

I tore my gaze away, feigning interest in the other dancers. But the figures brought us together again, and I was forced to acknowledge the stirring in my heart, the subtle shake to my hand as I reached for his. What had Isabell said about dancing and hands?

Something was different. *He* felt different. My skin filled with warmth, my fingers, my feet, my head. Instinctively, my eyes found his, and the room tilted.

Lewis Browning. What was he to me? My guardian? My coconspirator? My brother's murderer? Or something else entirely? My heart ticked to life in my chest. Isabell had been right about the music, about the dinner party. I'd made a discovery all right, only not what I had hoped to find.

Lewis lifted his eyebrows ever so slightly, and I was at a loss for words. Music floated about my ears. The room became a whirl of ribbons and lace and breeches and pumps. Laughter. Footsteps. Buried in the distance, I registered the bark of a dog that resounded over and over again as if far away.

Sophie? A lull of commotion followed, but my steps didn't hesitate, not until Adam faltered at the pianoforte, and I turned to see two strangers at the drawing room door.

Lewis thrust out his arm, forcing me away from the other dancers. "I do apologize, Rebecca, but I must cut the set short." His voice sounded shaken. "It is urgent, or I would never dream of doing so."

With as little fanfare as possible, he deposited me beside Aunt Jo and quietly made his way over to the new arrivals. The men hovered in the doorway and withdrew as Lewis neared. The first gentleman was eye level with Lewis, his black hair tousled by the wind. The second, an older man, had a patch of gray in his reddish hair and stood with his arms crossed, his broad shoulders tense, a riding crop still gripped in his hand.

Aunt Jo blinked. "Well, what is all this about?"

I managed a whispered, "I don't know."

"And in the middle of your dance. I could—"

"Lewis said it was urgent. He would not have been so rude otherwise." My gaze stayed on the door. "Have you seen either of those men before?"

"Only the wretched one with the gray patch in his hair. Lord Torrington is well-known in London, my dear." She pursed her lips. "Scandal follows that name. Mr. Browning would be well advised to steer clear of him."

"Or what?" The hint of a headache snaked across my brow. "He could lose his reputation? Really, Aunt, I don't believe that a concern at present. Why do you suppose they are here?"

"Who could know?"

I stiffened. "Well, I could." My eyes grew round. "Quickly, before the music ends. Take a turn with me about the room, or rather, to the door."

"You cannot be serious."

"I've never been more so. Now make haste." I latched on to her arm and smiled as we stood before sauntering off in the direction of the door. "You're doing quite

198

well," I said to Aunt Jo as I nodded to Colonel Hatcher. "Just a few more steps."

Aunt Jo squeezed my hand. "Your father would have my head if he were here."

"Thankfully, he is not." I gave her a knowing look and slipped through the open door. "Make my excuses. A headache perhaps." It wasn't far from the truth. Then I smiled and closed the door.

The quiet of the entryway swallowed me up as my careful footsteps faded into the gloom. The large front room stood empty. The candles winked as I passed. The hanging baskets hovered overhead, watching my movements like a cluster of owls. Lewis had likely taken the men to his study, so I headed there first, where I was rewarded by a flicker of light at the turn of the hallway.

I paced the long corridor and shrank against the frigid wall near the office, the narrow space a gray soup around me. Voices were audible at the library door, and I leaned down near the keyhole to make out what I could.

"It was a cursed setup I tell you. They were waiting for me, knew what I was about."

Lewis's voice sounded strained. "It is a definite setback. How long till you have the use of your arm?"

"Days, weeks, I cannot be sure."

Lewis's voice deepened. "Do you suggest we give it up then?"

A pounding resounded through the door, as if someone had hit the wall. "Not at all. Not when we are so close. My shoulder will heal. We must simply be more careful about our business."

A mature voice entered the fray. "Listen, boys, I'm new at this, but the report I brought you is credible. And it's not just information this time, but an actual person. I don't see how we can let this go."

"Sinclair has his own troubles, and Torrington, you must not get involved, not yet at least. You're too public a figure for this business. It will come to no good. I'd advise you to remain in the shadows for now." It was Lewis again, his voice on edge. "I'll see to this newest development."

"But you have done enough already."

"I have nothing else keeping me at home."

A voice sliced through the stillness behind me. "Why, Miss Hunter, are you lost?" Mr. Galpin's fingers circled my arm.

CHAPTER 13

The dancing had continued in the drawing room in my absence with the Hatcher girls making the most of the opportunity, giggling as they rounded their partners. Adam played with far more zest than he had earlier in the night.

Mr. Galpin ushered me inside, claiming Isabell had sent him to fetch me to save the dinner party, but I wasn't so sure I believed his desperate account. Everyone seemed quite busy enjoying their evening.

He led me straight to the makeshift dance floor and the top of set, then called out to Adam over his shoulder, "Won't you play 'The Marchioness of Blandford's Reel?'"

Turning back to me, he smiled. "I daresay you are free to partner me at last. You did promise after all." His dimple popped in and out on his cheek. "And this should be a favorite jig of yours, I would think."

I'd hardly danced a quadrille in company,

201

let alone a Scottish reel, and I loathed to mention the embarrassing fact that there wasn't a young man to be found in the tiny village where I'd lived with my mother. Clearly he was aware of my time in Scotland, for Mr. Galpin seemed far too pleased with his little arrangement. I kept quiet, a smile etched across my face.

I didn't mind the jig's lively steps, but our position at the top of the set left little time for talking and even less for a disagreeable subject like an inquest. Defeated, I blinked and cooed and made the figures as prettily as Isabell would have wanted me to. The deception made my stomach turn, yet I would need more time with the ineffaceable Mr. Galpin if I were to gain any answers about his time on the inquest.

The music ceased, and he led me from the set with the sort of smile I'd seen cross Isabell's face the day she met him in the folly, as if they had gotten just what they wanted. My fingers tightened into a ball at my side as I met Isabell's brilliant eyes and pert face. I supposed they had.

The irritating image haunted me the rest of the evening as we shared a dance here, a meaningless conversation there, all under Isabell's watchful eye. Mr. Galpin was most attentive. As I climbed the stairs at the close of the evening, my feet ached and far too many thoughts pained my mind.

I had been forced to remain in the drawing room until every last visitor departed and Isabell and her brother had taken their leave. Aunt Jo, however, had made her way upstairs hours before, leaving the hallway to my bedchamber dark and empty. Lewis resided in a separate part of the house, and even though our rooms had been aired out, the stagnant scent of disuse still marked the previously abandoned corridor.

Cautiously, I made my way down the carpeted hall with a candle thrust before me, hopelessly willing away the chill creeping up my back. A furtive wind had sprung up outside, and it howled against the window frame like a pent-up scream, shaking the leaded glass.

A few more steps, and I was at my bedchamber door. My feet froze on the threshold. The candlelight wavered, brought about by my twitchy fingers. The door — my door — was slightly ajar.

"Aunt Jo?" For a split second, I thought perhaps she had waited up for me. But as I tipped the door inward, I saw only blackness ahead.

My arm muscles tightened, and I lifted the candle, plunging it inside. I shall never forget the feelings that washed over me the moment I saw what awaited me — fear and utter confusion.

A cry bubbled up and poured out before I could gather myself. Through the door, a bulky shadow lay in wait where there should have been empty space. I tried to back away, but my knees locked. What was in my room?

I swept an arm across my forehead, staring at the dark shape that sat motionless on the floor. The thing could hardly be alive. I was being silly, surely. Shakily, I forced a step forward, then another, the light in my hand falling over the hidden corners of the room.

My shoulders relaxed a bit, and I took a deep breath. What I thought to be a beast bent on my destruction was only my desk turned on its side. My room, though ransacked from top to bottom, appeared empty of any threat, at least at present.

Aunt Jo came lumbering from her room, her robe dangling open and her nightcap askew. "Have you had one of your spells, Rebecca?"

"I apologize that I woke you, but I have not been to bed as of yet." I motioned to the room. "However, it seems I have been robbed."

My personal items had been stripped from

the wardrobe and lay scattered about the floor along with books and papers from the desk. The coverlet was in a heap beside the bed, my pillows handled and flung aside. Even the drapes had been wrestled to the floor. Not an inch of the room remained untouched.

"Heavens." Aunt Jo's fingers found her mouth. "How on earth could this have happened? During the party? Or when I was asleep next door?"

I grasped her arm, concerned she might faint, but Aunt Jo was made of finer stock than that.

Anger swarmed her eyes. "How dare they."

"Indeed." I toured the room, taking mental note of anything I saw missing, but I came to no conclusions amid such a mess.

Footsteps pounded down the hall. Lewis, still dressed in his evening attire, appeared around the doorframe and plunged his fingers through his hair. "I heard a scream. Is everyone all right?"

"You *heard* me?"

He mumbled. "I had not gone to bed."

"Well." I gave him a hard smile. "As you can see, someone has been in my room."

Only then did he look at what lay behind me, his eyes widening. "What the deuce?"

"Indeed." I dipped my chin. "Is this

perhaps a regular occurrence at your properties?"

We were both thinking about the London townhouse, and his eyes flashed to mine. "Not until you arrived."

Aunt Jo wandered over to the upturned desk. "What do you think they were searching for?"

I snatched my chemise and petticoat which were strewn across the middle of the floor, and I was forced to hide my face as I stuffed the articles behind a stray pillow. "I haven't the foggiest idea."

Lewis nosed around the papers with the toe of his pump. "That they were looking for something is certain now, perhaps in London as well."

"I can't know what. I have nothing of any consequence." I couldn't hide the bite in my voice. "Anything of any value was left to you."

Lewis cocked an eyebrow. "Personal then."

"What do you mean?"

He picked up a wrinkled sheet of paper. "A letter, information perhaps?"

I ripped Ellen's correspondence out of his hands. "My personal missives are none of your concern." I only hoped he hadn't seen his name penned several times throughout her words.

206

He seemed to think better of his actions. "I apologize for the intrusion."

The conversation I had overheard between Lewis and the other men coursed through my mind. What *were* they talking of? Could it have something to do with the search of my room?

I caught his discerning eyes and shrugged it off. "Regardless, we shall discover nothing tonight. I'm overtired and only wish for my bed. We can sort all this out in the morning."

Aunt Jo scooped up a pillow off the floor. "You can hardly sleep here."

Lewis leaned against the mantel. "Your aunt is right. I shall summon the maid to turn down another room as quickly as possible."

"Please." I held up my hand. "I do not wish to wake the staff. I have no problem sharing my aunt's bed for the remainder of the night. That is, if Sophie will allow it."

Aunt Jo gave a nervous laugh. "She shan't be removed, I'm afraid. We shall all just have to manage it together."

Lewis rubbed his forehead, still looking over the disheveled space. "If you are certain that will do."

"It will do quite well for me. Now, if you will excuse us, my aunt and I must gather my things for the night."

"Yes." Lewis backed away, but he seemed hesitant to leave the room. "I'll return first thing in the morning to help you make sense of all this."

"Thank you." My voice sounded clipped.

My aunt and I watched him leave before gathering up what we could. "You don't think he is somehow responsible, do you, Rebecca?"

I thought back to the dance and the blur of people I had seen. It could have been anyone. After my return to the drawing room, Mr. Galpin had consumed the whole of my time. I narrowed my eyes. Had Lewis returned as I'd assumed? And what about the other two men?

Lewis did look surprised when he entered the bedchamber and again when I brought his attention to what had happened, but where had he been in the house where he could hear my scream? The library, the kitchens, his room were all too far away. My maid had not even responded.

I turned to my aunt. "Do you remember the latter part of the dance? Specifically, if anyone stepped out after I left or rather, returned quite late?"

Aunt Jo bit her lip. "You know I'm hardly observant, but I do remember Mr. Galpin slipping out the door."

I shook my head. "That doesn't signify. He was coming to fetch me."

She added, "And Mr. Browning and those men were gone for some time."

"Yes. Yes, they were, but we cannot be certain they left the library."

"It wasn't long before the guests began departing, and I headed to my room. I do remember seeing Isabell walk several of the neighbors out into the entryway."

I pressed my lips together for a long second. "Unfortunately, there is simply no way to know. It could have been any one of them." I paused. "Except — Sophie! I heard Sophie barking while Mr. Browning and I were dancing."

"Are you certain, my darling? I don't remember that at all."

I paced over to the wardrobe, my mind ticking away with my newfound thought. "I'm quite sure of it." I gestured back across the room. "You remember. You were talking with Mr. Fernside" — my arm dropped to my side — "and likely distracted."

I secured a robe from the heap of clothes and a gown to sleep in. I ran the soft material through my fingers while I replayed the events of the dance, the feel of the room, the beat of my heart. "I'm afraid I was distracted as well. Lewis, he . . . You see, I was . . . 'pon rep, I know what I heard." Irritated at my fuzzy recollection and the reason behind it, I forced open a drawer to recover my tooth powder with far more force than necessary.

"Goodness, Rebecca. There is no need to throw the rest of the contents across the room. My nerves are rattled enough."

"I apologize. I'm just so angry my things have been tampered with."

Aunt Jo's eyebrows twitched. "Just your things?"

I shot her a sharp look, and she motioned for me to follow. "Nothing more tonight. Let us retire at present. We shall have plenty of time tomorrow to rehash this over and over again as you will insist on doing if I am not mistaken."

Another thought came to me as I crossed the room into my aunt's warm embrace. Sophie was awfully selective with her protective nature. If Mr. Galpin had been a part of the set, who else would cause Sophie to bark with such a marked distaste?

Lewis was true to his word. I was barely dressed before I heard him righting the furniture in my room next door.

I paused at the threshold, once again taking in the state of my bedchamber in the morning's fresh glow. His jacket was slung across the bed, and his fingers fiddled with every paper he came across on the floor.

"I thought you said we would do this together. My aunt will be here as well momentarily."

He glanced up and smiled. "I had a difficult time sleeping, so I thought I might as well get started." He slid the desk back into its proper place against the wall. "What do you make of all this?"

I had done a great deal of thinking over the night and come to one firm conclusion — Lewis must be told what I'd found in the woods to either gauge his reaction or elicit his help. "There is something I'd like to show you, something I discovered quite a while back, but I'm not certain it has anything to do with what happened here."

I walked to the fireplace and opened a satinwood box on the mantel where the handkerchief lay folded inside. Jacob had given me the box when I was thirteen, intending it for jewelry, but it had always been too small for that.

Securing the item, I turned to see Lewis's stark gaze and hooded eyes. He didn't trust me any more than I did him. His next words came out rough. "What is it? And how long . . . ?"

I shook out the torn material and shrugged one shoulder. "It's an embroidered handkerchief. I found it at the bridge."

I crossed the room to where he stood by the poster bed and allowed him to take it into his hands as I watched his eyes.

"Where at the bridge?"

"That's just it." I observed his fingers as they slowly traced the letter *B*. "A day after we spoke in the library, when you told me about Mr. Drake's body, my aunt and I went back to the bridge to investigate."

He cocked an eyebrow, his hands growing still. "You went back to the bridge to *investigate*?"

"As I said." I could hear Aunt Jo step into the hallway. She would be in here in only a moment.

He smiled as he balled the handkerchief in his palm. "And just what do you believe you have found? I can make out nothing from this ragged thing, and it could have been dropped by anyone."

"True, but it wasn't dropped."

Aunt Jo bustled in. Astute to our conversation, she faded into the background, gathering some papers.

He lowered his chin. "Go on."

"Well, while I was walking beneath the bridge, I happened to notice the dirt and twigs where Mr. Drake had lain had been depressed in a line, as if something had been dragged into the woods. Tell me, is that how they brought Mr. Drake back to the house?"

"Certainly not. He was gently lifted into a cart and brought straight here. I'd never have permitted him to be manhandled."

"As I supposed."

Naturally, I leaned back against the bed, taking a seat as I spoke. Lewis moved next to me, resting against the bedside table. A stony expression marred his face, and he shook his head. "I've not been back to the bridge. Not once." His voice slipped into a whisper. "As you can imagine, that place holds a great deal of pain for me." He paused, lost in thought, and a sickly calm filled the room. At first, unable to speak, he lowered his gaze. "I'm sure it does for the two of you as well." He reached out and touched my hand for several seconds before returning his own to his lap.

My vision blurred, the gentle honesty of his movement tugging at my heart. All at once I found it difficult to think. "The, uh, trail I found that day led a little way into the woods." I took a quick breath. "Which is where I saw the handkerchief in a tree, as if someone had placed it there and forgotten it. I believe that brown stain could very likely be blood."

Lewis rolled the square fabric in his hand again and eventually let out a long breath. "You may be right, but I cannot think of a soul who has a *B* in their name. I mean, besides me, and that's not my middle name, if it is indeed the middle initial. It's hard to tell because the others are so torn. They could simply be decorations, I suppose."

A cold chill washed through my body, and I'm certain he saw me flinch. Why hadn't I thought of such a possibility? I had been certain the other two embroidered marks were letters. Weren't they? It was a middle initial, right? I had dismissed all the Brownings out of hand because the *B* was in the middle. My mind churned for answers. What else could I have overlooked?

He leaned in close, his voice calm and steady. "It's not mine, Rebecca."

My pulse throbbed.

Did I believe him?

CHAPTER 14

Three days passed with little to no new information about the robbery. Apparently, the thief had snuck in and out during the dinner party without a single person the wiser.

Lewis said nothing more about the handkerchief, and considering I'd not seen him alone again, I was forced to swallow any questions I hoped to pose and move on. The fact that he might be avoiding me did cross my mind, yet he was in and out of Greybourne Hall at all hours, consumed with business he didn't intend to share with me. He could have simply been busy.

My room was cleaned and straightened by the staff, and Aunt Jo and I were able to make our foray into town within the week. The coachman Lewis provided for our short trip drew the carriage to a halt just inside the center of town where Aunt Jo and I were pleased to alight.

A slight breeze tugged on our bonnets, but we hadn't far to walk. Plattsdale's lending library was a two-story affair composed of tan stones and located in a prime spot in the square, sandwiched between the local jeweler and the accompanying bookstore, another business enterprise of Mr. Fernside. I assisted Aunt Jo up the steps, and we crossed beneath the two white arches. "I do hope Mr. Fernside is in."

She nodded quickly, the ostrich feather adorning her crape bonnet wiggling as we ascended the steps. Her eyes grew wide as we caught a glimpse beyond the door. "This looks to be quite a smart shop, does it not?" She grasped her parasol within her lilac-gloved fingers. "What a treat to have the use of so many books."

Dressed in a pale-blue walking dress with a matching spencer jacket, Aunt Jo looked years younger. She spent far more time on her attire for our outing than I did, adding a silver necklace and matching bracelet as if we were to attend a ball. Mr. Fernside could not be anything but impressed by her deft choices. Goodness, I'd thrown on my old green round dress and tan kid gloves with little thought.

A squarish gentleman on his way out of the library stopped short and held the paneled glass door for us to pass, bowing slightly as we walked inside. A whiff of pipe smoke filled the entryway, which opened up to a large reading room. Amid the various sofas and chairs reposed a few gray-haired gentlemen and well-dressed ladies, all catching up on the latest news in the papers and magazines.

Aunt Jo seemed nervous, glancing around the space as she fumbled with her parasol.

I leaned in close. "I am sure Mr. Fernside is in the back. Let us ask the clerk before you worry yourself into a fret."

"I just hope we have not wasted our day."

We crossed the room to the desk and waited for another customer to conclude his business. "Nonsense. Lewis gave me my pin money last week. In a pinch, we could always select a few novels to read."

The clerk motioned us forward with a curl of his fingers, his indifferent countenance meeting us head on. "The name of the book please and volume number."

I affected a smile. "We've not come for a particular novel per se. We were hoping to get a recommendation from Mr. Fernside. Is he available for —"

"I am well versed in all we have to offer, miss." The man wrinkled his nose. "Were you hoping for the latest novels or something else?"

Aunt Jo seemed to melt at my side, and I bolstered her back up with my arm. "I'm sure you are quite helpful, sir, but Mr. Fernside especially wanted to assist us with our selection today. Would it be too much trouble for you to fetch him?"

The clerk hesitated as the edge of his lip curled down. "If you insist." He smiled then — forced I assumed — and elevated his chin. "If you will excuse me." He pranced from the room as if we'd sent him scurrying to the prince regent, not the amiable Mr. Fernside.

" 'Pon rep." Aunt Jo flicked out her fan. "What a disagreeable man. I cannot imagine Mr. Fernside employing such a person."

Aunt Jo looked about ready to drop, so I directed her to a vacant sofa by the fire. We waited but a few minutes before Mr. Fernside's smiling face breached the side door.

Waving, he crossed the floor in a hurry. "Why, Mrs. Audley, Miss Hunter. I am so pleased you have come. I hope I find you comfortable." He motioned around the space. "This is our reading room, and we have a delightful selection of books in the back. Is there something I may interest you in today?"

His eyes never strayed from my aunt's

beaming face. I decided to speak first. "Your library is quite beautiful, and we shall be pleased to rent a book; however, I must tell you, I came about an entirely different matter today. Will you have a seat with us for a few moments?"

Concern dawned, and he settled into a slat-back chair next to us before pushing his spectacles up his nose. "What can I assist you with?"

I met his troubled gaze. "Please, don't be alarmed. All is well. I've come for information, actually." Where to begin? "You see, it has come to my attention that months ago you were the one who found my brother's body in the river. If that is true, would you be inclined to answer a few questions?"

Shock pierced his eyes as he considered how to respond. "I-I wouldn't wish to distress either of you." His gaze kept wandering to Aunt Jo.

Sweet, but not entirely helpful. "That is kind of you; nevertheless, not knowing the full story of what happened to my brother that day has been far harder to bear than whatever you might have to tell me. Please, I beg you to help us."

He rubbed his forehead, glancing toward the clerk at the counter, then back to Aunt Jo. "It was a monstrous time, but I will do

219

my best to enlighten you, if that is what you wish."

My shoulders relaxed a bit. "It is indeed. Thank you." I, too, stole a peek at Aunt Jo. "I — We have not been relayed the whole of the story, you see. None of the details." I lowered my chin, thinking of Mr. Browning's book from China. "I assure you, my nerves are in fine working order, so please, would you tell me what you found that day in the river, specifically?"

He swallowed hard, the lump in his throat bobbing up and down. "You mean, what I *saw*?"

I nodded.

"Well . . ." He wiped his forehead with his handkerchief, his fingers quivering. "I suppose I had gone down to Reedwick to fish, and quite by accident, mind you, I came upon a muddy lump on the side of the river. Birds were circling overhead." His eyebrows furrowed in the middle, then he turned back to Aunt Jo.

She encouraged him with a nod. "Whatever you can remember would be quite helpful."

He ran his hand down his trousers. "It was your brother, you see, or, what was left of him. It had been several days since he disappeared."

Considering what Lewis discovered about Mr. Drake, I was determined to learn more. "What exactly did he look like?"

"Look like?"

"Yes . . . specifically. I realize I am asking a great deal, but please, would you do us this favor?"

His eyelids twitched and his hands curled into fists. "I'll never forget, never. It would not be right of me to say."

Aunt Jo touched his hand. "Please. We need you to stand our friend. It is most urgent. Can you . . . describe what you saw?"

Mr. Fernside shook his head. "He was all swollen up." His voice deserted him, but he pressed on. "His hair gone, skin peeling in places, lips black. A part of his skull had been chipped off. I thought the injury strange at the time, but I didn't know who he was or where he'd come from."

I paused. "Was there anything else that stood out to you?"

He hung his head as if exhausted. "The whole town thinks Browning did it and the other one too." His hand found his wispy hair. "I-I cannot say I am certain myself." Then his eyes flashed open. "But if the two of you are in any trouble —"

Aunt Jo lifted her hand. "We are perfectly

safe under Mr. Browning's care. Thank you, Mr. Fernside, for telling us all. It took a great deal of courage. I shall not forget it." She stood, and Mr. Fernside hopped to his feet as well, reaching out his arm.

She gladly took it. "Now, I believe I would prefer a happier pursuit, like a book recommendation."

That was the end to our conversation. No more questions. Aunt Jo had had enough. But for me, our visit only made me more curious, more unsettled. Why was there a chip on Jacob's skull? The fall possibly. And why was his body swollen? Considering Lewis's knowledge of the dead, I would be forced to consult with him eventually. I only hoped he'd tell me the truth.

CHAPTER 15

Lewis avoided me for days, escaping all meals and sneaking out for walks with Sophie long before my maid could have me ready.

In fact, I'd heard and seen little of his presence at the house during the day. Once darkness fell, everything changed. Like clockwork, he was a steady rider, tearing down the front drive, night after night, streaking through the moonlit trees beneath starry skies.

Where did he go? And why do so at night? My curiosity had only grown over time, and I was determined to find out what he was up to. The villagers thought him a devil up to no good, but that didn't exactly fit what I knew of him.

Following the time we spent cleaning up my room, I came to the same conclusion I had before — the handkerchief probably wasn't his. Lewis's reaction had been far too genuine, his emotions a bit too real. However, I found I could not release him entirely of blame. No one around Plattsdale stood to gain from my brother's death, except Lewis — he had inherited Jacob's whole world. Had not Mr. Galpin said as much? Of course, Mr. Galpin could very well be lying, but to what purpose?

Lewis's odd behavior surrounding that awful night had done nothing to counteract Mr. Galpin's words. Why hadn't Lewis refuted him in public months ago? Or confronted even one of the angry villagers? He could have made clear his role in everything. Instead, he'd fortified himself behind the crumbling black stones of Greybourne Hall and shut out the world, leaving only under the cover of darkness.

A conversation with Lewis was the only balm to ease my growing anxiety. I needed to hear the truth from his lips. I would have to be the one to seek him out. Presently, I frequented the back grove of his garden, confident that if I entered unobserved, eventually we would meet. And on the fourth day, my luck held out.

The morning dawned unseasonably warm, a pulling breeze the only reminder of the chilly autumn we'd had of late. Far above, the sunlight feathered through wispy clouds, leaving a sparkling gray haze on the garden plants and dampened walls. The gate was slightly open when I arrived, and as I neared the back quarter, my chest lightened. Somehow, I knew he was there. Quietly, I pushed the mournful willow branches aside, retreating to the safety of shadows. It was Lewis all right, seated on the bench where we shared lunch. Arrested by his pose, I held utterly still, allowing myself a precious moment to watch him undisturbed.

Bent forward, he'd propped his elbows on his knees, cradling his head in his hands. His face held a haunting look to it, like he was lost. He intertwined his fingers and dipped his forehead against them as if in prayer. The desire to move closer tempted me, but I stayed where I was for a time.

He had a curious presence about him, the careless gift of a young man, yet at the same time, older somehow. His shoulders stooped with the weight of . . . what exactly? Regret? Fear? Pain? He remained in that position for some time — motionless, a cold statue engrossed in thought.

Gradually my mind ticked to Jacob, and I gave thought to the emotions I'd hidden for days. Lewis Browning did not seem at all like a murderer.

I could bear to remain silent no longer.

"Good morning, Lewis."

Startled, he looked up, his muscles twitching, but he stayed where he was, as if any movement would take far too much effort. "I didn't hear you come in."

I crossed to the far side of the small pond and took a seat at his side, then paused, gathering my words. "I do not mean to put myself forward, but I must say that you look distressed. Has something happened?"

He managed a wan smile. "No. Well, not today it hasn't." His palm found his forehead. "I'm only remembering someone — someone quite dear to me."

I raised my eyebrows, tempting him to say more.

He took a slow breath. "It was two months ago today that my Mollie died. I'm afraid the sudden memories have made me melancholy."

"Your dog."

He looked surprised. "How did you —"

"Mr. Galpin told me about her."

He slumped back. "Yes, of course."

"He said she looked a lot like Sophie. I'm sorry for your loss."

His gaze lifted to the sky, then back to me. "There have been too many losses of late. Your mother, your brother, Drake. Mollie was only a dog."

226

"But quite loved, I see."

"Yes, she was. And rather like Sophie in many ways, though not nearly as clever or determined." He shook his head. "You know, I never believed I would care for another dog, but Sophie coming here has done me a world of good. I'm glad to find I have room in my heart for another."

He allowed a gust of wind to roar across the garden before beginning again. "I'm not certain what I would have done if Sophie had not come back that day. The little mongrel has wormed her way into my heart, whether I wanted her to or not."

"She does have that way about her."

He hesitated. "Tell me, was everything all right with her when she returned?"

I narrowed my eyes. "Why do you ask?"

"I don't know if Galpin told you, but Mollie's death was not natural. She was shot. When Sophie disappeared, I thought —"

"That she had found the same fate." I pressed my lips together. "She did have a rather deep cut near her ear. But she could have gotten that anywhere, I suppose. Perhaps she was caught on a branch."

"I wondered if she had hurt herself. She seems a bit different of late, less eager to join me on my morning walks, flighty at times."

"Maybe that is because you leave so early these days. She has hardly the time to annoy Cook before you're off."

He smiled then, a real smile that transformed the grim lines on his face. "You may be right."

"I daresay you've been avoiding us all."

He must have sensed my quick glance, for he looked up. "Not exactly. I've been busy."

"With the two gentlemen who arrived during the party?"

His blinked. "Yes, if you must know."

I shrugged, trying to keep the conversation flowing. "You never did introduce them, and the party *was* in my honor — to meet all the young men in the neighborhood. At least, that is what Isabell designed."

Lewis lifted his chin. "Interested, are you?"

My eyes widened as I realized my mistake. "Don't be absurd. I saw them for a whole three seconds."

"I do believe Lord Torrington has made a conquest in far less time than that." He nudged my arm. "Or did you prefer Mr. Sinclair?"

Shaken, I scooted away. "Goodness, I do not prefer either of them. Now stop talking such foolishness. I only wished to know who they were."

His eyes brightened. "Little badger, I'm well aware why you asked." He took a quick breath. "The two gentlemen are friends, business associates. I'm afraid at present I cannot say more."

"Oh."

A hush fell between us, and Lewis tossed a rock into the pond that sent ripples in all directions. The water shimmered in the gusty breeze. "Rebecca, I have something to ask you, and I plead with you to take it in the right spirit." He closed his eyes for a brief second. "Did you perhaps fancy anyone? At the party, I mean. I am your guardian after all, and it is my duty to see you properly settled."

My toes curled in my half boots. Hadn't we been over this already? He'd even witnessed one of my spells. I was *not* on the marriage market. My words turned cold. "There was no one present at the dinner that I would ever consider."

He took a deep breath. "What about Mr. Galpin? He would not have been my first choice for you, but if you could tolerate him, Isabell seems to think the two of you would suit."

"And Isabell knows everything, does she?" I couldn't help but think of how she'd left Lewis for his younger brother.

His brows drew down. "That is not what I said."

"It sounds more like you two have arranged it all without a word to me. So Mr. Galpin is the chosen one who shall carry me off to Thorn Hall, and I shall be neatly tucked away. Hmm?"

"I did not say Galpin had to be your choice. If not him, then perhaps someone else. I could —"

"As long as it is indeed someone. Am I right?"

His fingers coiled into a fist. "Do be sensible, Rebecca. What other choice do you have?"

"Not many, I assure you, but I'd rather work at a dresser's shop till I'm old and gray than marry a man I barely know." I moved to stand, but his hand was on my arm.

"What is at the root of all this? Why are you so against marriage? Would you not consider it if I were to find you a respectable offer? If you had sufficient time to acquaint yourself with the gentleman?"

I pursed my lips. "And how, exactly, are you to do that hidden away, day after day, in the pit of Greybourne Hall? Can you tell me that?"

My comment struck a nerve. Lewis's voice flattened into a cold whisper, his face awash of emotion. "I still have some connections. Your father tasked me with —"

"My father. I might have known." Then I did stand, pushing roughly off the bench, my hands itching to throw something. Drawing in a slow breath, I measured my tone and met his gaze with all the wrath burning in my chest. "Understand me for the last time, here and now. I have no intention of marrying anyone. Not Mr. Galpin or any other hapless fool you bring my way — not ever. Good day." I turned and fled the garden, forgetting entirely that I had come for answers.

Aunt Jo found me rustling through my wardrobe several hours later, yet my anger had not completely subsided.

"What on earth are you looking for, my dear? You have the whole wall shaking."

"I'm in search of the paperwork I picked up at the Court of Chancery." I shoved the drawer shut, the heavy wardrobe quivering in my wake. "Where could that maid have stashed it? I've been through everything. I suppose it got misplaced after the robbery, but doesn't she realize the importance of an official document? I simply must find it."

Aunt Jo took my hand and led me to the chairs by the fire. After sitting and propping her arm on the side rest, she shot me a pointed glare. "What is behind all this? You've not mentioned altering your guardianship since we arrived."

"I have been foolish, Aunt Jo."

She dipped her chin. "Why do I get the feeling this has something to do with Mr. Browning?"

"Not you too."

"Then tell me what is bothering you."

I shook my head. "All this time, I have been eating his food, enjoying my pin money, searching for information about Jacob's death, but what I should have been doing was learning what I needed to do to apply to the Court of Chancery."

Her shoulders sagged. "To what end, Rebecca?"

"Independence, of course."

Aunt Jo smiled. "It was a nice dream — the two of us tucked away in a cottage somewhere, but it isn't to be, my darling. At least, not yet."

An empty feeling settled into my chest, and I tried again. "What about our plans? Surely you must agree my idea is preferable to a loveless marriage."

"Mr. Browning is a far cry from the man I once thought him to be. Your cousin Ellen should be brought to task over those ridiculous letters that set us on edge all those months ago. I daresay she could be a writer. Midnight devil indeed. All I've experienced is kindness and generosity from your cousin." She took my hand. "I do not believe Mr. Browning would ever force you into a marriage you did not agree to."

If only Aunt Jo knew how angry the townspeople were, had seen the look in that man's eyes on the edge of the woods. There was far more going on here than a silly story invented by Ellen. Perhaps I should tell her what Mr. Galpin heard Jacob say on the night he died. But did it matter? Aunt Jo would not believe me, not completely. Lewis cared for Sophie, and that alone made him a prince among men.

I took a deep breath. "I still have every intention of leaving, whether you join me or not. The sooner, the better."

"What about your investigation? How can you leave now?"

"I have come to believe Jacob's death was very likely an accident."

"And Mr. Drake's?"

"I don't know. But Lewis must fight his own battles. I won't stay here and let Isabell and him plan the rest of my life. I won't do it."

Aunt Jo leaned forward, a wise look filling

her aging eyes. "You care for him, don't you?"

I stiffened. "What do you mean?"

"Mr. Browning."

"Don't be absurd." I rose and paced to the fireplace. "I'll admit, I find him amiable at times . . . and clever."

"And handsome?"

"And infuriating." I jabbed the iron poker into the smoldering wood. "He means to marry me off as soon as possible."

"He said this to you?"

"Yes, he did, and I told him just what I thought of his little plan earlier today."

Aunt Jo stifled a laugh. "I'm sure you did."

"You all seem to think this a game — who I marry, who I don't. Well, I don't want to play anymore." Tears wet my eyes, and I wiped them away with the back of my hand.

Aunt Jo stood. "Do not accuse me of that. I have only ever had your best interest in my heart."

I let out a trapped breath. "I know. I'm so sorry. You're the one person in the world I trust completely. Please, forget what I said. I didn't mean it." My heartbeat accelerated and I pounded the palm of my hand against the mantel. "I just can't seem to escape this simmering anger — anger at the limited choices I've been given. Why must I have these spells?" A weariness joined my words. "Will you consider coming with me to London?"

Slowly, Aunt Jo shook her head, a curious look across her face. "Oh, Rebecca. I cannot."

Like a crash of thunder in a thick fog, understanding finally dawned. "It's Mr. Fernside, isn't it?"

"Yes. You and I share our own ideas and dreams of independence." She lifted her narrow eyebrows into peaks. "Mr. Fernside is mine. I never thought it possible to find love at my age, but I believe I have."

"Oh, Aunt Jo. I didn't realize. I have been terribly, terribly selfish."

"Stuff and nonsense. You have had much to concern you." Her smile brightened her face. "He took me driving earlier today, and I do not believe him indifferent to me."

I reached for her hand. "That is wonderful. And you are right as always. If he cares at all, we mustn't leave."

"You would stay here for me?"

I squeezed her fingers. "As long as it takes."

"But do you think you can manage Mr. Browning?"

I allowed a small smile. "I shall endeavor to do so. Perhaps he can be reasoned with."

She met my smile with a knowing look. "And what do you think Jacob would have advised if he were still here?"

I straightened. "I daresay he'd encourage me to follow my heart, whatever the cost. Passion and the fervor of life always came first with him. I suppose some would have called him ruthless in his endeavors for truth, but he was a man to be admired. If he were here today, he would challenge me to find the right path or carve one of my own, but to take it quickly, and to whatever end."

"Jacob was full of fire and purpose, but I beg you not to forget the importance of patience. In the end, my dear, there may be options that you have not even considered."

CHAPTER 16

I had a difficult time avoiding thoughts of Lewis — what he meant by his questions about my future and how I could route his plans to a more palatable end, which, if I were to be honest, could be nothing short of my absolute independence.

However, without Aunt Jo's jointure, there would not be enough money to enact any of my plans. The truth of my present situation loomed like a black cloud over everything, but I was determined to find a way.

In this steady fortitude of mind the next day, I encountered Lewis striding toward the kitchen door, a wine bottle in his hand. I forced a, "Good afternoon," as my gaze settled on the spirit in his grasp. "A little early for port, don't you think?"

He turned the bottle as if to read the label. "Yes, I daresay port is best after dinner, but this isn't mine." His brows pulled in. "No indeed, what I have here is a bit of a mystery."

"Oh?" I lifted an eyebrow, still uncertain as to whether I should engage him. "Regarding the wine?"

"In a way." The grim remains of our last conversation still hovered about his eyes. "Perhaps you are just the person to assist me." He handed me the bottle, which turned out to be empty. "Do you recognize it?"

"Goodness, no. Why should I?"

He hesitated. "It was from your father's private stash. While he was in residence years ago, he chose to drink only from a superior collection he furnished himself."

I looked again at the label. "As I said before, I knew little of my father. What he drank would certainly be beyond my knowledge." I thrust out the bottle, and he took it into his hand before turning it in his palm.

"Your father was prodigiously selective — particularly with port. When he was at Greybourne Hall, we kept the whole of his wines in a special place in the cellars, where it has remained to this day. Quite frankly, I'd forgotten his stash was even down there. The servants have long since given up that particular passageway, as they've declared it dangerous and utilize another section of the cellars for our daily needs." He leaned in. "Hence, my little mystery."

"The bottle?"

"Moreover, who took it out of the cellar and drank it?"

I shrugged. "I suppose it could have been anyone — one of the servants perchance."

"They all deny it."

"And that surprises you? Heavens, I daresay they do not wish to be reprimanded, or worse, turned out."

He tapped the bottle. "But why would someone partake of this now, after all this time, and carry it into the woods to dispose of it? Sophie nosed it up from where it was buried this morning. I cannot believe a servant would go to all that trouble. Not to mention, I keep a master key to the cellar room where they are kept, which has conveniently gone missing."

I took a step back as if looking for answers. "Missing? Knowles is meticulous in the extreme. Have you been down to the cellars yet to see if more has disappeared?"

"That is just what I was on my way to do." He twisted to the door. "If you will excuse me, I will be pleased to report back directly what I find."

"I most certainly will not."

He halted, glancing back over his shoulder, his voice a wry laugh. "What now?"

"I have decided to come with you."

He extended his arm across the arched door and dipped his chin. "You must have a remarkably selective memory. Moments ago I declared the cellar passageway dangerous, not to mention horribly dark. Not an ideal location for a lady."

"Fiddlesticks. Clearly, my father was not overly concerned if he saw fit to use it. He was here around five years ago. That is not all that long ago. And I am not so green as to faint in the dark."

"Possibly." A knowing look crossed Lewis's face. "I will admit that I believe that whole business about the instability of the cellar a hum. Cook swore she saw a ghost down there, and then the very next week, Knowles was declaring the passageway unfit to cross. I've been too busy to investigate myself. But I suppose now is as good a time as any. Only . . ."

On occasion, I found Lewis distantly civil or affected by a reserved charm, but today he was altogether different. A smile lit his face like an innocent boy bound for an adventure. A great deal like Jacob used to look when we were children. I returned his enthusiasm with a smile of my own. "If there are no further arguments, then I suggest we get on with it."

He paused, a twitch about his lips. "I daresay if I don't let you accompany me now, you're likely to follow me or come another time of your own accord."

"Exactly." I motioned into the kitchens. "Lead on."

The cellars were accessed through the butler's pantry beyond the kitchens, which is where we descended belowground on a narrow set of stone steps and into the pitchy darkness of Greybourne Hall's underworld. Lewis paused at the arched opening of the receiving cellar. "At present, we keep the wine for the house divided between here, the butler's cellar, and the Madeira cellar. Your father's private room is at the opposite end." He motioned into the depths beyond. "Still game?"

I swallowed hard, concealing the doubt climbing my spine, and nodded.

Though the dank air was stagnant, chills roamed at will through the various rooms and passageways — sweeping across the floor, swirling about my shoulders. Lewis held a candle ahead of us, which illuminated only a few feet at a time, the shadows shifting as we moved. I had to stay close — and not stumble.

Each section of the cellar had a wide

doorway, yet the rooms felt small, filled as they were with floor-to-ceiling brick shelves and bins, which had rows and rows of bottles stacked in each one. The fetid scent of disuse and neglect intensified with each turn, the dampened air thick going down my throat. The candle glinted and my heart thundered as I imagined myself alone and overcome by the crawling darkness. Lewis's hand sought my mine at the same moment, almost as if he had anticipated my fear, but his voice remained impassive. "Careful here. The final corridor has a low berth."

He paused before entering, and I remained silent at his side as I could not trust my voice, my mind arrested as it was by his strong fingers about mine.

With his free hand, he ran the candle's glow across the low stone ceiling and the support beams before eventually shifting it back to my face. We stared at each other across the flame for the merest second before he released my hand. "Your father's supply should be right through here. The passageway looks to be in fine working order. I feel confident we should be quite safe."

Ducking, I followed him down the length of the passageway, which eventually opened into a similar looking space. Lewis handed me the candle before advancing on the first shelf. "It does appear that more bottles might be missing, but I cannot remember the last inventory. I am convinced there were not so few as this. It has been too many months to know for certain. And there are others who have utilized the port. Mr. Drake, for one, had full use of the cellars, and I believe Adam took some bottles a few months ago."

"Perhaps it was Mr. Drake then, before his death."

"You forget he had been in London and did not have time to partake the day he returned. This bottle was not buried long. The label is still intact without a hint of fading. And there are still drops inside." He stepped closer to the wine shelf. "What I cannot understand is why a thief would come all the way back here to steal some wine. There are plenty of bottles up front they could have helped themselves to."

"Unless the robber did not want to be discovered right away. Those bottles would be remarked quite easily."

"Conceivably. There have been several people in and out of the house of late. I can hardly presume to determine who helped themselves." He kneeled on the floor, as if to search the lower shelves but sprang back to his feet. "Dash it all!"

"What is it?" Quivering, I extended the candle just in time to catch sight of a large hairy rat scurrying across the floor — straight at me. One sight of his slippery gray tail and I lurched backward, catching my elbow on Lewis's arm. The jolt caused the candle to tip against my gown, which I cradled just long enough for . . . disaster.

The flame leapt onto my overlay, and I screamed, dropping the pewter holder, sending the candle crashing to the floor in my wild attempt to extinguish the small fire. While I batted at my waist, Lewis stomped out the rest of the flame, then immediately turned to assist me with my gown. His hands were adept yet reticent, an awkward dance transpiring between us.

A lingering flicker, a few well-placed strokes, and the last hint of light snuffed into obscurity. Darkness fell absolute. Silence engorged the room. Lewis's hands hovered about my waist. I could scarcely breathe.

He let out a laugh. "Well, I was not expecting that over a blasted rat." He fumbled for my arm. "You weren't burned, were you?"

I reached for my gown one more time. "No. I don't believe so, only my gown, but . . ." My eyes darted from one side of the blackened cellar to the other, desperately searching for something to focus on. "How do we find our way out?"

"It shall be a clumsy business, but we can retrace our steps easily enough. Let us wait a moment to allow our eyes to adjust."

The tethered blackness only faded to shades of gray as amorphous as a disquieting dream. I had never been one to see well at night. Lewis pulled away.

My heartbeat pounded and a pain settled into my chest. The room seemed to narrow and dip around me. The feeling that I had been abandoned surged to life. "Wait."

"I'm right here." His voice was low and calm and but a step away.

I let out a shaky breath. "I suppose I am not as steady in the dark as I led you to believe." I grasped the fingers that brushed mine. "Nevertheless, I refuse to faint. Screaming, now, that might be a different story."

He gave my hand a reassuring squeeze. "We shall have no cause for that. I am at the wall. All we need to do is follow it out. Easy enough."

I wished I shared his optimism, but my mind was at work conjuring up deadly specters hovering somewhere in the blackened abyss . . . or better yet, something even more real. "What if the person who took the wine is still in the cellars?" I drew closer to his side.

"Nonsense. We would have seen the fellow on our way in." A tap, a scratch, and he stopped. "We're at the low passageway." His arm slid around my back. "You first."

"Me?"

"Yes, you. Or would you rather be at the back?"

I cringed. "Goodness, I'm afraid that could be far worse, exposed as I'd be."

"As I imagined."

"But . . . what if there is something . . . ahead?"

"There isn't."

"But . . . what if there is?"

"I can hardly go in front of *and* behind you."

I cast a sideways glare into the darkness behind me, glad he couldn't see my reaction. "Nor did I suggest such a ridiculous idea. I shall take the front if you would kindly refrain from being so pushy."

He let out a long breath. "May I remind you that it was you who forced me to bring you down here?"

"No, you may not. And when I agreed to come, I imagined a lit candle guiding our path. If you had not roused that horrid rat, we should be walking out now without the least difficulty. Oh! The rat. I had quite forgotten." I ducked into the passageway, drawing him behind me like a dead weight. "And don't say it was me who dropped the candle, for your elbow was certainly just as involved."

Somewhere in the darkness, I could feel the room open up around me, and the wall took a sharp turn. I followed it for several steps, then spun to face Lewis somewhere in the darkness. "Now what?"

His voice held a hint of a laugh. "Just follow the wine shelf across."

My pace slowed to a crawl as I felt along the cold bricks.

Lewis touched my back. "You don't suppose the rat pursued us?"

I pushed his hand away. "Don't you dare tease me at such a moment, for I shall have nightmares for weeks." I pressed my lips together and silently chastised myself. Why on earth had I brought up nightmares? I couldn't see Lewis's face, but his hand slackened ever so slightly. I'm quite certain he was remembering that day he found me in library.

Distracted and unprepared for the sudden appearance of an opposing wall, my boot's hard discovery of something large and solid sent me reeling back a step, tripping over the shelf's corner and careening straight into Lewis's chest. Instinctively he extended his arms, gently supporting me back to my feet, his hands remaining at my back.

"Rebecca . . . ," he whispered, yet I could see nothing of his demeanor. His voice sounded different. I-I couldn't place it. Did he mean to scold me or tease me again? Or something else, something far more alarming? His hands didn't move. Neither did I. Ridiculously, my heart began to throb as I caught a fleeting whiff of the tangy orange cologne I'd smelled that day in London.

I wondered what he'd meant to say beyond my name, but I was not to know as a flicker of light illuminated one side of the room, and we stepped back just in time to see Knowles pass around the corner. The old lines on his face jumped in the candlelight, and I hoped he'd not remark on our odd appearance.

Lewis immediately took the lead, and I was grateful for his presence of mind. "I do believe we have been saved at last, Miss Hunter." He clapped Knowles on the back. "Your appearance is well timed." He lingered on the last word then smiled. "Give me the deuced candle, man, and let us be out of this dank hole."

Knowles passed the light to Lewis without question, shock evident on his face at finding us lounging alone in the cellar. He probably thought we were Cook's ghosts, lying in wait to attack him.

Lewis motioned ahead of us. "After you, Miss Hunter — unless, you would prefer the middle this time."

CHAPTER 17

Mr. Galpin was awaiting me in the drawing room late in the afternoon the following day. Unaware I had a guest, I walked in without question or the convention of a chaperone.

Alone and unobserved, he'd made himself at ease, reclining against the cushioned chair with one leg propped up on the other, his callous, gray eyes trained out the bow window into the twilight beyond. He dangled a watch fob in his right hand, and his fingers pushed the golden orb back and forth like the meticulous precision of a clock. His face, though, betrayed something I'd not seen before, as if his usually calm exterior concealed something far more threatening, something he fought hard to keep at bay.

Draped in fine clothes and full of smooth words, Mr. Galpin remained a mystery. I moved to call out his name and alert him to my presence, but something held me back.

I could still see Isabell giggling in his presence at the dinner party, enraptured by his every word. Why had he been hand-selected from the men of Plattsdale to be *my* husband? Why had he not sought *her* hand?

The watch fob suddenly ceased its movements, and Mr. Galpin craned his neck forward. Curiosity moved my feet silently across the rug. What was it out there in the grim afternoon haze that interested him?

Close enough to smell the lingering scent of his snuff and hear his fluted nasal breathing, I stopped and followed his gaze out the window. There, beneath the cloudy horizon, I saw nothing unusual, not on the manicured lawns or hiding amid the leafless trees of the woods. The corner folly sat empty and the garden gate was firmly shut. The fog was thick in patches, but nothing moved, not for several seconds. Perhaps Mr. Galpin was waiting for something.

A distinct chill skirted up my arms as I looked back to his eager face. All at once, I wondered if I shouldn't wait for Aunt Jo to return from her ride with Mr. Fernside to engage Mr. Galpin.

Too late. He'd noticed me, and the smile he usually wore slipped back into place. He shot to his feet and cast a fleeting glance out the long window. "Miss Hunter, I have been waiting a time for you." He tugged on his tight-fitting jacket. "What kind of help does Mr. Browning keep around this horrid place?"

I doubted Mr. Galpin had sent anyone to fetch me. He'd probably devised a way to catch me by accident, and I'd fallen right into his scheme.

I took a hasty step back.

Like a snake, he moved to block my path to the door. His voice dipped into that sweet tone he used on Isabell. "Please, won't you sit with me a moment? I have something I'd like to discuss with you."

I crossed my arms. "It is rather late for visiting hours, don't you think?"

"I suppose it is." He angled his chin. "But not for one so well connected with the family."

Dinnertime was nearing, and I vastly preferred to let him have his say now before he fished for an invitation to stay. Then I'd have to suffer several more hours of his company. More and more, his intentions were becoming clear. Besides, now was the perfect opportunity to ask about the inquest alone. I motioned to the scroll end sofa, where he took a seat at my side, his legs inching a tad too close to mine.

I winced. Did he think I wouldn't notice

or that I welcomed such an advance? I scooted away and bolstered my poise for what I would likely endure over the next few minutes. Clearly, the man thought me wildly in love with him, as every other girl in town no doubt was. He deserved a good set down, but I needed to ask him about the inquest first.

I batted my eyelids. "I, too, have been wishing to speak with you. Something of great importance has been on my mind."

A gleam lit his face, and he straightened his back. "I apologize that I have been so long away, but I assure you, you have not been far from my thoughts."

"It is about my brother's death."

I watched as the joy ebbed from his eyes and left a dull stare within the framework of his smiling face. "I thought we discussed that in full the day of the party. What else do you wish to know?"

I went on, ignoring his pointed tone. "At the inquest, was there any discussion of whether the body had been moved prior to discovery?"

His brow twitched. "What are you getting at, Miss Hunter? Could Jacob's lifeless body have been moved after his death? Possibly. Mr. Browning could have seen to that. There was plenty of time. However, I don't recall any of the men on the inquest bringing up such an idea. I call your theory . . . unlikely."

"And the wound on the back of his head — did the members conclude this was caused by the fall?"

I had his attention now. He searched my face for where I'd discovered my newfound knowledge of the incident. I cocked an eyebrow. It wasn't like the details were a secret. "I spoke with Mr. Fernside but a few days ago, regarding what he found when Jacob was discovered. He mentioned a rather large wound on Jacob's head."

Mr. Galpin's cold fingers inched onto my arm. "Your brother fell from a bridge. You do realize he could have received that wound anywhere in the midst of the fall."

Of course, he was right. I had no proof of tampering or anything else. Mr. Galpin's discomfiture, however, pricked my nerves. Such a close neighbor, he could have easily been involved. Mr. Browning and he certainly didn't get along. And he was Isabell's favorite friend.

Mr. Galpin's grip relaxed into a caress, and my gaze darted to the finely manicured fingers stroking my skin. He lifted his other hand to my chin. "I have told you all I know. Now won't you let me discuss what I came to say to you this evening? Allow me to turn the conversation to something far more pleasant."

I recoiled, pulling my arm back to my side. Then I stood and paced to the window. "Please don't."

He followed me before walling me against the edge of the window seat. "What is it, Miss Hunter? My family name? My connections? You leave me scrambling for answers, my dear, for this is not going at all as I'd imagined. And I'm not usually disappointed."

"No, I —"

He leaned close, and I took in a quick breath. My heart screamed to retreat, his lips mere inches from mine. Then he laughed, pulling back. "All right, my dear, I shall give you some more time to know me. This has been a bit rushed, if you will. Nonetheless, if you are anything like your brother, I daresay, we shall suit very well." His hand slid along the small of my back, and I pulled away. "And the chase shall prove invigorating." A detached look crossed his brow, then he secured my hand for a lingering kiss, his thumb finding the tender interior of my wrist. "Till another day."

I'm not sure how long I stood at that window after he left or when I stopped quivering with revulsion, but a million thoughts coursed through my mind. I'd promised Aunt Jo to stay at Greybourne Hall, but the impulse to run away dawned heavy, and the longer I stood there, the more it grew — run to London, to obscurity among thousands of other people, to a time when my mother wasn't ill and she'd protect me from eager men like Mr. Galpin.

Settling onto the window seat, I pressed my forehead against the glass, allowing the cold afternoon to wash away the charged emotions coursing through my veins. I had overcome many trials in my life. This new one would be no different. Mr. Galpin did not control me anymore than Lewis . . . or Isabell . . . or Aunt Jo.

I would find a way to be civil with him, to probe his mind without falling prey to his wandering hands and whimsical notions. Regardless of Lewis's other faults, he, of all people, would not allow Mr. Galpin any liberties with me. In my heart I knew Lewis would never force me into an alliance with someone I did not approve of.

Calming at the thought, I flicked open my eyes, only to be surprised by the sudden sight through the window. A person, standing quite close to the folly, buried in the shelter of the north woods. I squinted into the haze, only belatedly registering Isabell's willowy shape.

My heart constricted. In all likelihood she was waiting for Mr. Galpin — to hear everything that had passed between us.

I swallowed what I'd observed beyond that window like bitter medicine, and I remained silent throughout a tight-lipped dinner with Aunt Jo as well as long into the quiet hours of the night, unable to give voice to the stormy thoughts circling my mind. Only in my bedchamber, tucked away from the prying eyes of the house, did I allow the images to resurface.

Mr. Galpin and Isabell. There was more than mere friendship to that relationship. My fingers found the back of my neck, working their way into my hair, lost as to what I should think or feel or do. As I sat on my bed, my gaze retreated to the pitchy darkness of the bedchamber. I mindlessly watched the moonlit shadows of water droplets wiggle their way from one side of the steely square on the carpet to the other.

Everything I'd examined and deduced about Jacob's death would have to be gone over again. Who exactly could I trust? Mr. Galpin? Isabell? Lewis? The thought made my stomach churn. How long had they been meeting like that? And what were they planning?

The tip-tap of rain on the window was replaced by a charged silence that filled the room like a dense mist, choking me from within. I needed to get outside. I needed to think. Throwing a heavy shawl around my shoulders, I fled the house for the terrace and the hope of stars. My expectations were dashed by the thick clouds that stretched across the heavens like a heavy blanket over the world.

The shawl proved poor covering for the icy fingers of the dampened night air, but I stood there, my arms outstretched, as I breathed it all in, Greybourne Hall looming ever present behind me. There was no light at the dower house, nor in the massive structure I'd left.

My arms fell to my side, and I shook my head in denial. Everything I'd learned since coming here had to be questioned. Even then I'd learned little about my brother's death, certainly nothing to suspect anyone had a hand in his demise. The clues led nowhere. I was no better off than when I'd arrived. What use was it to keep trying?

My eyes blurred with tears, and I finally let them come, coursing down my cheeks. I cried into the hush of the night, my sobs echoing into silence. For a second, all was quiet. Then the singsong of a bird broke through the chill air. The clouds seemed to open up, projecting a sliver of moonlight into the trees. My heart pounded as the bird's tweet transformed into an almost human-like whistle — a song taking shape in my ear — when all at once, the melody disappeared.

My ears buzzed with the sudden silence, like they did after one of my spells. My fingers curled into fists. There had probably been no bird at all. I shook my head then slapped my forehead. "No, no. Please, no. Not now. Not like this." It was the first thing I'd conjured while awake.

Unable to properly breathe for a moment, I digested what my mind had materialized. A bird whistling? In the woods? At night? The sudden change of my condition was far too much for me to process. How long did I have? How long had my mother dealt with her own demons before they grew too difficult to handle? The plunging temperature mixed with my own dread and invited a slew of shivers that wound through my body. It was time to return to my room.

I skirted across the terrace, pausing to glance back at the forest, the evocative song replaying over and over again in my mind. I knew the tune well. My mother had sung it to me at bedtime when I was a child to calm my fears of the night — and now it had returned to haunt me.

A few days later, Aunt Jo summoned me to the yellow-papered sitting room on the first floor, where she spent a great deal of her time watching for forthcoming carriages. The window gave a fair prospect of the approaching drive, and over the past week Mr. Fernside had proved an ardent suitor. I suspected a betrothal would not be far away, which was exciting, but I couldn't help but wonder where it would leave me.

Alone at Greybourne Hall.

Aunt Jo awaited me reposed on the settee near the fire, a rug tucked around her legs, her thin eyebrows arched in that disapproving way she'd used on us as children. I bustled inside, feigning nonchalance.

"Have a seat, Rebecca."

I did so, favoring the brocade chair at her left, my gaze a mix of wonder and concern. "Are you well, Aunt?"

She lowered her chin. "More than well . . . as you know. Nevertheless, that is precisely why I have brought you to task this morning, my darling." Her finger sought the pattern on the blanket. "I am not a fool, you know. Something is eating at you, and I will not be fobbed off any longer."

I opened my mouth to speak, then halted. I had taken great care to avoid her notice, yet my intentions and emotions were two entirely different beasts, both of which I found difficult to control. The latter usually won in the end.

My revelation on the front lawn had brought clarity of mind. I had made a decision, one that left me nervous and excited at the same time. I daresay the lift had returned to my brow as I pursed my lips to respond. "Whatever do you imply?"

A shrewd smile crossed her face as she settled back against the settee. "Do you mean to tell me that insipid creature who has been moping around this house for days is finally gone?"

My beloved aunt was the one person at Greybourne Hall who sought my happiness and my welfare above all else. I gladly leaned forward. "I daresay she is, for I have formed a new plan."

Her lip twitched. "Not again."

"Well, not a new one exactly. I simply mean to go about things a bit differently." I folded my fingers together in my lap. "I heard something the other day that startled me at first, but now . . . ."

"What do you mean?"

"Well, it was quite late, and I had left the house intending to look at the stars —"

Her brows drew in. "Never say you did so in your night robe, here of all places. 'Pon my word, Rebecca. What must they think of you —"

"Well of course I did. But rest assured, everyone was abed." I glanced up. "Goodness, I do not see why I cannot make use of an empty terrace after dark without calling my maid."

She took a deep breath. "My dear, I am afraid you may never learn the simplest notion of propriety." She shook her head. "Such a thing is simply not done. Not done at all. This is not a remote cottage in Scotland. What if someone were to come upon you out there alone at night? And —"

"And what? Ravish me!" I lifted my eyes. "We are not in London, Aunt. And I am more than careful that no one is about. Besides, I daresay no one in the house could possibly sleep through one of my screams. So there you have it, I am quite safe to stargaze."

"But, your reputation —"

"If you mean to bore me once again about how I shall not find a suitable gentleman to take care of me, I beg you would not." I glanced out the window, and she seemed to follow my sentiment.

Her voice took on a leaden tone. "Tell me instead of this plan of yours. What is it you heard?"

I leaned forward. "There was a bird singing in the trees — it brought to mind one of my mother's songs from when I was a child, 'Black-eyed Susan.' Over the course of the following day I recalled the words of the melody, and they reminded me why I came to Greybourne Hall in the first place. Jacob's death. Justice for him. Everything else has been nothing but a hideous distraction — Isabell, the dreadful dinner, Lewis — especially Lewis." I stiffened, finding Aunt Jo's eyes with a keen glare.

"I have made the decision not to wait for further clues, but to seek them out with far more daring than before." I paused, steeling myself for her reaction to my next words. "I realized the reason I have yet to find a clue that might reveal all is because there is one place in the house I dared not search, but I am prepared to do so now. I intend to search Lewis's bedchamber."

CHAPTER 18

I was careful to figure out the best time to search Lewis's room unobserved. Aunt Jo had been aghast at the suggestion, but she had also not explicitly forbidden me, which I found oddly reassuring. We both yearned to know what happened that terrible night, and Lewis was the only person who claimed to be with Jacob on the bridge. He might be the only person with answers.

I spent some time watching the movements of everyone in the house and decided my foray into Lewis's private bedchamber would be best accomplished when he left the estate on one of his nightly rides. Such a prime opportunity would provide me the longest period to search as well as optimal time to remain undiscovered by either him or his valet.

Three arduous days passed in which I waited by my window deep into the night. Finally I was rewarded by the harrowing sight of a dark figure galloping across the northern rise. The cloaked man was a bit farther away than I was used to seeing, but I was certain it was Lewis.

Still dressed for my mission, I crept from my room and made my way down the long, musty corridor, my slippered feet as quiet as a fox. Silence throbbed as I snuck down the halls, each closed door glaring at me as I passed.

The crawling night had descended over Greybourne Hall's moldering stones, chilling the drafty floorboards and charging each step with a hazy gloom. Soon enough, the landing appeared, and I tiptoed across it, regarding the distant hall with a wary eye. I'd seen Lewis's valet come and go from that direction over the past few days, and I was certain Lewis's room lay beyond the turn of the corridor.

A motionlessness clung to the opening of the hall. The faded portraits of long-dead Brownings glared at my progress in the uneven moonlight. I darted past the sitting room, and the chapel, leaving the familiar heart of the house for the dim unknown. The master's wing.

I'd purposefully left my candle in my room, counting on the full moon to guide my steps and the opposing shadows to hide my presence if need be, but all at once I felt its absence. The secluded corners dipped and retreated as I moved, the scents of ash and dampened wood lingering. My heartbeat settled into a demanding drum in my ears.

I stole from one alcove to the next and peered in lonely room after lonely room, a perverse sense of sadness slowing my steps. So this was where Lewis was forced to reside day after day, accompanied the last few months by only a handful of servants and one loyal friend.

A dark blue sitting room emerged beyond an open door near the end of the hallway. The dregs of a fire still smoldered in the grate. The chamber stood empty, yet I could feel Lewis's presence hovering about the paneled walls. A rag lay across the table by the door next to a half-burned candle not yet gathered by the servants.

The unlit walls stood guard over the room like a host of dragoons safeguarding a private space. The papered designs looked almost like eyes that tracked my movements as I passed. A sudden gust of wind surged and the panes cracked. My heart screamed. My gaze darted around the room, but I was alone. Quite alone. I forced a measured breath and continued toward the carpet, taking in everything around me.

Lewis likely spent a good deal of time here — brooding, no doubt. I could imagine him lounging by the white plaster lion statues at either end of the fireplace, his feet perched on the footrest, his jacket thrown across the sofa. I took a hasty step back, the scene I'd conjured suddenly all too real. The enduring scent of his cologne came alive, suspended about the room.

Though the apartment was clearly meant for his enjoyment, there were few pieces of heavy furniture beyond the chairs and sofa. After a quick going over, I determined the room held nothing of importance.

As I moved to leave, I caught sight of a flash of gold near the door, nestled between the desk and the wall paneling. I reached down and took the object into my hand.

A button.

I turned it back and forth as something twisted in my chest. This was not just any button. It was Jacob's. I could not mistake the odd pattern on the face of the button, for I sewed it onto his coat the last time he visited Scotland. Jacob had torn it off quite by accident, and I'd mended it easily enough. When one stares at something for a long period of time, it is not so easy to forget, particularly when it was the last time

I saw Jacob alive.

I stood unmoving, pondering my discovery as the window rattled behind me and the resounding silence of the room thrummed in my ear. Jacob lived at Greybourne Hall for over six months prior to his death. He probably spent many a night in Lewis's company in this very room. He could have lost it at any time. Yet, my hand quivered as I slid the button into my pocket. It was another connection between my brother and my guardian — one I did not fully understand.

I moved back into the hallway, halting at the door to the room far more likely to hide Lewis's secrets — his bedchamber. My fingers circled the latch as I drew in a breath and inched the heavy wood inward. I'm not sure what I expected to feel, but perched on the threshold, staring inside, my feet would hardly move. While I'd formed my plans with as much gusto as I could muster, crossing into Lewis's private space was going to be far more difficult than I originally thought — for I knew now I was breaking his trust.

His chambers were large enough for a dressing room, though not so grand as to bespeak the wealthiest of gentlemen. I couldn't help but focus on the bed, its massive bulk filling one side of the room. I forced myself to move on to the looming wardrobe and dressing table, where the valet's supplies were laid out ready for the morrow. The chamber had a lived-in quality, not the neglected feel of the rest of the house. It was as if Lewis's very presence lent the room a dignified air.

The small clock on the mantel reminded me of my urgency, and I threw open first the wardrobe, then every drawer of the desk and dresser as I searched both within and then behind each one with care. I'd heard of hidden compartments, so I had to be sure. My fingers feathered across white cravats and layered waistcoats then on to his coats and breeches. There was nothing in the desk or the dresser to note.

Heading over to the scrolled fireplace, I stroked every knob and curve, pressing each groove, hoping for a secret corridor, but none emerged. I poked through the embers in the grate for a partially burned slip of paper or anything that might provide me with a clue.

After running my hands between and beneath the layers of his bed, I paused, wondering where I should hunt next. Slowly, I turned and scanned the room. Where would I keep something I wished to remain hidden? Moreover, where would Lewis's devious mind take him?

I placed my own secret items in the box Jacob had given me. With such a thought, my gaze fell onto the mantel and the rose-colored vase near the end — flowerless and horridly out of place. I raced over and grasped the porcelain item. I turned it first one way, then the next. Nothing. It was simply an empty vase. Irritation and urgency rushed my next steps. I pulled books from the small bookshelf, rustled through his bed stand, ran my fingers between every crack in the paneled wall.

Again, nothing.

I blew a whiff of hair out of my face, then slid down the wall into a sitting position beside the bed. What was I even looking for? A confession? At that moment, I noticed the nightstand and Lewis's well-worn copy of the Book of Common Prayer.

Carelessly, I reached for it and opened the leather-bound volume, certain of what I would find printed in those thin pages.

Instead, I sat up straight, holding the book into the moonlight — for it wasn't printed pages that resided within, but handwritten ink. A journal of sorts.

Dates. Times. Actions. I selected a few passages and read.

February 16 — Bedchamber empty, no
  mention of whereabouts
February 19 — Torrington reports nothing
  for the night
February 20 — Robbery unsuccessful
February 21 — Jacob and Isabell . . .

Footsteps sounded down the hallway, pacing fast. I slammed the journal shut and slung it back onto the side table before scurrying for the door, only to turn back like a caged animal.

Lewis's voice boomed beyond. "I said immediately."

Being caught flashed through my mind as I slipped behind the crimson drapes and covered my feet beneath the folds on the floor. I was trapped.

Boots plodded inside, followed quickly by the rustle of items being dropped.

"Do you require a bath, sir?" It was Lewis's valet.

Silence, then Lewis answered, "Just a basin and pitcher. I don't want you to wake the house."

"If that is what you wish, sir. Only, with all this mud . . ." A muffled gasp broke through. "And all the blood."

Lewis's voice grew serious. "Steady yourself, Steele. It's merely a scratch. It will heal easily enough. Now, help me with these blasted boots before you go."

A shuffle and the valet's voice went on, "I fear your cheek will never be the same, sir."

Lewis chuckled. "Thank goodness I had most of it covered, but I shall be confined to the house for a few days."

A sniffle. "Were you at least successful, sir?"

A pause. "No. The man is still out there somewhere, and I'm at a loss as to how to find him. I thought . . . Well, my friends will not be pleased."

"May I suggest speaking with —"

"No. I shan't have anyone else pulled into this bramble."

A creak of the floorboards and the sound of pacing.

"Help with your trousers, sir?"

"No, just the water, if you please."

My hand crept to my mouth, and I shrank back against the wall. Pawing through Lewis's intimate things had been bad enough, but here I stood inches from . . . I couldn't even complete the thought.

"Hurry up, my good man, before we get mud on everything."

One set of footsteps faded away, and I stood in silence, perched to hear each piece of clothing Lewis removed. I bit my lip, cringing as something whooshed onto the bed. I would be trapped till he was asleep. What on earth had I gotten myself into? But, the journal. My time had been well spent even if I had to stand for the next twelve hours. The wretch had been keeping watch on someone. And to what purpose? I needed to read more.

I listened intently to Lewis's steps across the room and the creak of a chair. A door clicked, and the valet was back. "Here you are, sir. Would you have me —"

"That will be all for now. Ouch. Stop your fussing. It will cease its bleeding soon enough."

"But the scar. Dreadful. Dreadful, I say."

"And nothing but a deuced inconvenience. Now get on with you. I shall not require your assistance again tonight."

A long pause, then footsteps trailed into the sound of the door sealing shut.

Something splashed into water. I could imagine Lewis cleaning his face, removing the evidence of an eventful night. If only I could get a peek at what he meant to conceal. My fingers edged the drape to the side, just enough to catch sight of Lewis's lean back, his distressed countenance reflected in the looking glass.

It was a nasty slice across his left cheek,

curving ever so slightly downward. He dabbed a wet cloth against it and dissolved the remains of dried blood and dirt. A few wipes, and the jagged cut emerged in its entirety beneath the grime, and fortunately for him, it didn't appear all that deep. But it sat dangerously close to his left eye.

I retreated behind the drapes, my head pounding, my mind haunted by that moment in the library when he had a similar injury — when he'd looked at me with those piercing yet kind eyes.

This thing with Lewis was proving to be more than what I'd admitted to myself, more than a mere passing fancy . . .

Footsteps pounded hard across the room, at first tentative, then in a hammering rush. I had no time to think before the drapes flew open, and a pistol was cocked and aimed at my heart. "Lewis. It's me." I held up my hands, waving.

He narrowed his eyes, deadly focused on the perceived threat. After all, who but a dangerous person would be hidden in his bedchamber? A clock ticked from somewhere in the room. Then all at once, he lowered the pistol and raked his free hand through his dusty hair. "Rebecca, what the —"

My gaze traveled to his bare chest, and

my eyes widened of their own accord. Thank goodness he hadn't disposed of his trousers yet. I had seen Jacob often enough when I was a child and he a young man, swimming in the lake by our country estate, but I had never seen a grown man in such a way, his broad shoulders exposed, every curve of his muscles drawn tight. He had a sprinkling of freckles across his chest, and I have no idea why I kept staring at them, my tongue a tangled mess. "It's not what you think."

He stepped back, the merest bend to the corner of his lips. "You have no idea what I think."

"No. I suppose I don't." I edged past him, intent on the door, then paused and pointed to his cheek. "I'm afraid it's — uh — bleeding again."

"Dash it all!" He held up his hand. "Don't move. I have questions for you." He turned to procure the cloth he had been cleaning the cut with, and I rushed out the door without looking back.

CHAPTER 19

The following morning I was unable to face Aunt Jo or my smoldering conscience with any semblance of control. Lewis's discovery of me in his bedchamber was a colossal blunder on my part, undermining all my efforts for Jacob. But seeing him like that — goodness, I couldn't get the thought out of my mind.

The moonlight had likely been playing tricks with my heart, which kept me up nearly the whole of the night pondering the connection I felt in that room as he stood there *en déshabillé.* Yes, there was embarrassment about our awkward situation, but something more lay so enticingly invisible between us. I'd felt it in the library after my spell, during our dance, and then again in the cellars.

"Augh!" I cried out, balling up the letter I'd been attempting to write and heaving it into the fire.

My fingers itched for more to throw, but they engaged my forehead instead, my elbows clunking against the wooden desk. I would not accept the heightening attraction between us.

Us. What a simple word that carried such deep meaning. When had it deviously slipped into my vocabulary? And Lewis, what of him? I could still see the muscles on his jaw tightening and relaxing the moment he found me, the soft fall of his hand from his injured face. His eyes had held a latent ache I could not explore. Was it utter loneliness that lay beneath such a look? Or worse, lies?

The journal once again invaded the turn of my heart and buried my unwanted feelings beneath pounds of imaginary dirt where I was glad to let them fester and die. Lewis had been watching someone, recording every move they made. Was it Jacob? Possibly. But why would he do such a thing?

Earlier in the morning after watching Lewis depart on his morning walk, I snuck one last time into his room to steal the journal, but it had conveniently vanished. And now, returning to my desk, I'd embarked on the only thing that came to mind — writing to Mr. Galpin, begging him to meet me alone. If I could not learn what else was written in that journal, digging into Mr. Galpin's insight regarding the inquest was more necessary than ever.

Aunt Jo would certainly disapprove, but how much time did I have before Lewis would arrange for my departure? Days? Hours? He would never keep me at Greybourne Hall after what had passed between us. Of that, I was certain. After all, my first day here he had been adamant in his resolve. Marriage was not on his mind. And thank goodness. I, for one, did not want him for a husband, but I had put him in a dreadful position. A gentleman might find himself honor bound to offer, but Lewis was not a gentleman. Not really.

I grasped the quill pen and jabbed it back into the ink.

Dear Mr. Galpin,

I had hoped to find a way to meet with you in person, but as my time at Greybourne Hall may draw to an unexpected close, I find a letter my only recourse. Would you be so kind as to meet with me at four o'clock in the afternoon beneath the willow tree in the front garden path? I am certain we can be alone there.

Your friend,
Miss Rebecca Hunter

I could only pray I was making the right decision. I had no intention of being foolish, but the man still held answers I sought. And he would have to behave himself so close to the house, yet the thick hedgerows and tree canopy would provide us a certain level of privacy from the prying eyes of Greybourne Hall.

I sealed my resolve as I pressed the hot wax onto the folds of the note. I only hoped my impulsive maid would carry it off as she'd promised. Thankfully, Tabby proved to be a redoubtable girl, convinced she carried a secret love note to my ardent suitor. She tore off across the estate within minutes of me placing the missive into her hands, which left me to count away the hours and wait in agony.

Three thirty found me nervously embroidering a cushion in the drawing room with Aunt Jo, trapped in my own deceit. I had expected an afternoon drive with Mr. Fernside to keep her engaged, and the unexpected change in her situation had left me unsure how to make my escape.

She broke the silence after sipping at her tea. "Mr. Browning has been oddly absent today around the house. Don't you think, Rebecca?"

I glanced up from my lap, attempting to conceal any reaction. Yet, even the mention of his name sent warmth flooding my cheeks. "I wouldn't say it is all that unusual. He tends to keep to himself."

"Yes, but he and I have enjoyed a nice coze most mornings when he returns with Sophie. And, you know, I do not believe he even took the dear out this morning for her walk. She has been most rambunctious."

So he did not wish to face Aunt Jo either. Interesting. Perhaps he was hiding his cut. My heartbeat ticked a bit faster, and I recrossed my ankles. "I imagine he has work to attend to. He does run a rather large estate."

"I suppose you are right, my dear, but his land agent handles most of the villagers. The current state of opinions around here leaves him little to do these days. And he enjoys walking her, even if he never goes into town."

I wondered if he'd been busy writing letters to secure another place for me to live. We were both aware Aunt Jo would have a proposal soon enough and Isabell would hardly do for a chaperone. "Why don't you ask him?"

"Indeed. I believe I will."

I focused back on my embroidery. "Speak-

280

ing of gentlemen. Where is Mr. Fernside this fine afternoon? It is not at all like him to miss your drive."

She met my question with a sheepish gaze. "He has gone to London."

"To London?"

A faint smile lit her cheeks. "I do not think it wise to speculate on matters of the heart; however, Mr. Fernside's mother does reside there with his younger brother, and . . ."

I leaned in. "And he has gone to ask for her blessing?"

She laughed. "Of sorts, for he declares her quite silly. I am told she has a particular ring he means to have as well."

I tossed the cushion aside and raced over to my aunt's side. "Oh, Aunt Jo. Is it for you? For the wedding? How can you bear the suspense?"

"Quite well actually, for he told me he loves me before he left this morning."

My eyes grew wide. "You minx. Why did you not say so before?"

"Well, you have been acting so strange, and I could not find you at all when it happened. It has been a great deal to take in. I ended up sitting in perfect silence for nigh on ten minutes. It is certainly not the story I had imagined for myself just a few months ago." She touched my hand. "How very fortunate I have been that you agreed to come here."

The heavy iron in my chest lightened at the thought. If nothing else, my time at Greybourne Hall had not been wasted. I threw my arms around her neck. "Oh, Aunt Jo. I could not be happier for you." I smiled. "I only hope that he endeavors to deserve you."

"Heavens, Rebecca. All men are not the awful creatures you imagine them to be." She kissed my cheek. "And what of you, my darling? I shall not be settled until you are equally taken care of."

She stopped short of mentioning a husband, but the iron returned to my chest nonetheless. I cleared my throat. "I am taken care of. Papa and Jacob saw to that. Do you think Mr. Browning means to turn me out?"

"Of course not. Don't be ridiculous. Although, the situation is not ideal. Not for you . . . or him."

I drew back. "What do you mean?"

She lifted her eyes. "Only what I said."

The grandfather clock pinged out the hour, and I stiffened, realizing belatedly I'd lost track of time. "I . . ." What could I say? What an awkward moment to make my retreat, but I had best do so at once. Mr.

Galpin could already be beneath the willow tree, and Aunt Jo would absolutely forbid me to go if she had a hint of what I was about. "Goodness." I grabbed the shawl I had brought down in one quick swipe. "I do believe I should like to take a walk."

She glanced out the window. "At this hour? I urge you to think better of it. Evening shall be upon us soon, and I fear a bitter wind."

"Do not be overly concerned. I promise I shall not go far."

Her hand sought my wrist. "Rebecca, I do hope you are not running away from what I said. Difficult though it may be, options must be —"

"Not at all. I only require a bit of fresh air." And I meant it. "If you will excuse me."

She nodded as that horrid wistfulness I'd seen so often of late filled her kind face. "You know I only want the best for you, my dear."

"I do." I gave her a smile and made my escape.

Mr. Galpin stood grinning at me beneath the willow branches, a look of triumph about his face, his dimple as infuriating as ever. I swallowed my pride and ducked into the shadows.

He gripped my hands and drew me as near as propriety would allow. "Your letter was a surprise indeed."

I forced a smile. "Thank you for coming."

"Always. If you should ever need anything." His gaze drifted over my shoulder to the direction of Greybourne Hall. "Or feel the least bit afraid, I am but a short ride to the north."

"What a comforting thought." I pulled back a step.

He eyed my movements with a cautious gaze. "Now, what is this about you leaving Greybourne Hall? I assure you, I was never more shocked. Isabell will be vastly upset."

I hadn't the least notion my meeting with him might in effect alert her. I clenched my teeth. "It is not settled exactly, merely a thought I had. My aunt is soon to be engaged, and I imagine Mr. Browning will see me back to London."

Finding a groove against the tree, Mr. Galpin crossed his arms. "This is a development, although you know quite well I have other plans for your removal from Greybourne Hall."

My lips parted. What a peagoose I was. Why hadn't I anticipated such a reaction? Of course he would think I meant marriage to him. I took a deep breath. "Goodness, you shock me, Mr. Galpin. I should think it far more proper to speak with Mr. Browning before I considered anything of the sort."

Mr. Galpin gave a halfhearted shrug. "If you believe such a formality necessary; however, it was my understanding that you might be looking elsewhere for guardianship."

I hid a gasp, but my gaze shot to his. "And who told you that?"

"There has been some discussion of your safety in the village. Isabell has scratched the most of it, reassuring everyone you will soon be settled. She may have mentioned something of Browning's hold over you."

"My safety?"

"You are living with a suspected murderer, my dear. You cannot blame the poor villagers for their questions. And after what happened last night, I was never more glad of your letter. If you think it necessary, I shall be pleased to procure a special license and have you out of that house in but a few days."

My mind reeled with my own experiences of the previous night, and I tried to catch up. "What happened in town yesterday?"

Mr. Galpin's eyes narrowed and his voice took on a demanding tone. "Haven't you heard? There was a robbery at the post office. A masked man apparently stormed inside searching for something. Mr. Miller came upon him, striking him with a rock in the face. He fled, the watch called, but Miller thought he recognized the voice of the injured robber. He swears it was none other than Browning himself."

Leaves swirled in the breeze. My arms shivered beneath my shawl. "I cannot believe it."

"No? Tell me, by any chance have you laid eyes on your guardian this morning?" Mr. Galpin's hands found their way to my shoulders, forcing me to face him. "Did our good friend have a mark on his face?"

I felt the rush of anger in his voice, the command in his fingers. The setting light made his expression appear ominous as a slight smile played with his lips. "You know something, don't you?"

The candlelit gash across Lewis's face flashed to mind. I haven't the foggiest reason why, but I said almost crossly, "No, not at all. I haven't even seen Mr. Browning today." It wasn't a lie, but I'm not sure Mr. Galpin believed me.

"Then why the letter? Why the urgency? I have dropped all my obligations to be here with you."

I had been careless with my words, and

here was the reckoning. Who to trust? "I was in need of information about Jacob's death before I'm sent away, nothing more."

I'm certain his superior voice was meant to be reassuring, but it wasn't. "You shall never be sent away, my dear. Never. I am here — always. Remember that."

The finality of his statement sent a chill up my back. Lewis's duplicity rankled in the extreme, but I'd never felt afraid of him, even when he aimed a pistol at my chest. Mr. Galpin was a different animal — so difficult to read.

I fought for control. "Tell me about Mr. Browning's relationship to my brother."

Mr. Galpin let out a long sigh, the scent of brandy light on his breath. "It was not a pleasant one, I'll tell you that."

I stepped back a pace. "What happened between them?"

"I do not know the particulars, but Jacob was certain your guardian meant mischief for not only him but his inheritance."

"But Mr. Browning had no hold over my brother. He could have simply left."

Mr. Galpin lifted his brows. "I believe there was a debt of honor between them. I daresay, Jacob had lost a great deal of money in London before his arrival here."

So that is why Jacob decided to come to

Greybourne, to ask Lewis for some of his trust. After all, how could he continue to support Aunt Jo and me if he was short of cash? "Before Jacob died, did you notice anything about him, anything that would cause concern?"

"Jacob Hunter was hardly my responsibility. Isabell might be the better person to ask."

I looked up. "Isabell?"

He laughed. "She found him amusing, as a person would their pet. She likes men . . . or haven't you noticed? She keeps Browning on a lead often enough."

I cringed. I could just see Jacob enjoying those teasing eyes as well as the next man. I'd heard rumors about him in London often enough that I had been hard-pressed to keep from mother and Aunt Jo. I didn't like to be reminded of Jacob's querulous nature. Surely time and a happy marriage would have cured those particular evils — at least I'd hoped so at one time.

I stood there motionless as my mind spun in useless directions before retreating to the safety of the path. "I do apologize for rushing off, but it is time I should go. Aunt Jo will be missing me."

His chin dipped and his eyes betrayed the uncertainty raging in his mind. "Will you come to me tomorrow? Shall I seek the license?"

My heartbeat raced, my legs weak. "Not yet. Please, let me do this in my own time." I sought for an appropriate reason. "I would like to be free of Mr. Browning before making any decisions."

He cocked his head and stared me down. I was stalling and he knew it, but he stepped back. "Write me at the first sign of trouble."

"I will." I nodded, then turned away, hurrying down the dusty path without a glance back. I had no intention of ever engaging Mr. Galpin again. I only hoped Lewis would stand my protector — even after all that had passed between us.

Out of the mist, as if he heard my thoughts, Lewis appeared steps from Greybourne Hall's front portico, a wriggling ball of fur grasped in one hand, the cut still evident on his cheek. Sophie circled his feet, yipping as soon as she caught sight of me, darting back and forth between us.

Forgetting my earlier embarrassment, I hastened over to see what on earth was going on. "Whatever do you have there?"

A momentary flash of suspicion entered his eyes, then faded to vague amusement, but I couldn't mistake the bend to his voice. "Why, Miss Hunter, you are just the person

I have been looking for — and a hard one to find at that. I came upon your aunt earlier in the sitting room." He pointed to the wound on his face. "She was quite concerned about my accident with the, uh, tree branch late last night."

A tree branch, was it?

"She said you'd run off for a bit of fresh air, but I couldn't find you." He lifted his brow. "I began to think you were hiding from me."

"Don't be absurd. Who would do such a thing? I was merely taking a walk."

"A walk?" he said dryly before diversion warmed his tone. "Sophie found something for you on our hunt." He held up the scrambling bundle, revealing the black-and-white stripes on its face.

"Well, what is it?"

He shot me a measured grin. "A badger, actually."

My eyes grew round, as I remembered his pet name for me. "And Sophie caught it? A badger?"

"She did indeed, and I should have liked to give it to the gamekeeper, but I decided to let it go."

I moved in closer. "I don't believe I've ever seen one this close before. They are handsome little devils — for a hairy animal, that is."

"And reclusive, sly, and a blasted nuisance when provoked — who I daresay prefer to spend their time sneaking around than in more respectful pursuits."

I was unprepared for the seething wrath that filled my throat. "Perhaps the poor creature merely seeks to find her place in this world amid the vicious dogs and other nasty animals bent on her utter destruction. Good day, Mr. Browning. You may take the lowly badger wherever you please, but I shall not stay and watch you arrange her life for her in the way that pleases no one but yourself."

CHAPTER 20

That night the stars summoned me to the terrace and the crisp, chilled air to lose myself once again in something far grander than my pressing problems, something infinitely bigger than myself. I sprawled out nicely on a patch of grass before I heard him approaching.

The footsteps came from the stables, and I sat up with a start. Lewis seemed as surprised as I was to find me laid out on the manicured lawn, wrapped in nothing but a mantle, robe, and nightgown. I tucked the mantle as tightly as I could about my legs. It seemed he meant to engage me, so I headed him off. "Can I help you, sir?"

He shoved something into his pocket then idly crossed his arms. "This is hardly proper, Rebecca, but after last night I suppose none of your hoydenish behavior could astonish me." To my surprise, he lowered himself onto the grass beside me with a tight sigh before beginning again. "I hope this is not something you do often."

I pursed my lips. "Really, what I find to do in my leisure time is none of your concern. But if you must know, I only venture out when I long to take in the brilliance of the stars . . . and when I need to think."

"Ah," he said aloud. The deep timbre of his voice echoed off the far trees before the night wind swallowed it up. "And what is it that Miss Rebecca Hunter ponders on this lonely evening?" There was a restlessness about his movements, an edge to his words. "Your next adventure perhaps?"

I stiffened, all too aware how foolish I must appear sitting on the front lawn all alone, staring up at the sky. "I can scarcely expect you to understand."

He leaned close and nudged my shoulder as if in some sort of contrition. "Why don't you try me?"

Try him? I shot a glance his direction. "If you must know, I was thinking of Jacob, missing him as I do most days. I begin to believe he might be the only one who understood me."

"Yes, Jacob." Lewis's voice deepened. "It is convenient that your brother's name is never far from your lips when you prefer me to leave you alone."

Stung, I was struck silent for a bit before I glared up at him. "How dare you."

He had moved to rise but abandoned the idea and settled back onto the grass. It took a long moment for him to speak as he stared at the far trees, a tense scrutiny about his eyes.

"You're right, of course. I am an insensitive brute. It is long past time we discussed Jacob." He gripped a small stone he found at his feet and launched it into the rigid darkness. "His presence, so to speak, has resided over *us* since you arrived."

He said the word *us* with the same insidious ring I used in my thoughts. I shivered, and Lewis wriggled from his greatcoat before draping it across my shoulders. A gloomy silence followed his quick movement, filling the space between his words. His fingers made a path across his forehead.

"This shan't be easy for either of us, I daresay, but I would be willing to answer any questions you have regarding that night." Then, almost bitterly, "We're alone, a good deal past mere acquaintances. Let us put to rest what happened that night on the bridge."

There was a hint of self-preservation in his voice, and for the first time I wondered if he had not spoken openly before because it might be painful for him. I nodded, uncomfortably off stride at his surge of emotion. "That is just what I wish — answers."

Then his eyes caught the starlight. "But there is one thing I would ask in advance of our discussion."

"Yes?"

"That I may ask a few questions of my own."

His arm felt warm next to mine, his muscles taut, and for a dream-like moment I wondered if such a bargain was worth the taking. Yet what he offered was far too tempting to ignore. It was the secrets I had come for after all. Honestly, what could my guardian possibly want to know about me that would affect anything now?

I managed another quick nod. "As you wish, though I hardly think it necessary." I gripped his coat tightly around my shoulders, and the tangy scent of his cologne reached my nose. I focused in but found it harder to begin than I'd once planned. "When you wrote to my aunt and me, informing us that you struck Jacob from the bridge, you never told me the whole of what happened. How such a thing came about."

His voice slipped away as if the tendrils of

the night air had reached into his chest and stolen it. I had been wrong to think him heartless. His shoulders drew in, his answer sounding strangled at best. "I've asked myself that same question a thousand times, and I've never come to any sort of answer. My memories are quite hazy, you see. After it happened — nothing. I don't even remember finding my way home. I had been at the Rose Inn earlier in the night. That I am sure of, and I only had a little to drink. Perhaps it was the shock of what happened . . ."

He picked at a leaf pressed to his breeches and flicked it onto the silvery grass. "I remember darkness and urgency, and then Jacob appeared out of nowhere, standing stark still in the middle of the bridge the very moment my horse . . ." Lewis's hand shook as he pressed his cheek. "The collision caused the fall, Rebecca, and his battered body turned up days later miles downstream." His voice dropped to a whisper. "The word *regret* does not do justice to what you lost that night. Yet that is all I have to offer you."

I sat stone still for a great many seconds as questions swirled in my mind. More. There had to be more. Lewis's hand fell to the grass so near mine that we were nearly touching. I stared at his fingers, the curve of his skin, the roughened edges and subtle freckles. Over the past few months, I'd turned him into a monster in my mind, but he was just a man — a complicated man who had made a terrible mistake. One he would live with for the rest of his life.

And yet, everything I'd learned so far at Greybourne Hall told me there was more to what happened that night than what he revealed. It burned to do so, but I would have to pry further. "Do you not remember anything else, anything at all? You know me well enough now to realize, I shall never rest until I've had the whole from you."

He sighed. "As I have come to learn." He looked away, his jaw tight. "At first, I had hoped to spare you the details, but you must know it all." His eyes fixed on the silhouette of shrubbery in the distance. "There was a gunshot as I approached the bridge. I didn't remember it that first morning, nor at the inquest that followed, but I've grown certain of it over time. Things have been forming more clearly for a while now."

My body tensed. "What do you mean, a gunshot?"

He took a long breath as if stealing himself for what would inevitably follow. "I've an image that haunts my thoughts . . . It was

Jacob, Rebecca. Jacob aimed a pistol — at me. It was the sudden crack that caused my horse to bolt, and well, the rest you already know."

Jacob? A pistol? I couldn't believe it. Doubt seeped through my skin and consumed every inch of my body until I lifted my chin, my heart thundering in my chest. "What reason would Jacob have to fire at you?"

"Again, I cannot be certain. It's been eating at me for the past few days. It was one of the reasons I brought you to Greybourne Hall. I thought perhaps you alone knew something, something that would expose the truth." He paused. "But then you arrived, and . . . things changed. For the first time I saw the futility of dragging up the past, what such an upheaval might do to others beyond me."

Spare me the details indeed. This changed everything — if Lewis could be believed. Jacob was never violent, not beyond the normal play of young boys. Of course, I'd not spent any length of time with him as an adult. He could have been desperate, or — my eyes widened — perhaps someone else had been at the bridge. I pressed my lips together. Lewis heard a gunshot, yes, but he admitted his memory was not altogether reliable. What if someone else took the shot?

Lewis adjusted his seat on the grass, resigned to his version of the truth. "Is it possible that Jacob wrote you before his death? Anything that might help us understand his motivations at the end?"

"No," I said defensively. "It had been several months since I'd heard from him, and he was never a reliable correspondent."

Lewis shrugged. "Then we shall likely never know. Perhaps it's best if —"

"Wait. Jacob did speak to my cousin."

Lewis cocked an eyebrow. "You mean Miss Ellen Cooke? Do you honestly think she can be trusted?"

"I agree she is a bit silly and an altogether trying peagoose, but she did write to me and explain about a time she met Jacob before that night. She told me she found him odd and anxious, not at all his affable self. He had a great many debts, you see. Perhaps he got in too deep?"

"Possibly, but I promised him when he arrived at Greybourne Hall that I would do what I could to help him."

I glanced again at the stars and took a moment to trace the constellations with my mind's eye. Lewis could not entirely understand the motivations that drove my brother to act. He'd not grown up in our family.

Jacob would not have swallowed help so easily, particularly from the man my father chose to bestow his favor on. It was the one thing Jacob repeated over and over again in his letters — his anger toward our father and his relationship with Lewis.

Jacob's opinions had likely colored my own. "I find it equally possible Jacob would have tried to find a way through a fix — one that did not involve you."

There was a rustle in the underbrush a few yards away. A fox broke free of the hedgerow's damp leaves before it scampered across the lawn and into the safety of the trees. I felt Lewis's gaze on me before turning to face him.

His eyes were soft and steady, the merest quiver to his lips. "Rebecca, we have been at cross purposes for far too long. It feels good just to talk." He regarded me for a moment. "Might we call a truce?"

A truce. The word startled me, likely because I had been unconsciously leaning the same direction. But could I trust Lewis to help me find the answers we both sought?

He went on, "I daresay you find me a bit more tolerable than you did before."

I feigned interest in the lawn. "No, only a fool for not telling me the whole when I first arrived." He had meant to spare me the supposed fall of my brother's legacy, if what he said was indeed what happened, but I was not a child to be protected. The quicker Lewis understood that, the easier we would get on. I looked up with a new-found energy. "I would rather the truth between us — always."

The surging wind played with a lock of his hair, sweeping it across his brow, and I was plagued with the sudden notion to tuck it back into place. He shook his head, righting the strand. "I understand." A smile followed his words, and I found myself returning it. It was as if we had been granted the chance to start again, like two friends meeting for the first time without the weight of death hanging over our heads. What would I have thought of him if I had met him in a ballroom in London during my season?

I took a cleansing breath, aware for the first time of something I had not seen before. The kindness in his eyes, the sense of justice he imposed on himself, the fortitude he possessed amid the censure of the town. Lewis Browning had presence and character beyond any man I had ever known.

I inched my hand across the rough grass until it touched his. People say sometimes the body responds before rational thought, but I'd never experienced such a thing before. I needed to feel him, allow my subtle movement to say the words that I couldn't seem to form in my mind.

Seconds passed, my skin tingled. We were both hesitant to breach the wall we'd built so carefully between us. But suddenly, like a feathered breeze from the north in the heat of summer, everything changed — everything I thought I knew about him . . . about myself. My heartbeat drowned out all else, and I didn't move when his fingers intertwined with mine.

The two of us sat motionless as the pressing night air shifted, my beloved stars witnesses to . . . what? A tentative friendship? Or something more?

At length, Lewis broke the charged silence. "I believe it is my turn for a question."

"What? Oh, yes."

His hand clenched mine briefly then released. "Why were you in my bedchamber last night?"

My mouth slipped open, then I pressed my lips tight. Of course, that would be his first question. I swallowed the lie already forming in my throat. "Quite frankly, I didn't trust you. I went to look for information or a clue, anything about Jacob's death.

If you had only told me what you have tonight. And I certainly did not expect you to return so suddenly and in such a state." I hesitated. "Where had you been after all?"

I could tell he meant to shirk off an answer until he, too, realized we had promised each other honesty. "I had just robbed the post office, as you well know."

"So, it is true."

He held up his free hand, silencing me. "But before you ask more, will you answer me one more thing? Was that the first time you have been in my room?"

I jerked my head back. "Yes, of course it was."

"I am glad to hear it, but it still leaves me a bit lost as to all I have experienced of late."

I hesitated. "What do you mean?"

"I'm beginning to believe someone has been in and out of Greybourne Hall at will."

My eyes grew wide. "There is more than just the wine bottle and my disheveled room?"

"Yes, a good deal more. Books missing, papers moved, windows left open. Someone has been making use of the estate and not being all that clever to hide his tracks."

"And the robbery at the townhouse."

"My thoughts exactly. When I found you in my room, let's just say you caught me at my worst. I did not intend to frighten you so."

"You were rather quick with the pistol."

He laughed. "I thought I had found my intruder at last."

We fell comfortably silent for a moment, my heart innocently aware of his fingers as they wrapped around mine. "Who do you think would do such a thing? And why?"

"All my hunting has turned up nothing. Perhaps you are the very person who might be able to help me solve the puzzle. You seem to have a bit more affinity for these types of things than I do. Any ideas at present?"

I thought for a moment. "Nothing comes to mind, but you are right. We do need a truce. Maybe if we work together, we might come about how all this fits together. Mr. Drake's murder, Jacob's, what if it all is somehow related? We could share what we know, do a little investigation?"

"Like in the cellar?"

I popped his arm with my free hand. "Certainly, but only the part before you caught my gown on fire."

"Me?" He chuckled. "How easily the truth can be twisted." He gave a light shrug. "But I would like that very much. You may do all the difficult thinking between us, and I shall do my best to keep you out of trouble."

"Hmm . . . trouble." I cast him a sideways glance as he stood. "Before you scamper away, I believe you owe me an answer." I rose beside him. "Why did you rob the post office?"

He took a long breath as if deciding something before his shoulders drooped. "I didn't rob it, exactly. I needed some information is all."

"Information?"

"Don't look at me like that. I didn't touch anyone's precious correspondence and did nothing illegal. I was merely helping a friend." He pressed his lips together. "It was imperative that I did what I did, but I cannot tell you anything more at present. You'll have to trust me on this one."

Trust him? What grounds did he have to demand that? I opened my mouth to probe further, but his compelling gaze stopped me cold, which was followed by a heavy sense of calm. I did trust him. I cast a quick glance back at the house. Perhaps now was not the best time to test it. Besides, the emotional cost of the evening was adding up. "It's getting late. I better go."

He grasped my arm. "Please, just one more question, and then you may retire."

I managed a smile. "Oh, all right. Go on then."

But I would regret those words almost as soon as I'd spoken them. Lewis's face was usually so determined, a handsome mix of rugged carelessness and good breeding, but at that moment it all deserted him. He seemed almost hesitant as he rubbed a hand down his breeches. One pointed look, and I knew the question before it left his lips. "Why won't you consider marriage?"

The ease we'd settled into drew up like a snake ready to strike me back down. Had I allowed too much familiarity between us? I flexed my fingers, then balled them up at my waist, unable to meet his eyes.

"Please, Rebecca. I need an answer."

I shook my head. "But surely, you already know."

"No, I most certainly do not." He sounded irritated. "This idea you have of setting up on your own is madness."

I cringed. "Interesting choice of words." I thrust my hands to my side, turning at last to face him. "I daresay you are well aware that my mother went mad. Don't you see, I shall in all probability be just like her — I *know* in my heart I am. What sort of a wife would I make then? How could I agree to marry a gentleman knowing what I do of her illness and descent?"

The look he cast my direction spoke a good deal more than his words ever could. "I've seen no evidence of what you claim."

Anger crept into my words, feeding on the pain of the truth. "Haven't you? What about that night in the library? I assure you, those spells have become quite common of late. And only a few days ago, I heard a song whistled in the woods that dissipated right in front of me. How long? Hmm? How long before my appointed husband despises me, or worse, stays to fight the devastation of watching me slip further and further into madness till there is nothing left. I will not be a burden to anyone, least of all a man."

At length he took my hand again, grasping it as if that solitary act might change what I already knew to be true. "Such a future is daunting indeed, if it indeed plays out the way you suppose. But you are not your mother. You cannot know for certain that what you've experienced will result in the same end. Braving the unknown is what makes us all human and vulnerable. Every person has a past he or she must come to live with, as well as a future that is not yet written — do not give up the fight already."

I searched his eyes. "I —" He had to understand me. I needed him to stand my friend. "But it is not only my life, you see. I would be harming another. I should rather spend every day alone than knowingly deceive some hapless gentleman."

He grasped me with both arms and drew me close, but I stiffened, all too aware I could lose myself in his touch. My resolve, though loud as a trumpet on the outside, had already begun to crumble within.

He studied me for a long moment. His eyes crinkled at the corners as his face tightened. "That's not all, is it?"

I pulled back. "What would you know?"

"You're afraid, Rebecca. No, listen to me." He resisted my flight. "You're frightened, not only of your uncertain future, but of the startling truth that you just might find a man who knows his own mind, who might choose the path of happiness knowing someday it will certainly end. We men are not all haunted by the ghosts of your father and mother. Do not let your father's poor choices serve as a testament to us all. Answer me, what if the gentleman was aware of the risk and chose to proceed? What if your heart was engaged as well as his?"

His words were moving too fast for me to process. The issue far more complicated than he was willing to admit. Trembling, I buried my face in my hands.

His voice was soft now. "Rebecca . . ."

Unable to refuse such a heartfelt plea, I looked up and fell into a tender gaze.

"I don't mean to press you, but . . ." He looked a bit flushed, his words difficult to find. Then a steady look filled his face. "Tell me here and now that you do not feel what has taken possession of me, and I shall upset you no further."

Every last muscle in my body froze . . . except my heart, which, unbidden, hammered against my chest as tingles spilled into my fingers and toes. I'm not certain what I expected him to say, but not that. "I —" I had always assumed he meant someone else, some other gentleman of means he intended to marry me off to. How could I respond — to *him*? I placed my hand defensively between us, but it betrayed me and settled on his chest.

A quick smile and he reached out, his tentative fingers slipping into my hair, tucking a loose curl behind my ear. Then restless, they slid to the back of my neck, sparking a fresh wave of twisting emotions.

Closer. I inched closer. Had I been craving this connection since the very beginning? Yes. And how hard I'd worked to keep it at bay.

Lewis paused as if waiting for me. To do what? My lips quivered. The scent of his cologne tainted the restive air between us, drowning out what was left of any rational thought. I met his gaze, drinking in that impenetrable strength he always seemed to possess, before I rose up onto my tiptoes and his lips found mine.

There was a flash of silence, then pounding eagerness as my arms crept up his back and I drew him against me. His kiss was gentle at first, then urgent, as if we'd been granted something extraordinary and the moment might never come again.

A delicious warmth rushed across my chest, spilling onto my cheeks. More. I wanted more. I wanted Lewis. I wanted . . .

Suddenly, I jerked back, unable to think or feel as the galling pound of my pulse drummed wild in my ears. What had I done? Happiness was nothing but an illusion for me. There would be no *us,* no future. My feet itched to run, but I couldn't move, couldn't even take a breath.

Lewis's eyes narrowed, his arms as warm as moments before, but slack with confusion. And as I pulled farther away, I could feel the pain in his voice. "What is it? Is it me?"

My fingers retreated to my lips, and I

backed away. "I'm sorry, so horribly sorry, but you must know we can never be together. You were right. I am afraid, but it's so much more than what you imagine." I shook my head. "There is something that frightens me more than anything else, something you've probably not even given a thought to."

Emboldened by the fact I knew I was right, I met his pleading eyes with a level stare. "If I married you, there would be children, and I would never take the chance of passing on my mother's madness to them."

Stunned, Lewis's eyes darkened, and I turned away, fled across the terrace, and entered into the obscurity of the house, certain I had ended any possibility of happiness between us.

CHAPTER 21

Sleep, though late, proved a balm to my ruffled spirit. Upon waking, the autumn sunlight brought with it the feel of the previous night, yet none of the shame I expected to overpower me. Perhaps it was due to the comforting truth that I had shared such intimate kisses with Lewis. Yes, Lewis. I could still see the depths to his eyes, the way his mind turned like a clock. He would find his way to understanding.

My maid proceeded to complete my toilet with little to no conversation, a first since I'd arrived. I'm certain now that she must have suspected something lay heavy on my mind. At length, she took leave and abandoned me to my consuming thoughts. Listless, I settled into the chair at my dressing table and took a long look at the reflection in the looking glass. Lewis's voice resounded in my mind.

"Is it me?"

My eyes slipped shut. He cared for me. And I him, but what that meant beyond mutual attraction, beyond my horrid mistake, I could not fully grasp let alone mend the hurt feelings between us. My resolve to remain unattached had not wavered. I turned to look over my room. Living any length of time at Greybourne Hall was now utterly out of the question. I could not torment him so.

Unfortunately, there would be time before any arrangements could be made, time before I could be sent away. My stomach clenched. In the interim, I would have to face him.

I wasted a bit more of the morning, dallying in my room as late as I dared, but I knew I could not stay hidden forever. Swinging a shawl over my shoulders, I headed from my bedchamber intent on finding Aunt Jo. I wasn't sure I was ready to share the whole mistake with her, but the comfort of company, particularly a loved one, was just what I needed.

The hallways were as empty as ever. I crossed from one corridor to the next, but I couldn't escape the curious intensity that filled the quiet space as if the house itself knew of my discomfiture and enjoyed taunting me.

On the landing I scanned the lower floors over the railing, and I was heartened by the sight of an empty front room and even more so by the all too likely probability that Lewis would be closeted away in his apartment, plotting how to avoid me as well. The portrait of Lewis's great-grandfather that hung at the head of the stairs stood in his place, leering at me as if he, too, were privy to our time on the lawn, to the deep personal fears I had revealed. I glared back, daring the stuffy old man to say a word.

Silently, I made my way down the stairs and across the entryway as quickly as possible before ducking into the safety of the drawing room, hoping Aunt Jo was there ahead of me. Sophie, however, met me at the door and announced my entrance by lolling over in that particularly handsome way of hers that involves a great deal of tongue and wiggling of lower body parts.

Her warm welcome was not only heaven-sent but utterly distracting. If I had known anyone was there, I might never have taken those six careless steps across the rug. I certainly wouldn't have flopped down on the sofa as I did before urging Sophie and her endless happiness to join me.

"So, you decided to venture from your room at last?" Lewis leaned forward, seated in the same chair Mr. Galpin had found agreeable on his last visit. Dread hardened my stomach and my hand stilled on Sophie's head.

There was an edginess about his countenance that seemed at war with his easy words. "I have been awaiting you for some time now."

Irritated by Lewis's unwanted presence and more so by his pointed glare, I gripped the side of the sofa as if to rise. After all, what did I have to be ashamed of? His odd tone, however, arrested any further movement on my part. "I, um, apologize for any inconvenience I may have caused." I flashed a pert look. "Unfortunately, I was delayed . . . by a particular gentleman last night and retired quite late to my bedchamber."

He squinted. "Now who could possibly have been so careless?"

It was something of a relief to find the hint of wit in his words. "Who indeed?" I drew in a deep breath as the tension in my shoulders ebbed away. Humor suited Lewis much more than insipid pleasantries.

I caught the merest glimpse of last night spring into his eyes — hope, resignation, wistfulness — it was hard to tell, but he shrugged it off all the same. "Perhaps this particular gentleman was not himself, driven by a long, hard night that he found heartily improved by the sight of a beautiful woman lounging on his lawn. Tell me, did you find him desperate?"

I forced a laugh as he no doubt meant for me to, but it was not a comfortable one. "No, indeed."

"Agreeable then?"

"Certainly."

A slow smile formed on his face and the mood lifted. "Then I declare you as responsible for this egregious delay as the gentleman in question, and I shall probe no further into your private affairs."

I looked to Sophie, uncertain how to respond.

He had control of himself now, and the dreaded moment was past. Would we emerge as friends? He stood. "I am glad to see you rested. Have you had something to eat?"

His tone was friendly, his countenance genial, but I still felt off balance. "Yes, well, I chose to breakfast in my room this morning."

"Good, for I have something I wish to show you." He moved near the sofa and extended his arm.

I hesitated as I regarded the offer. I

316

thought he might have flinched, but he took a quick glance over his shoulder. "I promise you, I've had a word with the gentleman from last night, and he assures me he will not bother you any further."

"That is not what I meant —" I stood and accepted his arm. "I am more than pleased to see whatever it is you wish to show me."

Something sharpened in his eyes, and he motioned through the door. "It's on the second floor."

"Lead on."

Sophie's fluffy feet padded behind us as we climbed the grand central staircase and traversed the long gallery. I had never ventured this far into the house nor received the promised tour from Mr. Drake so long ago. One of my early walks had revealed an upper-floor room from the outside lawn, nestled into a sort of squarish tower at the northern corner of Greybourne. I'd wondered for some time what lay hidden there. The appearance of a narrow stairwell and a heavy door beyond the hallway only confirmed my suspicion that we were headed to that very room, but for what purpose I could not guess.

As we neared the stairs, the feel of the house changed so suddenly I nearly stumbled. It was as if we had stepped through

317

time into an older portion of the house. Mullioned windows of stained glass flanked the stairs and were interspersed with small, intricate alcoves. Carved beams climbed not only the walls but sprawled across the ceiling as well. The scent of past centuries met my nose as my toes disturbed clumps of dust, and cobwebs nestled in the upper corners of several steps.

At the landing, Lewis's voice dropped to a whisper as if the house demanded some sort of reverence. He pointed ahead. "This is the only remaining defensive tower on the estate. In my father's day, the housekeeper resided up here, but it has long since been abandoned."

I took a quick breath, intending to ascertain the purpose of our journey to the upper room, but decided to allow Lewis the mystery . . . at least for now. I couldn't shake the feeling there was something hidden behind this sudden idea of his to explore.

Though not large, the upper room with its high ceilings and textured walls had a grand feeling to it like the inside of a church. Weaponry — swords, dusty crossbows, iron plates, as well as a full suit of armor standing like a guardian in the corner — filled the whole of one side and surrounded a crenellated fireplace.

My eyes widened. "I certainly hope all this was not here when it was the housekeeper's bedchamber."

"No." He laughed. "A dangerous business, is it not?"

"Indeed. You have quite a collection."

"No Browning saw fit to dispose of a single piece over the years. We are collectors at heart. Now, if you would prefer to keep your head, you can follow me to the back window, away from all this."

The remainder of the room hid beneath a layer of Holland covers, which rested like little white mounds that reminded me of snow. At the far end, I noticed that the furniture had been pushed aside, the floor swept, and the drapes drawn back to expose a warm little nook.

Four large windows met there in a half-octagonal curve where a small desk had been pushed into the space below them, two chairs set to the other side. Upon the desk's smooth, wooden surface sat three spindly legs, which supported a long brass circular scope.

I slowed my approach, the truth of why Lewis had brought me here dawning. "Oh my! Is that a telescope?"

A smile curved Lewis's lips. "It is indeed."

I blinked, hardly sure I was not dreaming. "How ever did you come by it?"

"It was my brother's, actually. Until last night, I'd forgotten it was even up here. When we were sitting on the lawn, you mentioned how much you loved to study the stars. Charles, too, had a passion for the heavens. It was the artist in him, I suppose."

"This is extraordinary." Unable to contain my excitement, I lurched forward and squared my eye against the eyepiece before angling the scope toward the closest window.

At length, Lewis reached over my shoulder and lifted my hand to the far end of the barrel. "You can adjust the focus here."

I pointed the telescope first one direction and then the next, exclaiming with delight each time I alighted on something new. Then all at once I pulled back, my words coming out more like a child's than I intended. "Would you like a turn?"

Lewis had settled back against the desk, his eyes alight with mirth. "I've had plenty, thank you."

"Of course. I wasn't thinking." My finger fell to the brass stand, the awkwardness of the previous evening threatening to emerge. "This is amazing. Thank you for sharing it with me."

"Not at all." He gave me a quick smile. "Consider the telescope yours for as long as you are here. Unused, it is merely another item to attract cobwebs and a great deal of dust. Please, feel free to utilize this room whenever you wish, which I suppose will be best after nightfall to view the stars." He eyed the window. "No one shall bother you in this part of the house." He took a quick look back at me. "Although, I'd rather you not do so in your nightgown."

My skin tingled. So he had seen what I wore beneath my mantle the previous night. Embarrassed, I snapped back, "And if I prefer to do so?"

He shook his head. "Whatever will you say next, Rebecca?"

I answered with the hint of a shrug. "Who can say? I daresay I've never learned tact."

"Or propriety for that matter."

He meant it as a joke, but the memory of what we engaged in the previous night filled the motionless air around us like a hot air balloon, penning us into silence for a long moment. So much had happened between us, but now . . . now there was strangely little to say.

He surprised me by taking my hand. "There is something else."

I glanced up, hoping not to betray the

321

violent start his touch had produced. "Yes?"

He spoke then with what I thought must have cost him a great deal of strength. "You do know that you are welcome at Greybourne Hall for as long as you wish, for as long as you need, forever, if it comes to that. There will be no expectations on my part, no questions. I don't care a jot for what the world thinks." His thumb moved ever so slightly. "Only what you do."

The room seemed particularly warm all of a sudden, and I took a hasty step away from him, pressing my cool fingers to my cheek. My voice cracked. "That is good of you to offer, but I cannot think you really mean it."

He regarded the floor again for a moment. "Doubtful as always, Rebecca." Then he let out a sigh. "Certainly, I mean it, but do not feel compelled to answer at once. Just keep what I propose in mind when you are making those plans of yours." There was a trace of amusement buried in his last words, but I didn't allow it to rankle me as I usually did.

He made his way into the light of the window and turned his back to me. His lithe figure dropped in silhouette, and the room felt unnaturally quiet behind him. I watched him there as my hands found my stomach.

Father had been right. Lewis was a different sort of gentleman. I could hunt all over England and be unable find the equal to his steadiness of mind and character. If only things had been different. If only I were different.

He spun around, looking at me for a moment before saying in a dry tone, "The hour is likely advanced, and I'm afraid I've business to attend to below. Will you accompany me downstairs or would you rather spend some more time with the telescope?"

"I should like to remain here." I meant the room when I initially spoke, but I found myself inwardly agreeing to his notion about Greybourne Hall as well. Somewhere in the recesses of my mind I knew it was a foolish, risky notion, which would only complicate my resolve, but in that charged moment when the future seemed miles away from the wistful here and now, I didn't care. If Lewis asked me to stay, I would do so.

Late that afternoon, I sought the solitary confines of my bedchamber and the fresh afternoon air the eastern windows afforded. Aunt Jo had gone driving with Mr. Fernside, likely to return home with a new promise to revel in. Yet, such an idea fell on turbulent thoughts in my mind. What would happen to me?

Of course I was genuinely happy for her, but at heart we humans are such selfish beings. Earlier that morning, I fully intended to share her excitement, brought out by the note of his return from London and request for an afternoon drive. I thought I had put on an altogether convincing act, but my aunt was not a fool. She knew I was not entirely myself. And I hated that I let the situation get the better of me. Her subsequent engagement would be just as difficult to swallow.

I thought a novel would turn my thoughts from Lewis and the earnest look he shot me in the upper room, but the book I brought up from the library the previous night was *Camilla,* Jacob's favorite romance. I ended up flinging it across the room a bit more violently than I'd intended. Defeated, I flopped back onto the bed, one arm slung across my forehead.

Lewis Browning.

He was maddening and enchanting and handsome and I so horribly wrong for him. But I loved him — against my utter resolve. The thought stung with a fresh barb. I pounded my fist against the coverlet. He was the man my father had intended me to marry from the first. The man Aunt Jo adored like a son. The one man who made my heart quicken. I was at a loss.

Would it be so terrible to do as he said, to discard my anxiety for the future and fall into his willing arms? How good they felt, how safe. What a blessed release it would be to share my burden with someone beyond God and my adoring aunt. But the sight of my mother's twisted face crowded into my mind — the screaming sessions, the disordered thoughts, the heart-wrenching final few months. If I sought my own happiness, my husband and, more importantly, my children, would pay the price. They would be the ones to bear witness to my descent, realizing all too late their part in it as well.

Never. No one would be forced to experience what I did in Scotland. No one.

Determined I would not cry, I crossed the floor to the fireside, where the book I'd previously tossed aside lay crumpled in a heap. Jacob would have been quite angry if he knew I'd handled his book so. I reached down and straightened the pages before attempting to close the wrinkled mess. The spine of the book resisted the movement. I tilted the book first one way then the next, trying to right the twisted spine. Suddenly, a folded paper slipped from the book's damaged binding onto the floor.

I paused, regarding the paper. "What on earth?" I took one more hesitant glance at where it had emerged from the spine. The backing was split into two sections that created a small cove. My headlong throw had somehow dislodged the hidden contents. I reached down and picked up the paper.

It was a letter written in a hand I did not recognize and addressed to my brother. The scent of lavender still clung to the worn note. Clearly, Jacob had handled the thing a great many times. I knew of a few passing romances during his months in London, but I also knew our family was not well regarded by the ton. Who then would have taken a fancy to my brother? He'd never said a word. Perhaps it was only one of his light-skirts? I tapped the note. Yes, whoever it was could not be respectable.

I unfolded the missive, haunted by the intrusion into his privacy. But the letter had found its way to Greybourne Hall and into my hands, and I had promised to consider every clue that could possibly connect to his death. In a way, I felt his hand guiding mine, agreeing with my motives from beyond the grave.

My Dearest Jacob,

How lonely I will be when you leave for London, my darling. Lewis will bore me as always, though I shan't tolerate his censure in the least. And I certainly won't allow him to disparage you, my love. Perhaps I shall stay away from Greybourne Hall and drive him mad. He must always be in control of everything I do. As if I am his plaything.

A fortnight. How shall I ever bear the separation? I could cry only thinking of it. You are my one distraction from this horrid existence I've been forced to live, my secret indulgence. I know I've teased you in the past, but all that is forgotten now I hope. I meant what I said when you left this morning. Just remember that. Tell me you will come to me under the protection of night, my love, the very moment you are able. How I ache for you.

Isabell

I dropped the note, staring instead at the rose-papered wall. Oh, Jacob!

CHAPTER 22

Aunt Jo, bubbling over with news, found me in the drawing room upon her return. "Mr. Fernside and I are to be married as soon as the bans are read."

I fell into her excitement far easier than I had anticipated as we plopped onto the sofa like two young girls. More than anyone, Aunt Jo deserved to be happy. "Mr. Fernside is indeed a fortunate man."

"Oh, fustian. He is getting a silly old woman who doesn't know the first thing about running an apartment above a lending library."

I laughed and shook my head. "What a wonderful home — books everywhere!"

Her eyes twinkled. "There is that."

"I only wish Ellen and her family were in Plattsdale and not Bath. She would have loved to come to the ceremony."

"Yes. She would have made a lively addition." Aunt Jo dashed a smile, but it faded a bit as she turned to face me. "My dearest Rebecca, what you have meant to me all these years after my husband's death —"

"No more than what you have meant to me." I took her hands, appreciating the emotion behind her words, for I knew it well.

She took a long breath. "I am left wondering what will become of you, my dear?"

I had no intention of causing my aunt the least anxiety, not before or after her wedding, so I gave a little shrug. "You know me. I shall only need to form some new plans."

Her tone softened. "And what of Mr. Browning?"

My chest tightened. I had not told her about what happened on the lawn. That moment was for Lewis and me alone to share. Even so, Aunt Jo could always guess my feelings.

She leaned in. "I do not think him indifferent to you."

"Nor I."

Her eyebrows shot up, so I added quickly. "That is neither here nor there. My resolution remains the same." I could see the disappointment in her eyes. "You mustn't worry about me. He has kindly offered me a place in his household for as long as needed. It goes against my nature, mind you, but I shall simply have to find a new chaperone."

Aunt Jo watched me for a moment, her gaze peeling back far more than I wanted to reveal, then she squeezed my hand. "I do worry about you, Rebecca, but I shall do as you wish and leave you in Mr. Browning's capable hands. I do believe your father was wise in his selection of guardian after all."

I nodded, unable to give voice to my agreement.

Her own tone turned tearful as she looked about the drawing room. "It is all too likely that the hands of time will bring about change here at Greybourne Hall once I am gone. It always seems to do so, whether we plan for it or not." She touched my cheek. "What I see before me is not the same scared little girl who went willingly to Scotland with her mama. How different you have become — a grown lady with compassion, determination, honesty, and fairness. Your parents would be so proud."

She retrieved her handkerchief and dabbed her eyes. "Remember always my love for you. Wherever you go, whatever you do, you will be in my heart. And if I may leave you with one last thought" — she managed a smile — "don't plan too much, my darling. You'll miss what is right in front of you." Then she stood and wiggled to the door. "It is getting quite late. We must hurry and change for dinner."

Aunt Jo had never liked me to see her cry, so I gave her a quick nod. But I didn't move from the sofa, not yet at least. The truth of her words demanded my full attention. Aunt Jo was right. Change was indeed inevitable. Was I prepared to face it?

Lewis appeared quite suddenly the following morning on my walk from where he had been tarrying at the back slopes of the north field. The closer I approached, the more certain I became that he had been waiting to join me all along.

His welcome seemed full of ease, his movements relaxed, his attention merely that of a good friend, nothing more. He offered me an arm, and we settled into a comfortable pace and conversation. I suppose he'd found a way to move beyond his attraction, beyond me. I'd be lying to say my relief wasn't prodded by the sharp claws of disappointment, or should I say *regret,* for that which I would not know. It was in that moment, caught in his knowing gaze, that I realized I would never feel the same about another man. There was only one Lewis.

His hair lay a bit disheveled, his cheeks flushed with excursion. He smiled as I spoke, listening as if I were the most interesting person in the world. Life could be cruel at times.

He rested his fingers on the gloved hand I'd placed on his arm. "Your aunt has some happy news. I've just heard she will not be with us much longer at Greybourne Hall."

"Yes, happy news indeed." I added a smile. He could not know what her eventual absence would do to me. "I daresay she shall be quite content with Mr. Fernside, though I will miss her dreadfully."

I waited to see if Lewis would broach the uncomfortable subject of finding me a new chaperone, but his mind must have been elsewhere. Our steps slowed as we approached the fence that separated the back acres from the otherwise manicured lawns. We were away from the house and any prying ears — the perfect opportunity to tell him about my recent discovery.

I cleared my throat. "Though I would love to speak of my aunt, there is something quite different I wish to discuss with you. It has to do with Jacob."

He lifted his hand as he guided me over

the stile. "Oh?" Then he followed me over the rickety steps. "I, too, have been doing a great deal of thinking about something you said the other day — the part about Jacob being beholden to someone. You immediately thought of debt, but what if it was something else, something more sinister that drove his actions that day?"

I stopped short, processing his words. Was he somehow privy to the letter I had read? "What on earth do you imply?"

He held up his hand. "I hesitated to bring this up earlier, particularly because I was not certain it had any bearing on his death, and I did not wish to cast aspersions on his character. However, we did decide to be honest with one another."

"Go on."

"There has always been a great deal of smuggling in this area. I have reason now, as I did before, to believe Jacob might have gotten himself involved in something of the sort. He would not be the first young man to do so."

I thought at once of the journal and how Mr. Galpin had said Jacob held a debt of honor. Perhaps Jacob had been desperate, but smuggling? "I suppose he was romantic in his notions, but I cannot imagine him agreeing to something so dangerous."

Lewis grimaced. "Do you know if he had any connections in France?"

"Connections?" I stole a look up. "I should think not. Jacob was far too idealistic to spend any real time with those kinds of disreputable people, here in England or in France. You know, at one time I thought he was bound for politics, but our family was never situated for something like that. Our position in society angered him, I know, but what could we do? Unfortunately, he was forced to turn his energies elsewhere." I pressed my lips together. "Which turned out to be gambling houses and opera dancers."

Silence fell, and I peered up as the shock of what I'd blurted out filled my cheeks. "Goodness, you must forgive my cursed tongue. It does tend to go wild if I'm not consciously forcing it to behave. I meant no offense by what I said just now. I have come to understand it is all the thing in London. You may very well enjoy your fair share of gambling for all I know."

Lewis slowed before grasping my elbow and bringing us to a stop. "Let me be clear before we go one step farther, you little badger. I have never stepped one foot inside a gambling house or spent one minute with an opera dancer. The fact that you should not only know about them but feel free to speak so does unnerve me."

"Well, why on earth would I not be aware of them? Everyone is, you know, and it would be insipid to pretend otherwise."

Then he laughed. "I suppose you're right. In future, though, I must beg you to keep such indelicate thoughts to yourself, at least in company."

My shoulders slumped. "Let me assure you that I am not so lacking in judgment as to say such a thing in your drawing room." I shook my head. "I guess I felt at ease with you here, and it . . . it just fell out."

"Now that, my dear, sounded almost like a compliment."

"I suppose it was . . . in a way, but please do not depend on it too much. I find I'm distracted at present."

Turning to walk along the tree line, Lewis nudged my shoulder. "What else is on your mind?"

I hesitated to answer; trusting him still felt foreign to my lips. I patted the letter from Isabell to Jacob in my pelisse pocket. "There is more to this business than we thought. I need to show you something I found, and in a way, it involves you too — and possibly your assumptions concerning my brother. Yet, I don't want you to take it amiss."

He drew me into the shade of a large oak where the cool scent of an early winter lingered on the breeze. "Nothing could surprise me now. Out with it, my dear."

I fished the letter from my pocket and held it into the light. "I discovered this yesterday, concealed within one of Jacob's old books. He must have received it before he traveled to London a few weeks before his death. I'm not certain what to make of it."

A look of resignation preceded Lewis's reticent reach for the letter, and as his fingers closed over the worn paper, I wondered if he already knew what the missive contained. At any rate, he must have recognized Jacob's name scrolled in Isabell's handwriting.

Like the purveyor of a priceless antique, Lewis unfolded the paper and rested his back against the trunk of the sizable oak. I watched as his countenance faded from intrigue to revulsion before he smashed the ends together and thrust the letter back to me. He took one reckless step forward and paused. "I did wonder about them."

The wounded smirk on his face told me much of what lay beneath his controlled response. Isabell had been busy indeed. Mr. Galpin's words beneath the willow tree came rushing back to me. *She enjoys men.*

There had been Lewis's brother, Jacob, Mr. Galpin. I glanced up. And Lewis, years ago.

I regretted thinking on it immediately. My heart squeezed, and all I could see was the smile Isabell wore when she visited the house. I was forced to look away into the thick copse of trees where daylight rarely visited and shadows feathered the rough ground.

Somehow I managed to find a way to ease into the thought burning in my mind. "There is more if you will hear it."

He stiffened, casting a dark look at the horizon. "Go on."

"Just over a week ago I saw Isabell out the drawing room window. She met with Mr. Galpin in the folly."

His whole body seemed to sigh. "She is not very constant, is she?" He crossed his arms. "I am certain there are many men around here caught like a spider in her web."

"You, perhaps?"

His eyes shot to mine, and like the work of a smoldering fire, the years of bitterness made over his gentle features, twisting his lips and hardening his eyes. "She told you, did she?"

"Not exactly. At the dinner party, she mentioned that she had broken off an engagement. I don't think she meant to divulge your connection, per se. And I had already received a version of the account from Colonel Hatcher."

Lewis picked at the bark on the tree, his other hand clenched into a fist. "And I suppose you would like the whole of it from me."

"It seems only fair. You do know a great deal about me."

He let out a long breath. "It was some time ago, and I was quite young and foolish."

I willed away the image of the two of them and leaned against the tree before nodding for him to continue.

He looked a bit lost, as if he were reliving a period in his life when he was not yet sure of himself. "Isabell and I met at a country dance. Having inherited Greybourne Hall at an early age — my father died unexpectedly of a heart complaint — I had little time for town polish, let alone guidance, particularly when it came to affairs of the heart. I didn't prove much of a challenge for someone like her. Within days I'd fallen at her feet like the rest of Plattsdale. She was something of an heiress and the town's singular beauty, so I thought it only right she should be with me.

"At first, she went to great lengths to make

338

me believe she returned my affections. We became engaged shortly thereafter. It was then that she discovered the true state of my affairs — the enormous debt and disrepair my father had made of the estate — and her eyes began to wander. It has taken me years to rectify my father's mistakes. At the time, however, Isabell thought my situation a hopeless one. She figured she might as well have the more attractive and interesting younger brother if neither of us had any money.

"It wasn't long before I found them together, and I was expected to condone a quick marriage between them. I loved my brother, Rebecca. And as Isabell knew, I could never cut him off. They moved into the dower house without a qualm. In some ways, I'm glad Charles was not here to see her drift away into some other man's arms as she inevitably would have." He motioned to the paper in my hand. "That letter just brings all those feelings back. Not my affection for Isabell, mind you, but Charles. The hurt he caused by his betrayal will always be with me."

I didn't respond right away as the tugging wind slid around my arms and whipped my bonnet ribbons about. What could I say? Isabell used every person she came in contact with. "She lacks a heart, Lewis."

He lifted his chin in what seemed like resignation, then nodded coldly, the merest bend to his lips. "Yes, a heart." He moved as if to grasp my hand, then thought better of it. "I apologize for my dark mood. Thoughts of Isabell and Charles tend to rile me."

"Considering the letter, I am beginning to wonder if Isabell might have had a hand in my brother's death. If nothing else, she knows something — as well as her brother, Adam. Everything seems to point back to them, even if Isabell declared her love for Jacob in the letter. Could they be hiding something at the dower house?"

"Right beneath our noses? I find that unlikely."

"Then what do you think? What about Mr. Drake? She seemed awfully jumpy when I told her of his death."

"I will say she was never very friendly with Drake. He probably saw right through her practiced advances. I know he avoided her. Isabell has always thrived on being the only woman around here, enticing all the men, placing them under her power." He shot me a knowing look. "I half worried she would perceive your presence as a threat to her position here." His hands found his fore-

340

head. "But remember, she could not have overpowered Drake, and the murderer must have strangled him from behind."

"Yes, I'd forgotten."

"And I am convinced that no one else was on the bridge the night of your brother's death. At least, I don't remember anyone." He threw up his hands. "No, that tragedy can be laid squarely at my feet."

"Or can it?" I raised an eyebrow. "You said you remembered very little of what happened that night. Why?"

He shifted. "I don't know. Probably too much to drink."

"But did you? The other day you said you had not."

"I only remember one, but who knows . . ."

I matched his grave tone. "Let us think this through. Tell me, who else do you remember seeing at the inn that night?"

"Adam. Yes, Adam. I remember he was in a rare taking, angry over Isabell's pin money of all things. He acted as if he meant to call me out, slapping me with his glove. The whole scene was beyond ridiculous."

"Wait . . . Adam was there?"

"Yes, I'm fairly certain he was in his cups. He kept referring to me as 'old boy' as if we were the best of friends who'd had a falling out before suddenly turning the whole discussion into a deuced show. I wasn't falling for his game that night."

I remembered the strange feeling I'd had in the drawing room that day with Isabell and her brother. I tapped my fingers against my lower lip. "Do you find it a bit odd that you remember every single detail of your interaction with Adam, but little after you left the inn?"

Lewis's brow wrinkled and he pursed his lips. "I'd never given such a notion much thought, but you do bring up an interesting point." He paced back and forth near the tree, his eyes glued to a fixed point on the ground. "Do you suggest I was given something? That a drug was placed in my drink?"

I tilted my chin. "That is exactly what I suggest. By either Adam or someone else all too pleased by the opportunity he presented."

Lewis shook his head. "I cannot imagine Adam has the wherewithal to pull such a thing off, but I will admit that he could be used to some purpose. And if what you say is indeed true, whoever this person is may have intended for me to hit Jacob that night."

I spoke slowly as the harrowing truth struck me. My tongue felt numb to the words spilling out. "A subsequent shot in the dark, and your horse would be uncontrollable by a man not wholly in possession of all his faculties."

Lewis leveled his gaze. "In other words — murder."

"As I have always believed."

Without a bit of fanfare, long morning walks became a comfortable habit for Lewis and me, and our friendship, though tentative, blossomed in a way I never thought it could.

Beneath the bare tree limbs and overcast skies, freed from expectation, we began to share all we'd learned of the murders as well as any details we'd come by about Isabell. We had both noticed how she had been curiously absent from Greybourne Hall since the dinner party, and Lewis subsequently forbid me to go anywhere near the dower house. He decided it best to lure her into a feeling of safety instead — a place where she might betray something of importance.

If Aunt Jo had been aware of our arrangement, I'm certain she would have been quite pleased, for I rarely allowed anyone else to take the lead in anything. I was far too stubborn for that, but perhaps I did so now because it was Lewis. He alone listened in a way that I knew he heard me . . . and understood. I suppose maturity comes with experience.

By the close of the week, we had a working list of suspects. Of course, we reaffirmed our earlier conclusion that Isabell could not have murdered Mr. Drake with her own hands, yet Lewis clung to the thought that she was still somehow involved — at least with Jacob's death. I, however, could not get her brother, Adam out of my mind. His manner was presented as one of dissipation — a glass of sherry here, a silly quip there — but what if more dwelt beneath his glossy looks and seedy glances? The man was broad shouldered and strong, the perfect foil for an unsuspecting Mr. Drake. And he had been there with Lewis at the inn the night of Jacob's accident.

We also considered Mr. Galpin. He wanted to buy Greybourne Hall — quite badly — and the townhouse. Worse, he seemed to revel in the villagers' dislike of Lewis. Could he have had an ulterior motive for perpetuating the fear and mistrust of Lewis in town?

And then there was the elusive French connection, smuggling or something else, that Lewis somehow thought possible.

Intent on this, he decided to write to a friend in the government for more information.

But, Mr. Drake? I had a hard time seeing the connection, and I was convinced the murders were linked somehow.

Any one of the people we discussed at length could have ended Mr. Drake's life, yet there was one piece that remained elusive — why? Or Jacob, for that matter? A large part of the puzzle was still missing, and handkerchiefs and buttons would not provide us the answers we sought.

Several days whirred by before I thought of the telescope. I'd been hard at work on my embroidered cushion in the drawing room with Aunt Jo when she mentioned my stargazing with that infuriating bend to her voice. I was quite certain she meant to discover whether I still walked the grounds at night alone, and I daresay I enjoyed answering that I had done no such thing. Of course, I had been too busy investigating murder with Lewis to give a single thought to my beloved stars, but I kept that fact to myself. She would never understand my tenuous relationship with him.

It was in that moment with Aunt Jo, when her fingers jittered as she knit and her face scrunched up at the corners, that I realized why it felt so natural to be on such easy terms with Lewis. He was the first person in my life who treated me as an equal. Jacob spoke down at me as did my father before him, and my aunt — how to explain it — fretted all the time. With my father, I was forever acting foolishly, getting into scrapes, making trouble for the family, which I instantly felt guilty for.

Lewis didn't care a fig for any of my silly starts. It was not as if he approved of all I said or did. Goodness, no. I'd a lecture nearly every day, but he also found a way to laugh it off as Aunt Jo liked to do, and inevitably we'd continue with whatever we had been about. He was artful, engaging, and at times vexing. If I were to be honest with myself, I would have to continue to guard my heart.

In this state of mind, I began taking afternoon jaunts to the telescope. The large windows of the tower provided the perfect vantage point to focus in on the dower house, and I'd decided to watch it every day. Sophie joined me regularly, padding up the stairs before curling into a ball in the warm sunlight that splayed out across the floor.

I'm not certain what I searched for. It was nothing but a smallish two-story home, covered on one side by creepers and the other by the soft light of the setting sun, but I knew if I waited long enough, there would be something.

And at length, there was.

It was late in the day, the sun having already crested the small house. With the scope, I followed the path from Greybourne Hall as it curved along a small rise and took a turn beside a tight little garden to the east before terminating in a round drive at the dower house door. The elevated position of the tower room afforded me a unique view of the house where the windows remained shuttered across the ground floor.

When I directed the telescope up a level, I was surprised to find the corner room's window open. The drapes were tied back and the panes pushed out. The afternoon held a steady breeze, and the window had likely been adjusted for ventilation. I'd not been in Isabell's house as of yet, and in all probability, the apartment was a sitting space she frequented in the afternoon.

However, as I focused the scope to better see the inside of the room, I realized I could not have been more wrong. The foot of a heavy bed came into view and a large wardrobe on the far wall. There were no people within the chamber, but one thing caught my eye and sent chills up my arm.

At first, I took a step back and shook my head before leaning once again to the eyepiece, certain I had been mistaken. But it was not so.

There on a small dresser, barely visible through the leaded window, lay a red rag — a rag a great deal like the one I'd seen the man wearing on the lawn outside my window all those nights ago.

CHAPTER 23

I set out for the dower house the next day, confident the appearance of the red rag was reason enough to go against Lewis's instructions and poke around a bit. I first thought to discuss my hurried plan with him in detail, but I'd not been able to find him the whole of the previous night or this morning.

By afternoon my curiosity had boiled over, and I could wait no longer. After all, who knew when Isabell would pop back in at the main house. The rag confirmed she was a part of the mystery. Of that I was certain. And I was pretty sure the dower house was as well. A surprise visit might turn up a clue. At the very least, my sudden arrival might get her to betray something — something I could use.

The dower house sat but a few hundred yards from Greybourne Hall, boasting the similar dark stone patterns and curved porticoes as the main house. As I climbed the weather-beaten steps through the outer wall and breathed in the motionless air of the courtyard, I noticed what I had not seen through the narrow lens of the telescope — significant neglect.

The windows lacked trim. The creepers grew wild. Five large oaks had matured into massive beasts surrounding the house and stretched out their spindly arms to the sloping roof as if they thought it something to hide.

A tingle wriggled its way up my back. Perhaps it was foolishness that sent me calling on Isabell without a word to Lewis. I only hoped she would not question why I hadn't brought Aunt Jo. It's not as if I meant to keep the visit from my aunt, only I didn't wish her to worry, and she did so frequently. Now was not the time to turn her mind from happier pursuits, and a visit with Isabell would do just that.

A sliver of smoke laced the light breeze. The ghost of my footprints trailed behind me like a thin shadow, the ground still wet from the overnight storm. With each careful step, the crunch of gravel followed me to the door.

A wave of apprehension tickled my hand as I reached for the knocker, but I managed a loud tap. The sound echoed somewhere beyond the door. Silence reigned for several seconds as if I were the only person for miles, but then I saw the corner of the drapes flutter in a nearby window. If I had not been looking that direction, I surely would have missed the flash of color. Footsteps clambered through the house, first one direction then the next, but a great many seconds elapsed before anyone approached the door.

A metallic pop, and Isabell's brother, Adam, leaned lazily against the door's edge. "Why, Miss Hunter, what a surprise."

My eyes widened. I had expected a servant, not this disheveled mess that looked as if he had not slept the previous night. He wore no jacket, and his cravat lay unfolded around his neck. Wrinkles lined his brocade waistcoat, a brown spot evident near his shoulder. I cleared my throat, all too aware of the awkwardness of the situation. "Good afternoon. I have come to call on Isabell."

He raked his hand through a confusion of blond hair, yawning in turn. "Figured as much. Be deuced awkward if you was to come to see me." He laughed as his eyes toured my figure with all the tact of a hardened rake. Perhaps he was one.

My pulse quickened. The lout meant to

frighten me off. Well — I took a measured breath — he would find I was made of stronger stuff than that. I stepped forward. "Is she at home at present?"

He cast a quick glance over his right shoulder, mocking my tone with a half-hearted shrug. "Who again?"

I wondered if he was still in his cups. At this hour? I tilted my chin and spoke louder, emphasizing each syllable. "I-sa-bell."

His hands retreated to his ears, but he remained firmly planted against the door. "No need for dramatics, my girl. I can hear you well enough." He took another look behind him. "Suppose she's about somewhere. I'm hardly her keeper, you know."

I narrowed my eyes. "And yet you answered the door. Anyone would assume you meant to assist whoever stood on the other side."

His thick brows drew in. "What the devil are you speaking of? Dash it all! It's my sister's house. I'll do as I please."

I could see this was going nowhere, and a prickle of indecision crept up my neck. "I should like to come in and await Isabell, if I may."

A wry smile crept across his face. "Why the deuce didn't you say so? Been standing there gawking at me as if I could read your thoughts." He paused, pressing his hand to his forehead, a look of bewilderment about his eyes. "Don't agree with such a notion, by the way, them gypsies and such. Thoughts ain't written down like letters, you know. Can't just pull them out. If you asked me —"

"Who is it at the door, Adam?" Thankfully, Isabell's melodic voice stopped any further rambling.

"Says she's here to see you, though she keeps standing there jabbering like a bird. Haven't had a visitor in weeks, and it's blasted difficult to know what they want if they insist you read their mind." He grasped for his watch fob, but his fingers merely pawed the air, for it wasn't there. "Particularly at such an uncomfortable hour."

Isabell pushed past her brother. "Stand aside, love."

Though she was a bit more put together than Adam, Isabell mirrored his restlessness. Her face lacked its usual glow. Dark circles lay beneath her eyes, hastily covered with powder. Even her gown was absent the brilliance of jewels or ribbons, almost as if she had hurried into it and thrust a shawl about her shoulders.

She clasped my hand, her fingers ice cold. "How good of you to visit. It has been too long since I have been blessed with your company."

I allowed her to lead me into a darkened entryway, which was made only more pronounced by the cloudy day. My gaze fell to the gloomy hollows of the fireplace. I was surprised the servants had not lit the fires for the day. Isabell seemed to follow my thoughts and slid past the large, gray opening like a scared animal.

"We've not a single servant left at the dower house. Can you believe such a predicament? Oh my dear, I am almost ashamed for you to see how we live." Then to her brother. "Adam, love, could you see to the fire in the sitting room and then bring us some tea?"

The sitting room lay just to the right, and though it suffered the same economy Isabell had enacted all over the house, the furniture here was newer than I expected, the yellow wallpaper crisp, the heavy drapes free from fading. I was directed to a long sofa, fronting the curtained window where we watched Adam's feeble attempts at lighting the fire with the tinderbox he'd secured from its hiding spot on the mantel. He repeatedly struck the flint against the steel, but the sparks flew in all directions, none landing anywhere near the tinder.

"Blasted nuisance," he mumbled.

Isabell tittered in that way of hers. "Now, Adam, we shall have to make do until we can find another housekeeper." Then to me. "We have been simply lost since Mrs. Byrd went away. It was the oddest thing. She took offense quite suddenly four months ago and left us all in a lurch — Adam and me, that is."

More sparks but no fire. I cringed. "Perhaps your brother should bring a flame from the hearth."

"Nonsense. Adam will manage. Won't you, dear? Hopefully before he burns down the room." Again that nervous laugh. "Such an existence I could never have imagined a few short years ago. Charles would have been mortified to see me like this, reduced to a pauper. He would never have stood for it. He expected the best always, particularly for me."

She cast a tense glance behind me but smiled easily enough. "Ah, that's it, Adam. Wonderful. We shall be so much more comfortable with a fire."

I dipped my chin. "Have you told Lewis of your troubles?"

Adam took a sulphur match and lit a series of candles that brought light into the hazy room.

Isabell seemed pleased. "We have been far too busy of late, planning parties and such, to take our grievances to Lewis. He is not always receptive, my dear, but regardless of whether it makes him angry, I shall be forced do so directly. In part, I suppose, I didn't wish to burden him. First the murder of Mr. Drake, then the unrest in town. He has been saddled with a great deal of trouble over the past few weeks, and he was never as steady as his brother."

Adam trudged from the room, probably to get the requested tea, and I took the opportunity for a tête-à-tête, leaning in. "Isabell, I apologize for my sudden arrival, but I needed to speak to you about something in particular today."

Her sweet little mouth paused in the shape of an O.

I thought she would do very well on the stage at Covent Garden. "It's about Jacob."

She looked a bit dazed, a breathy laugh slipping out with her words. "What could I possibly know about Jacob that you are not already aware of?"

I'd placed Isabell's letter in Jacob's satinwood box in my room beside the handkerchief and the button. The words she had written, not only about my brother but Lewis, still burned in my chest. "I understand you knew Jacob well. You've hinted at such before."

She shifted in her seat, that edgy glance darting around. "We were friends. He was quite charming, and I was indeed lonely here." She stood and crossed the room to the fire before utilizing the poker to encourage a blaze. "He liked to visit me and make me laugh. He said it lit my eyes. We got on quite well together. There is no one like your brother."

"No. I miss him a great deal."

On the tail of my words, the room fell into an unnatural silence. I had to remind myself to relax my shoulders, but it was difficult to fight the eerie feeling that Isabell and I were not alone, that somewhere in the blackened corridors of the small house lurked someone — watching us. Adam, perhaps? I rubbed the chill from my arms at the same moment a creak sounded from beyond the wall.

Isabell gave a little gasp and went rather pale, but she hid her momentary discomfort in a stroll across the room. "I do wonder where Adam is with the tea."

She was frightened, and the crack to her practiced ease caused me to hasten my words. "If I may, I would like to ask you something a bit more delicate. About what we spoke of before . . . when you identified my brother's body."

She turned away from me, her hands shaking. "It was horrible. I-I don't like to think on that time."

"Please." I stood as well and drew nearer to the fire. "I can understand your hesitance, how difficult this must be for you to even remember, but it's vastly important."

"I do remember." Her eyes flashed. "Quite vividly."

"Yes. I imagine you do." I lifted my brows. "Is there anything that has come to mind since we last spoke, anything odd . . . with his body?"

There was a peculiar stillness about her. Her eyes seemed fixed in place, unblinking as she spoke. Only her fingers moved, twitching at her side. "I remember he was swollen all over, his beautiful hair in patches. I was wholly unprepared for what I saw that day."

She reached to steady herself on the mantel, closing her eyes. "He was wearing the waistcoat I had given him as a present just a few weeks before the accident. It was stained with blood, Rebecca — blood." Her hands covered her face. "And now you ask me to relive such a moment." Her frame shook as she moved to regain control of her emotions and pulled away from me. "I should like to sit back down. I've not been well for the past few days, and such questions are a trial for my nerves."

My stomach tensed. "Perhaps I should go and fetch your brother?"

Her eyes flashed open. "Certainly not." Then she waved her hand at the open door. "He is useless, as you well know." She seemed to recover rather quickly. "I've only the headache and a bit of low spirits."

Low spirits indeed. "Perhaps I should be on my way and return another day."

Her nervous laugh again. "Nonsense, there is no need for that. I am glad you came. I see now that I have sorely neglected you, and I shall be sure to visit you at Greybourne Hall quite regularly now. That is, until you've a change of address. Perhaps to Mr. Galpin's country estate?"

I stiffened, responding as if I'd not heard her last question. "I will be certain to mention to Lewis your need of a housekeeper on my return. I know he will agree it necessary to engage one at once."

Her hand clenched at her side. "That is very kind of you." Then, almost as an afterthought, "So thoughtful and quick. You do amaze me." She made a move for the door.

I was running out of time, and I'd discovered little of what I'd come for. I spoke quickly. "Did Jacob come here frequently before his death?"

She paused, blinking. "Nearly every week, I suppose. We enjoyed talking of politics and the like. He made everything sound vastly exciting."

Though she smiled and dipped her shoulder as if amused, something in the room shifted. Like a wave, the hair on my arms rose to attention. Another creak sounded from the shadowed hall. The candle on the table before me flashed as if a subtle whoosh of air played with the flame, but again no one emerged from that part of the house.

I couldn't help but look that direction. "Have you a great many rooms to keep up here?"

She didn't answer, her own gaze trained to the darkened corridor as well.

I asked again, "Have you many rooms to tend to?"

Her hand found her throat. "Oh no, my dear, all the bedchambers on the upper floor are under Holland covers. Adam and I keep up but a few."

My eyes widened. A lie. I'd caught her in a lie, for I had seen the room through the telescope. Why the secrecy? Pounding footsteps caused my jaw to clench.

It was Adam, of course, a languid grin across his face. "No tea today, m'dear. I'm 'fraid I ain't no cook. I 'spect it's back to the inn for dinner, or Galpin's again."

Isabell met my eyes before turning to her brother. "You make it sound as if we are incapable of cold meat and bread. Heavens, we shall do well enough here, or it's nothing but a quick carriage ride to dinner." Her eyes rounded on me. "I am sorry I cannot offer you anything further, my dearest Rebecca."

I was being dismissed. As I followed her to the door, something popped into my mind that ceased my steps.

"Isabell, before I go, I should like to meet the cat you and your brother spoke of in the drawing room a while back."

The evening brought Lewis home, and I found him poring over his desk in the library, a stern look upon his brow. I took in a cleansing breath in the doorway, for it was time to acknowledge my hasty venture to the dower house.

Certainly, there had been no cat presented by Isabell or Adam, and I was not surprised. Adam had laughed, but the look on Isabell's face worried me that I had pushed her too far. After all, Lewis had warned me not to go there.

Lewis motioned for me to enter, and I took a quick glance into the empty hall before pulling the door closed. "I may have done a foolish thing, but I couldn't help it."

"Of course you couldn't." A smile tugged at the corner of his mouth. "Good evening, Rebecca. I hope you are well." He tossed the quill pen he'd been holding onto the desk, his blue eyes smarting in the window's soft light. "What is it now, little badger? Have I a small fire to put out? Or is it more of a blaze?"

I strolled to the desk, keeping my fledgling irritation under control. I would not let him put me off stride, particularly when he looked so handsome sitting there like the king of England. "Well, you don't have to act all superior and whatnot. I made the conscious choice not to follow your instructions is all."

"Indeed?"

I dipped my chin. "I have been to see Isabell . . . at the dower house."

His brows peaked. "And?"

"I have much to tell you."

He gathered up some items before making his way around the desk. "Please, take a seat by the fire. I have something to discuss with you as well." He waited for me to sit before settling into a nearby chair.

It took all my willpower to let him get comfortable before launching into the story burning on my tongue.

I daresay the wretch knew he was making me wait and enjoyed every minute of it, his mouth quirking into a smile as he finally rested his arm on the armrest. "So tell me, what did you learn on your ill-advised journey to the dower house?"

"Well, first of all, were you aware Isabell and Adam are living in reduced circumstances? There are no servants in the entire house. Not a one!"

He froze for a second. "I find that hard to believe. After all, I've been paying for not only a housekeeper and cook but an upstairs maid as well — regularly."

"No servants have been there for some time. I can certainly attest to that. The house was a disheveled mess. Isabell said the housekeeper left months ago."

He narrowed his eyes. "I cannot imagine Isabell or her industrious brother managing without help, although we have seen very little of them in the last few weeks."

"I believe Mr. Galpin has been hosting them for meals."

"But what of the money I sent last week?"

I met his level glare. "Perchance it has

found its way to someone else."

He touched his forehead. "Indeed, you may be right. What else did you learn?"

I bit my lip. "Please, don't be angry with me."

"Rebecca." My name had turned into a whisper. He leaned forward and briefly touched my hand. "You say things sometimes, and I find I am at a loss as to whether you are simply being silly or you actually believe them. You know very well I could never be angry with you." He shrugged as he sat back. "Well, not really angry."

Trapped in his honest gaze, the room felt suddenly small. "I know. I do. I-I tend to ramble when I'm nervous. I wasn't thinking." He nodded. I felt fortified by that calming way of his, as if he were the only person who lay outside of my pressing troubles, a constant amid turmoil. A friend. My gaze fell to his lips and the memory of his kiss. No, not a friend.

He smiled. "Don't be nervous."

My heart responded as my cheeks filled with warmth. I was quite certain Lewis had uncovered what he'd been searching for since that moment on the lawn — the truth that I cared for him. Well, I did, and unfortunately no amount of rationalizing on my part was going to talk me out of it.

I had to be careful. Hiding from my own emotions, I picked a spot on the wall to focus on and told him what I'd seen through the telescope, what I'd experienced at the house.

At length, Lewis retrieved the journal I'd seen in his room and flicked open the first page. "Some time ago, I began following Adam's movements." He tapped the book. "As I told you before, I've been aware that someone hereabouts is involved with the French."

"How could you know that?"

"I thought it best not to tell you the whole before to protect your safety, but I cannot keep this hidden from you any longer." He tapped some papers in his lap. "I've just heard from my people in London, and the time has come for you to be apprised of everything." He met my eyes. "As you probably know, the villagers hereabout like to call me the midnight devil, but the truth is quite the opposite. I have been working with a group of men involved with the British government, who are determined to ferret out a treasonous spying network they have tracked through this area for some time. We utilize different ways of coming about our information. One of our main focuses at present is His Majesty's mail."

I crossed my arms, my mouth falling open. "So, you are a spy . . . for Britain. How? Why?"

He gave me a rather halting look. "It is a bit difficult to explain."

I leaned in. "I would appreciate it if you would try."

He took a deep breath. "After Charles died, I had a hard time coming to terms with his sudden death. I found myself retreating little by little within the walls of Greybourne, but my self-imposed isolation only worked to torment me. A friend of mine, Mr. Sinclair, offered me an unusual escape from my pain — spying." A slight smile lit his eyes. "The first night I rode out with Sinclair changed everything. I had a purpose. I had a means of channeling my sadness and anger into something that could help others. I owe him my life."

I had sensed something genuine and kind about Lewis, but in that moment I believe I finally understood him. His reservation didn't spring from being cold or inhospitable like Jacob had written in his letters. No. He was a product of tragedy. Like me, Lewis had simply learned to guard his feelings as best he could. He had to — to survive. The subsequent responsibility for Jacob's accident could not have been an easy weight to bear, and the townspeople had been cruel in their ignorance.

He seemed to follow my thoughts. "After your brother's death, I decided only to ride at night. I would not upset the townspeople any further."

"And the post office?"

"Though we have a man stationed in Deal, we have been forced to stage additional robberies of mail carriages and postal offices looking for anything that might identify the insidious network of French spies. They could be anyone, Rebecca. British citizens. Nobility. Commoners."

"Why would anyone risk death in such a way?"

"The reward can be sweet." A shrewd look filled his eyes. "Shortly before your brother's death, one of my fellow spies caught a man in Plattsdale who had been fleeing exposure to the coast, intending to return to France. He spoke of his own colleague whom he was to shelter with in town, but he could give us nothing conclusive, neither about this spy's identity nor what he looked like.

"I began to suspect Adam immediately. He kept far too many unsavory friends in the neighborhood, and Isabell expressed her worry about him to me at one time. But after following him for weeks, I discovered nothing, so I turned my search elsewhere. Soon, I had located a currier in Reedwick. I'd found the cursed French spy at last, and the night before your brother's death, I got a shot off, but after an exhaustive search, I never found the man's body. He must have escaped, injured or otherwise." The grief-stricken choke returned to Lewis's voice. "After learning what I have of the events of the following night and speaking with you, I begin to ask myself, could Jacob have been killed by this same man — the spy I never found?"

I sat up rigid, my thoughts racing. "The rag I saw at the dower house. The man I glimpsed from my window so late at night. You saw him, too, the night Aunt Jo and I arrived. Is he pretending to be you?"

"And we arrive at the same conclusion." He gave me a wan smile. "If this man were to use a similar rag, everyone in town would simply assume he was me, giving him free passage at night. I rarely use a mask here locally, but I do when I plan to leave the area. Our group doesn't work with the local authorities. Anonymity makes things far simpler." He rubbed his chin. "Your discovery through the telescope only strengthens my assumption about Jacob's murder. Accident or not, French spies were likely involved in his death."

"But how do you think Isabell fits in to all this? And Mr. Drake?"

He angled his chin. "I'm not certain. Drake had no love for the French. Maybe he saw something. I just don't know. But the activity that was in Plattsdale months ago has since moved to Reedwick. I have had a difficult time getting anywhere." He pressed his palm against his forehead. "I expect I shall have to keep searching." He grasped my hand. "But for now, I want you out of all this. If Isabell is indeed involved and thinks you have pieced something together, you may not be safe."

I opened my mouth to argue, but he shook his head before I could speak. "No. Not this time, little badger. You must allow me to do the digging. I will not risk your life."

"Where does that leave me, sitting in the drawing room perhaps?"

His thumb grazed my wrist. "Spend some time with your aunt. Enjoy the details of her wedding. It is only a few days away after all. I will be sure to tell you if I learn anything new. Now is not the moment to press things. Allow Isabell time to feel at ease. Trust me. I know how to handle her."

CHAPTER 24

The day of Aunt Jo's wedding was nothing but beautiful. The precious sunlight bathed the ground in warmth and sent droplets of dew sparkling along the front path to the church. The crisp morning air lent a spring to our steps and a happy caper to Aunt Jo's walk. Though she had been reserved within the carriage, I knew she was full of nervous energy.

Lewis and I accompanied her into the church, where Mr. Fernside took his place at her side, glowing. It was affecting watching them exchange their vows, two people embarking on a journey of life together with so much hope and love. At length, we each signed the register and embarked for Greybourne Hall where we'd further celebrations planned.

Lewis and I followed in his carriage alone, and it was the first real moment I felt bereft of Aunt Jo's company. I had been with

Lewis alone often enough, but never like this. Aunt Jo was Mrs. Fernside now. I had no companion at present, and regardless of what we did about that, as Aunt Jo had said, my relationship with Lewis would inevitably change along with everything else.

He remained silent across from me, keeping his head turned to the window. It was I who broke the cloying stillness. "Well, what do you intend to do with me now?" I asked in something of a light humor but followed up with more feeling than I meant to show. "Am I to stay at Greybourne Hall as you suggested?"

I'm not certain he meant to broach the subject just then, as my questions seemed to catch him off guard. "I have been giving your situation some more thought. There are a few different options to consider."

I didn't like the way he emphasized the word *different.*

"I have a cousin who writes that she might be willing to come for a month or two, but I'm afraid I have found no one who will be willing to stay on indefinitely. That is, if you would not rather return to London." He tried a smile. "And I don't mean to set up your own establishment."

I shook my head, tears threatening. "You know I don't . . . not for the season anyway."

He was well aware of where I stood on that particular topic. "At this point, I would rather be close to my aunt."

He tapped his leg. "I can certainly engage someone to come here, but it will take some time to employ a companion, to do the due diligence of inquiring after her character." He touched his forehead, and I could tell he found such an option as unpalatable as I did. "And I have had some difficulty of late finding people willing to work under my roof."

I dipped my chin. "Because of the murders?"

"Yes." He gave a halfhearted shrug. "My reputation is effectively lost, but I suppose there are always people who are desperate."

Then I noticed sweat at his temples. Strange, for the shadowed chill of the carriage left me quivering in the cold. He adjusted his jacket, first one direction then the next, running his fingers down his breeches in a vain attempt to find something for them to do.

"Rebecca, there is one more option I have been considering. That is, do you think . . ." His hand went to the back of his neck, a curious expression flooding his face.

Shaken by his sudden turn of behavior, I waited for him to continue, dreading what might come.

"You will think me mad." He took a tremulous breath as he leaned forward. "But would it serve, do you think? Rather, would you consider taking my name? It would answer nicely to our current predicament, and" — he met my gaze — "believe me when I say you would never be asked for anything further."

I stared at him in a sort of daze until my hands found my lips. "You mean a marriage of convenience?"

Now that his plan was out, he seemed to relax. "Why not?"

I studied his eyes, grasping for what lay behind the unexpected offer. All at once, my heart pounded. "This is not for my father, is it? A deathbed promise, perhaps?"

He shoved his hand down to the seat, causing a loud thump. Then he hesitated. "No, it is not."

The gravel crunched beneath the wheels. A muted squeak ebbed below the rocking of the carriage. Greybourne Hall rose up in the window like a black cloud. Could I be mistress of the rambling structure before me, destined to face Lewis day after day with no hope of ever being intimate? My body felt heavy as I imagined the opposite — a life in London. How would I be expected to interact with society? How long would I have before I followed my mother's footsteps? My eyes flashed open. More importantly, how could I possibly leave Lewis? Had I ever really thought I could?

And what of him? He was still young and handsome. An eligible match for many young ladies, regardless of his tainted reputation. That had all been exaggerated at any rate. No one in London had ever mentioned such a thing. I looked up into his earnest face and forced myself to ask the one question I didn't wish to know the answer to. "What if you find love with someone else?"

His eyes narrowed. "I have given up any possibility of that."

The finality in his voice sent a shiver winding through my bones, and I shook my head. He was wrong. He needed love, companionship. Didn't we all?

He held up his hand, staving off any sort of a rebuttal. "You needn't answer at once. Nor worry you might offend me. I don't want an impulsive answer. However, you know we haven't long to make a decision." His eyes pinched at the corners. "I have already procured a special license just in case you were in agreement."

A special license? Suddenly his proposal

felt even more real . . . more *desirable*? I looked to the floor as I shook my head. What was wrong with me? Was I actually considering his offer?

His voice was soft. "Rebecca, look at me."

Slowly, I lifted my eyes.

"I don't want you to leave."

The carriage drew to a sudden halt and the door flung open. The footman, eager to help me down, extended his arm, but I knew I couldn't depart without giving Lewis an answer. My heart thundered in my chest, and my hand quivered as I gripped the seat, but somehow I managed to meet his searching gaze.

"I will be pleased to accept your offer of marriage." I cast him a tentative smile and fled the carriage.

The wedding breakfast passed in a whirlwind of smiles and well wishes. The party was no crush, however, remaining firmly on the small side with so few of Fernside's friends willing to overlook the location. Isabell and Adam brought their usual acquaintances and presided over the room as always. Isabell in particular looked as keen as ever, the dark circles gone from beneath her eyes, the willowy bend to her arms attractive in her pale blue gown.

Though we said few words throughout the affair, she sought me out as soon as Aunt Jo and Mr. Fernside made their exit. I was emotional and cross, and all I wished for was the privacy of my bedchamber to have a good cry.

She settled her slender fingers on my arm. "I imagine you will be lonely without your aunt. Have you made any plans as of yet?"

I couldn't miss the twinkle in her eyes. She actually thought I was considering Mr. Galpin. I enjoyed giving her a tight smile. "My cousin has given me a very fine offer —"

Her pink tongue flit across her lips. "Is it London then? I shall be terribly jealous if that is true."

"I have no plans to leave Greybourne Hall. I —"

Her brows shot up. "Then what can you possibly be alluding to? Another companion perhaps? If so, I have been doing some thinking, and after speaking with Adam, I would like to offer my services. I see now how much you need a woman's guiding hand."

I stared for a moment, unable to process her words.

"Wouldn't it be wonderful?" She took both my hands. "We would get on famously,

I know, and Adam won't miss me a fig. I could have my things packed and moved within an hour or two. Now what do you say to that?"

I shot a darting glance at Lewis, who stood watching us from across the room. Did he know about Isabell's scheme? I didn't think so. And why on earth would she want to move to the hall? There had to be an ulterior motive. She would not want me watching her every move. Unless, she intended to watch mine.

Something cultivated in those eyes of hers. "Shall we go and tell Lewis together? He will be so pleased we have worked out all his troubles."

"No." I pulled back. "You didn't allow me to finish."

Her busy fingers came to rest on her throat. "Oh?"

"I have decided to accept Lewis's offer of marriage. We shall be wed as soon as possible by a special license."

The hint of a smile lifted the corner of her mouth as her eyes sought her brother. At first, she stood unnaturally still. Then as if on cue, she swayed on her feet and managed a pitiful, "Oh," before fainting onto Lewis's parquet floor in a dramatic heap of pale blue muslin.

■ ■ ■ ■

It took some time to revive Isabell. Smelling salts proved ineffective. When Sophie emerged from her prison at the back of the house and pressed her wet tongue firmly against Isabell's ivory cheek, it proved just the thing. She was up in an instant, gasping and batting her hands in the air before moping her way to the settee where she declared she had never been treated in such a fashion in her entire life. Considering she lived with Adam, I found that difficult to believe.

Lewis deemed it prudent to send for the doctor, and when the pudgy man arrived from Plattsdale, much to Isabell's apparent frustration, he lifted his spectacles and vowed her fit enough to return to the dower house under her brother's care. I wondered if Lewis caught the irritation in her voice or the muscles that tensed in her jaw when she thanked the doctor for his prodigious care. She'd been fully prepared to stay the night.

I would have enjoyed the show immensely if Aunt Jo had not just walked out of my life, I'd not just agreed to a convenient marriage, and the unsolved murders did not hang heavy over our heads. It was an unearthly moment, really, my life so horribly unsettled.

Lewis saw Isabell home, and for the first time since I'd arrived at Greybourne Hall I found myself alone — completely alone. Unsure what to do with myself, I sought the refuge of my bedchamber and the soft comfort of my pillow.

Aunt Jo came to mind almost instantly. I could not have asked for a better caretaker or friend. Mr. Fernside, of course, would be infinitely preferable over me to live out her dotage considering all my silly starts and ridiculous plans. She would be living in a library after all. Heaven. And we would not be separated forever. I was going to marry Lewis. Aunt Jo and I would be neighbors.

It was strange how the decision had flowed so easily off my tongue after years of fighting the idea of such a thing. Of course, it would not be a real marriage, only one on paper — even though I loved him. And oh, how I loved him — his searching eyes, the way his hair curled at the nape of his neck, the ever-changing countenance, which only sought to conceal a fine character few understood — one of strength, loyalty, and sacrifice.

I suppose that was the crux of it. I trusted Lewis to care for me when I could not, to hold to his word as a gentleman. There were few men whom I could have trusted in such a way . . . perhaps only the one.

I rolled onto my back on the luxurious bed. What would Jacob have thought of my sudden alliance? Lewis and he were so different. Jacob had always been driven by passion; Lewis sought truth in a steady way. They were never friends.

I rose to my feet and tiptoed across the rug, its fibers tickling my bare skin. My maid had left me a rolling fire, and I lingered in the heat for a long moment, breathing in the pleasant scent of woodsmoke. Before long my gaze traveled to the mantelpiece and Jacob's satinwood box. I took it in my hands and crawled back on the bed, dumping the pieces out on the coverlet. One, two, three. The handkerchief, the button, the letter — the clues I'd spent weeks collecting.

I hadn't the least notion of what secrets they held, or what on earth the person was looking for who had rummaged through my room. The items blurred before me as my mind wandered from one idea to the next. Why had Isabell suggested a move here to Greybourne Hall?

Her histrionics would suggest she wanted to be close to Lewis, that she hid an intense love for him, but I knew that wasn't true. The more I thought about her ridiculous movements, the more I could see the act.

If she meant to spend the night at Greybourne, she, too, must be looking for something. I thought back through days of actions and conversations, all I'd discovered, listing them off as if the key to the mystery lay somewhere buried within my mind. Lewis had called it a puzzle. Maybe I only needed to fit the correct pieces together to make sense of it all.

Isabell was certainly the corner piece, but what made up the four sides?

I began with what I knew. Two men were killed nine months apart, possibly in the same brutal way, certainly at the same spot.

Ellen wrote that Jacob had acted strangely before his death, as Isabell and Adam were now. Jacob had also come to Greybourne because he was in debt. He despised Lewis. And the night before he died, Mr. Galpin claimed Jacob was shouting about Lewis. What caused this sudden anger? Lewis's opinion had no bearing on Jacob, unless . . .

I jerked myself upright, a sudden thought taking root in my mind. Unless Lewis's ongoing spy work implicated Jacob in some way. My pulse raced. Restlessly, I shifted my hands through the covers before stopping dead still, my eyes trained to the window.

What if Isabell knew that Jacob was involved with the French?

But Mr. Drake had been killed as well. He was certainly no French spy. I suppose he could have learned something, something that put him in danger, but he was great friends with Lewis. He certainly would have told him if he'd learned anything, particularly about Jacob.

My mind raced back to the afternoon I spent at the dower house with Isabell and Adam. I'd been on edge because I'd sensed that someone else might be in the house — a presence we all sought to ignore, hidden in the shadows. The servants! Why hadn't I made the connection before? Isabell would have had to turn them all out if someone had taken refuge in her home — there would have to be no witnesses.

Desperately, I thought back through every moment I had experienced with Isabell. When I first told her of Mr. Drake's death, she had been shocked — genuine or an act? I wasn't sure. Regardless, she raced home to tell Adam. Adam, of all people? I couldn't imagine her valuing her brother in such a way, nor him being the least concerned about Lewis's solicitor. My mouth slipped open. Or perhaps Isabell rushed home to discuss it with someone else — the person in the bedchamber.

Riding on a wave of rapid heartbeats and exhilaration, I smoothed a stray hair from my face. I was getting closer to the truth.

The money — Isabell had taken money from Lewis for the servants. Could she be using it for something else?

And what about Sophie? She had been missing for a whole day.

What of Mr. Galpin? Could he be involved as well? He did want Greybourne Hall for his own. He would have had the opportunity and the means, though he would not be hiding at Isabell's.

I ran Jacob's button through my fingers as every word Isabell and I spoke in her sitting room came back to me in painful detail. She had been afraid, her nerves bound tight as a cord. She was a ghost of her former self. Conceivably something was not going as she had thought it would. They had not wanted me in that house.

Adam had been used as a foil for Lewis before, the night he was drugged, in fact. And that day, Adam had performed a ridiculous welcoming act. He'd distracted me for several minutes, and then I'd been offered tea. A cold shiver wriggled across my shoulders. Lewis had been right. I never should have gone there alone.

I pressed my fingers against my forehead, the initial spark of discovery transforming into a pounding ache. There had to be a clue that would launch the other pieces into place. What exactly had Isabell said in that sitting room? Something about Jacob visiting there often, how he made her laugh, and . . .

Jacob. My heart stilled as my gaze was seized by an item on the bed. Could it be? No. My head shook of its own accord as inwardly I screamed out a denial.

The room narrowed, the darkness growing hazy around me, almost as if I were experiencing another one of my spells, but it was not so. This was real — terribly real. My muscles tensed. My breath came out in ragged puffs. Feverishly, I reached for the handkerchief and spread it out on the bed, my quivering finger tracing the embroidered *B* over and over again.

My mind was finally in a position to digest the truth.

I would never find Jacob's killer, because Jacob was not dead.

CHAPTER 25

Jacob Bamber Hunter.

The words cut through my mind like a sharp dagger, leaving a trail of devastation in their wake. I had never even considered the fact that Jacob had the letter *B* in his name, nor that he could have lost his button in Lewis's sitting room while searching it recently.

Lewis said Jacob had taken a shot at him that night on the bridge. Isabell identified the body. Mr. Fernside said the face was not recognizable. I fought against the puzzle pieces that fit so nicely together.

People say thoughts can be as painful as fists, and I knew very well memories were. I'd seen much in my twenty years. The realization of the truth of Jacob's deception was unlike anything I'd ever felt before.

Nine months prior, his death left a gaping hole in my heart. I'd been robbed of not only a brother but a friend. The moment I realized Jacob may have left me on purpose, the hurt was just as acute and each subsequent thought far sharper than the last. Everything I thought I knew could be one horrible lie after another. If *this* were true, Jacob didn't love me at all, perhaps never had, and with one selfish decision, he'd stolen not only my future but my past as well.

I fought the truth well into the wee hours of the morning, but in the end, I could not rescind my conclusions; they only took root and grew deeper.

Jacob was the missing piece.

He was the one whistling in the night when I thought it was a bird. Who else would know my mother's song? Was he taunting me?

He must have also visited my bedchamber. I thought at the time I'd seen my mother, that it had been another one of my spells — Jacob's and mother's facial features were always so alike. Even Sophie would have remembered Jacob from the time he visited us in London.

I could hardly discern the particulars of exactly what happened the night of his supposed death, but Lewis had seen him fall from the bridge and was forced to live with the guilt of it all these months. Jacob's deceit injured more than me. And he had fled the area, possibly even England, because whether I wanted to admit it or not, Jacob was in all likelihood the French spy Lewis was looking for.

My fingers balled into fists. It all made sense — perfect sense. I could almost scream for not seeing it earlier. My indelible brother had always loved a cause, particularly one that worshiped a leader who had risen to power from humble beginnings. Napoleon had taken Europe by his own talent, shouting a pledge of social reform. Equality was indeed a concept to fight for, if it was not an empty promise. Like many others, Jacob had evidently fallen prey to Napoleon's grand schemes.

But why had he come back into Plattsdale at the height of the war? It had nothing to do with any familial feelings he harbored for me. Clearly, I was a bother he didn't mean to waste time worrying over. The thought hurt, but if I was to be honest with myself, it was not a new one. Everything had always been about him — all my life. Mother's favorite, Father's most despised. The heir. The idealist. Too bad his passionate whims led him to being taken in by a liar.

My mix of disappointment and relief at

Jacob being alive took a dark turn when I thought of Mr. Drake. Lewis's solicitor had been outside of all this, but there was one thing that might have gotten him killed — seeing Jacob alive. I closed my eyes and drew in a long breath. Deep within my core I still fought for my brother's innocence. Surely Jacob would never do such a thing. But in my heart I began to wonder if he could. If he thought the deed was only part of a bigger war, he might rationalize such a brutal death, and the remains of his handkerchief proved he'd been there, right where Mr. Drake's lifeless body had been dragged into place with the express purpose of casting doubt on Lewis's innocence.

What about the man who lay at the church beneath the gravestone with Jacob's name? Someone died in his place. Jacob could have easily slipped his waistcoat around another man and planted him downstream of the bridge. He'd had a few days to decide what was best to be done. And the scar? Isabell must have been involved as well.

I found my way back to the bed in a muddled haze and collapsed onto my pillow. In all likelihood, Jacob was even now at the dower house, plotting his next move.

The sun had peeked over my bedchamber's

window ledge long before I found sleep. And due to the late hour and troubled night, I didn't even wake when my maid lit the fire first thing in the morning, nor when she returned a good deal later to present my chocolate. Well, that is until the tray clattered against the desk as she set it down, triggering one of my spells.

Scrambling to my feet in a flurry of desperate confusion, I flung my fists for several steps before tripping over the edge of the coverlet. The fall brought me roaring to my senses, stunned by what I imagined I'd seen, what had disappeared into a haunting memory — Jacob with a rope looped about his hand. Tabby helped me back to my feet and properly ignored my strange behavior. Shaking as I sat on the bed's edge, I allowed my heartbeat to calm before managing a tepid, "Thank you."

It was just as well that Tabby should be privy to my secret. If I were to stay at Greybourne Hall, this would not be the last time she would witness one of my spells. I needed a friend, for Lewis would not be running into my bedchamber at night whenever it was needed. Aunt Jo had always known just what to say and do to calm me down.

Tabby nodded at my instructions, her face curiously placid. "Don't you worry, ma'am.

I'm awfully good at helping people after terrors at night. My mother had such things all the time. Drove us all to distraction, what with the screaming and all. We learned what helped her, and then it was not so hard to deal with."

I took a sip of hot chocolate. "What happened later? Was she sent to an asylum?"

"Cor, no! For a few bad dreams?"

I looked up. "You mean they didn't get worse when she was older?"

She shook her head. "Not at all. I suppose she still has 'em on occasion, but it's nothing to fret over."

For a delightful moment I believed her, considering what she'd said with all my hopes and dreams. But Tabby did not have my mother, who had most certainly gone mad. Our situations could not be compared.

I allowed her to dress me and leave before I, too, made my way down the stairs in search of Lewis. I located him in the drawing room at his desk, addressing a letter. He looked a bit drawn. His eyes lacked their usual directness. His face was a bit sallow in the morning light.

I walked to the window and leaned against the frame. "Good morning."

He stood but hesitated before responding. "Where were you last night?"

My brows drew in. "In my bedchamber, where else?"

He sighed. "I meant at dinner. I had Cook wait for you initially."

"Oh, no." My heart lurched. "I do apologize. I didn't realize you would be at home for dinner. You so rarely are. I should have thought."

His gaze sharpened. "I would never leave you to dine alone on the very day your aunt left Greybourne Hall." He looked away. "Rebecca, if I've caused you distress by my proposal, please allow me to —"

I touched his arm. "No, please, I was distracted is all. My mind was elsewhere. Oh, Lewis, I've been terribly thoughtless, but once you understand why" — I fumbled with my fingers at my waist — "I think I know who killed Mr. Drake."

"What do you mean?" His eyes rounded, that boyish determination I'd seen before taking over his face.

I forced my frantic nerves under control, using the wall to steady me. "I spent the whole of the evening digging through all we've learned about Jacob's murder, and I have come at a possible answer to our mystery." I hesitated but only for a moment. "I do not believe Jacob is dead."

He stared at me for several seconds, not

even blinking. "Impossible. I saw him fall from that bridge and float away with my own eyes." Then angrily. "Trust me, the scene is seared into my memory." He paused, frantically searching the room for answers. "What led you to believe such a thing?"

Carefully, I recounted all I'd pieced together the previous night before holding up the handkerchief. "I didn't recognize it at first due to all the stains, but I do now. My father gave it to him on his sixteenth birthday. It was a favorite of his." I crushed it into a ball. "No one else could have taken possession of it. And it places him near Mr. Drake's body."

Lewis withdrew into silence before shaking his head. "The handkerchief could have been left in that tree long before Jacob's death."

"Do you think so? Nine months or more? I cannot believe it would remain in such a pliable shape. Wind, rain, heat, snow. The fabric would not be so well preserved." I took a deep breath. "You asked me one time if Jacob had connections in France. Well, he didn't, not to my knowledge anyway, but he did think quite highly of French ideals. He grew up intending to take a grand tour, then the war raged on, and he was forced to remain in London by my father. At one time, he even sent me a book on social change he liked that was written in French."

Lewis shook his head. "Still, I find it difficult to believe Jacob is the man I've searched for all along. Remember, I had taken a shot at the person I believed responsible one night before Jacob's death. I'm fairly certain I hit him, even if it didn't kill him." He angled his chin. "Yet I will admit what you say is possible. And Drake, how do you suppose he plays into all this?"

"I am not entirely certain about Mr. Drake. However, I am convinced that Jacob is alive, has returned, and is residing at the dower house this very minute. I also imagine he's the intruder who has been making use of Greybourne Hall, searching the rooms whenever he can. He would be the only one with a taste for Father's port and the knowledge of where it was kept. He probably assumed it well hidden before Sophie nosed it up."

I could tell Lewis was coming about, the evidence overwhelming his earlier reticence. He fiddled with the signet ring on his left hand. "Let us suppose for a moment you are right. How do you presume Jacob survived the fall? My horse struck him quite hard into the River Grey. I am certain of that."

I took a measured breath. "I have given that a great deal of thought. As we have pondered, what if you were given some sort of a drug? You might have been fooled into thinking you knocked him from the bridge to his death, but in fact, he simply swam to safety out of sight. After all, why else were you unable to find his body? Unless he walked away from it all."

"It was foggy . . . and I did hit Jacob. But you are also forgetting the gunshot. I believed at the time it was the man I had shot the previous night. The known French spy."

I waited before glancing up. "You are assuming that there was another person at the bridge, yet you yourself admitted you saw no one else."

The muscles tightened in Lewis's jaw. "Jacob."

"Yes, as you said, Jacob took the shot. His fall from the bridge might not have been entirely planned, but he made use of it all the same."

Lewis nodded. "And I cannot be certain exactly what happened afterward, for I have very little memory of the search even though I'm told it went on throughout the night."

I grasped his hand. "There is only one way

to know for sure."

He cocked an eyebrow.

"We'll have to ask him."

He leveled a glare at me. "A surprise visit to the dower house?"

"Perhaps, or something else. Jacob's not leaving until he finds what he's come for."

"No, indeed. He took a great risk in returning to Plattsdale. It must have been for something important."

"Precisely. And I mean to find whatever it is before he does."

"But what is it? Do you have any idea what he is looking for?"

"No, but it must be something I possess without the knowledge of it. Remember, he went to the townhouse in London first, assuming whatever it is would still be there before he made his way to Plattsdale. Then once here, he went directly to search my room before starting in on the other parts of the house. In all likelihood he's getting desperate. And if Isabell's tortured demeanor proves an example of her own state of mind, I'd say she's feeling the same strain."

Lewis led me to the sofa and took a seat at my side, resting his elbows on his knees. "What exactly did you bring with you when you came to Greybourne Hall?"

"Very little, I'm afraid. Some personal items, my journal, little else. Most of the clothes were bought before we left."

"And your aunt?"

"Nothing of any consequence. I have been over every little detail of what I brought — all night, in fact. I begin to think whatever it is might still be at the townhouse."

"Not likely. He gave up rather quickly there, yet he has stayed here searching for some time. He must be certain it was moved."

"At any rate, I shall have to spend some more time thinking. It is merely a riddle that needs solving, and I am determined to do so."

He clutched my hand as a wistful look returned to his eyes. I thought he meant to say something of our marriage, but he turned the conversation. "Two of the men I have been working with are coming to Greybourne Hall this afternoon — the same two who were here the night of your dinner party. With your agreement, I shall tell them of what you know, and we can formulate a plan."

"Together, as in, all of us?"

He smiled. "All right. You may join us, but you do realize you force me to reveal that I've told you all, and after I swore the night of the dinner party that I would not. Even so, your insight will prove invaluable."

"Oh dear. I do not wish to cause you trouble."

He winked. "You are never trouble, Rebecca."

"Just infuriating, I suppose."

He laughed. "How quickly you have learned to read my mind."

I raised my eyebrows. "Well, what else do badgers do, but dig?"

CHAPTER 26

In the end it was only Lord Torrington who arrived at Greybourne Hall late that evening, a look of weary travel about his person, an urgency lining his face. He pushed his way into the library and spoke gruffly over his shoulder to Lewis. "I've come just now from Reedwick, and I've not much time."

It was only after he'd made this statement that he saw me hovering in the shadows, my hands gripped tightly at my waist.

Lewis motioned him forward then turned to me. "May I present the Earl of Torrington?"

I nodded.

"Lord Torrington, my ward, Miss Hunter."

Torrington returned a bow to my curtsy, adding a wry smile. "I did not realize you had company at present. Forgive me."

I could not forget what Aunt Jo had told me of Lord Torrington's character, and I was unable to hold off the warmth that filled my cheeks. He was a handsome man, well-practiced in all that might please a young lady in her first season, but I was no such lady. I took a determined step closer to Lewis and returned Lord Torrington's gaze with one of my own. "Mr. Browning tells me you have come to discuss the French threat."

There was something altogether attractive about Lord Torrington's eyes. "Indeed." He hesitated before carrying on, amused at my words. "Well, Browning, it seems we've a bit more to discuss than I had originally planned." A crease appeared across his forehead, and he crossed the room to the fire, where he warmed his hands in the flickering glow.

Almost as if protective, Lewis escorted me to a chair beside the fender and lurked at my side. "Miss Hunter has recently been apprised of our dealings. There will be no more secrets where she is concerned."

Torrington turned and cocked an eyebrow. "If you think that wise."

Lewis was the quieter of the two men, but his careful words and shrewd bearing demanded respect in a different sort of way. He rested his arm on the mantel at Lord Torrington's side. "I assure you, I do. But first, tell me the news of Sinclair. Why isn't he here?"

Torrington slanted one last look at me before responding, his voice tight. "I'd a letter from him three days past. The dragoons have him sheltered at the Towers for the present as well as his godmother's illness; however, he believes he is close to uncovering something there. I told him to stay put, that you and I would sort out our man here. He promised he would send word to you if help is needed, as I am to return to London as soon as possible. One of my girls is not well."

I was surprised by the mention of daughters. Torrington did not look so very old, and Aunt Jo had led me to believe him a man about town.

Knowles arrived with a tray, halting the conversation until the men had drinks in their hands and the door had swung shut, leaving us once again in tense silence.

Lord Torrington watched me as he took a sip from his glass before he slowly moved into the place Lewis had previously vacated. "I must admit, Miss Hunter, I find myself vastly curious as to your role in all this."

It wasn't what he said, but rather his tone. I cast a quick glance at Lewis before answering. I had no intention of being talked to as if I were a child. "Are you? Then allow me to speak freely. You see before you the sister of Mr. Jacob Hunter, who is currently not dead and is probably spying for the French as we speak."

Torrington's eyes grew wide. "Extraordinary." Then to Lewis. "Tell me, is she always this direct?"

Lewis laughed. "You haven't the half of it."

Torrington nudged him with his elbow. "No wonder you were forced to take her into your confidence." A devious smile transformed his face. "Well . . . if that is the case, I shall sit right here beside you, Miss Hunter, until you've told me everything." Then to Lewis. "What on earth have you been about hiding her away? I do believe she could have had this all figured out some time ago."

The two men shared a quick glance before Lewis dipped his chin. "Easy, Torrington, we've only made the connections today, and there is something else you should be made aware of — she is soon to be my bride." He crossed his arms. "She's no time for a rogue like you."

Lord Torrington's hand flew to his chest. "What a presumption. I vow I was never more shocked." Diversion laced his words.

"If you weren't a friend, Browning, I swear I should call you out immediately." Then to me. "However, I'm also all too aware my reputation precedes me. Perhaps it's best if we get on with the business at hand . . . hmm?" He patted my hand before whispering into my ear, "I promise I'll not tease him any further. You clearly have his heart."

The words were meant in jest, surely, but I could not control how my own heart slowed, pounding like a blacksmith molding an iron bar. Feigning nonchalance, I cleared my throat. "Allow me to tell you about Jacob then."

I recounted everything I'd already revealed to Lewis as quickly as I could. At length, Lord Torrington pulled back, a far more serious look taking over the curves of his face. Caught in that deep gaze, I wondered if my initial assessment had indeed been a bit hasty. There was more to this man than he would have one think. He shook his head. "If what you say is true, I can do nothing but caution any further movements."

"What do you imply?" Lewis asked. "We'll not sit here and wait."

Torrington raised his voice. "Take heed, man. If Mr. Hunter took that shot at you on the bridge, he would vastly prefer to see you dead. After all, an empty house might be far more easily searched than the one at present. And at any rate, Miss Hunter should not stay here any longer until the authorities can be notified."

Lewis paused, considering what he'd said. "I do agree about Miss Hunter, but Jacob has had plenty of opportunity to do me harm over the past few weeks. I do not think it likely he has that in mind. And I will not stand idly by knowing he could kill again at any moment."

I shoved to my feet. "Listen to the two of you — discussing Jacob as if he were a madman. I promise, neither of you could be more wrong. You have to understand my brother to anticipate his next moves. He is not some cold-hearted murderer. He is a man possessed by a cause. Trust me, he would only bring himself to pull the trigger if he thought it necessary and never, ever would he hurt me." I was angry now, driven by the last remaining shred of Hunter pride. "Jacob is not an animal. And I won't leave this house, not now when you need me more than ever."

Lewis reached out and took my hand, gently drawing me near. "It is an uncomfortable business, I know." He glanced down at my fingers resting within his. "I do understand your feelings, Rebecca, perfectly. But will you try to understand mine?" There was a look in his eyes that I had seen before — the night he'd kissed me on the lawn. Had Torrington been right about the depths of Lewis's feelings? He squeezed my hand. "Surely you must see that I cannot allow you to stay here, not when you are in danger." His voice faltered. "After all that has happened, I could not bear it if you were somehow caught up in all this. Please, leave with Lord Torrington in the morning. He will escort you to my cousin in London. She will be pleased to play your host." He was pleading now. "Rebecca, you must do this for me."

The intensity had left my voice. "And what of you?"

"I shall stay here and set a trap for Jacob. This all must end as soon as possible. I've lived under the crushing guilt of his death for the past nine months. I will not allow him the freedom to murder again. For you, for Drake. Jacob must be made to see justice."

I looked down at the floor. "I know." Then back up. "But is it wise to do so without knowing what it is he searches for?"

Lord Torrington stepped forward. "Miss Hunter does have a point there, Browning. Her brother may not be so willing to talk once he is in custody, and this hidden item, what if it could make a difference in the war?"

Lewis raked his hand through his hair. "What do you propose then? Tearing the house apart stone by stone? We may never find what he has hidden here."

"No, but we must at least try. Let us begin by informing me what you have searched thus far. If we could come at the answer tonight, I could notify Whitehall on my return to London."

I motioned to Lewis. "We might avoid an otherwise unpleasant confrontation. We have many hours before daybreak, and I cannot rest until we've done all we can."

The two men discussed every last detail that could prove important, spending a great deal of time on the items at the townhouse before focusing in on Greybourne Hall. I, however, had a hard time concentrating, my mind shifting from the fact that I would be forced to leave on the morrow to Jacob's horrid decisions. At one time, my brother had a brilliant mind. He could have been anything, so why had he chosen so poorly?

I wondered if Mother's departure in his life had caused more pain than I realized at the time. Father was certainly hard on him, and during that same period, my father was in no place to make concessions. Jacob had been as lost as me — lost to his own ambitions.

I thought back through the letters I'd received over the years, particularly the last letter he sent shortly after his visit to the townhouse, the one he'd included with the books he thought I might enjoy reading.

The books. My eyes darted about the room to the shelves filled with the volumes Lewis had shipped from London. Jacob's books. I sprang to my feet and grasped Lewis by the arm. "Where are they all?"

Their conversation halted abruptly, and Lewis stared down at me. "What do you mean?"

"Jacob's books." I pointed to the shelves. "You had them shipped here. Is this all of them?"

"I believe so."

I rushed to the shelf and pulled a few onto the floor. "Check the bindings — every last one." I allowed a hint of a smile as I met Lewis's questioning gaze. "Isabell's letter. Jacob hid it in the binding, remember? He could have done so with something else as well." I tore my gaze back to the books on the floor. "It would make perfect sense. He would have thought the books would still be in London or that I had brought them with me, but they are here . . . all of them."

Lewis knelt at my side and urged Lord Torrington to do so as well. "Quickly."

I showed Lord Torrington where Jacob had separated the binding to slide the letter into its hiding place before grasping the next book to do the same. Minutes passed like a slow-moving dream. Hands flitted over the leather covers and white pages, pulling and tugging. The casement clock ticked at our backs, an ever-present reminder of the time pressing against us.

Nothing. Each book was the same as the last — unadulterated.

Torrington shrugged and grabbed the last book from the top shelf, twisting it in his hands. "I thought you had something there, Miss Hunter. It seems we're at another impasse."

Lewis sat like a statue, his eyes trained to the empty bookcase. "It was a good guess."

I, too, paused, unable to believe we'd checked them all. Then my heart did a little jump in my chest. "Wait. I took *Camilla* upstairs to read a while back. Lewis, did you do so as well, perhaps with another book?"

He shook his head at first, then his eyes grew wide. "I did. *The Rights of Man* by

Thomas Paine." His eyes flashed. "I took it to my room weeks ago and forgot all about it."

Torrington took a deep breath. "Could it be that easy? A book defending the French Revolution?"

Lewis gripped his arm. "Wait here. I shall fetch it at once."

Frozen in place, I listened to Lewis's footsteps as he ascended the stairs, then turned to Lord Torrington. "What do you suppose Jacob's hidden inside?"

Lord Torrington's jaw clenched. "No way to know. Dispatches perhaps, although they would be grossly out of date." He let out a slow breath. "Hopefully it will be something we can use. This little band of spies that has been creeping through Plattsdale has proved a great difficulty for Wellington. He personally asked me to look into things and put an end to it."

Lewis's footsteps resounded once again before he burst into the library, a large book in his hand. He held it out to me. "It was you who figured out the riddle. Go ahead. Put us out of our misery."

The book felt heavy, the binding rather thick. We both knew something was inside. My fingers quivered as I turned it on end and peeled back the spine. I held my breath as I drew out a wad of wrinkled paper.

Money. A great deal of money.

Lewis took it into his hands. "He must have withdrawn it all from the bank when he came of age, before he left London. He wasn't in debt at all. He'd come to Platts-dale to spy. What a risk sending this to you in such a way."

My shoulders slumped. "He must have been desperate."

"Moreover, he meant to return," Lord Torrington added, shocking the room into silence.

"I suppose he wants to run away as soon as he gets his hands on this," I said aloud, thinking to myself, *Why shouldn't we just let him?* Then I remembered Mr. Drake's lifeless body. If Jacob had anything to do with that horrible death, we could not allow him to remain free. "What now?"

Torrington grasped the money. "I will be honored to escort you to London at first light, where I will go straight to the authorities at Whitehall. In the meantime, Browning will keep a watch on our man."

CHAPTER 27

The dead of night brought with it Grey-bourne's aches and pains — the popping, the creaking, the transient howl of centuries long past, driven by the ever-persistent wind. I pulled my mantle tighter about my neck as the anticipation of what I had decided rested heavy on my shoulders.

Flitting silently down the grand staircase and along the back hall like nothing more than a ghost, I paused only when I caught a whiff of Lewis and Lord Torrington's tight voices still deep in discussion within the library. I doubted either would sleep tonight, particularly if they knew what I meant to do.

It wasn't until I reached the side hallway a few feet from the north door that I considered one last time what I intended and what it would mean — for all of us. Jacob's amiable smile came to mind, the eager turn to his voice, which he'd employed the last time he spoke with me in London. He implied he had a plan. I'd thought nothing of it at the time. He always had plans, but now the sharp memories had taken on a far different meaning.

My muscles tensed, my body a torrent of hope and dread. We'd always trusted each other, Jacob and me. I had to be absolutely certain of his guilt. I could not leave for London without confronting him. If nothing else, I owed him that.

He was family after all, and no matter what he had or had not done, he would never harm me. Determined only in my desire to expose the truth, my fingers worked in frantic silence to release the bolt on the side door.

A loud crack. Then the unnatural feeling of hushed restlessness.

Pressed to the shadows and poised to run, I felt my heartbeat throb in my ears, but no one came. The twists and turns of the scrambling halls had hidden any sound.

I advanced through the door, and the cold night air met me in force, thick with an oppressive dampness that clung to my clothes and settled in my chest, the sticky scent of the earth filling my nose. Thick clouds hung low in the sky, choking out the stars, sealing the prowling wind with a dark cover. It would not be long before the fog would descend.

I kept to the shadows, darting forward in spurts until I was certain I could not be seen from the house. The path to the dower house was lined with darkened shapes, trees, which appeared hazy in the moonlight. Even the underbrush reared up like hairy animals that watched my progress, every looming shrub fighting to hide the imaginary danger beyond. Yet I continued, my eyes trained to the gravel at my feet, my mind steady on the task ahead. I would not be so easily shaken.

Soon enough, the dower house emerged like a black hill out of the darkness. I meant to find a way to see Jacob alone, and that did not include approaching the front door. I trailed the wall of ivy that wrapped the ground floor, and tried every window. To my great relief, around the far corner at what I assumed was the kitchen, a low window clicked open under my fingers. No servant would have made such a mistake. Thankfully, Adam's negligence had seen to that.

Carefully, I pulled the window open as far as it would go, glad it was just wide enough for me to shimmy through. I tucked my skirt, pushed my way inside, and dropped to the floor before crouching beside a cabinet. Gloom clung to every nook of empty space — pans thrown about, glasses on the floor, the hearth as cold as ice. I lifted my brows. The inhabitants of the dower house could not live like this much longer.

Dodging the various cookware, I made my way across the kitchen. Isabell's lavender scent laced every shallow breath I took. A poignant reminder of her presence not only in my brother's life but in his future as well. Silence throbbed in my ears. I could do this. I had to do this . . . or I would regret my cowardice forever.

My heartbeat echoed each tentative step, like a hammer urging me on. Down the hall, around the corner to the base of the stairs, where I kept firmly to the darkened sections. Then up the narrow staircase. I tested each worn board for the least sound, until at last, I crested the top and released a painful breath.

The upper, first-floor hall wore its own version of neglect — peeling paint, yellowed wallpaper. I turned right, knowing just where Jacob's room would be since the day I'd seen it through the telescope. Like a cat, I inched down the corridor and paused at the closed door of the last room. He was in there. I knew it.

My fingers wrapped the cold latch as my knuckles blanched white. A mere second of indecision descended into my chest, tightening every muscle against my heart, before I pressed inside like a whirlwind and slipped the door shut behind me, resting my back silently against the hard wood.

I breathed. I blinked. Nothing moved.

The small apartment was as dark as the hall, the heavy curtains drawn tight across the window at the back wall. And there on the bed lay the silhouette of a person, motionless.

Jacob.

Alive and well. Asleep on the bed. I crept forward, my arm extended, determined to prove what I saw was not a fantasy. The coverlet feathered under my fingers, and the curve of his arm took shape beneath the fabric. It was indeed a man facing the far wall. I pressed a bit deeper, and my other hand found its way to my throat. "Jacob," I whispered, almost afraid of my own voice.

The lump shifted then shot into a sitting position as his hands grappled for something on the bedside table.

I hadn't even seen the pistol lying there. Quickly I spoke, my voice barely audible. "No, Jacob. It's me."

His eyes appeared wild and gray in the moonlight, his hair far shorter than I remembered. A bead of sweat slipped down his gaunt cheek. A long moment passed before he lowered the pistol, and I waited patiently as he rubbed his face.

Draping his legs over the bedside, he paused to rest his elbows on his knees, a look of indecision about his grim face. He followed his sigh with an almost laugh. "Rebecca. What the devil are you doing here?"

At the same moment, a slender hand slipped over his shoulder, and Isabell's head popped into view.

I staggered back a step. My lips parted, my words lost to the cool night air. Of course, Isabell would be here with him. Why had I ever assumed he would be alone? What a fool I was.

Jacob's questioning look edged into a smile. "I've been wanting to speak with you."

I took in the nearly unrecognizable figure before me, and I didn't move as a slithering chill mounted my spine. Goodness, even his voice sounded different than I remembered. Why on earth had I come like this? I did not know this man.

Isabell giggled under her breath with that nervous titter of hers. "Well, I suppose we shall have to take your sister into our confidence after all."

The shocking numbness that had overtaken my body suddenly deserted me for tingling pain. "What confidence?"

Jacob stood and scratched his head before slipping on a dressing gown he acquired from the foot of the bed. Even in the shifting shadows I could see how thin he had become, how languid his movements seemed.

"Where have you been?"

He flicked his fingers as if irritated. "I thought you'd have guessed it by now, Becca. You always touted your fine intelligence." He pursed his lips. "France, of course." Then a mumble. "I had a delivery to make" — he shot a quick glance at Isabell — "before returning for what was mine." His shoulders drew back like a lion's, certain of its prey, then he crossed the rug to grasp my arms.

"I wasn't expecting you to come here, but I find that I am glad you did." His eyes brightened "Oh, Becca. You should have seen France. It is a glorious country. The artwork, the fashion. I simply knew I had to go there after listening to my friend, Ezra Taylor, describe it at Cambridge. And then in London when he finally let me in on his little French secret, I just had to be a part of the revolution."

Frozen for a moment, I searched his eyes, then jerked away, hiding the tremor in my voice as best I could. "I don't understand how you can stand here before me and speak so . . . after everything." Hurt was replaced by anger, which crept unbidden into my voice. "You allowed Aunt Jo and me to grieve your death . . . for months. And then at the house . . . It was you in my bedchamber, was it not? All along I thought I had dreamed up Mama, that I was having more terrors. How could you do that to me?"

His head seemed to bob as he drew closer to the empty fireplace, a look of impatience filling his face. "I can see you mean to be difficult. I had little choice but to check your room. Surely you know that. I had to have my book before I could do anything else. I didn't even think you would wake up." He paused, waiting for something — an agreement? He went on with more aplomb. "If you would only take one cursed moment to see things from my perspective, then you would understand."

My shoulders slumped. "That is just what I want to do — understand."

He hesitated, and his eyes narrowed as he

paced the room. "I had every intention of revealing it all to you eventually, when the time was right. I thought I could trust you, which is why I sent you the money for safekeeping in the first place." He stopped cold. "But Isabell has informed me that I was wrong, and you've grown quite close to our indelible cousin."

I tried to keep my voice light. "My friendship with our cousin does not signify."

"Does it not? Well . . . I'm quite certain Father would agree with him, perhaps even applaud our cousin's *work,* but I cannot."

I could see where he was going, and my throat felt dry. "Really Jacob, you do Lewis a disservice. He only means to protect our country."

Jacob cocked an eyebrow. "Lewis, is it now? How quaint. I do believe my little sister has fallen under his spell."

I turned away, my arms quivering with anger. "I don't know what you mean."

He forced his way back into my line of sight. "Lewis Browning, your fiancé, meant to see me hanged. What do you think of that? Oh, he hadn't worked out all the particulars, but it was only a matter of time till he did so. He was after the French spy. Don't you see? I had to kill him, or he most certainly would have killed me."

I stared at my once beloved brother, channeling the months of hurt and anger into something I could control. "So you drugged Lewis at the inn and shot to end his life on the bridge."

"Yes, I did. But his blasted horse moved at the last second then bolted. I was barely able to jump free into the water before the beast crashed into me in his haste to escape."

Isabell drew up beside Jacob and slid her arm around his back. Jacob kept his gaze steady as he kissed her hair and drank in her scent, his eyes trained on me. "You are bright enough to deduce the rest. I hid beneath the bridge until I was able to leave. Then I journeyed to Taylor's house. Only I found a dead body in place of my friend. Taylor apparently died from an earlier gunshot wound, which I am quite certain was Lewis's doing." Jacob rested his chin on Isabell's head.

"Though I honor Taylor's death, the timing was all too perfect for me. I dug the ball from his stomach, dressed him in my waistcoat, and placed him downstream on the river, hoping to implicate Lewis in the process. Instead, even with Isabell identifying the body as instructed and inciting the villagers to anger over Lewis's guilt, our cousin got out of it unscathed." Jacob laughed. "Although, I will say impersonating his highwayman persona proved helpful on my nightly visits to the Hall."

The air grew heavy as my chest heaved with each new breath. "Sophie knew it was you, didn't she? She must have followed you back to the dower house."

"Please, don't enact a Cheltenham tragedy." He motioned to the door with a lifeless shrug. "I only meant to frighten her. But she was determined to follow me, even after I shot into the air to scare her. Later, the shovel proved the only way to make her see reason. There was far too much at stake."

I cringed. Jacob was responsible for the gunshot so close to the garden as well. "Sophie must have remembered you as a friend. How wrong she was."

"Be glad I didn't have to take her life, like Lewis's little mutt, who wouldn't leave me alone when I first arrived back from France."

"Mollie." The word came out in a whisper.

Jacob reached out as if to appease me, but the feel of his cold fingers against my skin sent a quiver up my arm. He pretended not to notice. "Believe me when I tell you I wish I could have spared you the sorrow of my supposed death and all the things that have happened since then."

How much I wanted to believe him. "Why France when you had family here?"

"They were closing in on me — our cousin, his friends. After the incident on the bridge, I had no choice but to leave the country for a time. I thought it only right to deliver the missive my man was intending to take with him from our currier in Reedwick, particularly since I was borrowing his identity."

"And was it delivered?"

He laughed. "Of course. Would you expect any less from me?"

I pressed my lips together, fury fueling the constriction of my muscles. "What now? How can you hope to get free of all this?"

"Isabell and I are off to America, and you, my dear, shall marry our friend, Mr. Galpin. Isabell tells me he is not opposed to the match."

Isabell stepped forward, speaking as if we were simply having a coze after a ball, not creeping through the depths of my worst nightmare. "Oh, Rebecca, I wanted to tell you so many times about my promise to Jacob. He meant for you to be taken care of when we left. Galpin is the perfect choice for you — a widower, lonely. He was so easy to convince of your virtues. Of course, at the time, we had no idea you would fancy Lewis as well."

Startled, I shook my head. "The two of you have lost all your reason if you think I would ever marry a man arranged for me."

"Won't you? Well, you always were stubborn. I suppose Galpin is too much of a dandy for you? It is no matter, for I have decided here and now that you shall come with us." A smile crossed his face. "Yes." His eyes widened. "To America. Why did I not think of it before?" He patted my cheek. "There shall be plenty of young wealthy men in New England interested in an English lady of good breeding, particularly one with a dowry. Why shouldn't you come with us?"

Isabell laughed. "Don't tease her, Jacob. You shall only make her blush. She has seen very little of the world, poor dear."

He gripped my arm — hard. "I'm afraid there will be no time for you to gather your things from Greybourne Hall. I have already made arrangements to leave. I only need to get my book. Understand?"

Only then, as Jacob's tensile fingers dug into my arm, did I fully comprehend my plight. I was trapped. Adam was likely somewhere in the house. He and Jacob could easily overpower me. I would be forced to go with him that very night if he bid me to do so.

My mind raced for a plan as words spilled from my mouth. "You do realize that I would only be a burden to you and Isabell in America. Remember what happened to Mama?"

A dark look settled on his face. "Of course I do." He jerked me to the side. "Why the devil would you bring her into this?"

"She was mad, *mad,* and I have come to believe I suffer from the same illness."

He narrowed his eyes, a curious smile playing with his lips. "Syphilis? You have syphilis? Little Becca? I don't believe it."

I heard his words, but I didn't rightly process what he meant. "It is true. I've started having spells at night just like her. I fear I shall —"

"Do you even know what syphilis is?"

I glanced from Isabell's smirk to Jacob's amused eyes. They were laughing at me.

Jacob cleared his throat. "It is a venereal infection, my little innocent. It would be just like Father not to tell you what Mother contracted after you were born. Don't you see? Mother had a lover other than our unforgettable papa. Father sent her to Scotland more from embarrassment than anything else. And you actually thought you contracted it." Then he did laugh out loud. "What a ridiculous little creature you are, to be sure."

Thoughts jumbled in my mind. "But . . . before she died, Mama said I would be just like her. I-I thought . . ."

Jacob tilted his chin. "And you believed her? You really are gullible, Rebecca."

I shook my head, unable to fully grasp the sudden revelation. I was free — free from all those months of worry and doubt. But the happy release charging my heart hid the hint of a dark tale. Who else knew the truth of my mother's illness? Aunt Jo? Lewis? Why had no one told me of it?

As if to taunt me, Jacob went on, "The last time I was in Scotland, Mama whispered into my ear that you looked far too much like a woman for your own good. She saw you growing up, primed to repeat the same sins as her. I —" His smile faded. "You mean to put me off by all this, don't you?" He pressed his lips together, leaning in. "You always have thought yourself quite clever."

Hardly.

He regripped my arm. "No more distractions, my dear. You know just where it is, don't you?"

"Where what is?"

His voice dripped with ice. "The book."

I blinked. I froze. "I don't have it. Lewis, he —"

Jacob raked his fingers through his hair. "Lewis, of course. You would give it to him."

Isabell ran her hand across Jacob's shoulders and leaned in to kiss his ear. "Perhaps I can simply visit Lewis in the morning, and put him in a good mood . . ."

Jacob pulled away from her touch. "You've done enough of that already, and it has come to nothing time and again." He cast her a wry smile. "I've come to believe he doesn't want what you have to offer."

She looked affronted as she stepped away.

Jacob turned on me. "My sister will tell us where he has it."

My legs shook beneath my skirt, and my fingers curled into a fist. "A question first. You owe me that at the very least."

He seemed momentarily amused. "All right. Go ahead. What difference does it make now?"

My worst fears about Jacob being a French spy had been confirmed, but murder? It was a stab in the dark, but I had to try. "Why did you kill Mr. Drake?"

He pressed his lips together. "Worked that one out, did you?"

My heart sank as a cold wash of nerves splashed into my chest. He'd done it. My beloved brother was nothing but a ruthless killer.

His voice grew heady, direct. "As I said before, I had no choice, Rebecca. None." Then he was shouting, inches from my face. "How could I go on living as another man after being recognized by Lewis's best friend?" He covered his face with his free hand. "It was all so sudden, so hopelessly necessary. Don't you see? Drake walked away, and I responded on impulse, like a soldier. I had to help Isabell. She was counting on me to free her from this blasted prison Lewis has constructed for her. I couldn't abandon her after I had made her a promise. All my planning and work would have been completely wasted for what? A nosy solicitor?"

Tears filled my eyes. "Oh, Jacob."

"Don't you judge me. Don't you dare judge me. You don't know what it has been like to be me. Ridiculed in London for my unnatural mother, cast aside by my father for another more pliable 'son.' My ideas brought me nothing but mockery from my friends — that is, until I met Taylor. He wasn't laughing. France wasn't laughing. I had been betrayed by every last person in

Britain I cared for. Why shouldn't I support France and all the ideals I agree with?" He checked his pistol. "No more of this. I don't need to answer to you. Where is it?"

I crossed my arms. "Lewis moved the book to another hiding place in the library. If I were to come with you, I could show you where it is." Yes, Lord Torrington was there. He would help if I couldn't find a way to alert Lewis first.

Jacob stared at me for a tense moment before motioning to the door. "I daresay your frightened presence shall do nicely in Lewis's library — a pistol pointed at that pretty dark hair, and Lewis'll hand the money right over." He chuckled. "If Isabell is right, he is half in love with you already."

CHAPTER 28

A thousand ideas fluttered through my mind as Jacob grasped his breeches from the wardrobe and slipped into an adjoining room to dress. Isabell aimed the pistol as he'd instructed, and I couldn't help but notice how her finger lay loose about the trigger, how her face contorted into one of nervous indifference. Perhaps she was not as keen on the plan as my brother thought.

The solitary candle caused her shadow to dither across the wall. She adjusted her footing, first one direction, then the next. The transient light highlighted the ever-changing expressions on her face. Beyond the far wall, the floorboards creaked, sounds of my brother's hurried movements as he shuffled about the space. Isabell slanted a glance at the dressing room door.

Certain there had only been enough time for Jacob to be half dressed, I knew my moment had come. My pulse throbbed. My nerves swelled. In a wave of frantic energy, I shoved Isabell from her feet and darted through the bedchamber door, the ghost of the pistol chasing me from the room. I dared not look back as a high-pitched gasp echoed off the wall, then the fluttering of footsteps and the shouts of Jacob's name, but no gunshot. I'd gambled correctly. Isabell was no murderer.

I thrashed down the hall, driven by Jacob's declaration and my mounting fears about what it would mean for not only myself but Lewis. My shoulder crashed into the opposing wall, and I turned at the last second to descend the small staircase. Rushing blindly down the blackened steps, shouts resounded at my back. Footsteps pounded, swelling from somewhere beyond the hall. Tremors wound their way through every inch of my body, making my flight a skittish one and clumsy at that. I knew once Jacob was fully dressed, he would not be far behind. All I could think about was bursting from the dower house and escaping into the night. What a fool I'd been to come at all.

So keen on my thoughts, I never expected Adam, nor his shadowed figure that filled the bulk of the front door. He wore a lazy smile, his eyelids heavy with drink. I wondered if he had even been to bed. His jacket had been discarded, his cravat a tangled mess about his neck. Dazed, our eyes met. In his cups Adam was hardly a threat, but his presence could not be more ill-timed. He stood like a rock blocking the door, his eyes narrow beneath hooded lids.

My heart contracted. My muscles ached to fight my way through, but I forced myself unnaturally still, certain one wrong move on my part might set him off. I could not be certain how far he was involved in all this and I had precious little time. My voice shook as I spoke the only words that came to mind. "Adam, thank goodness you are here."

He grunted, wavering for a moment. "You say?"

I tugged at his arm. "No time for questions now. You must hurry. Your sister is in great need of your assistance upstairs, and you must go at once."

Like a floppy puppet, his gaze flicked up to the first-floor landing and took a slow tour of the empty space.

Then I screamed, "She said at once! You must make haste!"

A breathless second ticked away before Adam was able to process what I'd said and react. His slow movements stretched out like eternity as my jaw ached with tension.

A bang sounded, then a crack behind me. The room shifted. I didn't dare glance back as the air thickened in my throat. Silence pressed against my eardrum. Someone was creeping down the steps. I could feel it.

Adam seemed unaware of the charged silence as he lumbered forward and tripped on the edge of the hall rug like an oaf.

It felt as if I'd fallen into one of my spells. My mind was absent of thought, my muscles squeezing and releasing of their own accord. I fumbled with the latch before I thrust the door open. Panic heaved me forward, and I sprang across the threshold and into the night.

The front walk looked foreign at first as I bolted across the lawn. I had just reached the stone wall when I heard Jacob's voice behind me.

"Stop, Rebecca. You cannot leave."

Jacob would never shoot me, but he'd been a skilled runner since childhood. I would have only a few well-managed strides before he'd overtake me. My mind throbbed with indecision. Jacob was far too close to hide. I gasped for air, my side already aching with every agitated step.

I remember thinking how important it was not to lead Jacob to Lewis, terrified of what Jacob might do. My legs felt weak as I lunged first one direction then the next. I'd seen a cottage the day I met the farmer on my walk, and the place was quite close. The man had sworn to help me if needed. I only hoped he might stand my friend after all.

Without another thought, I tore left, straight through the trees to the road, darkness welling up around me. My feet felt heavy as I ran, and I tripped every few steps. Brush pulled at my gown. Rocks marred the way. But I wrenched ahead, driven by the fear choking my heart. I was the only one who could warn Lewis.

All at once I slammed hard into a tree. Startled, it took me a costly second to regain my bearings before beginning again. Compulsively, I checked the way I had come. Jacob's lithe figure was narrowing the gap between us.

Gangly branches lashed at my legs and the cold underbrush sought to bar my way, when suddenly the trees lessened and a road appeared. A cottage stood just beyond the bend, the few windows I could make out as dark as the rest of the night.

I tore across the gravel and crashed into the cottage door seconds before Jacob. I pounded against the wood with my fists and screamed for help. It was no use. Jacob grasped my arm and thrust me into the shadows like I was nothing but a doll. He was at my ear, his fingers entwined in my hair. "What do you think you are doing?"

"Let go. You're hurting me."

He gripped tighter, tugging me closer to his face. "Does it hurt? Well that is all you deserve, you ungrateful wretch. No wonder Father sent you away. When I tell you to do something, you'll do it from now on."

Gasping for air, I met his piercing gaze. "We are no longer in the nursery. You cannot tell me what to do." I attempted once again to pull free, but his fingers were like iron.

"No. I daresay I'm much stronger now." He jerked me behind him like an unwilling dog, and an oddly placed laugh laced his words. "And you can wipe that shameful look off your face, my dear. I am not the devil, just a loyal follower of Napoleon, and you are coming with me to get the money whether you agree to my plans or not. I'll not allow my ridiculous, hoyden of a sister to ruin it all now. There is far too much at stake."

"You're mad, Jacob. You know that — mad! I cannot reconcile this person you have become with the boy you once were."

Then he laughed, the deep timbre carrying like a bell on the wind, the ghostly growl of a specter haunting the night. I thought I heard another sound that sprang up from the shadows. Jacob's green eyes flashed in the moonlight and caused me to turn. At that same moment a round, dark projectile crashed into the back of his head. Jacob dropped lifeless to the ground.

I screamed and ran for the trees. My hands shook as a voice bubbled up from somewhere in the inky depths of the night. "I hit 'im. I did it. The midnight devil. We got 'im at last."

A toothy grin flashed amid the gloom. Then the farmer emerged, triumph written across his face. It took me a moment to process what had happened, but soon enough it became all too clear. Mr. Miller had mistaken Jacob for Lewis and deployed the rock he'd previously told me about. And he'd hit his mark, all right. Jacob, however, was already stirring.

Startled by the sudden change in his prey, the farmer turned to his fists and swung at Jacob as he rose from the ground. But the man was no match for my brother, who had trained in London. Jacob mauled over the man's slight stature with a few well-placed thrusts. I hesitated within the darkness of the trees, my heart in my throat, torn between plunging into the fray to put an end to Jacob's tirade or to run for help. Either action would be useless at this point.

Then Jacob struck again, his fist finding the man's jaw, knocking him motionless to the ground. He stood over him, eyeing the man with disgust before stumbling off in the direction we'd come. I caught a flash of Jacob's hard face as he turned to leave. Blood trickled down his forehead. He would need to bandage it at once. More importantly, he'd not seen the direction I'd fled.

Back on the ground, the farmer moaned and rolled onto his side. Though he'd taken a beating, I doubted Jacob did any lasting damage, and I was relieved to see his wife in the doorway ready to tend to his wounds.

A gust of wind whipped through the trees. My arms quivered. The numbing shock of what I'd witnessed rendered me momentarily fixed to my hiding spot — watching, waiting, unable to think or feel.

Then Lewis's steady gaze came to mind. My role in all this was not over. I had to warn Lewis. I backed into the shelter of the towering oaks, the moonlight creeping farther and farther away like a wave upon the seashore. I turned, my heart pounding, my palms wet with sweat, and bolted for Greybourne Hall.

There were only two people who could

stop Jacob now, and I hoped I was not too late.

It was near Greybourne's terrace where I finally succumbed to the emotions I'd kept carefully in check. I swiped my arm across my cheek, flinging the tears into the cold night. How I'd mourned for my brother, dreamed of seeing him again.

I had been utterly and completely deceived.

In the distance the hint of a shadow shifted beneath the portico. Instinctively I drew back, my heart thundering in response. Someone was watching me.

I edged in place, contemplating my next move. Could Jacob have already made his way to Greybourne? It took all my willpower not to retreat as the figure took shape in the moonlight.

"Rebecca, is that you? Thank God." Lewis paused, his uncertainty lasting only a second before he broke out into a run, his arms outstretched, his stride direct.

I saw relief in his face as he approached, the strength of his countenance. It took merely one light shake of his head for me to fall against his chest and bury my face into the folds of his cravat.

His hands traveled up my back, tentative

at first, then all encompassing, pulling me closer. His voice was at my ear. "I was about to storm the dower house or all of Plattsdale if it came to that. Where have you been?"

Slowly, I looked up, unprepared for what he might think of me. "I had to see Jacob."

The muscles in his jaw flexed. "You did not!"

"He's guilty — all of it." A tear followed the path the others had taken down my cheek. "He took your friend's life to save his own." I hesitated and watched as the storm filled Lewis's face. I took a quick breath.

"Moreover, Jacob's coming here. Right this minute. To get the money. He and Isabell have plans to travel to America as soon as may be." I swallowed hard, unable to bear Lewis's painful gaze any longer. "They mean to take me with them."

His fingers tensed against my back then released, his shoulders responding. "To America?" There wasn't much fight left in his voice. "What do you mean to do?"

I stepped away. "You ask me that after I've thrown myself into your arms?"

A wan smile peeked from the corner of his mouth. "You did do that, little badger." He laced his fingers around mine. "And I

437

wish we had more time to explore this sudden development."

"But we haven't." I retrieved my hand and crossed my arms. "Jacob could be on his way here as we speak. There was an injury, but it won't keep him away long."

"Injury." His smile vanished. "Are you hurt?"

"No." Only rattled.

His jaw clenched. "If he —"

"He didn't."

He let out a sigh. "I won't ask you to recount all that has happened thus far, not yet at least. It seems we haven't the time, but there will be a reckoning. You're certain he means to come here tonight?"

"Yes. And he does not value your life."

He turned to the far-off trees, his words slow to come. "I knew Jacob disliked me when he arrived at Greybourne Hall. My experiences with him have been so different from yours."

"And yet you put up with all my subtle accusations, my silly starts, my blind devotion."

"How could I not? When I've loved you since the moment you barged into my study, demanding a tour of the house."

A long pause charged the inevitable silence. I knew Lewis cared. He'd made that abundantly clear, but I'd never fully appreciated the connection between us, the relentless pull of one for the other.

His fingers found my neck, answering my unspoken question with the gentle touch. "I love everything about you. Your feisty spirit, your deft courage, the complicated way your mind ticks. You're beautiful to be sure, but what matters to me is the kindness in your heart. The way you look at me with that adventurous gleam of yours. The way you make me feel. I couldn't care less that you've demons to fight. Can we not fight them together?"

My throat grew thick as I basked in his words. Lewis loved me, all of me, regardless of my spells or my silly starts. And even if I hadn't learned the truth of my mother's illness and subsequent insanity, I knew at that moment I would follow him anywhere, love him for the rest of my life, take on his courage as my own. Whatever doubt I had at the dower house about Lewis's knowledge of my mother's illness faded away. He didn't know.

I rose up onto my tiptoes. "I have something to tell you, not now, just this — I love you too —"

A crack resounded in the woods. Lewis looked to the horizon as he drew me behind him. His voice sounded hoarse as he spoke. "We've tarried too long. Into the house at once."

I hadn't the time to say more as we raced through the side door, down the long corridor, and made for the library. Lord Torrington met us there, a look of danger about his otherwise handsome features. He eyed me as we approached. "You found her. Good."

"She's foolishly been to see her brother. We believe he's headed here now, and he has no intention of talking."

Torrington turned to secure his pistol from a nearby desk. "Not our original plan, but it might serve." He motioned to the door with his chin. "I believe I'll take a little stroll outside. Perhaps catch our visiting friend unprepared. Stay with Miss Hunter. She needs your protection. It is her brother after all. You know what he's capable of. Although I fully intend to apprehend him before he reaches the house."

There was something refreshingly reassuring about Lord Torrington's confidence. I could see why he was well regarded among the ton. He was the type who could convince you of anything.

He winked at me before shouldering his way through the door, leaving Lewis and me to the pitiful position most women are relegated to: waiting and praying for success. I wandered over to the fireplace. Lewis remained distracted, his eyes trained on the closed door. It was several seconds before he addressed me.

"We should not have stayed so long on the terrace."

I shook my head. "No, it was my fault. It was my decision to go to the dower house in the first place. I've beget this whole wretched business."

He cast me a fleeting glance. "Don't be absurd. You've provided us information we could never have obtained any other way." He made his way over to me. "Don't fret. Torrington will be successful."

I met Lewis's gaze, all too aware his voice lacked luster. "I'm sure you are right."

"However, since the first place Jacob will search is the library, I cannot be easy in here. Let us remove ourselves to the drawing room to wait and watch for his arrival."

Hand in hand, we made our way down the gloomy hall and refrained from speaking again until Lewis closed the drawing room door. I spoke at a whisper. "How long do you think it will be?"

"It is in Jacob's best interest to make an appearance before too long, and certainly tonight. He would not wish to give us time to make plans, let alone, enact them. Our only hope is that he is unaware of Torrington's sudden visit." He passed me a candle. "Here, light the sconces there while I thrust open the drapes on this window. If he is certain where we are, he may not account for Torrington. Jacob was always vain and impulsive. If my guess is correct, his confidence will be his downfall."

I did as Lewis said before taking a seat on the sofa, the long black window presiding over the room. The grandfather clock beside the fireplace ticked away, first the half hour, then the hour. Lewis grew more and more unsettled, first listening at the door, then peering out the far windows. He could not stay still. And could I blame him? My own foot bobbed beneath my gown.

At length, he stopped short in front of me. "I fear something has happened."

"Or Jacob is simply taking his time. He did have a rather large wound on his head."

Lewis's pacing began again — across the rug, around to the windows. He spoke over his shoulder. "Perhaps so."

He paused on his way back. "I suppose I am not all that good at waiting. Usually I'm the one galloping off into the night."

"And a very handsome rider you are."

He shot me a rough grin. "You think so?"

I moved to respond when a spine-tingling clatter resounded somewhere beyond Greybourne's thick walls, like a metal pot had been knocked to the floor. I rose, my hand pressed to my chest. "What do you suppose that was?"

Confusion lined his face. "I'm not certain, but I daresay it wasn't the wind."

Jacob or a servant? My stomach clenched, and my voice came out in a whisper. "If he is in the house, then he knows where we are. Surely we mustn't stay here. What should we do?"

Lewis cracked the door and we both heard the disturbing sound of footsteps retreating up the grand central stairs.

I made my way over to Lewis's side. "That could not have been Torrington."

Lewis shook his head. "No." Then glanced at the door. "Jacob cannot be certain where the book is now. He's planning his attack."

A searching moment and Lewis inched the door wide enough for him to pass through before reaching for my hand. "I want you to go for Knowles. Wake no one else. I don't wish to put any more lives in danger."

I thought of Mr. Drake and how easily Jacob disposed of him and nodded.

Lewis's words were direct, but I could see the hesitation in his eyes. "Knowles will assist you to the stables. Take one of the horses into Plattsdale and alert the authorities." One more look behind him. "Knowles will likely be surprised to see you, but he is well aware of my nightly pursuits. He will not hesitate to help you."

"What about you?" We both knew I was relatively safe. Jacob would not harm me. However, images of what might happen to Lewis if he were to be caught unaware flashed through my mind.

He tapped the barrel of the pistol. "I don't intend for it to come to this, but Jacob is well aware I'm a deadly shot."

I moved to stop him, but I knew no protestations on my part would diminish his resolve. He meant to protect his house and servants after all, particularly if I was out of harm's way.

"Please." I paused. "Be careful."

"Always." Lewis offered me a tight-lipped smile before motioning me toward the servants' wing. Numb, I took a few hesitant steps then cast a quick glance over my shoulder, terrified to let him go.

I watched as he ascended the curved stairs and vanished at the landing.

CHAPTER 29

Deep within Greybourne's narrow servants' wing, every creak sent my nerves exploding like tiny fireworks under my skin, my active imagination creating all kinds of dangers that might be hiding, waiting to pounce as I passed by.

My muscles screwed tight as I breached the dreaded silence of the kitchen area. The frigid night air held a smell to it, like the lingering scent of a wet rug. I skirted by the hearth and around the corner, a fresh wave of nerves washing over my body.

Steps before I reached the back hall, I halted — stone still.

The cellar door was ajar.

I shrank back against the wall, looking first one direction then the next. Surely Cook had forgotten to seal it. Or had she? The thought gave life to the shadows of the long room, each one leering at me from different angles. I closed my eyes for a brief second, certain I'd imagined the transformation of the room, when a rustle sounded ahead, followed by a tap on the floor.

My fingers found the edge of the wainscoting. Aunt Jo had left Sophie with us while on her honeymoon. Perhaps the little pup was merely roaming about. I tried her name quietly, "Sophie? Sophie, darling?" Whatever nerves I'd assembled just moments before vanished when she neither appeared nor responded.

Several gruesome seconds ticked by as I forced myself to press on down the back hall, intent on the servants' staircase. Knowles's bedchamber was just above.

As I neared the opening of the stairs, the air took a subtle shift across my back. The hair on my arms straightened, and the eerie feeling that I was not alone surged over me. For an appalling moment I could neither think nor breathe.

My resulting movements were jerky at best as I turned first one direction then the next, the candle still locked to my unsteady fingers. Of course, the gleam of the flame illuminated nothing but an empty room. I let out a trapped breath. Nothing but my imagination again. I was wasting time.

But then I heard it — footsteps on the stairs. I'd made a terrible mistake. I turned to flee, but a deep voice stopped me cold.

"Get ahold of yourself, my dear." Jacob's tone dripped with irritation. "I had no idea you were such a spineless creature."

His callous hand wrapped my arm. "You never could see very well in the dark, could you?" He chuckled. "I was watching you from right here the whole time."

I struggled to pull away, but it was no use. "You're hurting me."

"Don't be so dramatic. I only need your help." His hold tightened, his voice close to my ear. "Where's my money?"

I didn't answer, still shocked Jacob was not on the first floor as we had supposed.

He seemed to follow my thoughts. "Really, Rebecca, it is not so hard to confuse your lover. A quick dart up the central steps, followed by a dash down the servants' staircase, and here I find you sneaking across the kitchens."

"Don't —"

"Listen, this does not have to be so unpleasant. We are family after all."

I cringed.

"If you cooperate, I've decided to leave you here . . . with him. It seems Isabell does not wish for your company after all."

My heart lightened at his words. Perhaps if I did what he said and gave him the money, this could all be over. Lewis and I would be safe. But Mr. Drake's tattered body came to mind. There would be no happy ending for Jacob. He had made his choice weeks ago when he took an innocent man's life.

I steadied my voice. "Lewis stashed the money in the library."

"Good." He gave me a smile. "I had a feeling you'd be eager to help when you understood things a bit better." His hand tightened on my arm. "Though I'd love nothing more than to release you now, I daresay you must accompany me to the library. I have a feeling I haven't seen the last of our dubious cousin."

Jacob's movements seemed rushed, his lean body shifting like an imp's as he led us from the servants' wing into the front entryway. I had few ideas as to a plan, nothing beyond the knowledge that Lewis was somewhere in the house and Lord Torrington likely about the grounds. I hesitated a moment at the window, feigning interest in something beyond the glass.

I saw Jacob's smile in the reflection. "If you are searching for your friend, you mustn't bother. I daresay he shall be nursing the devil of a headache in the morning. That is, when he is able to escape the ropes about his hands."

My heart sank. Did he mean Lord Torrington . . . or Lewis?

Jacob tugged at my arm, forcing me to continue to the library. He meant to get his money and quickly. Of course, Lewis had given it to Torrington. How long could I fob Jacob off on a lie?

I held my breath as we passed through the library door, only to exhale a few seconds later. The room was as empty as I had left it hours before . . . or was it minutes? Time seemed lost to the miserable night.

Jacob played with the pistol in his hand, his first finger never far from the trigger. "Well, where is it? I'm losing my patience."

"We, uh, left it in the book. Let me find it for you." I crossed the rug to the rear of the desk and crouched down to fumble with the stack of books we'd previously left on the floor. I couldn't rightly remember where the French book lay that had housed the money, but I also made no attempt to find it.

Jacob seemed far more interested in the open doorway than my feeble attempts to thwart him with lies. He crept over to the wall beyond the bookcase, making himself invisible to anyone approaching the room. I choked down a hard swallow as I watched him lift the pistol. He already knew quite well I didn't have his money. Moreover, he knew who did.

My brother had us all right where he wanted us. Me, under his power. Torrington incapacitated. And Lewis . . . My eyes widened. Jacob was waiting for him. We both were.

The air in the room grew thick at the realization, each breath I took far more strained than the last. Oh, Lewis.

Then I heard it — footsteps approaching quickly. Boots heavy on the parquet floor. Instinctively, my fingers curled around a book, and I scrambled to my feet. Jacob had his arm extended, the pistol aimed straight at the opening of the door, a wry smile across his face. Whoever approached would be here in mere seconds, unaware of what waited beyond the closed door. He would have no time to react, no time to defend himself. And as my frightened gaze fell on Jacob's face, I knew he had no intention of allowing me to stay in England with Lewis — because he meant to murder him before he left.

One . . . two . . . three. My heart pounded in my chest until it shook my entire body. The library door lurched inward, and I thrust the heavy volume straight at Jacob's

head. My aim was off, but not entirely ineffective, as it crashed into his arm that supported the pistol.

Jacob cried out in confusion and anger as
he knelt to relocate the gun, but Lewis
crashed through the door at the same moment, taking in the scene before him. The
two men eyed one another for a breathless
second before Lewis rushed the room and
took a wild swing. Jacob was ready and
responded with a punch of his own, which
connected with Lewis's lower jaw. Pum-
meled backward, Lewis crashed into the far
wall. Recovering quickly, he utilized the
shelf as leverage and propelled himself back
into the fray.

Fists flew. The men were off stride, then
in control, dodging, grunting, swinging. So
terribly close to both pistols, which had
crashed to the floor. I edged around the
fight, keeping as close to the shelves as I
could. I had every intention of taking those
two deadly weapons out of play, or perhaps
ending the fight altogether. I skirted to the
side before dropping to my knees. Jacob saw
my plan at the last second and kicked the
first gun out of my reach. The movement
gave Lewis the upper hand for a moment,
and he forced Jacob back across the rug.

The other pistol. Where had it fallen? I

searched the floor, frantic to locate it, but found nothing. Was it beneath the chairs or behind the desk? I remembered it slipping from Lewis's fingers by the bookshelf.

Just then, Jacob hurtled into the base of the shelf. Lewis started across the room, his expression one of success, his stride intent, but Jacob looked up with a smile. "Sorry, old boy."

He laughed as he pointed the lost pistol at Lewis's chest. "Looks like I win this one."

Lewis went motionless, his eyes on the silver weapon.

Through my haze of fear, I heard a bark . . . behind me . . . beyond the library door. Sophie?

Jacob took a step forward. "The money. Where is it?"

Lewis scowled. "You know I have no intention of giving it to you. That money was made by betraying the very country I hold dear."

Jacob's hand twitched. "Give it to me now or I'll —"

"Take my life?"

Jacob gave a breathy laugh. "You think you are in a position to barter? I can see now why my father adored you. The great landowner. The gentleman of means. A man whose very existence is built on his respectability, his honor." A smile crossed his face. "I suppose you have enjoyed the past year. I had rather meant for you to take the fall for my murder, but returning a few months ago to see how they all hate you has proven just as invigorating." Then his smile faded. "My father was a fool in every way possible . . . and you are just like him."

I opened my mouth to speak, but Lewis's sharp look silenced me.

Jacob leveled the pistol at Lewis's chest, sweat dripping down his face. "Was there really any other ending to this ridiculous farce? You, my guardian, my friend? Absurd."

A whimper sounded at my back once again, then a scratch on wood. Sophie was indeed on the other side of the library door. I cannot say there was much thought to my sudden movement, but my instincts proved correct. As I thrust open the library door, Sophie tore at Jacob like a tiger, pouncing onto his leg, teeth bared.

It was the distraction Lewis needed. In a whirlwind, his palm slammed into the pistol, pushing the barrel at the ceiling the same moment Jacob pulled the trigger. The sound was deafening, the puff of smoke unearthly. Lewis had Jacob on the floor in seconds, and it took all my power to remove

Sophie's jaw from his leg.

Jacob writhed in pain, shouting, clawing at the rug until Lewis bound his hands. "That blasted mongrel. I should have killed her when I had the chance."

Suddenly weary, I straggled over to where my brother lay, towering over his pitiful form. I glanced up at Lewis. "They say dogs have keen senses. She must have known you were in trouble."

He nodded, offered a quick pat to Sophie's head, then turned back to me. Exhaustion filled his face, the toll of all we'd endured together rising to the surface. He didn't speak, but I knew just what he meant beneath that grim stare. Jacob would go to jail. Mr. Drake was avenged, but all we'd accomplished for Britain would not bring him back, nor fill the depth of pain we would both harbor for some time to come, perhaps forever.

In time, Lord Torrington stumbled into the library, a handkerchief pressed to his forehead. "I see you've routed the devil. Sorry I wasn't more help."

Lewis's voice came out in a whisper. "Nonsense. I'm only too glad to see you well. Perhaps you would do the honors of transporting this man to the nearest dragoons." He cast a quick glance at me, a spark of life brightening his eyes. "And by all means, do take the credit. I've a mind to get out of the spying business altogether."

Torrington laughed. "The credit, huh? That is just what you would want — to slip into anonymity, but I have no intention of keeping my mouth shut. You've a name to rebuild in the district, and I shall be the first to sing your praises."

Lewis shook his head. "None of that matters to me now." He reached out for my hand. "All I need is right here."

Torrington crossed his arms, hiding a knowing smile. "All right, you two. I can see when I am decidedly *de trop.*" He grasped Jacob's bound hands and lifted him to his feet. "Miss Hunter, have you any last words before we go?"

Anger, horror, desolation. I'd felt them all, but as I took in the sight of my brother, knowing the truth of who he really was, my heart turned in a way I was not expecting. I stepped forward and peered into the eyes I had admired as a child. "It will take a great deal of time for all of us to heal. You did the unthinkable, but for my part . . . I forgive you."

I felt Lewis's arm settle onto my shoulders as we watched them leave. Jacob never even looked at me on his way out, and I knew then and there I would not see him again. A painful final chapter to one long, difficult part of my life.

Lewis led me back to the drawing room where we sat in silence for a long while, neither ready to give words to the shock we'd experienced. He had lost a dear friend and I a brother.

At length, he leaned forward and took my hand in his. "I will have to go down to the dower house and figure out what is best to be done with Isabell."

I nodded in agreement, but an altogether different thought crossed my mind. I gripped Lewis's fingers hard, my voice lifting in anticipation. "Not yet. I have something I must tell you first." I smiled. "Something that changes everything."

The ocean. That's what Lewis's eyes reminded me of when he looked back at me with that boyish hopefulness of his. Not the sand-filled waves that crash against rocky shores, but the deep blue found only near the horizon, where the water touches the heavens.

I studied them for a moment before I took a deep breath. I was about to give it all to him — my worries, my hopes, my future. What would that feel like? I looked down, gathering my words, for I already knew the answer to that question. I had loved Lewis since the start.

"When I was at the dower house earlier this evening, I discovered something . . ." I paused, searing into my memory the feel of Lewis's hands wrapped around mine, the dear expression on his face. From here on there would never be a "me" or "I" again in regard to my future. Just "us." *Us.*

"Jacob revealed that my mother was ill, very ill, and it was that illness alone that caused her madness. There is no possible way she could have passed it to me. My dreams or spells are just that, nothing more."

He sat back as if processing what I said, then blinked. "Then that means . . ." He shook his head, his eyes wide. He sprang to his feet and drew me against him. "There is nothing preventing our marriage? I mean, a real marriage."

I pressed my lips together and shook my head. "I would consider it . . . if asked by the right gentleman." I cast a quick glance at the far wall. "I suppose Mr. Galpin's of- fer still stands —"

I was barred any further foolishness by Lewis's lips pressed to mine as he wrapped me tighter in his crushing embrace. There would be no mention of another man, not by me, not for the rest of my life. Without even looking, I had found the final clue, the last puzzle piece to my heart. And now I could see the picture in its entirety.

Love, companionship, children. It was all possible, even for me.

EPILOGUE

My Dear Ellen,

I know you have been waiting for this letter for some time, and I loath to have left you in suspense. However, the last few months at Greybourne Hall have been busy indeed. Rest assured I am well and happy — happier than I have ever been. Lewis and I were married by special license a week after I wrote to you of Jacob's arrest. And though it will be some time before we fully heal from all we've been through, I'm comforted to know we are taking the journey together.

Aunt Jo sends her love and begs you to visit us soon. She returned to Plattsdale with her husband following a delightful honeymoon, and I don't believe anyone was more pleased or shocked by the news of my surprise marriage. She visits the Hall as often as possible these days, particularly now because, oh Ellen, can you believe I am to be blessed with a baby? Aunt Jo intends to be a surrogate grandmother in every way possible, which only warms my heart. After all, any little one related to Mr. and Mrs. Fernside, whether boy or girl, shall never want for a book, nor question the fact that they are loved.

While I am determined to spend my days looking forward, I do sometimes look back and wonder what became of Isabell and Adam. Lewis raced to the dower house the night of Jacob's arrest and found nothing but empty rooms. I imagine they took Jacob's tickets and boarded the packet bound for America. But without many resources, I daresay they face a difficult time abroad. I don't believe we shall ever see them again.

Lewis and I decided to sell the townhouse to Mr. Galpin after all, so you may see him in London during the season. I imagine he is still in want of a wife; however, I can only caution you and your friends. Though Lewis never uncovered any connection between Mr. Galpin and the French, I was glad to see him relocate from the neighborhood. He was always too familiar with Isabell.

Little by little, the shroud of lies has

been lifted from Lewis's shoulders, and the townspeople have returned to do business as they did before. In effect, Greybourne Hall has been transformed and my husband along with it. Though he will always be a bit reticent in his actions and emotions, I find him smiling without provocation, riding into town at all hours of the day, and encouraging my fledgling ideas of entertainment.

Lewis also thought to move the telescope to our bedchamber, and I've been able to view the stars every night from our lovely balcony. Yes, I said "our" balcony. We decided to forgo separate rooms due to my nighttime spells. Although they come seldom now, I thank God every frightful occurrence that he placed Lewis beside me to share my burden — his gentle words, his calm strength — it has made all the difference in the world. In the darkest hours, I've only to look in his eyes and know that whatever happens, we will face it together.

Please write again soon. Aunt Jo will love to hear all the on-dits of Bath and the preparations for your upcoming season.

Your friend and cousin,
Rebecca

ACKNOWLEDGMENTS

Travis, the love of my life, I could not have written this story without you because Lewis gets all his best traits from you. Thank you for being my real-life hero with your unending patience, abounding love, and enthusiasm for all my ideas. Handsome, suave, articulate, I could not ask for a better partner in life.

Megan Besing, you continue to be an incredible critique partner and bosom friend. This crazy writing journey would not be the same without you. #iheartyou

Audrey and Luke, Bess and Angi, you all mean the world to me. Thank you for sharing my joy.

Tony and Ronda Smith, you guys have been my biggest fans. I'm blown away by your passion and kindness. There are some friends you just know you will have for your entire life.

The entire Wilson clan, thank you for loving and supporting me.

Nicole Resciniti, my amazing agent. Thank you for your shrewd wisdom and heartfelt enthusiasm.

My editors, Becky Monds and Jodi Hughes, this book would not have been the same without the two of you. And to the entire team at Thomas Nelson, you guys have given me such wonderful support. I am thankful every day I get to work with such an awesome group of people.

And to my Lord and Savior Jesus Christ. To you alone be the glory.

1. Lewis deals with quite a bit of guilt during the story. How do you deal with your own mistakes?

2. Rebecca is afraid to trust anyone with her future. Is there something that holds you back from making decisions?

3. What do you think caused Jacob to change so much from his earlier ideals? Was it a slow, insidious process? Or something more dramatic?

4. Rebecca is forced to reassess her assumptions about Lewis and Jacob. Have you ever made up your mind about someone only to realize later you were wrong?

5. In what ways did Rebecca change throughout the book?

6. What characteristics does Rebecca possess that will help her heal after all she's been through?

7. What do you think happened to Isabell and Adam?

8. Would you have handled any decisions Rebecca made differently? Why or why not?

ABOUT THE AUTHOR

Abigail Wilson combines her passion for Regency England with intrigue and adventure to pen historical mysteries with a heart. A registered nurse, chai tea addict, and mother of two crazy kids, Abigail fills her spare time hiking the national parks, attending her daughter's gymnastic meets, and curling up with a great book. In 2017 Abigail won WisRWA's Fab Five contest and in 2016, ACFW's First Impressions contest as well as placing as a 2017 finalist in the Daphne du Maurier Award for Excellence in Mystery/Suspense. She is a cum laude graduate of the University of Texas at Austin and currently lives in Dripping Springs, Texas, with her husband and children.

Connect with Abigail at
www.acwilsonbooks.com
Instagram: acwilsonbooks

Facebook: ACWilsonbooks
Twitter: @acwilsonbooks

The employees of Thorndike Press hope you have enjoyed this Large Print book. All our Thorndike, Wheeler, and Kennebec Large Print titles are designed for easy reading, and all our books are made to last. Other Thorndike Press Large Print books are available at your library, through selected bookstores, or directly from us.

For information about titles, please call:
  (800) 223-1244

or visit our website at:
  gale.com/thorndike

To share your comments, please write:
  Publisher
  Thorndike Press
  10 Water St., Suite 310
  Waterville, ME 04901